The Te

"A dark, richly imagined tale . . . a thoughtful meditation upon the dangers of fanaticism and the strength of the human spirit . . . Louise Marley deftly creates a detailed world full of complex characters so believable that they make you feel all their emotions with them: rage, powerlessness, rebellion, terror, determination, and hope."
—Sharon Shinn, author of *Heart of Gold*

"The beautiful Zahra is a young wife, a talented medicant, and a murderer. Sickened by a world of abusive husbands, Zahra's choice to kill is believably righteous, but it is fraught with treacherous subsequent ramifications . . . Marley realizes Irustan in dynamic detail . . . Marley's acclaimed, exquisite prose and her universal themes of feminist heroism light the book brightly."   —*Booklist*

"Thoughtful and effective."   —*Kirkus Reviews*

"Marley shows a real feel for the elements that make fantasy (and science fantasy) popular."   —*Locus*

continued . . .

"Louise Marley is a natural fantasy writer . . . Marley's world tinkles with music, light, and creativity . . . to produce a *Midsummer Night's Dream* feel. Her writing is ethereal and touching, and her plot is irresistible."

—Glodowski's Bookshelf, *Deja News*

"*Sing the Light* is . . . a science fiction/fantasy crossover style novel. On the colony of humanity, the cold, bleak, harsh planet with an unusually long year has produced a human psychic mutation . . . a guaranteed good read, pure entertainment. You'll never be able to tell it's good for you by the way it tastes."

—Jacqueline Lichtenberg

"*Sing the Light* [is] a highly crafted science fiction tale that makes authentic use of the author's extensive musical background."

—*Bellevue Journal American*

Ace Books by Louise Marley

SING THE LIGHT
SING THE WARMTH
RECEIVE THE GIFT
THE TERRORISTS OF IRUSTAN
THE GLASS HARMONICA

The
Glass Harmonica

Louise Marley

ACE BOOKS, NEW YORK

THE GLASS HARMONICA

An Ace Book / published by arrangement with
the author

PRINTING HISTORY
Ace trade paperback edition / September 2000
Ace mass-market edition / August 2001

Visit our website at
www.penguinputnam.com

Check out the ACE Science Fiction & Fantasy newsletter
and much more on the Internet at Club PPI!

ISBN: 0-441-00836-4

ACE®
Ace Books are published by The Berkley Publishing Group,
a division of Penguin Putnam Inc.,
375 Hudson Street, New York, New York 10014.
ACE and the "A" design
are trademarks belonging to Penguin Putnam Inc.

PRINTED IN THE UNITED STATES OF AMERICA

10   9   8   7   6   5   4   3   2   1

For our darling Zack
Joy of the past, hope for the future

Acknowledgments

This novel, and all my offerings, have been deeply influenced by Dr. James Savage, Director of Music and Liturgy at St. James Cathedral, Seattle. His musicianship, his pedagogy, and his scholarship are beyond compare, and I am most grateful to have been his student and his colleague.

This book also owes a great debt to William Wilde Zeitler, contemporary virtuoso of the glass armonica, whose playing, music, support, and advice have been invaluable.

Thanks are also due Brian, Cathy, Dave, Jeralee; and Niven, Jake and Zack Marley; June Campbell; Dean Crosgrove, P.A.C., and Nancy Crosgrove, R.N.

The Body of
B. Franklin, Printer
Like the Cover of an Old Book,
Its contents torn out,
And stript of its Lettering and Gilding,
Lies here, Food for Worms.
But the work shall not be wholly lost:
For it will, as he believed, appear once more,
In a new and more perfect Edition,
Corrected and amended by the Author.
He was born Jan. 6, 1706,
Died 17—

Epitaph composed by the young Benjamin Franklin in 1728

———————————

Thus shall ye think of all this fleeting World:
A star at dawn, a bubble in a stream;
A flash of lightning in a summer cloud,
A flickering lamp, a phantom, and a dream.

The Buddha

I

London, November 1761

"PLAY it again, child."

Eilish Eam looked up from her rickety stand of glasses into the watery eyes of an old lady who peered at her from beneath powdered curls. The lady leaned on a carved ebony stick, and the broad panniers of her skirt blocked the wooden walk. Behind her the fashionable citizens of Mayfair and St. James, wrapped in furs and woolens against the fog, sauntered through Covent Garden piazza in colorful ranks.

Eilish rubbed her reddened hands together. Her chosen spot under the east portico of St. Paul's Church was the warmest in the whole square, but the chill fog crept in just the same. She pushed her little collection basket forward with her foot.

The water in her copper basin was greasy with the cold, and it stung her chapped fingers when she dipped them into it. Only thirteen glasses remained in the crooked wooden stand that served as her instrument case. Just last week a passerby had broken three of the glasses with a careless brush of her widely framed skirt, and Eilish hadn't enough pence to replace the glasses. She had to rearrange her melodies to accommodate the loss. She could only dream of a full complement of twenty-six, such as Richard Pockeridge played, or Maestro Gluck.

The old lady had stopped to hear "Barb'ry Allen," and Eilish began it again, slowing her circling fingers to draw out the sweet refrain, singing the words half under her breath. She glanced up hopefully at each cadence, gauging her listener's response.

> *"In Scarlet Town, where I was born*
> *There was a fair maid dwellin' . . ."*

"Ah," the lady said when she finished. "Lovely." She opened her eyes wide to fix Eilish with a rheumy stare. "How old are you, child?"

Eilish dropped a curtsy as best she could while bracing her unsteady case with her hands. "Ten, milady," she lied.

"Oh!" the old lady cried. "Only ten, and so talented?"

"I'm Irish, milady," Eilish said, as if that explained all. Perhaps it did. "You mustn't call me milady," the old woman said. "I'm only Mrs. Tickell." She looked behind her, and took one gloved hand out of her thick muff to gesture to someone. Her breath wreathed her wrinkled face with mist.

Eilish pushed the basket again, trying to make her two seed coins clink together. Talk bought no food. 'Twas money she needed. She made the basket rock on the uneven cobblestones, hoping to get the woman to make her donation before some sourfaced escort came along to tell her not to waste her pence.

But Mrs. Tickell wanted conversation. 'Twas better than what some wanted, at least.

"Where are your parents, child?" the old lady pressed.

Eilish gave a small, practiced sigh. "With the angels, missus," she said in her smallest voice. " 'Twas the fever carried 'em away, God rest 'em, and left me behind. And three little brothers to care for!" She sniffed noisily, a real enough sniff. She caressed her glasses with three fingers, bringing out a little swirl of harmony, a triad that shimmered and evaporated into the mist like the passing of a shade. Eilish shivered, and that was real, too.

Mrs. Tickell sighed theatrically. "How sad! We live in terrible times, do we not?"

At last, fumbling and scrabbling through the reticule hanging among the folds of her ample gown, the woman brought forth a ha'penny. She held it up with such a flourish, one would have thought it a shilling. Eilish held out her hand, and Mrs. Tickell, wary of the dirty palm, dropped the coin from several inches above. Eilish snatched it from the air with a nimble flash of small fingers. "Ta, missus." She held the coin for a moment, to feel its history, but it was cold and dead. She thrust it into the little flat purse she kept inside her bodice, and pulled her cloak more tightly about her shoulders.

"Why, Aunt, I did not know you were fond of music!"

The sour-faced escort had arrived.

She wasn't truly sour-faced, though. She was young, and buxom, and the hand she tucked under the old lady's elbow was warmly gloved. Her skirts were far more practical than Mrs. Tickell's, being only moderately framed and of simple pressed wool. She wore no wig, but a close-fitting bonnet.

"Just think, Polly!" the old lady quavered, waving her stick at Eilish, narrowly missing her row of glasses. "This poor girl has lost both her parents, and she's only ten years old!"

"Ten, is it, Aunt?" Polly said. She looked at Eilish with sharp brown eyes beneath curving brows. Her cheeks were round and pink, her chin dimpled.

Eilish's own eyes were the vivid blue of the Black Irish. She blinked, all childish innocence. "Shall I play you a tune, milady?" she asked. "Irish, Scotch, or English?"

The young woman's smile made her plump face very

pretty. "Oh, Scotch, I think," she said. To her aunt she said, "Mr. Franklin does love the Scottish airs."

Eilish bobbed once and dipped her fingers into the basin. She began "Bonnie Laddie, Highland Laddie," modifying the melody to suit the paucity of her glasses. She kept her head down, avoiding the young woman's gaze, watching her own fingers circle the rim of each glass. The sleeves of her dress were tied back with grimy ribbons to keep them out of her way, and her thin wrists embarrassed her. Her dress, lacking even a petticoat, hung straight as string from her narrow shoulders. Her cloak was threadbare, its collar torn, and she with no needle to mend it.

When the tune was ended, she glanced up to see the younger woman frowning again. Eilish took her hands from the glasses and thrust them under her arms for warmth. She had grown so much that her skirt barely reached the tops of her shoes, and the cold reached beneath to freeze her ankles. She would have to visit the Rag Fair for a second time this year, if she could scrape together a little money. She toed her collection basket again, but without much hope.

The old lady's eyes strayed away from her, down King Street, searching for some fresh attraction. "Come, Polly," Mrs. Tickell said. "Let's see what Mr. West is showing today."

She hobbled away in the direction of the milliner's. Her niece hung back a moment, still fixing Eilish with her sharp gaze. "You're not really ten, are you?" she asked.

Eilish wished the woman would move along if she had no intention of broaching her purse. "It's a close enough number, miss," she said. "I might be."

"You're an orphan? Truly?"

Eilish was on certain ground here. "Truly," she said, lifting her chin. "Soon after we came to London, me ma died. Me da followed the very next year."

"No doubt you should go back to Ireland, then," the young woman said.

"Ireland's no better, I can tell you, miss," Eilish answered in a peppery tone. This one had no mind to offer her a penny. "Food and money and work are short. So here I am."

"Hmm." Polly eyed Eilish, and Eilish stared right back. Polly took a step after her aunt, saying, "I must go. But perhaps—Is this your special corner, or any such practice?"

"If I'm early enough, 'tis mine, miss. Unless some dirty buffer pushes me out." She shrugged. "Then I find some other corner. But I like it here, just by this column. 'Tis warmer."

"Where do you live?"

Eilish hesitated before she said, "Seven Dials, miss. Down Monmouth Street."

Polly drew back a little, full lips pursed with distaste, but still she did not leave. "Tell me—Will you be here tomorrow? Are you working tomorrow?"

A juggler began a noisy show in the center of the piazza, turning the heads of passersby. Eilish, afraid of losing her audience, dipped her fingers into her little basin of water and began to play "Planxty McGuire." She said, her fingers circling, circling on the glasses, "I work every day, miss. The little ones, you know."

Polly tilted her head to one side and regarded Eilish doubtfully. "Oh, of course, the little ones," she said. "Well, perhaps I will see you tomorrow. There's someone who should hear you play." Without farewell, she turned away to follow her aunt. She lifted her long skirts as she stepped over the edge of the wooden walk, showing very clean, embroidered damask shoes.

Eilish glared after her. "Bring money next time," she muttered. Her fingers were almost numb, but they slid around and around the tuned glasses, spinning their plaintive melody out from under the eaves of St. Paul's and into the bustle of Covent Garden market.

•   •   •

SEVEN Dials was as dark and close as Covent Garden was bright and spacious. Eilish, her assortment of glasses wrapped and carefully stowed in rags gone gray with age, lugged her wooden case across King Street, down to Garrick, and on to Monmouth. It was a long walk, and she stopped several times to catch her breath and ease her aching hands. At least the effort made her warm for the moment.

Home, for Eilish Eam, was little more than a cupboard granted her by the aging whore who paid rent on one corner of the courtyard tenement. Dooya O'Larick walked the streets of Seven Dials and the Strand by night, and slept by day. Her son, a big-eyed boy of three, crept about during daylight hours in the cramped flat above the Clock and Cup Public House, careful not to wake his mother. Eilish stayed with him nights while Dooya went about her business.

Dooya had known Eilish's da before he died, and had taken her in to help with the boy. Though of the opinion that Eilish would be better off pursuing her own chosen trade, Dooya tolerated the girl's skimpy income in order to have her in the flat by night.

The sounds of London changed as Eilish made her way into Seven Dials. The lilt of spoken Irish flowed from crowded buildings and cramped shops to mingle with the syncopated chatter of the Cockneys, the calls of the costermongers, and the shouts of children. The buildings leaned so closely together that neighbors could shake hands across the street from the upper windows. The slanting tenements closed out the worst of the wind and fog, and captured the smells of cooking soup and rotting garbage, making the narrow streets as noisome and cozy as a fox's den.

Eilish much preferred her own end of Monmouth Street to the wide boulevards of Covent Garden. Few swells dared the streets of Seven Dials, for fear of having their pockets picked or their heads broken. And Eilish was known here. She was Raffer Eam's daughter. No one grasped at her skirt or groped at her chest to see if she was worth hauling into some corner.

"So, you're here at last!" Dooya cried when she staggered up the dark stair, her case banging against her knees. The boy, Mackie, came to greet her, wobbling on his crooked legs.

Eilish leaned her case against the inner wall of the tiny room that was hers, and pulled off her bedraggled cloak. Soup was steaming on the hob, and Eilish hurried to put out her aching hands to the coal fire. There was no other heat in the room. She and Mackie slept on Dooya's bed, curled together for warmth like orphaned kittens. On the coldest nights, Eilish piled her cloak and an old dress, too short now to wear, on top of the worn blankets.

"And how much today, me lass?" Dooya demanded, holding out her hand.

Eilish pulled the little purse out of her bodice and emptied it into Dooya's palm. Dooya picked over the few coins with dirty fingernails.

" 'Tisn't much, is it?" she snapped. "Wasting your time! Oughta follow my example."

Eilish tossed her head. "And who'd be staying with your spalpeen, then, Dooya? While you're playing the trull?"

Dooya only grunted as she bent over the kettle to ladle oyster stew into a wooden bowl. She set the bowl on the crooked table and put a spoon beside it. Mackie pulled on Eilish's hand.

"Hi, Eilish," he piped. "Soup! Soup!"

Eilish smiled at him, and kissed the top of his head. Dooya gave her a bowl of stew, then sat down with her own. Dooya was thirty-five, with faded red hair, and freckled skin ravaged by hard living and poor food. She was missing one front tooth, and two bottom ones.

Mackie was redheaded, too, his face round and white, his freckles standing out like flyspecks. His short legs, it seemed to Eilish, were even more crooked than they had been the year before. He was cheerful and affectionate, though he often screamed with night terrors, making Eilish irritable with fatigue the next day. It was perfectly true, as she had said to the well-fed Polly, that she played her glasses every day of her life. Even then there was never enough to eat, and she was cold, always cold.

Dooya finished her stew and sopped up the broth with a heel of bread left over from the day before. One slice was left for Mackie. It was dry, but he chewed on it, anyway. Eilish had the dregs of the stew, the last oysters, and a few scraps of scorched potato. Dooya, as always, finished off her meal with a big glass of gin. Gin, at least, was cheap and plentiful.

The flat's grimy window looked out into Monmouth Street, where one block to the northeast the clock stand, Seven Dials, marked the intersection of seven roads. Eilish watched from the window as Dooya made her way through the courtyard and disappeared into the evening traffic. Dooya would go to the pillar of the seven clocks, and lounge about until someone approached her. If her customer wasn't particular, she would satisfy his needs right then and there, in the shadows. If he was a bit more discriminating, she might lead him back up the road to her rooms, in which case Eilish would take Mackie into her cupboard to wait until the work was done. The sounds and smells of such work made Eilish swear never to follow in Dooya's uncertain footsteps.

Eilish and Mackie slipped under the blankets in the bed Dooya slept in by day, and Mackie snuggled close to Eilish, his shaggy red head tucked under her chin.

"You're cold, Eilish!" he complained.

"You just stay close and make me warm," she said. "And I'll tell you a story."

"A long one," he said.

"Right. A long one."

They curled together, and the noises outside, calling voices, crying, laughing, sometimes screaming, faded away as Eilish whispered the old Irish tale about the little girl carried off by the fairies to Heaval. There was a song about it, "O Little Sister," and she murmured the refrain, "Hu ru, hu ru," in Mackie's ear. He grew still when the story was only half finished. She let her voice trail away, bit by bit, until she was sure he was asleep. Their little nest of blankets grew warm, and Eilish thought she might have been comfortable if she were not still so hungry. Her belly ached, demanding food. *Tomorrow*, she thought drowsily, *tomorrow I'm keeping some of those pennies to buy me own bread.*

2

London, November 1761

THE bells of St. Mary-le-Bow chimed four before Dooya O'Larick staggered up the stairs behind the Clock and Cup. Eilish knew she was home by the reek of gin and the sour cloy of that other, alien smell. She sighed and groaned when Dooya slapped her rump through the blanket. "Off you go, me girl."

Groggily, Eilish detached Mackie's arms from about her neck. She moved blindly, only half waking, to her own tiny room as Dooya fell heavily into bed next to the child. Eilish's cot was icy cold, and she shuddered as she laid her head on the rag pillow. Dooya's snores filled the tiny flat. Eilish lay shivering, her belly empty, her feet aching with cold. She tucked her feet up under her bedgown, but still it seemed an hour before she slept again.

When the first finger of wintry sunshine poked through the flat's window, Eilish climbed wearily from her cot. She dashed water on her eyes and face, gasping from the cold. She found herself thinking of the young woman, Polly, who had said she might return today. Silly, that. People said a lot of things on the street, and they never signified. Still, Eilish took care to make her face and hands as clean as she could with the frigid water and a grimy sliver of soap. She took up the old cracked tortoiseshell brush that had been her ma's and brushed the black cloud of her hair, slicking down errant curls with water, tying the whole up in a scrap of kerchief. The last thing she did before leaving, the last thing she always did, was to touch the little square of Irish linen, embroidered with tiny silken stitches, that she kept folded neatly on her single shelf. It used to be white, but was now a delicate beige. Eilish couldn't read, but her da had said 'twas an Irish blessing, left her by her ma. She touched it once each day. 'Twas all the religion she had.

Mackie still slept, tucked up against Dooya's wide back, as Eilish tiptoed across the creaking floor. Dooya had shed her clothes in a messy pile, her night's earnings, several pennies and one or two shillings, spilled about on the floor. "Silly clart," Eilish said under her breath. She bent down and nicked tuppence from the scattered coins. She would buy a fall apple from the costermonger for her breakfast.

As she was picking up her case of glasses, Mackie's big eyes opened.

"Oh, Mackie! Your mother bought a half loaf," Eilish whispered. "It's on the table. Shall I slice you some?"

Wordlessly, Mackie nodded.

"Come on, then." Eilish put down her case and went to cut a chunk off the day-old bread. She scooped up a ladle of cold oyster stew as well. She would have liked to make some stirabout for Mackie, but she dared not start up the fire for fear of the boy stumbling into it on his twisted legs, and Dooya such a sound sleeper she wouldn't know if the chimney fell down. The wee lad's legs were as rickety as Eilish's glasses case. He wriggled silently out of the bed now and staggered to the table, his bedgown dragging on the splintered floor.

Eilish wrapped a blanket around him from her own cot. "I'm off, Mackie," she whispered. "Don't wake your ma, now."

He shook his head, his mouth full of bread. "No, Eilish."

He knew well enough the back of Dooya's big hand that would warm his cheek if he woke her too early.

Eilish kissed his ragged head. "That's fine, then," she said.

She turned to go, but the little boy clung to her. "Mackie, too," he begged. "Take Mackie, too."

She looked down into his freckled face, and her heart fair turned in her breast. "I can't, sweeting," she said sadly. "I can't watch you while I'm playing the glasses. And it puts off the swells."

He nodded, dull-eyed. Eilish patted him, and picked up her case of glasses once again. As she maneuvered it down the narrow stairs, she felt cold and weary as the winter sun. What life was this they had come to find in the great city? Mayhap plump Polly had the right of it, and they should all have stayed in Ireland.

POLLY appeared just as she said she would, walking up under the portico of St. Paul's in the company of a man of perhaps fifty or fifty-five years of age. It was late in the day, perhaps an hour before teatime. Though the mists had cleared, the sky over the city was still gray, in the way of November, and most of the shoppers had gone off to their homes. Eilish had been thinking of giving it up. Her little basket held fourpence. Thruppence would satisfy Dooya, though she would lay about with the sharp edge of her tongue. Eilish would keep a penny for herself.

"Ah, here she is." Polly's voice was firm and carrying, announcing her arrival as she rounded the corner of the churchyard. Her hand, in an elbow-length silk glove, was tucked warmly under the arm of the gentleman. She wore a fur-lined, hooded pelisse over a wool sack gown, and her cheeks were pink with warmth. Eilish was certain her own were red from the cold, as red as her wet fingers. If the man with Polly had not looked so prosperous, with a lovely fatness rounding his waistcoat, she might have snubbed

them both. But another penny to take home would be a
blessing and might even soften Dooya's scolding.

Eilish began "Bonnie Laddie, Highland Laddie" right
away, remembering what Polly had said about the Scottish
songs. Indeed, the gentleman's wide, thin-lipped mouth
curved in a smile of pleasure. His eyes twinkled through
round spectacles, and he patted Polly's gloved fingers
where they curled over his arm. It was a gesture of fondness
such as Eilish herself had rarely known. She tore her eyes
away from it and concentrated on her tune.

Before she had even finished the air, tuppence dropped
into her basket with a sweet clink of coin against coin. She
played on to the end, adding a little skirl at the cadence,
just to say thanks. When she looked up, the gentleman was
nodding as if he knew exactly what she meant.

Eilish sketched a curtsy. "Ta, sir," she said.

The gentleman gave her a small bow. " 'Tis for me to
thank you," he said. His accent was odd, neither English
nor Irish nor Scottish, nor any other she knew. "The Scotch
airs are the finest, as I believe," he said. "They will never
be forgotten, I'm certain of it."

Eilish tilted her head, looking at the pair of them, taking
their measure. Surely the gentleman was too old to be the
young lady's husband, or fiancé, but there was some affection between them. He was old, sure enough, but there was
an air about him that drew the eye, commanded attention.
Her da had said often and bitterly, "Takes more than a title
to make a lord, 'tis the truth." In the Irish toft where Raffer
Eam had labored, the very bread from their table vanished
into milord's accounts. But Raffer Eam would have liked
the cut of this gentleman.

"Perhaps you know this one, milord?" Eilish began "The
Misty Mountain." Polly tossed her head at her gentleman,
but Eilish could only guess at the meaning of that. She
played on, her fingers cold, but her heart warmed by the
tuppence. She tried her best not to sniffle. She knew the
swells didn't like it.

The gentleman was nodding, listening, pressing Polly's hand tight to his side with his arm. He wore a modest brown wig and a fine green waistcoat with charcoal wool breeches and topcoat. He looked a gentleman given much to smiling, and when he smiled at Eilish at the end of her song, she had to smile back. She scrabbled in her pocket for a bit of rag and wiped her nose as genteelly as she was able.

"Well, Polly," the gentleman said, "you were right. She's very good." He nodded to Eilish. "Where did you learn to play the musical glasses?"

"Me da," she said. "And he learned from Mr. Pockeridge."

"Oh, yes," came his response. "Richard Pockeridge, that is," he said in an aside to Polly. "And have you heard Mr. Gluck play? No, no, you're too young by half. But he had many more glasses than you do here."

"I know, milord," Eilish said. "I had three more than these, but they got broke by a lady."

"Well, well, a shame. And what's your name, my dear?"

"Eilish Eam, sir," Eilish said, and bent her knees again.

"Polly says you're ten years old . . ." The gentleman eyed her carefully through his spectacles. They were odd, those eyeglasses. They had a line through the middle, from side to side, such as Eilish had never seen before, and he had the habit of dropping his head to peer through the top half. Generous flesh folded beneath his chin when he did that, and his eyebrows went very far up his high forehead. "I expect you're a bit older than that, hmm?" he prompted.

His easy ways were disarming. His canny dark eyes tempted Eilish to tell him the truth about everything. She clenched her teeth hard, to stop herself. When he reached in his pocket and drew out a shilling—a whole shilling, by the angels!—and put it in her basket, she could have wept with joy. She curtsied a third time. "Would you like another tune, milord?"

He chuckled. "I think you know I'm not a lord, don't you, lass?"

Polly frowned at Eilish, her full lips pinched together. Eilish noted with some satisfaction that the sour expression made her face plain as plain. "You mustn't deceive Mr. Franklin," Polly snapped. "He may present you with a proposition, and you must start as you mean to go on."

The smile faded from Eilish's face. She didn't like the sound of "proposition." Just this morning, one of the swells had sidled up and rubbed himself against her as if she were as easy as his own dirty hand. The memory still made her furious. Only the appearance of one of the Bow Street Runners, twirling his baton as he strolled the road between St. Paul's Church and the piazza, had prevented worse. And the bounder hadn't left so much as a ha'penny for her pains!

"That's as may be," Eilish muttered, half to herself.

Mr. Franklin surprised her by laughing aloud. "Quite right you are, Miss Eam," he chortled.

Polly sniffed. "Treat Mr. Franklin with respect, Eilish Eam," she said. "He's a great man, greater than any you'll ever meet again, I vow!"

"Now, now, Polly." The gentleman gave her hand another pat. "Our Miss Eam has spirit. And well she might, working here on the street as she does!" He dropped his head again to peer at Eilish over his spectacles. "Tell me true, now. You're orphaned?"

Eilish looked at the two of them with deep suspicion. Stories of slave traders and whoremongers flew about the Clock and Cup, and Eilish had no doubt there were even more tales she'd never heard. But Polly, and her aunt Tickell, and this impressive gentleman . . . they hardly seemed like slavers. More like they were in search of a servant. Eilish tilted her head and arched her brows. "Why d'you want to know?"

Polly drew breath again, but Mr. Franklin was already

speaking. "A fair question," he said firmly. "Young ladies with no family must protect themselves."

Eilish stared at him. No one in her short life had ever referred to her as a young lady. Lassie, yes. And colleen, or chit, or, often enough, brat. Not young lady. Her cold cheeks burned with confusion.

Mr. Franklin seemed to read her every thought in her face. His smile grew more gentle, his dark eyes warm. She had to struggle to feed the flame of suspicion burning in her breast. There was a kindness in his face that could persuade a girl to foolishness.

"Miss Stevenson is in the right of it," Mr. Franklin said. "I do indeed have a proposition for you, an offer of employment, if you will. An honest offer, without dishonor to you or to me! But it means I would want you to come with me—with us, that is," he added quickly. "I'm doing an interesting bit of work, and I need a musician. A musician like you."

Musician. Young lady. It was too much for Eilish, altogether too like the blandishments of the young men who begged her to toddle off into a dark corner of the Clock and Cup to give up her favors. " 'Tis already working, I am," she said, lifting her chin. "Just look at my basket!"

Mr. Franklin laughed again. "Yes, indeed! And it looks much the better for my visit!"

Eilish lowered her chin. " 'Tis true, that," she said bluntly. "And I thank you, sir. But as you says, I have to watch out for meself as there's none else to do it."

Polly Stevenson protested, "You haven't heard Mr. Franklin's suggestion yet!"

"Come now, Miss Eam," said Franklin with a gentle smile. "You know, I have a daughter of my own, though far older than you, and I wouldn't wish harm for anyone, could I help it. 'Tis just that I have need of someone with your special skill."

"You mean my glasses?"

"I do." Franklin lifted one arm in a summons. A carriage, very neat and small and drawn by a single horse, came clopping up from the corner of King Street. Eilish goggled as a rather short, quite well-fed black man leapt down from the driver's seat to open the door. She had seen blackamoors, of course, but only the little ones who trailed after their mistresses like tired lapdogs. She had never seen one full grown.

Franklin saw her stare. "That's my slave, Peter," he said. "You can see I am a man of substance, and not some rogue seeking advantage over a feckless girl! Come with me, Miss Eam, see my home—our home—" He nodded to Polly. "Let me show you what it is I want with you."

Eilish hesitated, torn near in half by indecision. The inside of the carriage looked wonderful warm, and she was shivering. Polly Stevenson twitched her muff impatiently. "Please do hurry, Mr. Franklin. It's ever so cold out here this afternoon."

Mr. Franklin said, "I've no doubt Mrs. Stevenson— mother to Polly, here—will serve us some tea, Miss Eam. Wouldn't you enjoy some nice hot tea and scones, perhaps some chocolate?"

That did Eilish in. She was, after all, only thirteen, and had not had a full belly in her memory. She said, stiffly, "I s'pose I might."

"Good, good," Franklin said easily, as if he had just invited an old friend for a ride. "Come, then, pack up your glasses, and we'll be off."

In her nervousness, Eilish's chilled fingers were clumsy. It seemed to take half an hour to pack up her case, especially with Polly Stevenson fidgeting before her, but she finally got it done, carefully packing the rags around the glasses. Her earnings she slipped carefully into the little purse inside her bodice, and it hung nice and heavy against her narrow chest. Soon after, she was tucked into the carriage with a lap robe over her knees.

It was as warm inside the carriage as it looked, and made the warmer by the bulk of Mr. Franklin and the generous sweep of Polly's woolen skirts. Scents of bay rum and face powder tickled Eilish's nose, and she grew drowsy with the unaccustomed heat, the delicious ease that came with being carried rather than doing the carrying. She had meant to watch carefully where they were taking her, but instead her eyelids grew heavy, and her chin fell down on her bosom. The jouncing of the carriage was like being rocked, back and forth, up and down. The afternoon began to seem like a dream, warm and comfortable and wondrous, and Eilish's sense of time slipped away.

"And here we are!" Mr. Franklin's jolly voice woke her all at once. The sky wasn't much darker outside. It must have been a very short journey.

"Number Seven Craven Street!" Franklin announced as he leaped out and held his hand to Polly and then Eilish. "And a more hospitable home you won't find in London."

Eilish looked up at the long, two-story house with its tall windows glowing in the gathering dusk. She didn't know what awaited her inside Number Seven Craven Street, but it was certainly a respectable, even grand-looking, house. And it did look like a place where they might have scones for tea.

She fetched her case from the carriage and followed Mr. Franklin and Miss Stevenson up the short walk. The black-amoor held the iron gate open for her to pass through as if she were a real lady. She glanced up at the yellow rectangles of the windows once again and took a deep breath. "Oh, well," she whispered. "In for a penny, in for a pound, eh, Da?"

3

Seattle, April 2018

TWO polite taps on the dressing room door. "Five minutes, Miss Rushton."

"Thank you." Erin Rushton washed her hands one last time, and dried them carefully on a fresh towel as she checked her reflection in the dressing room mirror. The long, narrow dress was black, to set off the ragged halo of her silver-blond hair and the whiteness of her slender arms. The bias-cut neckline draped loosely around her shoulders, making her small breasts disappear in artful folds. Her shoes were flat, so she would be no taller than her five feet five inches. No jewelry, very little makeup. She looked about fourteen. Just what Mal wanted.

She used the towel to turn the doorknob, keeping her fingers squeaky clean, then dropped it as she walked backstage, flexing her fingers. The oboe's A floated through the hall, and Erin felt the familiar thrill of nerves in her arms and shoulders as the other instruments took up the pitch, passing it from the winds to the strings, the strings to the brass. Her soft pumps were silent on the bare boards as she moved to the wings.

Lewitt was waiting behind the stage left proscenium, his

cork-tipped baton under one arm. The gold threads in his tux jacket glittered under the worklights. He smiled when he saw Erin. "Ah, there's our girl! You look lovely. Need anything?"

"No, I'm ready, Maestro."

"Good, good. Full house tonight."

"Is it? Wonderful."

The jumble of sound from the orchestra subsided. Lewitt counted to three, winked at Erin, then strode out to center stage. A wave of applause rose from the house to greet him. The conductor bowed into it, then turned to stretch out his hand to Erin.

She stepped quickly past the proscenium, leaving the coolness of backstage for the hot glare of the footlights. She walked with her head up, smiling. Black silk swirled around her ankles, skimmed the toes of her shoes. The applause swelled and she bowed, keeping one hand on the drooping neckline of her dress. The audience in the concert hall was invisible to her past the white lights, but she could hear their murmurs as the clapping died away, feel their eyes on her, sense the energy of their anticipation in the darkness.

She stepped behind her instrument, adjusted the position of her bowl of distilled water, touched the power with her foot to begin the spinning of the glasses. As always, she looked to the stage-right proscenium for Charlie. He was there, watching from his silver chair. He grinned and gave her a thumbs-up.

Erin dipped her fingers into the water, nodded to Lewitt, and the concert began.

The first half of the program was the usual, the Mozart Adagio and Rondo, the Reichardt Rondeau, the mad scene from *Lucia*. The soprano for *Lucia* was tall and large-breasted, wearing a sparkling blue dress and flashing earrings. She threw out her arms as she sang, her bosom heaving, the dress and earrings glittering with each movement. Erin knew Charlie would have something to say

about that, but the audience seemed to like it. As Erin answered the singer's staccati with precise fingers, tiny drops
of water flew from her spinning glasses to sparkle in the
lights as they fell. The echoing passages rang nicely in the
clean ambience of Sokol Hall, and the ovation at intermission was solid.

The soprano bowed, Erin bowed, Lewitt bowed, the orchestra stood, and Lewitt bowed again. He brought the
singer out for a second call, and then, without warning, he
waved Erin forward. She was caught by surprise, having
already moved behind her instrument to turn off the power.
She took an awkward step to the side and bowed quickly,
knowing better than to waste a moment of applause.

She forgot about the dress. The neckline drooped, offering a flash of white skin, a glimpse of black satin slip.
Too late, she pressed her palm flat against her chest. *Oh,
dammit. Not again.* She smiled and nodded as if nothing
had happened, but she felt her cheeks flame as she preceded
Maestro Lewitt from the stage.

Erin went straight to her dressing room after the curtain,
avoiding the chatter of the orchestra as they left the stage.
The stage manager brought her a cup of tea, and she sat
sipping it through intermission, trying to convince herself
the bow didn't matter, that no one could have seen. When
the program resumed, she listened over the monitor as the
orchestra played Barber and Ives. Just before the *Requiem*,
she washed her hands once again, and went backstage to
wait for her cue.

The stage darkened gradually until it was completely in
shadow except for the little pools of white cast by the orchestra's stand lights. A hush fell over the hall. The holographic projector came on, focusing a point of vivid light
above the stage that bloomed swiftly into colored images.
The shining wood of the violins and cellos glimmered, reflecting blue and vermilion and scarlet. The audience exclaimed, and then quieted. Erin flexed her shoulders as the
excitement rose in and around her.

The *Requiem for North Korea* contrasted the crystal voice of the glass harmonica with a double quartet of strings and a trio of winds. Charlie knew exactly how to elicit an emotional response with glass music, how to draw the nerves to a fine edge, to play with the human ear as if it were an instrument itself. At the premiere of the *Requiem* in Boston, people had cried out, moved by the music, anguished at the heartbreaking scenes above their heads. More than a few had wept. The net reviewers had been at a loss to describe the effect.

The glasses began to spin, glittering with refracted color from the holograms. Erin waited, hands poised, breathless with concentration, for Lewitt's downbeat.

The downbeat wasn't quite right. It was hesitant, too slow. The harmonic movement of the first section, the *Dies Irae,* would be lost. Erin sensed Charlie's twinge of dismay from the wings as clearly as if he had called out to her. She had the melody, so she pushed the tempo. Lewitt glanced at her, surprised, and she nodded the beat she wanted, subtly but clearly, hoping only he could see it. There! There, now he had it, and so did the strings. The violins were perfect. The cellos gave just the right balance in the forte section. Now the piece moved, it sang, it came alive.

Erin forgot about Lewitt. She forgot the audience and Mal and the dress, forgot technique and tempo and fingerings. Charlie's melodies came in fragments at first, blossoming in ever-longer phrases from the spinning crystals beneath her fingers. The orchestra followed her, she felt it with her as if it were part of her own instrument. Everything became instinctive, automatic. The music seemed not so much to come from them as to come through them, flowing like a wave from the sea, like a current of electricity, the musical ideas borne from Charlie's mind to the waiting listeners, transmitted through the synchrony of fingers and lips and breath, strings and reeds and glasses.

Erin's mind was set free. Her consciousness opened like

ripples in a lake, widening, growing, expanding in concentric circles from her moving fingers and the singing glass beneath them. The hall, the world, the universe resonated. Time and sound and thought were one.

Lux Aeterna, the last movement.

And there it was again.

The image was insubstantial, little more than a thought, a waking dream. A vague cloud of hair, a half-seen silhouette, the pale oval of a face. Thin arms extended, reaching . . .

It was a ghost, a vision, a wraith. It shimmered against the downstage right curtain as if hiding itself behind the proscenium arch, its outlines so delicate it seemed any movement of the curtain would disperse them like a passing mist. It was almost, yet not quite, real. Erin's forehead tingled like a receiver vibrating. Her mouth went dry, and the skin of her arms prickled.

Fear broke over her like a wave of icy water. She caught a sobbing breath, and forced her eyes away. She struggled to ground herself, to be in the present, to see only the stage, the music, her instrument. Her eyes fastened on Lewitt's white baton and followed it desperately, shutting out everything else.

Her training sustained her, the long hours of practice that made her the greatest of the contemporary glass harmonica players. The final bars of the *Requiem* required that her fingers skitter from the widest cups to the narrowest, her hands crossing and crossing again. Hardly knowing how she did it, she played on to the celestial cluster of sounds that represented release from torment, the end of suffering. And now the cadence, the final resolution. The end of the piece.

Breathless, she lifted her fingers from the spinning glass to let the sound, undampened, die away. The holograms faded gradually, leaving empty shadows above the stage. The ensemble sat with instruments still in place, bows arrested. There was a silence. Had it been all right? Erin couldn't tell.

In the quiet she lifted her eyes, and saw that the wraith had vanished as if it had never been there. The silence in the hall was deep and mesmerizing. Charlie would like this, would be delighted that the audience let the last notes decay against the curving walls of Sokol Hall before they began to clap.

At last they did applaud, slowly at first, then harder and faster, a thunder of hands. Cries of "Brava! Brava!" leaped from every corner. Erin bowed, her throat tight with emotion and satisfaction.

Lewitt brought Charlie from the wings. The cries changed to "Bravo!" for the slender blond youth bowing from his silver wheelchair. Someone brought Erin a huge bouquet of yellow tulips and white mums, and she laid them in her brother's lap, winning more applause. Lewitt brought the orchestra to their feet one more time, and then, at last, it was over. Erin and Charlie left the stage together.

Backstage, out of sight of the audience, Charlie hissed, "What happened? In the *Lux*?"

Erin only shook her head, stunned, trembling. Lewitt hurried up and seized her hand to pull her away, saying "Great! Great!" Erin apologized to Charlie with her eyes as she hurried after the maestro, following him into the greenroom.

Lewitt led Erin to the front of the room to receive their admirers. Compliments, hands to shake, introductions to the wealthy supporters of the orchestra. Elderly women in long dresses exclaimed over Erin, speaking to her very clearly and rather slowly, as if she were a clever child. A board member in a black period tux was taking still photos with a camera no bigger than a multicard, showering Erin with fragmented light. Younger people, middle-aged women and men, some children, stood watching.

One woman, tears streaming down her cheeks, wrung Erin's hand. "Miss Rushton, that was—I hardly know how to say—completely magical—I've been ill, you know. But tonight—"

Erin hated these confessions. She never knew what to say. She was grateful when someone else interrupted, and she could decently take back her hand. Perfume and aftershave and bodies too close together made the room stuffy and hot, and Erin began to long for fresh air.

Charlie rolled in, and he, too, was inundated by the crowd. Mal, in a beige- and gold-patterned tux, relieved Charlie of the flowers and found a stagehand to take them to the dressing room. He patted Erin's shoulder and mumured, "Good job. Really fine. And the dress is charming."

She flashed him a look. Behind her, Charlie snorted with suppressed laughter.

"Just one more, Miss Rushton, right there with Maestro Lewitt, all right?" the board member begged. Lewitt put one arm loosely behind Erin's back and smiled into the camera.

By the time Erin was free, the stage was empty and the houselights had been turned off. All the orchestra members were gone. Her instrument was packed in its cases under Mal's supervision and had been dollied to the stage door. Charlie and Mal followed as she trudged, exhausted, into the brilliant light of her dressing room. Unspent adrenaline throbbed in her temples. She unzipped her dress and let it fall to the floor in a puddle of black silk. "I hate this dress," she said.

"You look divine in it," Mal told her.

"Mal, it drives me crazy! It's too loose at the neck, didn't you see?"

Defensively, Mal said, "It gives the perfect impression."

"And ever such a nice peek at your little nippers, E," Charlie added wickedly, grinning.

Erin spun around, hands on her hips, and glared down the front of her satin slip. "Charlie! You could see them, couldn't you?"

Mal said, "If you'd just wear a bra, for godsakes, Erin!

And the dress makes you look an absolute waif, very pale and young."

"Except for the nippers," Charlie murmured.

"Oh, jeez. That's great." Erin turned away to pick up a pair of jeans from the floor. "Both of you scram so I can get dressed, okay? I'll be out in a minute."

She put one leg into the jeans.

"Not jeans, Erin!" Mal held out a hanger with a silvery blouse and skirt. "I brought this for you. For the reception."

Erin sighed. "Oh, Mal, I'm so tired. I don't want to go to a reception."

"You need to go. We're negotiating for next year's contract. You gotta do some p.r."

"But I hate doing p.r.!"

"No kidding?" Mal said in feigned surprise.

Erin had a recycled fabric T-shirt in her hand. Mal snatched it away from her. "No reff clothes, okay? Really, Erin, you have to go to this thing," he said. He thrust the blouse forward, and the silvery fabric rippled.

She didn't take it. "Why do I have to go? They're going to hire me again. Didn't you hear them in the greenroom? They like me in Seattle!"

Mal ran one freckled hand over his thinning gray hair, and rolled his mournful eyes. Puppy dog eyes, Erin and Charlie called them privately. "Never believe anything said in the greenroom, Erin. Just do this, okay? I wouldn't ask you if it weren't important."

Charlie said, "Let's compromise. Erin wears the jeans—anyway, Mal, they're very waiflike"—with a wink at Erin—"and the silver blouse. It's a very child prodigy kind of ensemble. And I'll wait at the hotel and order up some food."

Erin wiggled out of her slip, letting it drop as she buttoned the blouse. Mal picked up the slip and the black dress and hung them in a garment bag. The silver skirt he put in the bag, too, with one last aggrieved look at her jeans. Moments later they were crossing the darkened stage, Charlie having to negotiate around abandoned chairs and music stands. The limo was waiting, and Mal and the driver loaded the long instrument cases into the trunk.

Charlie spoke to his chair, then toggled the joystick to maneuver it closer to the open limo door. He reached for the door frame, and stood, shakily. Erin reached out to him. "Charlie! Let me help you."

"Thanks," he said. He leaned on her shoulder as he struggled into the car. Erin felt the shaking of his hands as she supported him. He was tired, too. Usually Charlie's hands were reliable. She stroked his cheek as he settled himself, and he gave her a weary smile. She pressed the autofold on his chair and slid the collapsed frame into the trunk beside the instrument cases.

The limo was a vintage Mercedes, long and black, circa 1950s. It had been retrofitted with a fuel cell and hot- and cold-servers in the interior, but in all other respects it looked exactly as it had when it rolled out of the factory. Erin settled back against the old leather upholstery, breathing the faint, pleasant smell of lanolin. Mal climbed in to sit facing her.

"We won't stay late, I promise," he told Erin. "You've got the netcast tomorrow, anyway."

Erin made a face. "Oh, dammit. I forgot."

"Don't say 'dammit' at the reception, okay, E?" Charlie said.

"Or 'jeez,' " Mal added dourly.

A tart response was on Erin's tongue, but she restrained it for Charlie's sake. She hadn't mentioned her wraith to him yet, either, but she would tell him tomorrow. He could rest now. She took a small velvet pillow from the seat beside her and tucked it behind his head. He leaned against it and smiled at her.

"The *Requiem* was beautiful tonight, E. The best ever," he said softly. "Good job with the *Dies Irae*."

She smiled back at him. His face was very like her own, except for the eyes. Hers were sharper, she knew, a brighter blue. The blue of his eyes was soft, gentle—sad, she supposed, though she hated to think that. A sad, sweet blue. "Thanks, Charlie. They loved the *Requiem*."

"And they loved you."

She whispered, "Never believe anything you hear in the greenroom," and they laughed together. Erin gave Mal an apologetic smile, and turned to watch the city slide past.

At least they hadn't put viewwindows in the limo. Sokol Hall had been built on the crest of a steep hill that looked west over Elliott Bay and east to the sparkling, microbe-scrubbed waters of Lake Union. The car swept down the wide street to roll slowly past tidy businesses and neat period storefronts to the exclusive hotels and condominiums lining the waterfront around the Pike Place Market.

Seattle, like most American cities, was a model of urban reclamation. The original façade of the Market had been carefully restored to look period, though the interior, of course, was contemp. At a stall in the entrance, men in canvas aprons slung great silvery fish back and forth as they had a hundred years before, except that now the fish were made of recycled plastic. City workers in green-and-white jumpsuits bustled here and there, picking up bits of trash, scrubbing bird droppings from benches and walkways. The street performers stationed in several spots around the Market and on the street were all appropriately costumed.

Their limo was waved to a stop at an intersection by a white-gloved policeman. Erin rolled down her window to hear a slender barefooted black man, wearing a straw boater and trousers shredded below the knee, strum an acoustical banjo. Behind him was an ice-cream shop with white scrolled-ironwork tables and a young soda jerk in a white cotton hat lounging behind the counter. A young couple in anachronistic jeans and reff T-shirts sat at one of the tables sipping from tall glasses.

"What is this? Nineteen hundred?" Erin asked.

The limo driver said politely, over his shoulder, "It's 1906, miss. When the Market first opened. That allows cars to drive in the area. First automobile rolled on a Seattle street in 1900."

"I like it," Erin said.

"You always like it," Charlie said, chuckling. "The older, the better, for you."

"Well, it's not just me, Charlie. It's everybody, isn't it? The cities, the neighborhoods. Everyone. I love it."

"You should love it," Mal said casually. "It's made your career."

Erin, tired, tense from the evening, felt her temper fray. "Oh, is that it, Mal? It couldn't be the music, maybe?"

Mal spread his hands and shrugged. "Showbiz," he said gloomily. "They like to see the little girl who plays the mysterious old instrument. It's not all about art, unfortunately."

Charlie patted Erin's hand. "Never mind," he said softly. "It's not important."

"No, of course not," she muttered. "Just showbiz."

The policeman waved his gloved hand and the car began to move again.

Mal said, "Close the window, will you, Erin? It's cold."

She pressed the button and the window rolled up smoothly, but she stared over her shoulder at the barefoot man with the banjo until the car turned a corner and she couldn't see him anymore.

4

London, November 1761

EILISH followed Polly's straight back up the stairway from the street to the ground floor of the house. A shining brass number seven fixed to the door proclaimed the address. A fat maid in mobcap and spotless apron opened the door at their approach, and a gust of warm air, fragrant with yeast and flour and hot sugar, welcomed them. The maid took Polly's pelisse and muff, but her cheeks turned an outraged red at the sight of Eilish, and she hurried away in a flurry of gray wool skirt and long, lace-edged apron. Eilish stood with her sad cloak in her hands, uncertain what to do next. Her mouth filled with water at the scents of baking wafting from the basement.

Polly said, "I'll let Mother know we're home, Benjamin. Why don't you show Eilish the laboratory, and then we'll have tea in the sitting room."

"Good, good," Franklin said. He gestured to the stairs. "This way, Miss Eam."

Eilish swallowed, and followed Franklin's substantial figure as he climbed another set of stairs to the first floor. Two doors stood open to the landing. Half-a-dozen umbrella handles bristled from a tall porcelain vase set between them. The door to the right opened onto a parlor crowded with dark wood furniture and chairs and couches covered in velvet. Eilish glimpsed a brass nautical clock, tall windows, and a gently smoking coal fire in a huge fireplace.

Franklin entered the room to the left, and went to light a floating oil lamp. As it flickered and glowed, Eilish looked around the room with wide and wary eyes.

An odd sense of recognition made her skin prickle. Rows of glass tubes reflected the lamplight, and an involved apparatus of jumbled wires and oddly shaped jars filled most of one wall, but none of this was familiar. She put her hand on the doorjamb, fighting a sudden disorientation. There was something, something about the tall windows, the shape of the room—a knowing, a ken—a remembering. She was relieved to see that there was no couch, nor any furniture except for a stool tucked under a rolltop desk. The fey feeling subsided in seconds, leaving her trembling and breathless.

Franklin lighted a tallow candle and held it high. "Over here, Miss Eam. Come and look."

He was standing by a waist-high table on which a won-drous assortment of glasses was laid out. The glasses, thirty or more of them, were arranged by size, from a tiny cup to a great beaker, and everything in between. Each had been turned on its side, and all were pierced by a metal rod. Two forked brackets supported the rod, which was bent at the ends into sharp angles. Beside this contraption was a glass bowl full of water. Eilish stared, not understanding.

"This is going to be my armonica," Franklin said with a nod of his head at the contraption. "My glass armonica." He put his hand on the rod. "Please," he said to her, ges-turing at the bowl of water. "Try it for me."

Franklin began to turn the rod with the angled end, and Eilish perceived it now to be a handle of sorts, like a pump handle. The rod revolved like the axle of a carriage, and the glasses began to spin. Glass and metal glowed in the warm lamplight, and Franklin grinned with delight, like a small boy with a wonderful toy, as he turned and turned the rod.

All at once, the pieces of Franklin's little puzzle fell together, and Eilish saw what he was about. She dipped two fingers into the water and put them out to touch the spinning glasses. At first the pressure was wrong, or Franklin didn't spin them fast enough. But in a moment, their efforts coordinated, like a right leg working with a left, and a strange sound emerged, two random pitches, unrelated, a dissonant chime as of heavenly bells. Eilish thrust all her fingers into the water and pressed down four, and then eight, to the spinning glasses. A delicate cacophony of pitches jangled sweetly together. She touched her thumbs to the glasses and ten crystal tones sang, echoing against the high ceiling, ringing off the wooden floor. There was no key and there were all keys. Eilish exclaimed at the beauty of it. "Oh, sir," she cried. " 'Tis a wonder!"

"Nay, my dear," he answered, but laughing too. "Not yet! 'Twill be soon, though. With your help!"

THE sitting room on the ground floor, just beneath the laboratory, held so many chairs faced every which way that Eilish hardly knew where to put her feet. The coal fire glowed cherry-red, and the heavy spiced air made her head spin.

"Please, sit down, Miss Eam," Franklin said cheerily. "Mrs. Stevenson will be along in a moment, I'm sure. She's no doubt down in the kitchen fussing over our tea."

Polly was already seated on a short, hard-looking sofa, and Eilish gingerly sat next to her. Polly's nostrils twitched, and she moved a little away. Franklin sank into a fat chair opposite them, and put both feet up on a small stool. "Ho, that's better," he said. "These boots have pained me all the day."

Polly said, "You must go round the bootmakers for a

new pair, then, Mr. Franklin, lest you ruin your feet."

Eilish hardly comprehended the idea of going to a boot-maker for boots. Her own dilapidated shoes came from the Rag Fair, like everything else she wore. She stared around at the overfurnished room, the shelves and tables, even the polished lid of a harpsichord crowded with snuffboxes, clocks, and figurines, the velvet cushions, the stern ancestral faces looking out of carved frames. Any single one of these gilt or enamel or porcelain gewgaws would have fed Dooya and Mackie for a week, a month perhaps.

She felt Franklin's gaze, and turned to see that he was regarding her over the tops of his strange spectacles, his eyebrows lifted. "Different to your own home, Miss Eam?" he said.

"I never bin in a room like this," she replied.

"And do you like it?"

"It's proper warm," Eilish answered carefully. She had no word for the abundance of things that met the eye in Mrs. Stevenson's sitting room. Their number overwhelmed her. She didn't know if they were beautiful or ridiculous.

Franklin chuckled richly. "That it is," he said. "Proper warm. Proper warm, indeed."

The maid returned bearing a laden tray and followed by an older woman in an open gown and a lace cap. Polly stood up. "Mother," she said, and went to kiss the woman's cheek.

Mrs. Stevenson looked very like Polly, though two stone heavier and with carefully arranged gray hair. The sharp brown eyes were rounder in the mother, softer, the back not so straight, the chin sagging now, undimpled. Eilish wondered if she resembled her own ma. What would it be like to look into another's face and see what you might look like when you were old?

"Ah, Margaret," Franklin said, waving his hand. "The tea smells wonderful. Just put it here, will you, Bessie? Good, good. You see, Eilish Eam? As I promised. Choco-late!"

The maid placed the tray on a little table in front of Franklin. Eilish gazed longingly at the hot dark chocolate and the fresh bread and scones. Again, when she lifted her eyes, Franklin's were on her. Without looking away, he said, "Margaret, this is Miss Eilish Eam, a young musician. She's had a long day and is very hungry. I'll just give her a plate, shall I?"

Mrs. Stevenson came to sit at Franklin's right hand. "How do you do, Miss Eam?" she said, her voice high-pitched and dry.

"Hello, ma'am," Eilish said carefully. She tried to nod to the older woman, but her eyes stole to the plate Mr. Franklin picked up. He buttered a thick slice of bread, spread red jam on a small scone, and added two iced cakes and a comfit sparkling with sugar. He poured a tiny cup of the thick chocolate and fitted it into the center of the plate. He held it out to Eilish, and she took it in her hands gingerly, fearful of dropping it.

Franklin said easily, "Just hold it on your lap, Miss Eam. *Bon appetit.*"

"What?"

"I was only wishing you good appetite, my dear," he said.

At the endearment, Polly frowned so hard that Eilish could fair hear her eyebrows draw together. "It's French," Polly snapped. "I don't suppose a girl like you speaks French?"

Eilish's temper got the better of her appetite. She held her plate firmly on her knees and said, with a toss of her head, "Girls the likes of me speaks Irish. And if I wishes you good appetite in me own tongue, will your tea taste better?"

Polly drew a sharp breath between her teeth. Mr. Franklin coughed and hid his face behind his hand.

Mrs. Stevenson said quickly, "Now, now, Polly. This is Benjamin's guest." She turned to Mr. Franklin and put her hand on his arm. "Now tell me, Benjamin. To what new project do we owe the honor of Miss Eam's visit?"

"It's my armonica," Franklin said, his wide mouth twitching. "I've been searching for a musician to help me, and Polly found this young lady down in Covent Garden."

As Franklin was speaking, Eilish tasted the chocolate in her cup. Polly sipped her tea delicately, not making a sound. Eilish tried to emulate her, but the chocolate was so sweet, and warm, and rich that she couldn't hold herself back. She downed it in three great gulps, and looked longingly at the sediment left behind. Franklin whisked the cup out of her hand and refilled it. She smiled at him gratefully and drained it again. When she took a bite of buttered bread, her eyes closed with ecstasy. Such bread, cloud-white and soft, could only have been made this very day. The sweet butter melted on her tongue like icing on a Christmas cake. Oh, Mackie would weep over such a taste!

The thought of Mackie made Eilish glance out the window. It was so dark outside! Dooya would be furious. Eilish stuffed half the scone into her mouth and chewed quickly. She didn't want to miss a morsel. Ah, but it was hard to think of leaving this warm room, this sumptuous feast.

Polly was saying, "I would like to see your progress before I have to return to Essex. But Aunt Tickell will be impatient if I delay."

"Oh, yes," Mrs. Stevenson said, "you really must go to Mary soon, Polly. I believe she must be home by now."

Franklin grumbled, "Silly business, making a young woman miss out on city life, just for a bit of inheritance!"

"But there it is, Benjamin," Mrs. Stevenson said. " 'Tis all the inheritance Polly is likely to have, other than this house."

Eilish's plate shone, empty of the last crumb. The comfit she dropped in her pocket for Mackie. There was still food on the tray, but she feared she would be sick if she ate any more. She glanced at the darkness beyond the windows once again, and Franklin saw her look.

" 'Tis growing late," he said, rising from his comfortable

chair with a grunt of effort. "If you've finished your tea, Miss Eam, perhaps we could discuss my proposition?"

"Bessie," called Mrs. Stevenson. "Come and remove Miss Eam's plate and cup."

A haughty Bessie returned to take Eilish's crockery with reluctant fingers, bearing it away at arm's length as if it were covered with ants. Eilish was too full and sleepy to care at this moment. She rose and followed Franklin out of the sitting room and back up the stairs. They passed the laboratory and continued up, past the second floor and on to the third.

Two small rooms occupied the third floor of the house. Franklin waved at the smaller one. "That's Peter's bedroom," he said. "And this one"—he indicated the slightly larger room at the front of the house—"is my son William's room when he's in England. I propose that you use it while we work on my armonica. Should William return, you can sleep in the little room behind the kitchen, in the basement."

Eilish blinked in perplexity. "Sleep here?" she said. "You want me to sleep here?"

"Yes, indeed," Franklin said with a generous smile. "I often keep strange working hours, and I would want you near at hand! It will all be quite proper, I assure you." He made a small bow. "You are well chaperoned, since Mrs. Stevenson lives on the ground floor, and Polly owns the second. And you will be the first, the very first, to play a newly invented musical instrument!"

It was too much for Eilish to comprehend. To live here, in Craven Street, far from the noise and smells of Seven Dials, to eat this wonderful food every day, to be warm as toast every night—surely the very angels could not be more comfortable! And the instrument, that beautiful, crystal creation with its unearthly sound—it was all beyond her.

"Come now," Franklin cried gaily, ebullient with excitement. "Let me show you where your concerts will be held!" He clattered ahead of her back down the stairs to the first floor, indicating his large parlor with a flourish.

"Right here!" he exclaimed. "You see, we will set up the armonica there, before the windows, and we will have a *salon* just as they do in Paris! You will play for my friends of the Royal Society, for my foreign visitors!"

Eilish stared at the spot he indicated. Three great windows, draped in heavy velvet ran from the floor almost to the ceiling. Her head was afog with food and drink and warmth, and as she gazed at the dark velvet folds, the present blurred. She saw herself standing beneath those windows, the strange little instrument before her, her hands stretched out over its spinning glasses. But this could hardly be Eilish Eam, wearing such a lovely long skirt, a clean white scarf tied about her shoulders . . .

She gave her head a brisk shake. She needed her wits about her, and for certain. This was no time for one of her trances. She breathed deeply, and the present returned to her.

Franklin beamed, immensely pleased with himself. Eilish faltered, "I-I don't know." She could hardly credit the offer. Was it opportunity, or peril? And how could she ever explain to this great man about Mackie?

"Well!" he said, clearly disappointed that she did not immediately seize upon his proposal. "I suppose you could think it over for a day or so. But no longer! I wish to press on with my invention without delay."

Eilish pressed her hands to her cheeks. "Mr. Franklin, I'm proper grateful, truly I am. But I have—'tis my—I hardly know—"

"There, now, never mind," he said. He put his hand under her elbow and propelled her swiftly to the stairs. "We'll send you home now, in the carriage, and I'll have Peter come for you tomorrow. If you've decided not to work with me, you can tell Peter. Otherwise, pack your things, and by tomorrow night, Number Seven Craven Street will be your home!"

•   •   •

DOOYA railed at Eilish the moment she stepped through the door. "Ye ungrateful wench! D'ye know the hour? And if I'm not about the work, who's to be feeding this house?"

She threw her voluminous cloak around herself and stamped to the door. "I saved ye no dinner, and serves ye right! What was I to do, go off and leave Mackie on his own?"

"I'm sorry, Dooya," Eilish said. "But I work, too, don't I?"

"Hah! For tuppence, thruppence. How much today, my girl? Enough for a loaf, or a few sardines? You call that work, playing on those glasses all day? Hah!"

Mackie, still seated over his porringer, began to sob, and Eilish went to soothe him.

Dooya said, "That's right, all sweet and loving now, aren't you, little drab? But you would have left him stay by himself all the night!"

"You could have called Rose Bailey up from the pub! She could stay with Mackie."

"And pay good pennies out of my earnings? Yer daft!" Dooya slammed out of the flat. Her heavy footsteps slapped against the bare wood stairs as she descended.

Eilish took off her cloak, and pulled the comfit out of her pocket. "Look, Mackie, me darlin'," she said. "I've brought you a treat."

"Candy?" Mackie said through his tears. "Candy, Eilish?"

She put her arm around him and wiped his nose with a bit of his bedgown. "That's right, me darlin', me little gossoon. Candy. Just for you." He sniffled and slurped on the comfit. She put her cheek against his ragged hair. The flat seemed colder and darker than ever, ugly and mean after the warm comfort of Number Seven Craven Street. Eilish looked at her rickety case of glasses, so few, such silly glasses, and she could have wept from indecision and longing.

5

Seattle, April 2018

WHEN Erin woke the morning after the concert, the phone console was flashing, telling her she was an hour late getting up. She groaned and rolled out of bed. She would have to hurry to dress for the netcast, and there would be no time for breakfast. "Charlie? Charlie!" she called from her bedroom. There was no answer. She pulled on a robe and explored the suite. Charlie wasn't there.

It had been late after all when she and Mal returned from the reception, and Charlie had been asleep. Now he was gone again. She still hadn't told him about her vision.

She found no message from Charlie, but he had hung out a dress for her, a blue-figured sheath with scarf sleeves and neckline. It made the ragged fronds of her hair look like spun silver. She showered and dressed, and was rooting through her disorderly closet for shoes when Mal knocked at the door and came in.

"Where's Charlie?" she asked him immediately.

He shrugged. "Haven't seen him." He eyed her critically. "You put lipstick on."

"Yes, and mascara too," she said. "I'm twenty-three, Mal. Legal in all fifty-two states."

He sighed. "Look, honey, I don't want you to be a baby. Just young. It's part of the package. And don't mention your age, okay?"

"What am I supposed to say if they ask me?" She straightened, a pair of sandals dangling from her fingers.

Mal looked mournful. "Can't you just say what those opera singers always say? About how you never ask a girl her age, all that stuff?"

"Oh, Mal. Opera singers!" Erin tossed the sandals to the carpet and thrust her feet into them.

Charlie showed up a moment later, looking dapper in a loose white cotton shirt and jeans. His hair, almost as pale as Erin's, was windblown and slightly damp. Drops of moisture shone on the arms of his chair.

"Hey, E, you look great! You ready?"

"Where've you been, Charlie?"

"Tell you later. Get a move on, they're all set up down in the lobby."

"Charlie, I haven't even had coffee. I'll be dumb as a duck."

"There's an espresso stand in the lobby." He waved his multicard. "I'll buy you a jolt while they do lights and sound."

Erin followed Charlie out, and Mal trailed behind them. They emerged from the elevator into a crowded lobby. Armchairs waited in a semicircle under a modest array of netcameras, and hotel guests loitered about, watching. One entire wall of the lobby was a long viewwindow in which Model T's drove on narrow streets, and women with bobbed hair and enormous fur collars strolled the sidewalks, casting coy glances out into the room.

A tall woman in a white silk jacket over black jeans tried to take Erin's hand to lead her to a chair. Erin, offended, pulled her hand away, and the woman looked around for help, spreading her hands in confusion.

Mal hastened across the room to them. "Erin, this is the producer."

The woman turned back to Erin and gave her a wide smile, cooing, "Hi, there. We're going to have some fun this morning, I just know we are. Can I get you something? Juice? Cocoa?"

Charlie rolled up and handed a cup to Erin. "Hi," he said to the producer. "I'm Charlie Rushton. There you go, E, caffeine as ordered."

The producer glowed at Charlie. "I love your music," she said in a confiding tone. "I have both your discs, and I just absolutely treasure them. And your playing, of course, Erin dear." Charlie rolled his eyes behind her back, and Erin bit her lip to keep from laughing. The woman said to Mal, "John will ask some questions, we'll cut to the concert footage, then come back to tie it up. Okay?"

"Sure, sure," Mal said. "Okay with you, Charlie? Erin?"

"Fine," Charlie answered. Erin nodded.

A makeup woman in a smock draped a towel over Erin's shoulders and used a large soft brush to lightly powder her cheeks. She eyed Erin's lipstick doubtfully. "It's a little dark, perhaps? Considering?"

Erin sipped coffee. "Considering what?"

"Well, I mean—it seems a little old for you. Do you mind if I change it?"

Erin scowled. Charlie said quietly, "Let her change it, E. Choose your battles, hmm?"

She sighed and shrugged. "Okay, I guess. Whatever you think." The woman leaned forward quickly and wiped away the lipstick with a cotton pad, painting on the new shade with deft strokes. Erin turned to Charlie, brows raised, for his assessment.

He grinned. "Not bad, actually. Very näif."

She threw the towel at him. The makeup woman took her cup away before she could finish her coffee.

John, the host, had large, unnaturally white teeth, and deep wrinkles disguised by a heavy, greenish foundation. He sat on Erin's left, Charlie on her right. Lights were moved and adjusted, the netcameras raised and lowered and rolled about, the viewwindow frozen and dimmed. Mal stood just beyond the lights, watching.

"This young lady sitting next to me," the host began, "is Erin Rushton, the reigning virtuosa of the glass harmonica." He made his voice deep by forcing his larynx very low. Erin felt a giggle rising in her throat, and she carefully avoided Charlie's eyes.

". . . debut with the Boston Pops at the tender age of eleven," John was saying. "Next to her is her twin by birth and by talent, the composer Charles Rushton. Tell me, Erin, Charles, how old were you when you knew you wanted to be musicians?"

It went on in the usual vein. They talked about Erin's early training. Charlie spoke easily about the Friedreich's ataxia that had put him in a wheelchair when he was eight. They talked about life as children on the concert circuit, tutors, studies, growing up in hotels. Erin tried desperately not to yawn, and longed for the vanished coffee. It seemed forever before John asked a musical question.

At last he said, "So, Erin, Mozart wrote a piece for glass harmonica, didn't he?"

"Two, actually," she said. "Adagio and Rondo in C Major, and Adagio in C minor."

"And what about the Donizetti piece, from *Lucia di Lammermoor*?" The host's smile was directed at Erin, but his eyes were fixed on a screen past her shoulder where his questions were displayed beyond the reach of the camera. She was used to that.

"It's the Mad Scene," she said, "from the last act."

"But," he went on blandly, "isn't that usually played by a flute?"

"Not in the original score." Erin would have bet her multicard John had never heard the opera in his life, but she tried to smile pleasantly. "Donizetti wrote it for glass harmonica."

"Now, that's curious, isn't it?" the host rushed on, looking past Erin's face to his prompt screen. "Why did that change?"

Erin felt the rising heat in her cheeks, and she took a deep breath. She dared a glance at Charlie and saw him studying his fingernails, lips curling. "That's an old story," she said carefully.

"Tell us about it."

"Oh, it's silly," she said. She crossed her legs. One foot began to twitch. "Really, uh, John, nobody believes that stuff anymore."

"What—*stuff* would that be?" He smiled indulgently, showing all of his beautiful teeth.

Erin's fingers began to drum on the arms of her chair, and she folded her hands together. "Nervous breakdowns, illness, that old stuff. It was idiotic." She uncrossed her legs and leaned forward, then realized she was blocking the prompter.

John wouldn't give in. "Well, it is a mystery, isn't it?" he pressed. "I mean—" He leaned back in his chair to see past her. "The glass harmonica fell out of use around 1830. It was banned in some places, I understand, and those who played it died mysterious deaths. Do you ever worry about that?"

Erin knew her cheeks were red, and she could feel her voice rising. "Does anyone ask if Stradivarius got slivers, or how many elephants died for the sake of a Steinway? If I played the piano, would you ask me how Schumann ruined his hands?" She crossed her legs again, and tried to sit still. "The glass harmonica is a wonderful instrument, and there's some fine music for it! Can we talk about Charlie's work?" Her throat was tight, and she was afraid she would burst into childish tears. "Jeez, do we have to go over these stupid stories?"

"Cut!" the producer cried in a desperate tone.

The host threw up his hands. "What? What did I do?"

Erin collapsed against the back of her chair, mortified.

Charlie was laughing, but Mal was furious. He strode into the light, his sagging jowls trembling.

"Erin!" he hissed. "Do you have to do that? This is for a netcast! Can't you behave?"

She protested. "I didn't say anything wrong."

Charlie murmured, very softly, "Jeez."

Erin felt stretched tight by fatigue and hunger and frustration. She needed coffee, and food, and more sleep. "We were supposed to talk about the music!" she cried.

The producer came to stand beside Mal, her vivid smile rigid. "Now, now, everyone, it's okay. We can use most of that . . . Well, maybe we'll just trim that last little bit. Erin, dear, can I get you some water or something, give you a moment to relax? And then we'll start again."

ERIN fled to the suite the moment the interview wrapped, avoiding Mal's scolding and Charlie's teasing. She ordered breakfast sent up, and went to the wall panel to turn off the viewwindow and turn up the lights. She set the music stand beside the glass harmonica and put Charlie's newest score on it.

Moving Mars wasn't finished yet, but it was already a challenge. Erin was eager to get at it. Dizzying key changes were going to require abrupt movements of both her hands, and the fingerings looked impossible. Erin scrubbed her hands and began at the beginning.

She played the first passages slowly, experimenting, feeling her way through the harmonic progressions. She stopped when her tray arrived, and ate quickly, turning the pages of the score. Charlie's broken bits of melody were scattered at wider intervals than usual, and she searched through the music for them, seeking to understand the structure, the connection, the forward movement of the piece.

She washed her hands again and resumed her practice, gradually approaching the tempo Charlie indicated. She found ways to shift her hands quickly, finding the new chords under her fingers, her palms. The music was daring, full of contrasts. It was utterly different from the *Requiem*. It was wonderful. Hours passed without her noticing.

At the opening of the door, she started, and missed a fingering. "Dammit!"

"Happy to see me?" Charlie said mildly.

"Oh, sorry," Erin laughed. "Hi." She straightened her back and rubbed her stiff neck. "What time is it?"

"Time for dinner. I'm starving. What have you been doing all day?"

"Trying to learn your bloody score, you beast. Whatever made you think you could modulate from D to B flat without any preparation?"

Charlie chuckled. "You'll get it. You always do. You can't move a planet without some surprises, can you? I have more surprises, too."

"What? Is it going to be even harder?"

He wiggled his eyebrows, trying to look mysterious. "Nope, nothing to do with you. But I have an idea—don't ask, because I'm not ready to say."

"Listen, Charlie. I have to talk to you. I have to tell you what happened last night."

"Better tell me later. Mal's waiting downstairs."

"But, Charlie—"

"Come on, E. We'll talk after dinner. Let's try to make Mal happy for now. He's had a bad day."

IN the viewwindow of the hotel dining room a yacht with burnished teak sides and gleaming brass rails floated gracefully on twilight waters. From a lakefront park, picnickers waved as the vessel passed. Charlie pointed and said, "The maitre d' tells me that boat belonged to Al Capone." Responding to the movement of his arm, one of the figures in the scene waved in the direction of their table. Charlie chuckled and waved back.

Mal was studying his multicard. "It's an early plane tomorrow, kids. The limo will be here at eight. You better pack tonight."

Charlie turned away from the viewwindow and put down his fork. "Listen, Mal. Erin. I'm not going to San Antonio."

Erin's fingers slipped on her water glass, spilling drops of water across her plate. "Charlie! What do you mean, you're not going?"

Mal looked aggrieved. "They're doing the *Requiem.* You have to be there!"

Charlie shook his head. "No, I don't. Erin can handle the rehearsals."

"But why?" Erin demanded. "Why aren't you going?"

"I'm staying in Seattle." Charlie patted her hand. "Come on, E, you can manage. You know the piece inside out."

Mal sighed and leaned his chin on his hand. "What's up, Charlie?"

Charlie pushed his plate away and leaned back in his wheelchair. "I have an appointment with a doctor. A clinic. Here in Seattle."

"When did this come up?" Erin asked.

"Today. This morning."

"But, Charlie—"

He folded his arms, and set his sensitive mouth in a stubborn line. "I have to try this, E. Something different. New."

"What is it? Who is this doctor?"

"His name is Berrick. Neurophysiology. It's experimental."

Erin bit her lip. There had been so many doctors, so many different therapies. So many disappointments. She could hardly bear the idea of fresh hope, and the tears and rage and dejection that followed each attempt. "What's he do that's different?"

"It's kind of complicated, actually. It's a sort of retraining of the brain. With augmented sensory emissions. Rerouting the neural impulses, to bypass the damage in my brain."

"Augmented sensory emissions?"

"Tiny electrical impulses applied to the brain. To the cerebral and cerebellar cortex."

"Is that safe? And why didn't you tell me?"

He shrugged. "Didn't seem much point till I knew if Berrick would take me."

"But how did you find him?"

"I read a paper of his on the net. 'Clinical Applications of Augmented Sensory Emissions and Binaural Beat Research.' "

"Jeez. The net. Couldn't it at least be JAMA?"

Charlie made a derisive noise. "Please. Mother and her friends."

Mal had to ask, "Speaking of whom, does Sarah know?"

"I'll tell her later," he said.

"But won't you need a referral? From your doctors in Boston and Philadelphia?"

Charlie's fine mouth twisted, and he made a small, tight gesture over his legs. "I think these are referral enough. So does Dr. Berrick, apparently."

Erin put out her hand and took Charlie's. "I'll stay with you, then. Cancel San Antonio."

Mal choked on his coffee. "Erin, you can't cancel! What would we say?"

"She's not going to cancel," Charlie said. "Erin will go to San Antonio, and I'll stay here. No big deal."

"Then Mal has to stay with you," Erin said.

"No, he doesn't," Charlie insisted. "I can't walk, E. That doesn't make me helpless."

Erin felt a quick flush burn her cheeks. "Oh, Charlie, of course not! You know I never meant that! But you—" She looked away. "I'll worry about you."

"Don't," he said gently. "I'm not a child, either, Erin. Not if you're not!"

"Oh, yeah," she said. She turned back to him, tried to smile. "I forgot for a moment."

He grinned at her.

"But what about your physical therapy?"

"Erin. Stop worrying. Dr. Berrick has a physical therapist in his clinic, and all the machines. He's young, and he's new. He's not incompetent."

Erin had heard all of this before, in one form or another. She sighed, and looked into the shining evening scene of the viewwindow, the unlikely beautiful people and the sleek boats on the lake. Not a wheelchair in sight.

6

London, November 1761

EILISH lay awake most of the night, her back freezing, her right arm afire where Mackie's hot little head pressed against it. Her mind danced with visions of Mrs. Stevenson's home, the clean, full-skirted dresses, Polly's warm muff, the starched apron of the maid, Bessie. Her stomach roiled with the unaccustomed rich food, the sweet and stimulating chocolate. Every time she thought she would sleep, her stomach gurgled again, reminding her of scones and iced cakes. And through it all, above and around and beneath, floated the ethereal strains of music from Mr. Franklin's armonica, that beautiful, that tempting, creation.

Toward dawn she dozed, but woke soon after to the sounds of Dooya's heavy feet on the stairs. Pale light glittered on the rime-laced window. Eilish rolled sleepily out of the bed, and was halfway to her own bed when she realized Dooya was not alone.

She turned back to the big bed to get Mackie. Dooya laughed drunkenly on the landing, and a deep voice echoed her. Eilish's feet burned against the icy floor as she hurried to her own room with the sleeping boy in her arms. She pulled the curtain across her doorway and lowered Mackie to her bed with a little grunt at his weight. She climbed in after him, shivering at the cold bedclothes.

"Eilish! Hi, Eilish!" Dooya pounded on the wall with a heavy hand. "Eilish! Get ye out here, lass!"

Very slowly, with a sinking heart, Eilish got out of bed. She tucked one blanket in around Mackie and took the other to wrap around herself. She held it to her chin, and it dragged on the floor as she went to the curtain and peeked out.

"What d'ye want, Dooya?" she whispered. "Yer lad's asleep."

The curtain was pulled roughly aside, and Eilish jumped back. Dooya leered at her in the half-light.

"Get yer lazy bones out here," Dooya said. Her lips were loose and wet. The smell of gin roiled from her as if she had bathed in it. "Earn yer keep, ye little do-naught!"

"Close yer mouth, ye great sot!" Eilish said, still keeping her voice low. "Ye'll wake the kid!"

Dooya's thick hand closed on Eilish's arm. " 'S time you did some real work, lassie," she said. Her cheeks were aflame with gin, her eyes unfocused. "Time and enough fer you to learn."

Eilish tried to pull her arm free, but Dooya O'Larick was as heavy as three of Eilish. She tugged the girl out of her tiny room and into the flat.

A smallish man lay on his back on the bed, his black and gray beard stuck up like a flag, a brown glass bottle in his hand. He lifted his head as Dooya dragged Eilish across the room.

"Aye, and she's a sweet little piece, Dooya!" he cried. "Where ye bin keepin' yerself, sweetheart?"

Eilish gaped in horror at the man, and then at Dooya. "No, Dooya," she said faintly, and then more strongly, "No! No!"

Dooya pulled harder. Eilish caught at a chair with her free hand and tried to set her heels against the bare wood of the floor. "I said no!" she screamed.

Dooya rounded on Eilish with a stinging openhanded slap that made the girl's ears ring and her vision blur. "Time ye earned yer keep, me girl," she growled. Her hand rose again, and Eilish ducked to avoid it.

The motion twisted her arm out of Dooya's grasp. She scuttled backward, to the table, holding the chair out before her. Her ear burned from the slap, and she had caught a sliver in her foot. She tried to blink away the black stars that littered her vision.

The bearded man swayed to his feet. "Here ye go, little darlin'," he said. He staggered toward Eilish, waving the bottle. "Here, now, we'll have a little drink, and you won't feel a thing! I hardly feel anything meself!" His braying laughter blew spittle over his beard. He stumbled and grabbed at Dooya's shoulder to right himself.

Eilish crouched, panting, the chair in her hands. Her blanket had fallen away. The ragged shift that served her as a nightdress was far too cold, and despite her fear and fury, she began to shiver. "Leave me be," she chattered. "The both of ye, leave me be!"

The bearded man leered at Eilish. "Come on, now, lass! We're all ready, see?" He tugged at his trousers, and they gaped open. Eilish looked away from the sight of the dark hairiness, the grotesque tumescence. It was the more frightening for being half-seen, mysterious in the darkness, Mackie's little winkie grown monstrous.

He whined, "Dooya, 'ave ye played me fer a cully? Ye never said she wasn't willin'!"

Dooya pushed the man toward her bed. "Put yer needle away fer the minute," she said. "I'll deal with this little minx."

The man stumbled back to the bed with his bottle, falling heavily onto it, mumbling to himself. Dooya loomed over Eilish.

"Listen to me," she thundered. From Eilish's room Mackie began to scream. Dooya ignored him. "I've given you a roof and a table these four years, Eilish Eam," she shouted. "It's time and past ye did a bit o' work, and this is the work o' this 'ouse!" She grabbed at the chair and pulled.

"I won't!" Eilish cried. With all her strength, she shoved the chair at Dooya, striking her full in the chest.

Dooya fell backward, hitting the floor hard on her tail-bone. "Oh, me ass!" she shrieked. Mackie screamed louder, a hopeless monotone wail.

Dooya got to her feet again with difficulty, grunting, swearing. Eilish still held the chair, waving it before her, heart pounding in her ears. "Stay away from me!"

Dooya grabbed the chair in her two hands and flung it into a corner. Eilish cringed against the table. There was no place to hide. There was nowhere she could run. Dooya grabbed a handful of her hair and wrenched her toward the bed, growling, "Old enough now to do a woman's work!" And she thrust Eilish on top of the bearded man.

He smelled, if possible, worse than Dooya. The empty bottle he let fall, so as to have both hands for Eilish. He seized her right hand and forced it over his hot and swollen phallus. She shuddered with fear and revulsion.

"There now, me darlin'," he said in her ear. "Ye'll be all the happier for a bit o' fuckin'!" He fumbled at her nightdress with his other hand.

In the background Mackie howled on and on. Eilish twisted her head away from the man's stinking beard, and in so doing she spotted the gin bottle.

It was made of heavy brown glass, and it lay on the bed within a hand's-breadth of the man's shoulder. Eilish grabbed the bottle with her left hand and whacked the little man a great blow across the bridge of his nose.

He yelled in pain. Blood flew everywhere, over Eilish's hair, her shift, her hands. Free now, she scrabbled backward through the bedclothes, brandishing the bottle. "Don't touch me!" she screamed. "Don't ever touch me, ye bloody bastard, or I'll bash yer roger as flat as yer ugly nose!"

Her victim cried, "Dooya! Damn ye, Dooya, this little bitch's broke my nose!"

Dooya came flying, the still-screaming Mackie in her arms. She saw the mess of the man's face, the bedclothes, and Eilish still with the brown bottle in her hand. "What've you done?" she shrieked. Holding Mackie on one hip, she backhanded Eilish with her free hand. Caught by surprise, Eilish fell backward to the floor in a jumble of blankets, Mackie wailing at the top of his voice all the while. From the flat beneath came a thunder of pounding and voices shouting for quiet. For a long moment they all stayed where they were, Eilish scrabbling at the blood on her face, trying to wipe it off on the blanket, the man moaning and pressing the sheet to his ruined nose, Dooya cursing long and fluently under her breath.

At length, with most of the blood off her face and hands, Eilish got warily to her feet. She and Dooya stared at each other, both panting, open-mouthed. "Give me the lad," Eilish said, and Dooya, exhausted now, worn out by drink and exertion, handed him over. "Ssh, ssh, now, Mackie, me darlin'," Eilish said, pulling his head down on her shoulder. "Ssh, now, 'tis all over."

Dooya fetched a wet towel and began to mop up blood from her client's broken nose, the man wincing and then groaning like a woman in childbirth. "Great ninny," Dooya muttered. "Worsted by a slip of a girl. What a chucklehead."

Eilish soothed Mackie into silence while Dooya repaired her visitor as best she might. When peace reigned at last, Dooya and Eilish eyed each other. Dooya was a horrific sight, mussed hair, eyes red and cheeks purple, clothes awry, and Eilish supposed she herself didn't look much better.

"I told you," she said truculently. "I won't do it."

"Aye, and I'm tellin' you, me lass," Dooya said sullenly, "ye'll do it or be out on yer bum."

The knock at their door came immediately, as if ordained. First there were two polite raps, then four impatient ones in rapid succession.

"God's body!" Eilish swore. " 'Tis a madhouse!" Mackie began to whimper again.

Dooya threw the door open. "What d'ye want?" she demanded, before she even saw the visitor.

Peter, Franklin's blackamoor, stood on the narrow landing. In the darkness of the stairwell, his teeth gleamed white as he smiled and bowed. He held a modest tricorn hat in his hand, and looked past Dooya to Eilish. "Mr. Franklin bids you good morning, Miss Eam. His carriage is waiting below."

Dooya goggled.

Eilish stepped forward, putting Mackie into Dooya's arms. "Indeed!" she cried. "Do come in, Mr. Peter!"

The plump Negro hesitated, and then followed the disheveled Eilish over the threshold. He looked around at the chaos, the bearded man moaning on the bed with a wet towel over his face, the red-faced Dooya, a whimpering Mackie hiding his face in her shoulder. Peter took one step beyond the door and stopped, standing with his hand in the pocket of his braided waistcoat, his wide eyes showing white in his dark face.

Eilish teetered on the verge of hysteria. "Oh, I'm coming, I'm coming, to be sure, Mr. Peter," she cried. Behind the blackamoor she saw Rose Bailey, come up from the pub to see who had arrived in the nice carriage. Eilish seized her hand to pull her into the flat.

"Rose, wait here!" She ran to her room, blanket trailing, and returned. She pressed fourpence into Rose's hand, all the money she had in the world. "Rose, you watch Mackie tonight, all right? And tomorrow night! Make Dooya pay you after that. I'll come back to see Mackie, and I'll make sure."

Rose was staring at the blackamoor in his bright scarlet wool overcoat. "But why, Eilish? Where are you going?"

"I have an expectation, I do," Eilish declared. "I've a

chance, and I'm meant to take it!" She retreated toward her room. "Will you, Rose? Will you watch Mackie?"

"I will if that one minds her manners," Rose sniffed, indicating Dooya with her head.

Mackie lifted his head from Dooya's shoulder. "Eilish? Go to play?"

His piping voice tore at Eilish's heart.

"Aye," Eilish answered. "I'm going to play in a different place. Rose will be here with you while yer ma's gone, though. You know Rose, Mackie."

"Eilish go to play?" Mackie said again.

"Aye," she repeated. She put out her hand to his cheek, and then pulled it back. Her chest ached. She could hardly wait to be away from Dooya's smell, Dooya's cold flat, her empty table, her vile customers. But Mackie . . .

"Candy?" Mackie asked.

Eilish gave him a tremulous smile. "Aye. I'll bring Mackie some candy!"

Satisfied, Mackie lay his head against his mother's neck. Dooya picked up the chair from the corner and sat down in it, Mackie in her lap. A bubbling snore came from the bearded man, and a moment later Dooya, too, was asleep, her chin on top of Mackie's head.

"Mr. Peter, just give me a minute," Eilish said. She ran to her room and threw on her clothes as quickly as she could. Her few small possessions she stuffed in a sack. Moments later she was following Peter down the stairs, Rose Bailey trotting after them.

"Eilish, where ye off to? What will I be telling Dooya?"

"Never mind Dooya." Eilish climbed into the little carriage. "I'll be back when I can."

Rose wrung her apron and shook her head back and forth as she watched the carriage pull away. Eilish waved at her, once, from the window. Then she turned her face forward, into her future.

* * *

THE little room at the front of the house in Craven Street was nicely appointed with printed cotton curtains over the window, a painted iron bedstead with a thick mattress and a puffy quilt, and a wide bureau with four drawers. William Franklin's linens and ties still filled the bottom drawers, but the top two had been lined with fresh paper and left empty for Eilish. " 'Tis little enough I have to put into these," she said.

The maid, her arms folded, stood in the doorway. "Never mind that, miss," she said haughtily. "The first thing for you is a bath."

"A bath?"

"Aye. Mrs. Stevenson's orders. Follow me, please." Without waiting to see that she was obeyed, Bessie hurried down the stairs, her back straight, her neck stiff. Eilish paused only to put her little bit of embroidered linen, her mother's linen, into the empty top drawer, and then hurried after her.

Four floors below, in the basement kitchen, a hip bath was being filled with steaming water. Soap, brushes, and towels were laid ready, and Mrs. Stevenson was giving instructions to the cook. She looked up when Eilish entered.

"Ah, Miss Eam," she said. "Cook here, and Bessie, will see to you. In this house, each person bathes every week, head to toe. Your baths will be here in the kitchen."

Bessie stood beside the tub and said, "Off with your clothes, then, miss."

Eilish stared at her, open-mouthed. "Take—take off my clothes? All of them?"

"Of course, all of them! What did you think, you would bathe in your shift?"

Eilish was at a loss. She had never, that she could remember, been completely naked. But all of them were watching her, waiting. Slowly, unhappily, she undid the tie at the neck of her cloak, and stepped out of her battered shoes. Cook said impatiently, "Come on, now, my girl, your bath's getting cold. In you go!"

Eilish pulled off her shapeless dress and then her even more shapeless shift. Beneath these she wore nothing, and she looked down at herself as she stepped into the hip bath. She was surprised to see that her breasts had begun to fill out, though the rest of her body was thin and flat. She shivered with cold and flushed with embarrassment all at the same time.

Bessie picked up her clothes, holding them at arm's length, and disappeared with them. Mrs. Stevenson had already left the kitchen on some other errand, leaving only Eilish and Cook. Cook was even plumper than Bessie, with red cheeks and soft brown hair. She gave Eilish a cake of fragrant yellow soap and a brush with a long wooden handle, and then turned away to her baking.

Eilish took the soap and brush and sank slowly down into the water. She had never felt such a warm wetness, and after her first fear, the sensation was delicious. The water reached just to her chest, and her bent knees poked out above it. Little by little, she began to lather herself. When she had soaped her whole body and rinsed it, she did it again. Bessie came in with a pile of clothing and stood beside the tub. "Hair," she said shortly.

Eilish said, "What?"

"Hair," Bessie repeated sourly. "Wash your hair, too."

Eilish didn't bother arguing. She dropped her head backward into the water until it was thoroughly wet, and applied the soap to her tangle of black hair. So pleasant was this new experience that she didn't even mind Bessie's tone. Not until the water began to grow chilly and slightly scummy with the soap did she want to think about getting out.

When she was dried, and her hair wrapped in the towel, Bessie began to hold out items of clothing. They were obviously well-worn, but clean. There were bloomers, a scratchy wool shift, cotton stockings, and the loveliest pale blue petticoat. Over it all went a dark blue wool sack gown, much too long, but marvelously warm. Bessie took the towel and rubbed Eilish's head briskly. It hurt, but Eilish was too proud to say so. When her hair was mostly dry, Bessie tied it in a thick horsetail in the back, and pulled a lappet cap over it, tying the cap with strings beneath Eilish's chin. She stood back then and looked at her handiwork.

"You'll do," she said. "Here's a pair of Miss Polly's shoes. They'll be too long, but you can stuff the toes if you need to."

They were soft calf leather, worn and pliable. Eilish put them on with a little sigh, and Bessie sniffed. "Indeed," she said.

Cook laid out a cup of tea and a plate with hot fresh bread on it. "Here you are, my girl," she said gruffly, but not, Eilish thought, unkindly. "A bite to get you through the morning."

Clean outside, warm inside, Eilish sipped the hot tea and then took a huge mouthful of bread, sweet and soft. It was so much whiter than the hinder end loaf that would be Mackie's breakfast. At the thought, her gorge rose suddenly, and she put down the thick slice of bread. Would Mackie haunt her every day here?

She looked up and saw Cook's inquiring glance. "Oh, it's ever so lovely," she said sincerely. "Thanks." And with Cook's eye on her, she finished the snack.

7

San Antonio, May 2018

A LARGE, red-faced woman met Erin and Mal's plane in San Antonio. As Mal supervised a skycap in the removal of the instrument cases from the first-class cabin, the woman chatted endlessly to Erin, calling her "honey," rattling on about the heat and the orchestra and the hotel. Erin stood nodding, trying not to look bored. They set out through the airport at last, Erin keeping an eye on the motorized cart carrying her instrument, glancing around occasionally at the renovated terminal. Phone consoles and information booths were set into the stucco walls like saints' niches in a Spanish mission, and all the seats had curving, solid arms like church pews. Imitation moss draped every corner.

"Honey, isn't it hot?" the red-faced woman asked. "You must be tired. We'll just have to get you a nap. Would you like some ice cream?" Erin hadn't caught the woman's name, but it didn't seem to matter, since there was never a break in the stream of words. It was a relief to reach the limo. As they drove away, Erin gazed out at Texas in springtime and tried to breathe away the hollow feeling in her solar plexus that came from missing Charlie.

The limo, a gray contemp, rolled past fields delicately tinged with green, where cattle and horses grazed. In one pasture, Australian emu paraded on long thin legs behind a tall electrified fence. Erin didn't know what they were for, but she smiled, thinking what Charlie might have said. A few minutes later they drove past a tented enclave that sprawled over many acres, the smoke of outdoor cooking fires rising in slender streams into the still air.

In the city the central neighborhoods were styled with wooden spikes topping stone walls and glassphalt driveways cut to look like cobblestones. The maintenance workers wore loose cotton shirts and trousers and broad-brimmed sombreros. The rooms at the Riverwalk Plaza were furnished in white wicker and tiled in brick-red. When Erin went into her room, she found a large bouquet of irises and orchids sent by the Chamber Music Society, and a fruit basket waiting near the hot- and cold-server. The red-faced woman peeked into the room, nodded satisfaction, and said, "You need some lunch, Mr. Oskar?"

Mal, opening the door to the room next door, said, "Thanks, but we ate on the plane."

"You okay, too, honey?" the woman asked Erin.

"Yes," Erin said. "Thank you for the flowers. And the fruit."

The woman was talking even before she finished her sentence. "You just call room service if you're hungry. I'll be by to pick you up for dinner. You just have a little nap, now, honey."

A bellhop, costumed in belted leather trousers and a wide-sleeved shirt, set Erin's suitcases on the valet rack and pressed the button to turn on the viewwindow. "Shall I unpack for you, miss?" he asked.

"No, thanks, I'll do it." She gave him some money, and he closed the door on his way out. Sighing, Erin kicked her shoes into a corner, took a Japanese pear from the basket, and turned to survey the room.

In the viewwindow a dancer in a flaring red dress twirled

across a bougainvillea-draped patio. A man on a wrought-iron bench bent over a large guitar, his face hidden by a stiff, silver-trimmed hat. Beyond the hacienda, brown fields stretched beneath an empty blue sky. The dancer swayed and stamped, soundlessly snapping her fingers. Erin watched her for a moment before she went to the realwindows to open the latticework shutters.

The room looked directly down on the Riverwalk, where heavy tree boughs hung over smooth glassphalt paths. Between them the San Antonio River ran green and clear, its slow-moving waters microbe-clean. Erin nibbled at the pear and watched pedestrians in shorts and sleeveless shirts stroll in the sunshine. The Riverwalk was lined for miles with umbrella-shaded restaurant tables and covered kiosks. Waiters and vendors wore long dresses and bonnets, or leather pants and sombreros. It was all quite lovely and silly. How nice it would be if Charlie were here, if the two of them could go down to the Riverwalk, sit, and watch the river and the people flow by, laugh together. She could go alone, of course, but it wouldn't be the same.

The phone console chimed and said, "You have a call, Miss Rushton. It is a Seattle number. Do you wish to take it?"

"Yes!" Erin threw herself across the bed, stretched out on her stomach facing the phone.

Charlie's face filled the screen, and she grinned at him, waving the pear. It was the first time all day she had felt cheerful. "Hey."

"Hey," he answered, smiling back at her. Looking at his familiar face was like looking into a mirror, the same fine bones and slender chin and white-blond hair. Sometimes he threatened to grow a beard so people could tell them apart. "You made it, I guess."

"Here we are," she answered. She gestured around her at the hotel room. "Another city, another suite."

Charlie followed her gesture. "Nice flowers. What's that? In the viewwindow?"

She rolled a bit to the side so the camera could see it. "Flamenco dancer, I think. From 1836. The Alamo and everything. You remember from the last time, don't you?"

"That was three years ago. Most of it was still under construction. How does the city look?"

Erin shrugged. "Like Texas. But a lot cleaner."

Charlie laughed. "What, no dirt roads?"

"Only in the viewwindows." Erin sat up, cross-legged, dropping the half-eaten pear on the bedspread. "Charlie, we never got to talk."

"Let's talk, then."

"It was at the concert. During the *Requiem*."

"You saw it again, didn't you?" he said.

"Yes. In the *Lux Aeterna*."

"I figured it was something like that. Same as before?"

Erin's lips trembled suddenly, and she pressed her fingers to her mouth. It was a moment before she could go on. Suppressed tears stung her eyelids. "It was a bit more distinct this time. Such a strange sensation—like it came through my forehead." Vaguely, she touched her brow. "It's like dreaming, Charlie. But of course, I'm awake, and I'm still playing." She pulled her bare feet closer beneath her.

"What happened? When did it fade? Did it move?"

"I don't know. I looked away—looked back at Lewitt. I was afraid I was going to lose my place. And then, at the end—it was gone." She hugged herself, feeling suddenly cold. "What do you think it is?"

Charlie made a wry face. "Not a clue, E. Unless you're seeing a ghost."

She shivered. "That's what I'm afraid of. But do ghosts follow you around? I've seen it in Boston, and Minneapolis, and now Seattle!"

"I was kidding," Charlie said gently. "I don't believe in ghosts, and you don't either."

Erin gave a shaky laugh. "You know what I'm afraid of."

"Yeah, but I don't believe it," he said.

She held up her arms. "Look. Goose bumps. Dammit, Charlie. It's scary."

"Don't worry about it, E. Just blame it on Dad—all that fey Celtic blood."

"You mean, you do think it's a ghost!"

"Whatever it is, at least it can't hurt you." Charlie leaned back in his chair, and Erin could see the silver arm and the dark gray arch of the wheel. He was still in the hotel suite in Seattle. "Speaking of our late father . . ." he said.

"Oh, Charlie! Did you go? Did you meet this doctor? What's he like?"

"You have to meet him," Charlie said. "That's the best way. I could never explain him."

"But he's going to take you? Is there anything new?"

Erin, watching the flicker of hope that crossed her brother's face, felt a sharp ache in her breast. She was sure, even through the phone, that his eyes reddened, and her own tears threatened again. "Oh, Charlie," she murmured. "Did he say he can help?"

Charlie blinked hard, and glanced away briefly. Erin pressed her own tears away with the heel of her hand. "Oh, well," Charlie said lightly. "He said maybe. But I liked him, E. You have to meet him."

"What's his name again?"

"Berrick. Eugene Berrick. M.D., Ph.D."

"What schools?"

Charlie gave a bitter chuckle. "Watch out, E, you sound just like Sarah."

Erin said, "Sorry. Reflex. Tell me about him." But Charlie wouldn't say anything more, and she had to resign herself to waiting. When they said goodbye, she put out her hand to touch the screen, but the cool glass was nothing like her brother's smooth cheek. After he broke the connection, the pretty hotel room seemed as cold and empty as the blank screen.

•   •   •

AT the first rehearsal the next morning, Erin was preoccupied. Mal had seen to the delivery and setting up of the glass harmonica, and she scrubbed her hands in her dressing room and then went to the stage and turned on the power. She tested the treadle, and rather absently warmed up her fingers while the orchestra set up behind her. Mal brought the conductor to her. "Erin, this is Lucas Underwood."

Underwood put out his hand. "How do you do, Miss Rushton."

She shook his hand without thinking, and then muttered, "Oh, jeez."

Underwood raised his eyebrows in surprise.

"Sorry," she said casually. "It's my hands." She held them out as if they had caught some disease. "Now I have to wash them again."

Underwood cleared his throat, and Mal said hastily, "She always has to wash her hands, Maestro, for the instrument, you understand. Otherwise we have to clean the cups constantly."

Underwood said in a chilly tone, "Certainly." He turned away to speak to the first violin.

Mal glowered at Erin. "For godsakes—" he began.

She said with real contrition, "I'm sorry, Mal, really. I'm distracted. I'll just go wash, okay?" She knew she had been gauche. She hadn't slept well, and her dreams had been haunted by specters that seemed to linger in the light of day. She went to her dressing room to soap her hands, and hurried back to the stage, hoping not to delay the downbeat and give further offense.

Underwood was new to the orchestra. Erin knew her contract had been negotiated before his arrival. She offered him a conciliatory smile as he lifted his baton. He was a stiff sort of man, with a sharp gray beard and a brush of gray hair standing straight up above his forehead. He nodded at her, his neck as stiff as the rest of him. She looked down at her music, resisting the urge to roll her eyes. Not a great start.

Underwood rushed through the Mozart with only minor brushings-up here and there. Erin thought he could have rehearsed the strings considerably longer, but she kept her silence. Mal was watching from the front row of the house. At the premature end of the Mozart, Erin tipped her head to one side and gave him a saccharine smile. His lips twitched, and he covered them quickly with his hand. Erin chuckled, and felt better.

The Röllig Quintet in C minor was next. Erin was pleased about the choice, as it wasn't often programmed. Röllig, a late eighteenth-century composer, had played the glass harmonica himself, and his quintet was a fine one, with a lovely first violin part. If only Underwood wouldn't rush the tempo! Neither the violinist nor Erin could work with the melodic material at the speed he chose. She cast a glance out into the house, longing for Charlie's diplomatic voice, but there was none but her own to speak.

"Maestro—" she said hesitantly, when the first read-through ended. "Would you mind a slower tempo? The melody . . ."

Underwood dropped his baton on his music stand with a faint clatter. "Well, Miss Rushton? What tempo would you like?" The bristling beard quivered, and there was emphasis on the "you."

She felt her cheeks warm, and her chin came up. Mal came to his feet, but she put up her hand to stop him. "I'll take your tempo, of course, Maestro," she said lightly. "You have the baton. But as this is a rehearsal—" She smiled as politely as she knew how. What would Charlie have said? "It might be nice to try a different approach."

He stared at her, his features unmoving, for five long seconds. She held his gaze, her cheeks burning. Behind her, the orchestra members stirred uncomfortably. At last, with a flicker of gray eyebrows, the conductor picked up his baton. "Well, people," he said, "shall we indulge our guest artist? Let's try it a bit slower."

Erin held her smile. The first violin gave her a slow

broad wink. She let her eyelids drop, once, in acknowledgment, before she turned to her score, but still she felt exposed and alone. They played the piece through, at a more leisurely tempo. Erin made the turns of the melody expansive, expressive, trying to prove her point. At the end, she lifted her hands from the spinning crystal cups and waited for Underwood to speak.

"Bit romantic for my taste," he said to the room at large. "But we'll leave it there for the time being."

At the break, several members of the orchestra came to stand around the glass harmonica and talk. The first violin was a thin man of about thirty-five with long, spidery fingers. "Beautiful playing, Miss Rushton," he said.

"Please call me Erin," she said. "Listen, your tone is terrific. The vibrato's perfect, just enough."

"Not too romantic?" he asked, and she giggled. One or two of the others laughed, too, but cautiously, glancing around for their conductor.

Erin was glad of a chance to talk to the other players, but in moments Mal came on stage with the orchestra manager to bear Erin away to schedule a netcast. Underwood was back on the podium by the time she returned, turning the pages of a score. The gray eyebrows came up again.

"I'm sorry, Maestro," she said. "Had to do some business."

"Perfectly all right," the conductor said frostily. "We must sell those tickets, after all."

The first violinist winked at Erin again, but she sighed. It was going to be a long and lonely week. And they hadn't even begun work on the *Requiem*.

8

San Antonio, May 2018

"YOU have to take out one cello," Erin repeated. "The balance is wrong."

Her cheeks were flaming under Underwood's glare. She stared down at her feet, embarrassed, but determined. She wouldn't—she couldn't—let him ruin the *Requiem*.

Mal gazed helplessly at the ceiling of Underwood's dressing room. The conductor had thrown down his baton and stalked from the stage. Mal had hurried after him, and Erin, after an agonizing moment, with the eyes of the orchestra members burning into the back of her neck, had followed the two men into the dressing room and shut the door behind her.

Underwood snapped, "Listen to me, young lady. This is my orchestra. I'll judge the balance!"

Erin's temper strained at her control. "Please go out and listen," she said tightly. "I know the way my brother's music should sound."

The conductor's lips thinned. "I like to hear all the ensemble, you know. I'm not interested in featuring a star."

"Maestro," Erin said. "This isn't about me. It's about

the *Requiem*. If you drown out the glasses, the affect is ruined. Don't you understand that?"

"I like the effect the way it is."

Erin's temper snapped like a wire stretched too thin. She folded her arms and stuck out her chin, and Mal fairly groaned with tension. "Not the effect," she said, her voice rising, "—the bloody *affect*! Do you even know the word? The emotional impact, the *feeling*!"

Underwood's head swiveled to Mal. Erin could have sworn she heard his neck creak. "Mr. Oskar," he said, "I inherited this program, and I have to make the best of it. But I understood you would be here to keep your prima donna under control!"

Erin squeaked, "*Prima donna*? Just because I want Charlie's piece to be musical—"

Mal said faintly, "Erin, take it easy . . ."

"Look, Miss Rushton." Underwood's features were rigid, only his lips moving. "This concert isn't just to showcase your little antique instrument! Every musician here is important."

"Of course," Erin snarled. "But if the cellos are too damned loud, no one will hear anything but the low strings!"

"Erin—" Mal said desperately.

"I'm going to call Charlie." Erin whirled and stamped to the door of the cramped room. "I'm going to tell him he should withdraw the piece."

"Erin—"

"You have a contract, Miss Rushton!" Underwood said loudly.

She turned at the door and faced him. "Business, is that all it is to you? Dammit, send somebody out into the hall to listen! Send your concertmaster—now, there's a musician!"

Mal moaned, "Erin—" one more time, but she was already out the door.

. . .

THE morning's rehearsal was shot, but by afternoon Erin and Underwood had reached a truce. He did, in fact, send the first violin to the back of the house to listen to the *Dies Irae*. He wasn't happy with the report, but he took one cello off the part, and they moved forward. They made it to the *Sanctus* before she had to leave for her interview.

The red-faced woman came to take Erin and Mal to the radio station, and Underwood's relief at their departure was palpable. As she followed Mal and the escort up the aisle, the crisp strains of a Haydn sinfonietta, Underwood's own choice for the program, followed them.

The interviewer at KTXI was short and square, with blunt-cut brown hair and sharp brown eyes, wearing vivid scarlet lipstick and what appeared to be a vintage suit of beige linen, midcalf skirt and long jacket. She shook Erin's hand briskly. "Hi, I'm Ashley Adams." She saw Erin's glance at the suit and chuckled. "My Golden Age of Radio outfit," she said. "Brings me luck." She looked Erin over. "You're young to have compiled such a long résumé," she said.

"I'm older than I look," Erin said.

"Lucky you." Adams indicated a door. Mal stayed behind with the escort as Erin and Ashley Adams went into a tiny room with carpeted walls that soaked up every vibration of their footsteps, of the rollers on the chair feet, of the keys on Adams's slimscreen. No camera operators here, no crew at all. Automated netcameras crowded the room. Little windows looked out into the reception room where Mal and the escort were being served coffee by a receptionist.

Ashley Adams put an unlit cigarette between her lips. Erin raised her eyebrows, and the woman laughed heartily. "Don't worry. I've signed the form, but I won't light it in here. They won't let me have a personal ventilator in the studio." She pushed some buttons. "Now, since we're going to netcast in realtime, let's plan the questions, okay? It's interactive, but we always screen input for content, so don't worry about that. Tell me what you'd like to make sure we talk about, let me know if there are any sensitive issues. Emphasis on music, of course, but as much personal interest as possible."

Adams' straightforward manner was a relief after the battles of the morning. "Can we avoid talking about my age?" Erin asked bluntly.

Adams chuckled. "I usually get that from older women. What's this about your age?"

Erin spread her hands. "It's this child prodigy thing."

"Good or bad?" Adams asked. She tapped on her slim-screen as she talked, one eye on the notes, one eye on Erin.

"Good for business. Bad for life," Erin heard herself say, and gave a small laugh. She hoped she would remember that, to tell Charlie. Or maybe he would watch the netcast.

"Got it," Adams said. She looked at Erin, waiting. "What else?"

"I hate all that nonsense about the curse of the glass harmonica."

Ashley Adams took the lipstick-stained cigarette out of her mouth and gazed closely at Erin. "We'll do it your way, because I promised. But you know it's what people like to hear. Folks love a mystery."

"I know," Erin said. "But it's moronic."

"Why?"

Erin shrugged. "They're just stories."

"*Grove's* thought they were real enough."

Erin made an exasperated noise. "I know. I wish they'd update the entry."

Adams pulled a photocopied sheet from a file, put on a pair of glasses and peered down at it. "Here it is: 'There is ample testimony that the practice of eliciting sounds from the revolving bowls of the glasses was apt to have a deranging effect on the nerves of the player.' *Grove's Dictionary of Music and Musicians*."

"Idiots," Erin said.

Adams chuckled and waved the cigarette. " 'The instrument was banned by police in Germany,' she read. 'And physicians warned against anyone with a nervous condition playing the armonica.' "

"Or pregnant women attending concerts, or small children listening!" Erin could see Mal through the window, his brow furrowed, his jowls trembling delicately as he sipped his coffee, and she felt a pang of remorse. "Look, if we have to talk about it, we can, but let's make it clear. There's no evidence for any of this stuff. It was a rumor that got started, and grew. People got nervous. But lots of people played the instrument in the eighteenth century—Benjamin Franklin himself, and Anton Mesmer—they didn't go crazy. Or have nervous breakdowns."

"Or die prematurely?" Ashley said.

"Of course, some of the players did die, like Marianne Davies. But they had symptoms of lead poisoning—there was lead in everything! Face powder, medicines, all kinds of glass and china, paint, ink—I don't see why the glass harmonica gets the blame."

"So you don't think there's anything to the tales about the vibrations—the high partials—causing *crise de nerfs*?"

Erin snorted. "No. Not a damned bloody thing."

Ashley Adams's boisterous laugh made the window vibrate. "Clear enough! Okay, then, you'd better tell me some things you would like to discuss, or I won't have a thing to say." She tapped on the slimscreen. "Your training, your early career? The program you're going to play Friday at the Crockett, of course. That will lead us to your brother."

Erin smiled, thinking of Charlie. "It's too bad he's not here. He's so good at interviews."

"Is he?" Adams typed a few words. "He's in a wheelchair, isn't he? Do you mind talking about that?"

"I guess not—he never seems to mind. He has Friedreich's ataxia. An inherited neurological disorder. Our father died of it, before we were born." Erin's voice faltered the tiniest bit. She could have lost her brother, too. As always, she tried not to think about that. "Charlie was given an engineered virus, and that stopped the progression of the disease."

"Okay, I'll ask one or two questions about that. And now, tell me about the *Requiem for North Korea*. The holographic projections are real photographs, aren't they?"

ERIN wore the black dress, hoping to appease Mal and to salvage what she could of her standing with the Chamber Music Society. She wore only a faint glossy lip color, and so little mascara it was almost invisible in the glaring makeup lights. And she wore a little black bra under her gown and secured the neckline with a pin she begged from the stage manager. She fluffed her hair into a silvery nimbus and pouted into the dressing room mirror. About twelve this time, she thought.

She stood waiting backstage as the orchestra tuned. The orchestra manager smiled at her rather nervously. "Nice interview today," he said.

"Oh, did you see it?" Erin asked.

"Sure. And we sold a hundred tickets after the netcast," he told her.

"Ashley's terrific."

"Yeah, she's great." The orchestra grew quiet. He whispered, "Good luck, Miss Rushton." Erin nodded her thanks. The conductor was making his entrance.

Underwood led both the Mozart and the Röllig Quintet at his original tempo. All improvements were gone, all rehearsal wasted. Erin couldn't tell if he did it deliberately or was simply so inflexible he couldn't change. The lovely melody of the Röllig became nothing more than a nervous riff of notes, and all Erin's efforts to lead a gentler tempo were in vain. Underwood either didn't hear her or deliberately ignored her. The first violin's face was dark with anger after the final cadence. He stared down at his music stand, avoiding both Erin's and Underwood's eyes.

The applause was no more than adequate. Erin bowed carefully, one hand at the draped neckline of the black dress. Then she strode to her dressing room and slammed the door so hard the vase of flowers sent her by the red-faced woman slid an inch down the makeup counter.

She kept her dressing room door closed during the Haydn. Over the monitor she heard the applause at the end, and she scrubbed her hands one more time while the orchestra retuned for the *Requiem*. As she emerged, she saw the orchestra manager hovering anxiously in the corridor near her door.

"Don't worry, I'm coming," she said tersely.

Underwood was waiting behind the proscenium. The two of them made their entrance together without speaking a word. They bowed, and Erin stepped behind the glass harmonica. Underwood lifted his baton and looked at her expectantly.

Erin made him wait. She kept her hands at her sides and closed her eyes, trying to focus her thoughts. It was the music that mattered, Charlie's music. Underwood didn't matter, even she didn't matter. It was the *Requiem* she cared about. She opened her eyes and looked up into the projected images, seeing the dark colors, the heartbreaking scenes. At last she poised her hands above the cups and nodded at Underwood. She didn't miss the slight twist of his lips as he raised his baton, but she looked away from him, out past the footlights.

It was Erin who led the performance of the *Requiem*. She did it deliberately. She thought ahead, anticipating each section of the *Dies Irae,* the *Lacrymosa,* the *Sanctus.* There was no question of losing herself in the music. All her concentration was required to force Underwood to follow her, to gather the orchestra behind her. There were moments when the ensemble was shaky, when cadences were not quite together, but she persevered. She played like a

prima donna, without regard for her conductor's prefer-
ences. She played for Charlie.

When it was over, perspiration ran itchily down her ribs,
and her hair clung damply to her forehead. Her shoulders
trembled with tension.

The ovation was solid. Underwood and Erin and the
concertmaster each took two bows. Erin shook Underwood's hand, shook the concertmaster's hand, bowed once
more, and left the stage. The only good thing about the
evening was that no ghostly vision had haunted the downstage curtain.

Erin was half-undressed when Ashley Adams knocked
on her dressing room door.

"You skipped the greenroom," Adams said when Erin
opened the door.

Erin held the door wide. "Come in," she said. She
turned, stripping off the now-wet bra and picking her reff
T-shirt off the floor. As she pulled it over her head she
added, "I couldn't face it tonight."

"I thought I detected a bit of tension," Adams said comfortably. She sat down in one of the padded easy chairs and
crossed her legs. Her thick figure was encased in a beaded
dress, her legs in black silk stockings and uncomfortable-
looking pointy-toed shoes. "In the Röllig, particularly."

Erin pulled on her jeans. "The Röllig was putrid."

Ashley Adams gave her rollicking laugh. "I won't quote
that," she said when she caught her breath. "What would
you say about the *Requiem*?"

"Are you writing a review?" Erin asked warily.

Adams pulled out a cigarette. Her lips were painted a
deep plum color this evening. "Yes," she said, the cigarette
bobbing between her teeth. "I'm writing a net follow-up to
the interview. Just checking whether what I heard is what
you thought you played."

Erin turned to the mirror and picked up a hairbrush.
"Ashley, I'm in enough trouble here without my negative
remarks being repeated on your program."

"Okay," Adams said easily. She stood, adjusting the beaded dress so it reached her plump knees. "Do you want to know what I'll probably say?"

Erin pulled the hairbrush once through her hair, then finished the job with her fingers. "Sure."

"I'm going to say that the tempi in almost every piece were so brisk, I could hardly follow the music. That the ensemble was poor, except in the Haydn. That the florid passages in the Röllig were almost too much for the first violin. That only the *Requiem* made any musical sense, and in that it seemed as if the soloist and the conductor had completely different ideas of how the piece should go."

Erin dropped her hairbrush on the makeup counter and turned. "That's close enough," she said. "A little unfair to the concertmaster. And Underwood will be convinced the bad notices are my fault."

"You play beautifully, Erin," Adams said, taking the cigarette from her mouth and turning it in her fingers. "I wanted to tell you. It was a treat for me to hear you. I'm not sure my review will reflect that, but I'll try."

"Thanks," Erin said. She managed a wry smile. "I guess it doesn't matter, anyway. I doubt the Chamber Music Society will be hiring me again in any case."

"That's too bad. Our loss."

"That's nice of you to say. It's a shame you won't hear Charlie's new piece."

Adams put the unlit cigarette in her mouth and sucked on it for a moment. "Did you see the woman in front, in about the third row?"

"No. Can't see anyone past the footlights. Why?"

Adams shrugged. "Oh, looked like some kind of breakdown. During the *Requiem.* She was crying, shaking. The man with her took her out, but she clearly didn't want to go. It was strange."

"That happens a bit. There are usually one or two like that—it's an emotional piece."

"You're sure it's not the glass harmonica?" Adams

asked. "The vibrations?" Erin cast her a look, and Adams grinned and waved her cigarette. "Okay, okay. I'll leave it. Just curious."

A moment later, Mal came to the door, and Ashley Adams excused herself. Mal set about picking up Erin's things while she went to fetch her scores. She paused on the darkened stage and looked about her.

The chairs were left turned this way and that, the stands empty, their lights off. The hall was deserted, only the floor lights glowing redly in the dimness. Erin sighed, looking out into the shadows, and wondered if she'd ever appear in this hall again.

9

London, December 1761

EILISH quickly gained weight in the first month she lived at Number Seven Craven Street. She grew like a starving puppy well-fed at last. Polly's cast-off gown almost fit now, though it would always be too long. She admired herself in the glass above the bureau. Her cheeks were smooth, her hair shone, and even her fledgling breasts were rounder and fuller. Cook had given her a bit of grosgrain ribbon that went well with the blue dress, and she used it to tie her hair into a fall of black curls down her back.

On her way to breakfast, she peeked into Mr. Franklin's laboratory. He worked at odd hours, and it would not have been surprising to find him bent over some experiment or other, his spectacles smudged and his hair wild from having stayed up all the night. This morning, though, he wasn't there, though the scent of his bay rum still lingered. They had worked till midnight the night before, Franklin fussing with the glass cups, asking Eilish to try them over and over again, searching for the right tuning. Several cups still lay on the worktable next to the flat grinding stone.

The scent of toasting bread drew Eilish on flying feet

down two more flights of stairs to the kitchen. Polly and Mrs. Stevenson, having no guest this morning, sat at table drinking coffee. A wheel of the English cheddar much beloved by Franklin rested on the table, and a small pot of chocolate and a charger of fried bacon were warming on the cast-iron Pennsylvania Fireplace that dominated one end of the kitchen. The stove, like Mr. Franklin's odd spectacles and many other newfangled objects in Number Seven Craven Street, was an invention of Franklin himself.

Cook smiled at Eilish's entrance. "Good morning, m'dear," she said. She brought the charger of bacon and set a cup for Eilish. "Had a bit of a lie-in, did you?"

Polly looked sidelong at Eilish, her full lips thinning to a sour line. It was fascinating to see how quickly Polly's pretty face could turn plain.

Her mother said hastily, "They were up late, weren't you, Eilish dear? You and Mr. Franklin?"

"Aye," Eilish said. She took a sip and fair shivered with pleasure. "Oh, ta, Cook. Such lovely cocoa!"

Cook patted her shoulder. "Have some bacon, Eilish. The toast is just coming." Cook pulled the bread toaster away from the cookfire and slid two thick slices onto a plate. She set them before Eilish with the butter dish and jam jar.

Polly put her cup down. "How is the work going? Is the armonica ready?"

Eilish chewed with gusto, and spoke at the same time. "Nay," she said, crumbs falling from her lips. "The tuning won't come right. Mr. Franklin says the lead glass is the best, but he has to grind it slowly. Once it goes sharp, it's ruined."

Polly's eyebrow rose. "So what are you doing at all hours? You surely don't grind the cups yourself?"

Eilish dipped jam with her butter knife. "Nay," she answered. "But my ear is better than Mr. Franklin's. He grinds, I play, and then I tell 'im if it's in tune yet." She took a huge bite of jammy toast, and spoke around it. "Mostly it's not."

"Mr. Franklin is attending a meeting of the Royal Society today," Polly said. "And Peter is going to escort me to Essex, to my aunt Tickell. You should make yourself useful in Mr. Franklin's absence, Eilish. Help my mother, or Bessie." Her voice was sharp with resentment.

Eilish thought Polly very silly to be jealous of the time she, Eilish, spent with Mr. Franklin. And the whole thing her own idea in the first place! Eilish dabbed delicately at her mouth with a napkin, and made her eyes round, her voice sweet. She said, "Mr. Franklin bid me practice on the armonica whenever I could. As it's so different from me own glasses."

Polly gave an unladylike snort. Dooya could have done it no better.

Mrs. Stevenson cleared her throat. "Now, Polly, Eilish must follow her instructions, mustn't she?"

Polly dropped her napkin. "Where's Peter?" she snapped. " 'Tis time I was off."

Cook merely pointed to the back of the house, where the horse was stabled and the carriage kept. Mrs. Stevenson cast her eyes up at the ceiling and sighed, then rose with Polly. "Go get your things, dear," she said mildly. "I'll get Peter to carry them out for you."

Polly's back was stiff as a poker as she marched away.

Cook crossed her eyes at Eilish and Eilish giggled. She was just draining the last of her chocolate when Peter came into the kitchen.

"Good morning, miss," he said to her, just as if she were a nob like Polly.

"Hi, Peter," she said, smiling at him. She loved the blackness of his eyes, the shine of his dark skin, his gentle address. "Did you see Mackie last night, then?"

"I did, miss," he said, flashing his white teeth. "I gave the boy your gift. 'Twas eaten before I departed!"

Eilish laughed. " 'Tis just like him! And how did he look? Is he all right?"

"He looked like any dirty three-year-old, miss. He seems all right." Peter didn't mention Mackie's legs. Eilish supposed he knew, like everyone in Seven Dials knew, that crooked legs often came with poverty, especially in the dark slums of London.

"Here, Peter," Cook said softly. "Quick, before they come for you. A nice cup of tea to keep you warm on your cold journey." She set a cup and saucer before the blackamoor, who pulled a chair up beside Eilish.

They passed a pleasant ten minutes before Peter was called away. Eilish helped Cook tidy the kitchen, putting the crockery away, setting the butter dish in the sill to keep cool. Cook handed her an embroidered tea towel to wipe the table. It was stiff with age, and stained, though it must once have been cloud-white. Eilish started to rub the tabletop, but then slowed, and stopped, feeling the old cloth in her hand, drawing it through her fingers. The world around her blurred, and she let it disappear. She floated gently into a dream of the past, when the cloth was new and soft and clean.

" 'Twas a kind person, this," she mused.

"Eh? What's that? Who was?" Cook asked.

"The one who stitched this tea towel," Eilish murmured. Her eyes were closed, and she rubbed the worn embroidery with her fingertips. "Aye, kind, and loving. But tired. So tired."

Cook was staring at her. "Eilish? Are you touched, child?"

Eilish blinked, and the world returned to her, the world of today, all hard-edged and cold and real. She looked at the dingy towel in her hand, its frayed embroidery and raveling edges. "Aye," she said again. " 'Twould have been nice to know such a person."

Cook came close to peer into her face. "Are you fey, child?" she whispered.

Eilish shook herself and grinned at the older woman. "Aye, Cook, I am! And me grandmother before me, so me da said." She bent over the table and wiped it vigorously with the old tea towel. "And her grandmother, and hers, and on back to Saint Brigid herself!"

EILISH was at the armonica when Franklin returned from his meeting. Three men made a noisy progress up the stairs and burst into the laboratory, laughing and clapping each other on the shoulder. Their cheeks were pink with the cold, and they cast their heavy overcoats here and there on stools and chairs, filling the room with the smell of wet wool. Eilish rose, wiping her wet fingers on her apron.

"Miss Eam," Franklin exclaimed. "Meet my dear friends and colleagues, Dr. John Pringle, the royal physician, and Mr. Richard Jackson, of the Royal Society!" He came close, putting his hand under her arm to urge her forward. She was immersed in a wave of the bay rum he splashed on after shaving, and his breath was rich with spirits and garlic.

Eilish dropped a brief curtsy. Both men bowed from the waist.

Franklin gestured to the armonica. " 'Tis right here, gentlemen," he said with relish. "Come, Miss Eam, a demonstration of my little invention!" He thrust the bowl of water at her, spilling a good bit across the floor. "Now, mind you, my friends, the tuning isn't perfect yet. But see here, each of these cups represents a pitch in the diatonic scale, and we have three full octaves, every half step!"

Eilish seated herself again at the table holding the armonica. As she adjusted the stool, its legs crunched on the lead glass dust coating the floor. She dipped her fingers into the water, and put her foot to the treadle. The visitors drew close to watch the cups revolve. When she touched her fingers to the rims and the glassy sound swelled in the room, they cried out in admiration.

It was a lovely sound indeed, and Eilish never tired of

it. It was very like her glasses, though ever so much easier, and the variety of pitches was as satisfying to her as the rich assortment of dishes Cook laid out in the basement kitchen each day. As she had been starved for food, she had also been starved for music, for real music, without compensating for the shortcomings of her paltry water-filled glasses. Now each of the sweet old melodies was fully realized. Her crystalline triads rang against the high ceiling of the laboratory, and drew answering vibrations from the unused glasses waiting on the shelves.

Eilish played one of the Scottish tunes Franklin loved, harmonizing it with the left hand while she picked out the melody with her right. She couldn't read music, of course, any more than she could read written words. But she knew the tunes, and her ear supplied the harmonies. She was talented, and she knew it. She reveled in the use of her gift, and in the playing of this precious instrument. She felt it was hers, hers alone, that no one could ever understand it, could know it from the inside out, as she did.

When she finished her tune, the men patted their hands together in a little frenzy of appreciation, saying, "Wonderful, Franklin, just wonderful! How fresh, how charming!" and other things. Eilish rose and stood away from the table, watching them. They were warm now, but still red-faced, and laughing together. The smell of spirits almost overwhelmed the dankness of their wet coats. Still, it was lovely having a proper audience, even for a short time.

Franklin pointed to the armonica. "See here, gentlemen, this largest glass is G, the lowest tone, and this smallest one is G, three octaves higher. I'm going to paint the glasses with prismatic colors—the C will be red, the D orange, the E yellow and so on through purple and then red again, so that glasses of the same color will make octaves with each other. The semitones will be white. I've ordered some good paint from Purpool Lane, and Mr. Charles James is coming round to do the work himself. He's going to measure the armonica for a case as well, mahogany, to match the wheel." He stood back with his arms folded, beaming.

It was a beautiful sight, Eilish thought, the crystals gleaming in the soft winter light, the mahogany wheel polished to a deep glow. Even the treadle was good hard mahogany. She liked best to remove her shoes and feel the smooth wood under her stockinged feet. The case, Franklin had assured her, would have lovely curved legs like a harpsichord, and an arching lid to pull closed, to keep the dust out when the armonica was not in use.

Pringle and Jackson moved close to the table, reaching out to stroke the cups with their unwashed hands. "Oh, nay, sirs!" Eilish cried, putting out her hand to stop them. "Your fingers must be clean!"

Franklin frowned. "Miss Eam, you overstep yourself."

"But, sir—" she began.

He scowled now, and his face grew redder. "Thank you, Miss Eam. That will be all."

Eilish snapped her mouth shut and spun about. Her overlarge shoes caught on the carpet and she stumbled, making her even angrier. No one noticed. As she stamped out of the laboratory, she heard the two visitors scraping their thick dirty fingers across her glasses, laughing boisterously at the squeal of sound they made.

" 'Tis all well and good, Mr. Royal Society," Eilish muttered as she went down the stairs. "And now ye'll have to clean 'em yerself. Nor will ye be raggin' me about it, neither!"

She spent the rest of the afternoon in the kitchen with Cook, hearing the laughter of the men above stairs, and then, later, the closing of the front door. Franklin's bedroom door swung shut with a bang just moments later, and there was silence.

Cook winked at Eilish. "Sleeping off his dinner now," she said easily. "He'll be a new man after tea. 'Twill be no more malbehavior, I promise!"

Eilish's own temper subsided after tea. When Franklin

called her into the laboratory to resume their work, she was as eager as ever. He was jolly again, too, asking her to stroke the glasses, compare the pitch with the harpsichord, and stroke them again. Over and over he slid one of the cups off the iron spindle to carefully grind it against the stone, then slid it back on and repeated the whole process. Eilish cleaned the glasses as he worked. Crumbs of lead crystal flew everywhere. When she judged a glass had reached the right tuning at last, he would cry out, "Hurrah!" and clap his hands, and they would laugh together. Then he would seize the next one and begin again.

Far into the night they worked. Eilish's eyes were red and weepy from the lead dust that fell from the grinding. She wiped her running nose repeatedly with her apron until her nostrils were sore. Franklin sneezed several times himself. "Bessie tries to sweep this room," he said, "but I've told her not to touch it. I don't want anything disturbed!"

"Aye, Mr. Franklin."

Eilish sneezed and yawned, all at the same time, making her jaw crack. Franklin looked up at the clock. " 'Tis late, my dear," he said. "You be off to your bed. I'll finish up."

"Nay, Mr. Franklin," she said. "I'll stay as long as you!" But another yawn spoiled her brave words.

Franklin brushed the glass dust off his green waistcoat and pushed his spectacles up on his head. " 'Tis enough for tonight," he said, smiling. He blew out the lamp, and led the way into his little sitting room. At a sideboard he poured a generous dollop of brandy into a wide-bellied glass. He held up the bottle to Eilish. "A sip of brandy, Miss Eam?"

She said, "Nay, Mr. Franklin. I don't care for spirits."

" 'Tis a great aid to sleeping," he said, taking a swallow. He patted his round belly. "And to digestion!" He fell heavily into his favorite stuffed armchair and put up his gouty foot. "I do believe and declare, Miss Eam," he pronounced, "that it is time for a concert!"

Eilish's mouth dropped. "A concert, sir? Already?"

"Indeed!" Franklin squinted up at her. "Let us say two

weeks from now! 'Tis time to present my armonica to the world!"

"Oh, aye, Mr. Franklin!" Eilish cried, all sleepiness forgotten. She laughed and then coughed. "Oh, aye! The Scotch tunes, you think?"

"The Scotch, the Irish, the English," he said. "We will plan the program together." He waved his hand. "Now, off to bed with you! You will have a great deal to do—including acquiring a new dress!"

"A dress? Another dress?"

"Yes, indeed, my dear Miss Eam! You must have a dress—an afternoon dress, for an afternoon concert. I shall speak to Margaret about it myself."

Eilish climbed the stairs to her attic bedroom in a fog of fatigue and ecstasy. A concert, a real concert, indoors, with an audience! And a dress! She washed her face and dragged the tortoiseshell brush through her hair. It was almost more than she could take in. Would she be nervous, self-conscious? Did Mr. Franklin mean, perhaps, a new dress, made just for her? She reached to touch her ma's bit of embroidered handkerchief, and then fell into bed with a happy sigh and pulled the quilt up to her chin. *Oh, Da. If you could see me now! 'Twould make the very angels sing for joy!*

10

Seattle, May 2018

TWO of the glass harmonica's cups had worked loose on the spindle. The morning after the San Antonio concert, Mal flew with the instrument to Boston, to have the cups remounted and the others inspected at Finkenbeiner's. Erin flew to Seattle, and Charlie.

He insisted on meeting her plane. She hurried up the jetway to him, and bent for his hug, anxiety fluttering in her throat. He looked thinner, and he was pale, with dark patches bruising the skin under his eyes. "What's the matter with you, Charlie?" she asked. "Are you sick? Not sleeping?"

"I'm sleeping okay," he said. "Here, give me your bag."

"It was too much for you, wasn't it? Being alone."

He shook his head. "It wasn't too much, and I didn't mind being alone. I'm a big boy now, Mommy." He smiled up at her. "Come on, E. Let's get out of this crowd."

He balanced the bag on his lap and set off. Following his chair as he weaved through the streams of people, Erin saw that it had changed, too. The joystick was gone. Charlie wore gray leather gloves she hadn't seen before, and he was powering the chair entirely with his arms. She had to trot to keep up with him.

"Charlie—what happened to your chair?" she panted.

He winked at her. "I'm in training."

He led her to an elevator which carried them up two floors. They exited the terminal through a skywalk, and rode one more elevator to the top of the parking garage, where double glass doors opened into a flood of chilly Seattle sunshine and the bustle of the SeaTac monorail base. Erin's eyes watered from the sudden brightness, and she shielded them with her hand. A racket of public announcements and the muted roar of monorail cars on their magnetrans cables confused her. She didn't know which way to turn. Shining silver cars descended from every direction, and people carrying suitcases or briefcases strode between a dozen boarding platforms.

Just as she found a directory on an enormous flickering screen, Charlie said, "Here, E. This one." He rolled to one of the platforms and slanted his wheels. Before she could follow him, the moving platform caught the wheels, and he was suddenly several feet ahead. He laughed over his shoulder as she hurried after. The monorail car slowed to match the speed of the platform, and Charlie rolled easily over the sill. He slid his multicard through a scanner, flipped an empty seat to a vertical position, and secured his chair to the base with a heavy nylon latch. Erin used her own card and took the seat next to him.

The car was topped with a translucent hemisphere of plexiglass. The track lifted steeply away from the airport to climb above the green hills and neat houses of the suburbs. The black line of a bike path wound beneath, paralleling the freeway, and off to the west, the green and brown roofs of a tent city ranged in crooked rows. They passed over a narrow harbor where container ships crouched like enormous black spiders, then swooped down into the silver and gray towers of the city. The track wound between highrises and sank to occasional stops on the roofs of lower buildings. The sun-spangled waters of Puget Sound framed the cityscape, and the old Space Needle glittered in the spring sun. To the north, Erin glimpsed the circular roof of Sokol Hall. "This is wonderful, Charlie!" she breathed. "I had no idea."

"Monorail's great," he agreed. "When it's not raining, anyway. Beats riding in limos all the time."

"But how did you figure all of this out?" She gestured around her at the car, at the latch that secured his chair.

He shrugged. "Practice, that's all. Wait till you see the condo."

"Whose is it?"

"Some doctor friend of Mother's. She arranged to borrow it for a while—he's off on an exchange fellowship."

"Sarah? How did you ever get her to agree to all this?"

"Well—she didn't like it much, but I told her I was staying anyway. And she didn't want me to stay in a hotel."

"Is it nice?"

"Very. You'll see. But first—" Charlie reached behind him to unhook his chair as the car descended to a smooth stop on a moderate shrubby hill. "First you meet Dr. Berrick."

Charlie worked his way deftly out of the monorail car onto the moving platform. This time when he slanted his wheels the platform itself propelled him onto the fixed sidewalk. Erin followed, catching up with him outside the kiosk. He began laboriously wheeling his chair up the sloping sidewalk. The glassphalt was just rough enough to provide traction, but the sharp incline made Charlie struggle.

"Charlie, use the motor," Erin said.

"I uncoupled it."

"Let me push, then." She put out her hands to the back of the chair.

"No, Erin," he said between gritted teeth.

"At least give me my bag."

"Nope."

There was nothing she could do but walk helplessly be-

hind him as he thrust his chair forward, biceps and triceps
ridging as he turned the wheels. He stopped at the top,
panting, not looking at her. Scarlet patches stood out
against his pale cheeks.

"Is this what's the matter with you, Charlie? You're trying to push your chair everywhere on your own?"

"Ted says I need to strengthen my muscles. No more
pushing, no more motor."

"Who the hell is Ted?" Erin wailed.

Charlie managed a breathless laugh. "Physical therapist
in Berrick's clinic." He turned right, down a street that was,
mercifully, a downslope, and now Erin had to trot to keep
up.

The sidewalk ran past tall white houses with columned
balconies and porches painted green or dark red. Repro
cars, with curtained windows and spoked wheels, waited in
neat driveways. The only anachronism in the scenery was
the monorail, sewing the city together with looping silvery
stitches.

"What period is this?" Erin asked.

"Runs from 1910 to 1920," Charlie said. "It's in the
neighborhood covenants."

"It must cost a fortune to keep it this way."

Charlie nodded. "You can bet your multicard it does.
Keeps out the rabble, I guess."

The clinic, when they came to it, was indistinguishable
from the houses around it. Drapes hid the interior from
view, and camellias in bloom and rhododendrons in bud
snuggled close to the walls, almost hiding the tiny sign in
the front window:

Eugene Berrick, M.D., Ph.D.

Applied Neurophysiology

Erin said doubtfully, "It doesn't look like much."

"Well, it can't. The covenants. But you'll see."

Charlie pushed himself up a short ramp and held the door for Erin. She went past him into a room that was a perfect Edwardian parlor, appointed with a Tiffany lamp and brocade-stuffed chairs and a loveseat beside a piecrust table. Charlie rolled past these and went to a door in the far wall. He pressed a button beside the door and grinned over his shoulder. "Ready to meet the mad scientist?"

Erin didn't answer. She had met a lot of doctors. There was her mother, of course, and occasionally her mother's friends. And there had been a long, long list of Charlie's neurologists, geneticists, and virologists. She remembered every one of the various alternative practitioners Charlie had tried in his longing to walk again. She wasn't looking forward to meeting one more, and she couldn't pretend she was. The door opened, and Eugene Berrick appeared.

He was tall, with black hair prematurely streaked with silver, combed straight back from a narrow, dark face. His eyes were incongruous, a startling clear gray behind old-fashioned round, rimless glasses. He didn't look familiar to Erin, but she experienced a strange feeling of recognition, disorienting, like the odd little shock of déjà vu. She blinked, and the moment passed.

Berrick said, "Oh, good, Charlie. Come in, I've been waiting for you to try this," and disappeared immediately. He didn't seem to be aware of Erin at all.

Beyond the inner door of the clinic all traces of period decor vanished. The room was a long rectangle, crowded with monitors and keyboards and fullscreens that lined the white walls. A door in the back opened onto another room full of what looked like exercise equipment, where a technician in a white jacket was working on an exercise mat with an older woman in sweatpants. Berrick closed that door as he passed it.

Everything in the clinic was spotless, glass and chrome and enamel. A track of modular light fixtures shone directly on a high-backed white wooden armchair. The chair sat in the center of a tall construct of supporting rods dripping wires and cords in rainbow colors, and a wheeled walker stood near it.

Erin's stomach turned at the sight of the walker. On Charlie's eighth birthday, *their* eighth birthday, Charlie had tried to walk to the table where a birthday cake and presents were waiting. She could still see him, leaning on his pediatric walker, struggling to make his legs move. His legs had refused to obey him. It was the first time it had happened, that he couldn't force them, manipulate them somehow. Charlie had cried. Erin had cried. The cake was never touched, the presents never opened. Sarah Rushton had stood frozen, watching her children, not touching either of them. The twins had clung together in a mutual grief. They were very young, but they both knew that when Charlie could no longer use the walker, he was confined to his wheelchair forever. It had seemed weeks before he smiled again.

And now, Erin thought, it would begin all over.

Dr. Berrick touched a switch to extinguish the overhead light. Small lamps in the corners of the room cast muted shadows across the gray biocomposite tiles of the floor. Erin stood by the door, not sure what to do. Charlie rolled himself forward, to the white wood chair.

"Dr. Berrick, this is my sister," he said. "Erin Rushton."

The doctor was seated in the only other chair in the room, leaning over a piece of equipment. Erin recognized the Moog 105 synthesizer, but not the array of emitters that had been added to it.

Eugene Berrick appeared to be about thirty. He wore jeans and a white shirt, like Charlie, and a white coat over that. He had long, delicate fingers that flicked over the sensing pads of the synthesizer. He looked up briefly to nod and say "Hi" to Erin. And then, abruptly, "Ready, Charlie? A new progression I want you to try."

Charlie locked the wheels on his chair and lifted himself on his arms. Erin moved automatically to help him, but he gave a sharp shake of his head and she stopped, hands outstretched, feeling awkward. Neither Charlie nor Berrick noticed. Berrick's attention was on the Moog, and Charlie was occupied with working his way into the wooden chair. Erin wanted to look away, hating to see him struggle. His expressive features twisted with effort, carving lines around his mouth like those of an old man. He maneuvered one foot at a time, the typical ataxic motion, wide, inaccurate, like wading through waist-deep mud.

Charlie took three torturous steps, supporting himself on the arms of the wheelchair and then on the back of the wooden one. He fell heavily into the seat, and wiped the sweat that trickled down his temples. He smiled bitterly at Erin. "Pretty, isn't it?" he said.

At that Berrick did look up. He thrust the round spectacles up on his forehead and stared at Charlie. "What's that?" he said. "Are you okay, Charlie?"

"Yes," Charlie said quickly. "I'm ready."

He pulled a pair of headphones from one of the rods above his head and put them on. Berrick crossed to him to attach two tiny black remote-sensing electrodes to his temples and two more behind his ears. He reached up to adjust the wireless receptors in the frame. Charlie leaned his head against the back of the chair and closed his eyes as Berrick went back to the synthesizer and pulled on his own set of headphones. He adjusted several dials, his eyes on the projection monitor at his elbow.

An image sprang to life above the monitor, a three-dimensional, hemispherical blue sponge with small red lobes swelling to one side and at the bottom. An elongated shape, gray and dull, trailed off from the other side like a sort of holographic gingerroot. Tiny spears of light flashed through the sponge, clear and white against the blue. The spears came in a quick and fiery rhythm at first, then quieted gradually to a regular pulsing. Charlie's eyelids flickered. His hands lay open on his lap, palms up, fingers twitching.

The image projected by the monitor rotated slowly,

rather elegantly, above a graph projection. The flashes peaked at intervals like snowy spires against a winter-blue sky. Berrick watched them, his fingers constantly moving over the synthesizer. Erin sighed suddenly, not realizing she'd been holding her breath. There was almost no sound in the room. An ancient Bulova rested on top of one of the idle computers, and when she caught sight of it Erin realized it had been almost half an hour since they first came into the clinic. What could be happening? And what was it for? Charlie's color was high, red spots in his cheeks garish against his pallor.

A few minutes later the track lighting came on, gradually brightening the room. Charlie lifted his head and opened his eyes.

"Okay, Charlie," Berrick said. His eyes were still on the projection. His long fingers touched the dials once, rose, then touched them again, like a musician playing his instrument.

Charlie pushed himself up, and reached for the walker. Erin stiffened, but restrained herself. Trembling, Charlie leaned on the crosspiece of the walker and extended his right foot. He took a slow, wobbly, swinging step. He placed his right foot on the floor, shifted his weight, and began to extend his left foot. Erin heard him grunt. His left foot found a purchase, and he began all over again with the right.

Erin wrapped her arms around herself. She wanted to look away from Charlie, but she couldn't. She was terrified he would fall, would collapse. It was like watching someone climb a horizontal cliff, each new foothold achieved at enormous cost. Now Berrick's attention moved back and forth between Charlie and the monitor projection, the blue of the projected field reflecting in his round glasses.

For fifteen minutes Charlie labored, and in that time he covered perhaps ten feet. At a point when Erin was sure he must fall, when his arms and hands seemed to be collapsing with strain, Eugene Berrick pulled off his headphones and tapped the power switch on the Moog. "Good, Charlie, very good," he said. "Back you go, now."

For an instant, Charlie's eyes met Erin's, full of shame and pain, and her heart turned over in her chest. It was like being six once again, watching her brother stumble and fall, lose his balance, tumble from a chair or collapse without warning on the play surface at the Llewellyn School. How many times had she helped him up? She took a step forward.

Dr. Berrick snapped, "No!"

Erin stopped as if she had been slapped. Hot blood rushed to her cheeks.

Charlie pulled off his headphones, letting them hang in their plastic cradle around his neck. His eyes were on his feet as he turned back toward the white wooden chair. Erin could hear each harsh breath whistling through his clenched teeth. He took one agonizing step, and then another. Erin bit her lip till it stung.

Charlie's arms and shoulders shook. He took another step. Perspiration stained his shirt. Another step. His breath became a whimper, almost a sob.

Erin closed her eyes at that, and she didn't open them until she heard Charlie fall into the seat of the chair. His head was thrown back, and he panted through open lips. Berrick was leaning over him, testing his pulse, wiping his brow with a tissue.

"Good, Charlie!" he said. "Significant improvement." He looked up at Erin as if seeing her for the first time, his gray eyes alight in his dark face, radiating power and drive. "Do you see it?" he demanded, pulling his glasses down on his nose to peer at her above them.

She stared at him. What was she supposed to see? Could he not see Charlie's suffering?

A spurt of anger rose in her breast. "Well . . . well . . ." she stammered, trying to hold on to her temper. "Charlie? Does it seem better to you?"

Charlie nodded. "Sure," he said, his voice choked and hoarse. "Better."

"But what is it?" Erin asked. "What did you do? What are you doing?"

Charlie sat up straighter, and Berrick released his wrist. He pushed his glasses up again, to inspect his patient at close range. "You okay now, Charlie?"

"Getting there," he rasped.

Berrick nodded to Erin. "I'll explain it," he said. "Just let me fix Charlie up with something to drink." He went to a small fridge at one side of the room, and came back with a tall glass. "Here, Charlie, drink this while I talk to your sister."

Slowly, feeling reluctant, Erin followed Eugene Berrick to the desk. He held the chair out for her. "Sit down," he said. His tone was uninflected, neither warm nor cool. "I'll give you the brief lecture on augmented binaural beats and neural restructuring."

He bent over her to reach for the headphone set. His eyes were luminous behind the circular glasses, the color of sun through a mist, and his skin was as fine-grained as dark satin. Oddly, she wanted to touch it, until he turned those eyes on her. Then she felt transfixed, like a small nocturnal creature caught by some bright light. He handed her the headphones. She glanced back at Charlie, but he had closed his eyes again. The glass in his hand was half empty. Almost unwillingly, she looked back into Berrick's eyes. "What's he drinking?" she asked.

"It's high-powered fruit juice, essentially—electrolytes, potassium, sucrose, fructose. Bring his blood sugar back up." He adjusted the headphones over her head, his long fingers grazing her cheek. They were very clean, the nails short and shining. He pressed a pair of electrodes to her temples, brushing back wisps of her hair to do so. Another pair he fastened to the base of her skull, one behind each ear. Then he bent and touched the sensing pad of the Moog.

A deep sound began in her left ear, a slight, rhythmic

pulsing, barely audible, too low for her to discern the pitch at first. She listened, wrinkling her forehead in concentration. Just when she thought she had it, another sound began, in her right ear. She couldn't identify that pitch either. She shook her head, irritated, confused. A moment later she realized there was something coming through the electrodes, too, some sort of mild pulse of energy. She looked up, and saw Eugene Berrick watching her, the round glasses thrust up on his forehead, his lean dark features unreadable. She felt her lips part in a breathless moment of anticipation.

The pitch changed, becoming higher, more intense. She still couldn't identify it. Her perfect pitch had deserted her, it seemed. The sound was not really music, and not even really in her ears. She felt it in the center of her head, as if the sounds from each earphone pierced her skull to meet in the middle. And the electrodes—was that electricity, some sort of low-amp stimulus? It didn't hurt exactly, but it wasn't pleasant. The pitch in the headphones rose again, and pulsed faster. She scowled, annoyed, feeling as if mosquitoes were flying around in her head. The monitors flashed, but the patterns didn't appear to have any connection to the sounds she heard. After a moment the pitches dropped and slowed, then dropped again, lower and lower, until they were out of the range of her hearing. The pulses she felt at her temples also stopped. She pulled off the headphones, shaking her head.

"I don't get it," she said.

Berrick said, "That's what the lecture's for." Charlie was back in his wheelchair, and he rolled across the room toward them, looking considerably stronger now, the red patches in his cheeks subsiding.

Eugene Berrick pointed to the Moog. "I'm feeding a different pitch into each ear, but pulsing them at the same rhythm—binaural beats. The cochleae in the ear vibrate in response to the sound waves, and pass that energy along to the brain in the form of electricity. The brain translates the different pitches into one pitch it can understand—sort of splits the difference. In the process, the brain waves—patterns of electrical impulses through the cortex—are affected. They change in response to the binaural beats, in order to process them. I can speed them up, slow them down, coax them into alpha states for relaxation, beta for concentration, theta for learning. I'm doing that for Charlie, working him through a progression of brain-wave states in order to help his brain find new neural pathways to his legs."

"And the electrodes?"

"That's a small electrical charge, extremely low voltage, but specially designed to match the neural impulses of the brain. Charges to the cerebrum, here at the temples, and to the cerebellum, here behind the ears. They're to stimulate the regrowth of the neural paths. Auditory cortex doesn't have a direct path to the motor cortex—the augmentation boosts it along."

"But it was so hard for him. He's exhausted."

"It's not easy," Berrick agreed. "And he's spending a lot of time with Ted, too. He needs to be a lot stronger physically, to be ready to walk. But it's the connection between body and mind that we're working on. It has to be both physical and mental. Pointless to do one and not the other."

Erin eyed Berrick doubtfully. "Are you sure it will work? Putting him through all this?"

He stiffened, and his eyes flicked away, then back. She was afraid she had offended him, but his dark features told her nothing, showed no emotion. He said, "Friedreich's causes ataxia because there's degeneration in the thalamus and the cerebellar cortex. You probably know that. Charlie was lucky—the damage to his brain was halted by the engineered virus he received. His intentional tremors are limited to his legs. He wants to walk, his brain sends the signal through the motor cortex, but the route by which the intention is transmitted is too damaged to pass along the command. What I'm doing is creating new routes. Bypassing the damaged area. Can I be sure? No. It's experimental. Charlie understands that."

Erin pushed back from the desk and stood up. "I don't like seeing him so tired, Dr. Berrick," she said.

Berrick's eyes glinted like newly washed windows. "Would you rather see Charlie stay in that chair?"

Erin felt her cheeks warm. What did this man know of how hard she had fought for Charlie? When they were children, it was she who had waited for him on the Llewellyn soccer field when he couldn't keep up. It was she who pulled him up when he fell on the safety surface of the playground. She had punched a classmate for calling Charlie a cripple, and earned a scolding from her piano teacher for bruising her hand. Erin had been the first to do battle with Charlie's disease.

Still, she hadn't been able to drive away the truth. Nothing she did made Charlie better. Nothing she could do had ever helped him.

"Dr. Berrick," she said. "I would do anything to help my brother walk. But I don't want to see him suffer for nothing. He's endured too much already."

"E—" Charlie began.

"No, it's okay, Charlie," Berrick said. He took off his glasses and polished them on his white coat. "Erin, I assume you've been tested for the gene?"

"What does that have to do with it?"

"I know your mother refused to be tested. When your father developed Friedreich's."

Erin stood stiffly. "How do you know that?"

Charlie said, "Erin, for godsakes! He's my doctor, I told him all that, of course."

"It's unusual, you know," Berrick said. "Your father was forty when he became symptomatic. Very late onset. One would think your mother would have wanted to know."

"Would it have made a difference? To Charlie?"

There was a moment of silence before Berrick said slowly, "We won't ever have the answer to that."

"Mother was furious," Charlie said in a wry tone. "Because our father contaminated the Rushton gene pool."

Berrick's eyes were still on Erin. "Friedreich's is the prototypal spinal ataxia, and like most others, hereditary. Your mother's a physician. I'm sure she was aware that if she was a carrier, one of you, or both of you, could inherit the disease. And when Charlie became symptomatic, she had to know immediately that she carried the recessive gene."

Erin remembered very well when her mother had made that discovery. Sarah Rushton had come to the Llewellyn at the request of the head, and Erin had watched her as six-year-old Charlie struggled across the schoolroom, his brows knit, his head bent, arms out for balance, short legs swinging in clumsy circles. Erin had seen the recognition that distorted her mother's perfect features, had seen and understood the naked fury. There was another, more complex emotion, too, but Erin, at six, had no name for it.

Now she said shortly, "I've been tested. I don't have the gene."

"It's just Charlie, then," Berrick said.

Erin's throat closed suddenly, and her eyes burned. She had to look away from the doctor's piercing gray gaze. "Yes," she whispered. "It's just Charlie."

He pressed on, relentless. "But that's not your fault."

"I know that!" Erin said in a raw voice.

His voice was level. "Nor would it help Charlie if you also had the gene."

Erin felt Charlie's eyes on her, too. She looked down at her hands clenched in her lap. "Of course not."

"And you can't make this easier for him." There was no softness to Berrick's tone, yet she somehow felt that he was offering her a kindness. She thought she had never met anyone so utterly controlled. He was like a frozen lake, the surface hard and smooth, the depths dark and deep. What would it take, she wondered, to see below the frozen surface of his character? And how could she know if he could be trusted with Charlie?

11

Seattle, May 2018

CHARLIE still refused to use the power on his chair or to let Erin help him as they worked their way up the slope to the monorail stop.

"Charlie, you're beat," Erin scolded. "What good does it do to wear yourself out?"

"Ted says I need to use my muscles," he said.

"But you have your own physical therapist in Boston!"

"She never made me work like this. I want to do it, E. I'm getting stronger. Stop worrying."

She kept a surreptitious eye on him as they waited at the monorail kiosk. His voice was thick, and she saw that his hands trembled on the wheels of his chair. Fronds of hair, dark with sweat, clung to his neck and temples. As they boarded the car, he caught her looking. "I said stop it, Erin," he repeated. She turned away to look at the scenery, feeling helpless and vaguely hurt.

It was a short ride. At the very next stop, Charlie led Erin out of the kiosk and across a broad street, up a semicircular drive to a large boxy building topped by a copper roof gone green with exposure. The entryway was dim and cool. Mild spring light filtered through colored glass win-

dows to cast pastel patterns on the dark wood fixtures and
pale marble floor. Charlie peered into a scanner, and a small
elevator opened. As he rolled into it, a metallic voice said,
"Good morning, Mr. Rushton." Charlie grinned at Erin and
said, with a flourish of his arm, "Welcome to St. Mark's,
Miss Rushton."

The third-floor hallway was dominated at one end by an
enormous rose window that cast jigsaw rainbows on the
white walls. Charlie opened the last of six doors spaced
along the corridor, and Erin followed him into a large, airy
apartment.

Couches, an oak table and chairs, shaded lamps, and a
sparkling brass spittoon all sported the curving parallel lines
of art deco. A viewwindow filled one entire wall. Opposite
it a broad, deep-silled realwindow looked west to the peaks
of the Olympic Mountains gleaming with late snow. Erin
went to look down on a generous slice of lake with boats
moored around it.

"Isn't it pretty?" Charlie said. "Lake Union."

"Lovely. What's the point of a viewwindow when you
have this?"

He lifted a small switch cover in the opposite wall and
touched a button. "Observe."

The viewwindow glimmered to life, showing large
wooden yachts making creamy wakes across a sun-starred
lake. A tall ship tacked in the wind, white sails billowing.
The topography looked the same as the lake in the realwindow, except with considerably fewer buildings. The hill
was shown as a greensward bisected by narrow brick
streets, a handful of houses scattered here and there. "Oh,"
Erin said. "All that space!"

"No kidding," Charlie said. "Nineteen thirty-one. Hardly
built up at all." He moved to the center of the viewwindow,
and the perspective adapted to his presence, shifting south,
toward the center of the city. The cityscape was sparse, too.
Heavy-looking, round-nosed cars rolled on narrow streets.

Charlie pointed to the empty hillside on the opposite shore. "That's where Sokol Hall is now."

Erin strolled around the room. An ornate walnut piano on three double legs filled one corner, and Charlie had rolled his Akai S3X synthesizer underneath it. She sat on the piano bench and traced the fading gilt letters over the keyboard. "Chickering," Erin said. "They don't make these anymore."

Charlie said, "It's a 1927 parlor grand. Doesn't sound too good, but it holds its tuning."

Erin touched the middle C. The tone was dry, but more or less accurate. She glanced around. Everything in the apartment was old and obviously expensive. "I guess medicine pays well in Seattle."

"I suppose," Charlie said. "Especially in the city. Probably not on the fringes. But then you wouldn't find one of Sarah's friends treating public patients."

"What about Dr. Berrick?"

Charlie chuckled. "Dr. Berrick lives above his clinic and handles his own appointment schedule. I don't think he's making a lot of money."

Erin played an E flat triad, then tried a full two-handed chord. One of the hammers clunked, and she sighed. "Charlie."

"What?"

"What did that feel like, today? What you were doing with Berrick."

Charlie twirled his chair toward a tidily arranged, quite modern kitchen separated from the room by a carved mahogany bar. He tapped buttons on the cold-server and juice poured out into a tall cut-crystal glass. Glass in hand, he came back to Erin. "It feels like learning a new instrument," he said thoughtfully. "Like when you're trying to learn the fingerings, train the *embouchure*, coordinate your breathing. The binaural beats irritate me, but I guess irritation is one kind of stimulus, like a grain of sand annoying an oyster into making a pearl. But I'm sure I feel something happening, something changing." He watched Erin for her reaction. "Really."

She swung her legs around the piano bench, putting her back to the keyboard, and smiled wryly at her brother. "You can probably guess how weird it seems. From the outside."

"What do you think of Dr. Berrick?" he asked.

Erin left the piano and crossed the room to look down on the real Lake Union. Small drops of rain smudged the window and obscured her view. When she turned back, she saw that in the viewwindow the day was sunny, with boaters in white clothes and straw hats waving at each other across blue waters.

"Tell me," Charlie prompted.

"He's very focused," Erin said carefully. "Single-minded. As if all that's important is the work, the results."

"Works for me," Charlie said lightly.

"But it's so hard on you."

He shrugged, eloquently.

"He's awfully young."

Charlie smiled. "I like that. He's just beginning, still full of energy, willing to take a risk."

"You're the one taking all the risks!"

He shrugged again.

"What if it's all for nothing?"

"I don't believe it will be," Charlie said.

"And what . . ." She had to say it. "What if you get worse?"

He looked down into his glass. "I can't think about that," he said quietly. "I have to try."

"Oh, Charlie." Erin wandered through the kitchen, tracing the deco patterns on the glass cabinets, fingering the reproduction toaster and coffeepot that masked contemp appliances.

In a brittle tone he called after her, "You don't believe him, do you? You don't think we can do it."

Erin finished her circuit of the room, and returned to

stand beside his chair. "I don't know," she said. "Why didn't anybody else ever try this, if there's anything to it?"

"First time for everything." Charlie rolled away from her to a low table beside a divan with an asymmetrical back. He held up a sheaf of papers. "Look at these."

She followed, taking the stack in her hand. It was the coarse, thin paper, many times recycled, used for making copies. The print was a muddy black against the dull gray surface. "What are these?"

"Research papers, clinical studies, stuff like that."

"Have you read all of this?"

He nodded. "Every word. Did you know that classically trained musicians have more cerebellar volume than non-musicians? The practice, the coordination of mind and fingers or lips or whatever, actually increases the area of the cerebellar cortex." He gave a little laugh. "I should have plenty to work with."

"But Charlie, walking is complicated!"

"Maybe it's not, E." He took the stack of papers back from her, tidied it, and laid it on the table. "You know how the minds of deaf or blind people reroute to compensate for the loss of one of the senses? It's the same thing with stroke patients who rehabilitate their speech—they develop new pathways in their brains. Maybe this is a bigger leap—but I think we can do it."

Erin didn't know what to say to her brother. Charlie had wept when hypnosis failed him, raged at the pain of physical therapy and neuroshock and spinal injections that left him with shaking limbs and blinding headaches. Sarah Rushton had refused to sanction these attempts, or even to hear the results. Erin wondered how Charlie had talked their mother into supporting this one, but she didn't want to ask. She hoped for a few days of peace before she had to fly off to Boston.

Charlie showed her to a lovely bedroom, all white and pink organza and elongated glass fixtures. They would share the bathroom, which was fully outfitted with a bath lift, shower seat, and grab bars. A brass handrail, gracefully curved at the corners, was set at waist height on every wall. "See?" he said wryly. "Art deco for the handicapped."

"Bad joke, Charlie," she said.

"I know," he said. "Sorry. It's been a long day."

"It's okay. What about dinner?"

He looked up at her from his chair. His blue eyes were reddened, his mouth bracketed with lines of fatigue, but his grin was merry. "For dinner—we cook!"

She clutched at her throat in mock terror, and followed him out to the kitchen.

Berrick, it appeared, had even taken over Charlie's diet. The fridge was stocked with whole foods only, not a package or can in sight. Fruit, soy yogurt and tofu, organic cheeses, and natural-yeast bread crowded the shelves. Charlie laid out the ingredients for a supper of steamed local clams, a green salad, a tiny loaf of dark bread, and a fragrant bleu cheese. Erin rounded up dishes and flatware, and laid the table. She found a candelabra and brought it to the table, dusting the candles with a tissue before lighting them.

When the clams were ready, Charlie opened a bottle of white wine. "He lets you have wine?" Erin demanded. Charlie looked up at her in surprise, and she regretted the edge of resentment in her tone.

"If it's pesticide- and sulfite-free," he said mildly.

She gave him a rueful smile. "So what's with all the health food?"

Charlie put two crystal flutes on the table and poured the wine. "One of the problems with neurological conditions is the blood-brain barrier," he said. "It's not as strong as it might be in a healthy person. Mine may be okay, but to be on the safe side, Dr. Berrick doesn't want me taking in anything that might cause further damage."

"So you turned into a cook in one week?"

He smiled at her. "Sit down, little girl," he said, with a flourish of his hand. He rolled his chair close to the table. "Let's find out."

To her surprise, Erin found the dinner wonderful. To her
left, the picnickers of the 1930's waved and laughed under
a vintage sunset. To her right, the real view was gray and
wet, the lights of the city coming on one by one to glimmer
through the rain. She and Charlie sat in a cozy circle of
candlelight, tossing the clamshells into a bowl between
them, sipping chardonnay, savoring the sharp bite of the
cheese. When Charlie yawned, his eyelids drooping, Erin
was sorry to see the evening end. She sent him off to bed
while she cleaned up.

When the dishes were in the washer, she poured the last
of the wine into her glass and went to stand by the realwindow looking out at Seattle's contours. It could almost
have been the city of a century ago, most of the lights
obscured by rain, the streets empty of traffic. Sokol Hall,
on the other side of the lake, was dark and invisible. A red
warning light flashed somewhere above the mist, but otherwise everything was a soft, ageless gray. Erin found herself wishing she could stay in this gentle city, stay here
with Charlie in this clean, orderly, comfortable apartment.

She drank off the last bit of chardonnay. In two days
she would be in Boston, for a matinee performance at the
Early Music Festival, and then she was off to London, to
play with the Atheneum of Ancient Music. It would be
hard, going without Charlie. She hoped this Dr. Berrick
knew what he was doing.

12

London, January 1762

EILISH'S dress, ordered for her by Mrs. Stevenson, was a lovely charcoal wool, new and clean and crisp. The skirt just brushed her toes. Knife-thin pleats on the bodice exaggerated her meager bosom, and there was a fine white linen scarf, trailing wisps of fringe, to tie around her shoulders. Cook helped her to put up her hair beneath a tiny embroidered lace cap, then stood back and looked her over. "You're a vision, child, right enough," she sighed. "Such eyes, and your wonderful curls! No girl in London could look better."

Eilish sighed, too. A nervous butterfly fluttered just beneath her breastbone. 'Twasn't anything like getting ready to play outside St. Paul's. This was to be a proper concert, with people sitting in chairs and listening to every note. 'Twas no use pretending it was just like practicing, because it wasn't the same at all. Her every bone, her every shivery fingertip, knew the difference.

Polly had returned from Essex for the occasion, and had made a great show of bringing Eilish a gift, a little tin of the face powder she herself used. She splashed some on Eilish's face with a big cotton puff. Eilish, caught by surprise, gave a convulsive sneeze. More powder filled her lungs as she gasped, and she choked.

" 'Tis a bit too much, I think, Miss Polly," Cook said hastily. "Here, let's brush some off." She smoothed Eilish's cheeks and brow and dusted the excess powder from her fingers. It spilled across the dresser in a drift of white, reminding Eilish of the glass dust covering everything in Mr. Franklin's laboratory. " 'Twas a lovely thought, don't you think, Eilish?"

"Oh, aye. Ta, Miss Polly. Such a lovely little tin."

Polly stood back a bit and looked Eilish up and down as if she were a carriage horse for sale. " 'Twas a good choice Mother made," she said. "Not above your station, but quite presentable. Now see you present Mr. Franklin's creation to its full advantage!" She nodded to Cook, and made an imperious exit.

Cook tweaked Eilish's earlobe affectionately. "You look lovely, no matter your station! The white scarf makes your eyes such a bright blue, like the Thames in summer!"

"Ta, Cook." Eilish went to the basin on the washstand and began to scrub her hands.

"Surely you're already clean, dear?" Cook said. "You bathed this morning."

"Oh, aye, but 'tis a funny thing, Cook. The glasses sing better when my fingers are cleaner than clean," Eilish said. "Always if people touch my glasses, I have to clean them after, or they won't sing at all!" She dried her hands and then went to gaze into the looking glass.

She hardly knew the girl she saw. A proper nob she looked, her hair up, her cheeks powdered white. Her dress was not so fine as Polly's, whose painted cotton gown was nipped at the waist, low in the bosom, and busy with lace and pleats. And of course, Polly wore a wig, and pearl earrings! But still, Eilish thought, for a girl from Seven Dials, she was a sight for the angels.

She turned away from the glass and immediately forgot about her appearance. It was the music that mattered. It was the reason she was here. Her armonica would make its debut today. Her fingers longed for the touch of its crystal bells, for the transcendent feeling that came when the two of them, the little shining armonica and the Irish orphan, made music together. She started to go down the stairs, but then turned back to open her top drawer. She stroked the embroidered blessing on the old linen handkerchief. "For luck," she whispered. Then she hurried down to Mr. Franklin's rooms.

Perhaps a dozen people were gathered around the armonica. Fortunately, Mr. Franklin was standing in front of it, holding forth on its special properties. The bit of *écru* silk they had draped over it was undisturbed. No unwelcome fingers were touching its sensitive glasses, but still Eilish would have preferred they kept a greater distance.

"Ah!" exclaimed Mr. Franklin when she entered. "Here is our musician!"

Every eye turned to Eilish, and her step faltered. So many unfamiliar faces, rich gowns and waistcoats and powdered wigs! For a moment she could scarcely breathe, as though the scented air was too thick for her lungs to inhale. But she lifted her chin, and walked very deliberately to the armonica. Her place, after all, was at her instrument. She was the star of the day, or at least, she and the armonica together. If she had to be jittery as a shoo-fly on a sheep's rump, then so be it. She had waited for just such an event all her short life. 'Twas worth a nasty case of nerves to be the one standing just here, ready to play, to be the center of attention.

Eilish had met Dr. John Pringle and Mr. Richard Jackson before, and of course Polly and Mrs. Stevenson. Franklin introduced the others. The gentlemen smiled. The women nodded, their lips pursed, their nostrils flaring delicately. Bessie moved among them, pouring wine into fluted glasses, as they resumed their interrupted conversations.

Franklin patted Eilish's hand. "A bit nervous, my dear?"

"Nay," she said, straightening her shoulders. "Not a bit of it."

He chuckled. "Just a few more minutes, then." He was drinking wine, too, and he held out his glass for Bessie to refill. "We'll begin in about five minutes."

The five minutes stretched to fifteen as Franklin laughed and talked with the assembled guests. Eilish stood beside the armonica, her hands by her sides. It seemed she was invisible. Her butterfly fluttered beneath her new dress, and she breathed to calm it. She waited. 'Struth, there was naught else she could do.

At last the guests ceased talking and found their seats. Franklin, his cheeks grown red and his voice loud, returned to Eilish. He thrust his spectacles up onto his head and held his hands out wide, palms up. "Now, now," he exclaimed. "We have kept Miss Eam waiting long enough! Quiet, now, quiet, everyone. This"—a dramatic pause—"is my glass armonica!"

He pulled off the *écru* silk with a flourish. The crystal glasses gleamed softly in the afternoon light, and the mahogany case glowed golden brown. There were feminine cries of "Lovely!" and "Oh, Mr. Franklin, how charming!" The men made various admiring comments while Eilish poured water in the crystal bowl and positioned it below the cups. She sat down on the little velvet-covered stool and adjusted the position of the foot treadle as Franklin stepped back and took a seat with the others.

At last. Eilish closed her eyes for a moment. *This is for you, Da.*

"Bonnie Laddie, Highland Laddie" was her first tune, because it had a lovely lilt and rhythm, and because Franklin so loved the Scottish melodies. The armonica responded to her fingers, the pressure just right, the speed of the treadle smooth and flexible, the glasses singing out as if they, too, had been awaiting the moment. When she finished, the audience applauded with soft pats of their hands, nodding enthusiastically to Franklin. Only Margaret Stevenson smiled at Eilish.

Eilish told herself that didn't matter. It was natural, they were Mr. Franklin's guests. She smiled back at Mrs. Stevenson, and began the ballad "Barb'ry Allen," a slow, sad song Da had loved. He had sung it to her in his crackly tenor when she was wee. The words hadn't meant much to her then, but the emotion of the melody had sunk into her very soul, and she poured it out again now, giving all of herself to the music. The armonica answered the pressure of her fingers with a delicate drag, that perfect resistance that made the crystal ring so sweetly. It was a moment all hers, hers and the armonica's. When it was over, the last plangent note died slowly, as if reluctant to fade.

Another little burst of muted applause startled her. She had forgotten her audience. She looked up, seeing their smiles, the gentlemen nodding to each other, Franklin beaming, several ladies whispering together. Only one, a middle-aged woman with cruelly lined eyes, sat staring at Eilish, or the armonica, it was hard to say which. Tears streaked her powdered cheeks, and her lips trembled uncontrollably. She brought her handkerchief to her face to hide her eyes. Eilish didn't know what to make of it, and she had no time to think about it.

Franklin had left his chair to stand beside her. "You see, my friends," he said with a grand gesture, "how clever this is! We have the same sound of the musical glasses, as made so popular by Mr. Pockeridge, but without having to adjust the water in them at every turn! Here we have smoothly turning glasses, never needing tuning once they're ground, and an easy time for the performer. Miss Eam already played the glasses, and it was merely a question of becoming accustomed to this new arrangement." Smiling, he thrust his hands into his waistcoat pockets. "The brilliant thing was turning the glasses on their sides. That was the spark of genius!"

The applause was more energetic this time. Eilish hid a

little smile at Mr. Franklin's pride. He often boasted like a small boy, and Cook and Peter chuckled about it in the kitchen. But 'twas certainly true he was a clever man. Eilish was not inclined to feel critical of him, but rather grateful for her beautiful instrument and the opportunity to play it.

Then Franklin took his hands out of his pockets and, without so much as wiping the crumbs of cake from his fingers, he put his hands on her armonica. "Observe, how simple it is to play!" He stretched his leg under the case to pump the treadle, bumping Eilish's feet to one side. He played two or three chords, and a bit of clumsy melody. Eilish heard the deadening of the tone, the slippage of his fingertips as the cups became greasy. "Anyone can do it, really!" Franklin cried. " 'Tis a wonder, is it not?"

After a time he allowed Eilish to go on with her program, but 'twas too late. Her glasses no longer sang. They squeaked at times, and left spaces in their crystal tones. She played her songs—"The Unfortunate Rake," "The Massacre at Glencoe," and "Dublin Lass"—but the magic was gone. The applause was generous. No one else seemed to notice the difference. And at the end, Franklin stood up again, and asked her to take a bow. Eilish smiled and curtsied carefully. She knew about putting a good face on a bad performance.

Bessie came around with more wine, and Peter came in with the tea things. Conversation rose again amongst the elegant company.

Eilish stood beside the armonica, not sure what she was to do. No one spoke to her, though they crowded round Franklin. It was as if she had disappeared when the music stopped.

She waited a few minutes, watching the gathering. Not even Franklin glanced her way. He stood with his chest thrust out, receiving compliments from the ladies, questions from the gentlemen. When a little cluster of them came to the armonica and began to rub their dirty fingers across its glasses, Eilish picked up her skirts and hurried from the parlor.

She knew Cook would be holding her tea for her in the kitchen, but for once she had no appetite. Weary now, dejected, her head aching slightly, she trudged up the stairs to her bedroom and closed the door. She went to the bureau and looked into the glass.

"So, yon ninny," she whispered to her reflection, "did you think to make a silk purse out of a sow's ear?"

She pulled out the long hairpins and let her hair tumble down around her shoulders. Stretching her arms behind her, she undid the buttons of her fine dress, and hung it carefully in the wardrobe. She took out the old, overlarge blue dress and put it on, and tied her hair back with a plain ribbon. She nodded sharply toward the looking glass. "There you are again, miss," she said. "And don't go putting on airs again."

13

Seattle, May 2018

A T Charlie's next appointment, Berrick pulled out an extra set of headphones and offered them to Erin. "Care to follow along?" he asked.

She accepted the headphones and put them over her head when Charlie did. Berrick brought a chair for her, placing it just behind Charlie's so her headset could pick up the binaural beats. He didn't give her the electrodes. He bent into the construct around Charlie to adjust a bit of wiring. He looked just as he had the day before: white shirt, long, lean legs encased in jeans, hair combed straight back from his high forehead. Erin watched him work, thinking how beautiful his hands were with their dark, elegant fingers, and how arrogant his manner, giving orders to Charlie, to her, touching Charlie without permission, shoving things here and there without regard for anyone else. Somehow, even so, he managed not to offend. There was something—*essential,* was the odd word that came to her—something essential in the way he worked, the way he addressed them both. She understood why Charlie trusted him.

When the tones began, she felt the same things Charlie had described. At first the sounds in her head were calming.

Her breathing slowed, her heartbeat settled into sync with
the low-pitched pulses. As the tones came faster, the pitches
began to rise. They concentrated, irritated—like an itch—
right in the center of her skull. She closed her eyes, examining the feeling, wondering if she could channel that
nervous energy into her legs. She wanted to experience
what Charlie was experiencing, to sense what he might be
sensing.

She was surprised to hear Berrick's voice telling Charlie
to get out of the chair. It seemed only moments had passed.
She opened her eyes and watched Charlie struggle into the
walker to begin his painful progress across the floor.

Erin tried to project her mind out of her own body and
into her brother's, to lend him her own strength, her energy,
and especially her natural, instinctive knowledge of how it
was done. You pick up your right foot. You bend your
knee, you flex your ankle, your foot comes down like this,
heel and toe, and your weight shifts. Now the left. Pick up,
bend, flex, place. So simple. So hard.

Only the corner lamps were lit. Chrome and glass and
steel gleamed softly in the dimness. It was easy to let the
room fade into background, an indistinct *mise en scène,* a
setting like the vague backdrops that mask backstage chaos
from concert audiences. Erin sighed, her eyes on Charlie,
but not really seeing him anymore. Not seeing anything.

And there, in the gloom beyond her brother, her wraith
appeared.

Erin caught her breath, held it. Though her eyes were
open, the image seemed to flare in her forehead, in a re-
ceptor not fed by pupils and irises and optic nerves. *Then
by what?* her mind cried frantically. And was the shape
more distinct than usual, or was it that there was nothing
to distract her from observing it?

The image wavered, trembled, black and white and gray
and—what was that color? Blue? How could she know it
was blue if it wasn't her eyes perceiving it? Could she feel
blue, sense it, as if it were an emotion, or an idea? The

shape was graceful, a long, sweeping skirt, a cloud of black hair above a pale profile, and those slender arms . . .

It was clearly a woman, perhaps a girl, so slender, the waist so tiny. The arms were reaching, white hands turned down, fingers curled. And as Erin watched, frozen, hardly breathing, the face turned, ever so slightly, the neck bending in the shadows. A glimmer of light from a nearby full-screen caught wide eyes, a curve of cheek . . . Erin took a shuddering breath.

"Charlie . . ." she whispered.

"Quiet," Berrick ordered. Erin's eyes flew to him in surprise. She suddenly remembered where she was, what was happening. She found she was shaking with cold, that her stomach was quivering with sudden nausea. Despairing, reluctant, she turned back to her vision.

It was gone. The cold reflection of blank glass and white enamel machinery mocked her.

Charlie had reached his goal, unaware of Erin or anything but his legs. The tones in Erin's earphones subsided. She wrapped her arms tightly about herself, shivering, swallowing bile. Charlie pulled off his headphones, took a deep, shuddering breath, and turned to work his way back to the chair. Erin closed her eyes, fighting her own battle.

She was crazy, that was it. She was losing her grasp on reality, unable to tell dream from substance, fiction from fact. Tears burned her eyelids. Her deepest fear rose from within her, a dark bubble rising, ascending inexorably through even darker water. Allowing it to surface, to burst in her consciousness, almost made her ill, right here in this impersonal room, hiding behind her closed eyes, ears stopped by state-of-the-art-headphones.

It was the terror that lurked in her nightmares, that stalked her when she was weakest, most vulnerable. It was the fear that made her snap answers to stupid questions, made her impatient and angry at the probing and pushing of interviewers and reporters and historians. She was afraid. She wasn't afraid of her wraith, of ghosts or visions or

manifestations. What she feared was that, like her prede-
cessors, like the ancestral virtuosi who had first played her
precious and mystical instrument, her nerves were breaking
down. She was afraid she was going mad.

She hugged herself tighter, trembling and sick, not even
knowing that tears were making glassy tracks down her
cheeks. It was Charlie's exclamation that brought her to
awareness.

"Erin! Erin, what is it? What's wrong?"

She opened her eyes to see Charlie, restored now to his
wheelchair, rolling swiftly toward her, his hands strong on
the wheels despite his fatigue. Behind him Eugene Berrick
frowned.

Erin leaned forward into Charlie's arms and buried her
head in his shoulder. "Oh, Charlie! She was here, she was
right here! Omigod, Charlie. I'm losing my mind!"

THE juice was salty-sweet and thick on Erin's tongue. She
was surprised to find that it banished her nausea almost
immediately, that the pounding of her head subsided. She
drained the glass and looked up to see Eugene Berrick's
dark face above hers. He bent over her as he had over
Charlie, checking her pulse with two long fingers placed
gently under her jaw. The crystal gray of his eyes had the
irresistible pull of clear, moving waters.

"Better," he said as he took away his hand. Not a question, but a statement, as if he needed no corroboration.
"Better."

He took the glass from her, and the one Charlie had
emptied, and carried them to a small sink beside the fridge.
Charlie reached to comb sweat-damp fronds of hair from
Erin's forehead with his fingers, and she leaned her cheek
into his hand. "God, Charlie," she whispered. "She was so
clear."

"Take it easy, E," he said. His voice was steady, but she

felt the trembling of his hand. "We'll talk about it when you feel better."

Berrick returned, and stood close to the two of them, peering over his glasses at Erin. "What was it?" he asked. "What did you see? You're not surprised, are you, Charlie?"

Charlie shook his head. "She's seen it before," he said. "In concert. I didn't really think—well—" He spread his hands. "You'd better tell us, I guess, E."

She rubbed her eyes. "It's so weird."

Berrick said, "Let's hear it." His gray eyes held hers, and she wanted to look away, but she couldn't.

She took a deep breath, and tightened her fingers on Charlie's. "I see this—this figure. This girl—I mean, I know she's not really there, she can't really be there, can she? But I see her."

"What does she look like?" Berrick asked. He seemed neither shocked nor perturbed.

"It's—it's hard to say. It's mostly an outline, a silhouette, sort of. Hair piled up, long skirt, very narrow waist. Arms out—like this—" Erin put out her arms and curled her fingers, and then froze, staring at her own hands.

"What, E?" Charlie demanded.

"It's as if she's playing an instrument! I just realized!"

Berrick said, "How often have you had this experience?"

Erin said slowly, "Three—no, four times. Counting today."

"When did they start?"

"Last year," Charlie said. "Right, E?"

"Triggering event?" Berrick asked. Erin realized he was making notes on his slimscreen.

She said, blankly, "What?"

"Something happened, to start these psychic visions, right? Some event, some turning point or crisis?"

"Psychic visions? You're saying I'm psychic?"

Berrick took off his glasses and wiped them with a tissue. "Everybody's psychic. Everybody has a mind, and a psyche. Some have better access, that's all. Now, what happened?"

Erin shook her head, and looked to Charlie for help. "Well—nothing I can think of. Nothing, really."

Charlie said, "When was the first one, E? Boston?" She nodded. "I can think of something," he said slowly. "Two somethings."

Now Erin stared at Charlie. Why was he so eager to give this strange man what he wanted? He behaved as if everything Eugene Berrick said was gospel.

"Think, E," Charlie said. "Boston was the premiere of the *Requiem*."

"So?" she said, more sharply than she intended. Berrick actually lifted a finger in warning to her, the same finger he had raised earlier. Erin felt her temper spark. It felt better than being afraid.

Charlie didn't notice. His eyes were unfocused as he remembered. "It was the first performance," he said. "And we worked so hard, going over and over it—and then, the same day of the premiere, Mal booked you to perform at the State House, at the Franklin exhibit. Same room you first saw the glass harmonica. Same instrument, actually."

"Did something happen at the exhibit?" Berrick asked.

Charlie glanced at Erin. "They let her play the old one, the one they never let anyone play. They brought it up from Philadelphia. The man from Finkenbeiner's cleaned it up, and oiled the treadle, and she played it, just for a moment, but the real thing, the one Franklin himself played."

Erin remembered. It had been strange, going into the exhibit where all the old, old things were so carefully preserved. There had been a coat of Franklin's, and some china of Deborah's, and silver that had belonged to William Franklin and his English bride. And of course, the armonica.

Erin had been careful with it. She was unfamiliar with the archaic foot treadle, the uneven thick glass cups painted to identify the notes. Its tone had been odd, almost crude compared to the crystalline perfection of her own instrument. The glasses had revolved reluctantly, the spindle complaining against the ravages and rust of two hundred and fifty years. And touching it had been oddly painful, the nerves in her arms aching obscurely as she played. She had been relieved to step out of the exhibit area, to see them close and relock the glass doors on the controlled atmosphere that protected the artifacts. She had gone to her own gleamingly new instrument and played easily, fluently. And afterward, in the car, she had wept with fatigue and nerves.

She looked up to find Berrick and Charlie watching her. "What?" she asked shortly.

"Tell us about it," Berrick said.

"I don't know what to tell you," she said. "I played Franklin's instrument—the *armonica,* he called it. It wasn't called the *harmonica* till the Germans took it up, you know—that *h* just came naturally to them, I guess. I played only a few phrases. It's fragile, and not in very good condition. Then they locked it up again, and I played a bit of Mozart and Reichardt and Zeitler on mine, and we went home to rest before the concert. That was it."

"Erin." Charlie squeezed her hand. "Come on. There was more than that."

She glared at him, not wanting to reveal her weakness, her nerves, in front of Eugene Berrick. Not wanting Dr. Berrick to think she was mad.

"She was crying," Charlie said to Berrick. "In Mother's car, on the way home. And shaking like a leaf."

"Why was that?" Berrick asked.

Erin gave a dramatic, wide-handed shrug. "Who knows? I was tired. Nervous about the premiere."

Charlie laughed. "Come on, E! Nervous?"

Berrick had turned away from them, restlessly, striding back to his desk and the scan projector. He switched off the Moog and stood hipshot beside his desk, staring down at its scarred wooden surface. "Fascinating, fascinating," he said, almost under his breath. Then, abruptly, he turned back to them and said, "Let's try it again, see if we can repeat the event."

"Fantastic," Charlie said with enthusiasm.

Erin stood up, scraping her chair against the tiled floor. "No."

Berrick was suddenly still, his glasses in his hand. "What?"

"I said, no." She thrust her hands in her jeans pockets and stuck her chin out. "I don't want to do it again. It's freaky, and I don't intend to repeat it if I can help it."

There was an awkward moment of silence, and Erin knew Charlie was embarrassed, but she didn't care. This man was not going to bully her into some bizarre head game. She was startled at the sincerity with which Berrick said, "But—don't you want to *know*?"

She didn't answer. She turned away to the door. "I'll wait outside, Charlie."

She walked with deliberate steps out through the little parlor into a misty afternoon. A weak sun was trying to pierce a thin, persistent layer of cloud. The camellia had dropped all its blossoms, and the rhododendron was afire now with pink blooms. Erin waited, pacing, feeling resentful, then confused, then just anxious. When Charlie emerged from the clinic, they set off up the hill for the monorail stop without saying a word.

Once Charlie had secured his chair in the car and it had lifted away, he smiled at her. "It's okay, Erin. It's no big deal."

"Oh, right." Her throat tightened again, and she swallowed. "So if I lose my mind, it's no great loss?"

Charlie chuckled and patted her knee. She grabbed his hand and held it as tightly as she dared, staring out into the fog, trying not to think of anything.

14

London, January 1762

EILISH woke the day after the concert with a headache and shaking hands. When she appeared in the kitchen, pale and trembling, Cook exclaimed over her.

"Aye, dear, and you with neither tea nor supper last night! 'Tis no surprise to me you feel poorly this morning!" She set a cup of tea and a plate of thickly buttered bread before Eilish, pressing it on her. Eilish tried, but could swallow no more than half a slice of bread, and even that churned in her aching stomach like bees trying to escape their hive.

"I'm sorry, Cook," she muttered at last, pushing away from the table. "It pains me to eat. Just the tea, I think."

"You're so wan, Eilish," Cook said in a worried tone. "Perhaps we should ask Mrs. Stevenson to send for the doctor."

"No, no, please, Cook," Eilish pleaded. "No doctors." She knew about doctors, though she had met only Dr. Pringle. Doctors meant ghastly sharp tools and blood and screaming and pain. In Seven Dials, medical care was well known as a frequent cause of death.

"You'd best rest today, at least," Cook said, untying her

apron. " 'Tis the best thing for you." She hung the apron by the sink and bustled out of the kitchen and up the stairs.

Eilish leaned her head on her hand. She wanted air, and perhaps some clear water, but a great fatigue oppressed her. She laid her aching head on the table and closed her eyes. "Oh, Da," she breathed. " 'Tis just as ye said. Pride goeth before the fall."

She rested so for some moments, her cheek on the clean scarred wood. Presently she began to feel a bit stronger. Above her the house was quiet, and she remembered that Franklin had been summoned to the King's Council. The men at the concert had spoken of a second Parliamentary grant. Eilish had no idea what a Parliamentary grant was, or that there had even been a first, but there was some problem, something about money, that Mr. Franklin was worried about. She didn't care about that either, not today. Serve him right, she thought ungratefully.

Eilish lifted her head. On the sideboard she spied the remains of a sweet seed cake, left from the refreshments of the day before. She had no doubt it would sit there, mostly uneaten, until it went stale. What a waste that would be. And how Mackie would love a bit of seed cake! A sudden urge seized her, an aching need to see the little boy, to hold him in her arms. The desire was so strong that it brought her to her feet. She moved slowly, only a bit unsteady, toward the back of the house in search of Peter.

She found him in the stableyard, on his knees between the empty hames of the carriage. The horse put his head out of his box and snuffled at her approach. Eilish stroked the long muzzle, and breathed deeply of the fresh air and the pungent smell of straw and horseflesh. The air sparkled with thin winter sunlight, cold and clear. Her nausea began to subside.

"Hi there, miss," Peter said cheerfully. He put down the ballpeen hammer he was holding and straightened, groaning a bit as he stretched his back. "The footboard was loose," he said. "Rattling like a pebble in a tin. Can I do aught for you?"

"Oh, aye, Peter," Eilish said. "If you're not too busy— would you take me to Seven Dials? To see Mackie? I haven't seen the wee one in ever so long. Could you?"

Peter tugged his vest down over his round belly and smiled. "Seeing as how Mr. Franklin's gone off to White-hall with Dr. Pringle, I don't see why not, miss. He'll be there all the day, he said. Fetch your wrap, though. There's a breeze, and a bit o' fog coming off the river, though we see the sun just now."

"Oh, ta, Peter! I'll be no more than a minute!" She felt worlds better as she trotted upstairs for her cloak. She heard Cook's voice in Mrs. Stevenson's parlor as she passed. With her bonnet on and her cloak over her shoulders, she hurried down the three flights to the kitchen. Her hands trembled as she picked up a broad knife, but she tried to ignore them. She wouldn't be playing today, in any case. She cut three thick ragged slices of cake, spreading them with sweet butter and layering them together. She wrapped the whole in a clean napkin and tucked it under her cloak. She could hardly wait to see Mackie's pleasure as he ate them.

When she returned to the stableyard, Peter had hitched the horse to the little carriage. He tipped his hat to her, his cheeks creasing cheerfully. "At your service, milady."

"Oh, la, Peter," Eilish said tartly. "Me lady, indeed. Me da would've said you've been on a visit to Blarney Castle!"

He wore a heavy cape-collared overcoat and brown leather gloves. He opened the door of the carriage and held it for her. "Can't I ride up top with you, Peter?" she begged. "Since it's just the two of us?"

"Nay, miss. 'Tis not seemly. And too cold! In with you now, and no arguments."

Peter was right, she found. She felt snug and warm inside the closed carriage, away from the bite of the wind. She sank into the seat, and gave in again to her weakness and fatigue. She leaned her head against the red plush as they left the stableyard and rolled up Craven Street to the Strand. Her eyes were heavy, and she slept a little. When a jolting of the carriage woke her, she saw they were already in Monmouth Street, almost to Seven Dials. They had driven into a heavy fog that obscured the leaning tops of the buildings. She sat up abruptly. How long had it been since she had seen Seven Dials? She had come to Craven Street in November, and it was now January! She hadn't been back once in all that time.

The Clock and Cup appeared out of swirling mist, its slanted walls and cracked sign dully familiar. Peter pulled the carriage up before the pub and climbed down, grunting a little in his tight waistcoat. Eilish stepped gingerly out, mindful of her shoes and the dirty street. Her headache had returned, and with it the ache of her stomach. She hesitated, suddenly fearful of the dilapidated buildings, the suspicious eyes watching from grimy windows. For one terrible moment she was sorry she had come.

She gave a shake of her head, rejecting her own foolishness. She lifted her chin and picked up her overlong skirts, keeping the packet of cake tucked under her arm. With Peter following, she strode purposefully into the pub. Several voices rose in greeting, then fell when they saw her escort. Eilish nodded to those she knew, then walked straight back to the narrow, dark stairway that led to Dooya's flat.

The odor of overcooked oysters, of potatoes on the verge of rot, of unemptied chamber pots and never-washed bodies filled her nostrils, and she wished for one of Polly's scented handkerchiefs to stop her nose. How was it she had never noticed that smell before? How quickly she had become refined enough to be offended by it—aye, and what a pain 'twould be were she forced to return to Seven Dials for good!

She stood with her hand raised to knock on Dooya's door, casting her eyes sideways to Peter for support. The whites of his eyes flashed nervously in the gloom. She felt just as wary, and with good reason. To awaken Dooya O'Larick in the middle of the day was to loose a banshee. Eilish thought better of knocking. She dropped her hand and put it on the latch.

She opened the door carefully, remembering how it scraped against the raw boards of the floor. She saw the mound of Dooya's wide hips under the blankets on the bed, and heard her burbling snore. She pushed the door a bit farther. The air in the flat was no warmer than the air in the stairway. Her breath misted before her face, and she saw that Peter had tucked his hands, gloved though they were, under his armpits.

She could see the empty table, and the remnants of a fire, now dead. She pushed the door all the way open, wincing as wood squealed against wood, but Dooya snored on. Eilish stepped into the flat with Peter just behind her.

"Mackie?" Eilish whispered. Then, a little louder, "Mackie?"

At first there was no answer. Then Eilish heard a rustle, a little tumble of blankets and bare feet, and Mackie appeared in the doorway of the cupboard that had been her room only two months before. His red hair stood up in every direction, stiff with oil and soot. His freckled face was moon-white, his eyes wide and staring. He gazed at her for a long moment as if he had never seen her before. Then, with a loud wail, he flung himself across the floor, staggering on his thin, crooked legs. "Eilish! Eilish! Hi, Eilish!"

She fell to her knees and held out her arms. Mackie threw himself against her, still wailing. "Eilish! Hi, Eilish!"

Dooya's snore came to a strangled end and she choked out, "Damn ye, Mackie!" Peter took a step back, right to the wall, as Dooya struggled to sit up. Eilish hugged Mackie tightly, his face buried in her shoulder. "Shush, shush, now, Mackie, let your ma sleep. Shush, now."

Dooya, the blankets under her chin, glared blearily at

Eilish. "So 'tis you," she growled. "I might know you'd come back right in the middle of me rest!"

"I've just come to see Mackie," Eilish said. "Go back to sleep. We won't be long."

Mackie lifted his head to look up at Eilish. Dirt tracked his round cheeks, and strands of hair stuck fast to his forehead. He smiled the old sweet smile, and begged, "Candy, Eilish?"

Laughing, she untangled herself from him and stood up. "Aye, Mackie. I've a bit of a treat for you, right enough." She pulled the napkin parcel from under her cloak.

Dooya watched with gummy eyes, her lips loose with drink and sleep. "Y'see how the child is starving, miss high-and-mighty! Ye might have thought to bring a bit o' cash."

"So you can drink it all up, ye great tart?" Eilish snapped. Peter, still waiting beside the door, shuffled his feet and cleared his throat. Eilish cast him a look of apology for her sharp tongue. 'Twas bad enough he had to stand there suffering Dooya's rancid smell. Eilish carried the parcel to the table, sat down, and pulled Mackie up into her lap. "Who stays with Mackie by nights, Dooya? Rose Bailey? You'd not be leaving him alone, would you?"

"And what do you care, Eilish Eam?" Dooya made a rude noise and threw herself back on her pillow. "See, the child knows ye care more for fine clothes and food than you do fer him."

Eilish looked down at Mackie, who already had stuffed his cheeks with seed cake. His round blue eyes were dark with tears that formed even as he chewed. She pressed her cheek against his unwashed hair. "Oh, Mackie, darlin', darlin', you know it's not true, don't you? You're me bonny lad, just like always!" She dropped some coins on the table. "D'ye see, Dooya? There's all the money I have in the world! See you spend it on food and not gin!"

The child wriggled on Eilish's lap. "Mackie go with Eilish!"

She shook her head. "Oh, Mackie, I'm so sorry. You can't. I can't take you with me."

He stopped wriggling, swallowing, tears spilling. His voice cracked as he said, "The swells, Eilish?"

"Aye, darlin'." Her throat tightened. " 'Tis the swells. Me life's not me own, even now."

"Hah!" shouted Dooya. "Yer breakin' me heart, ye little drab!"

Peter cleared his throat again. "Please, madam—" he began.

Dooya barked with laughter. "Madam, he says! Madam! Eilish, take yer blackamoor on out of here! We don't need yer charity. Madam, 'struth! Mackie, come here, come to yer ma!"

Mackie stopped chewing. He hung his head, sitting still with both hands full of cake. " 'Tis all right, Mackie, dar-lin'," Eilish whispered. If Mackie defied his mother now, he would pay for it later, she knew that well enough. Eilish kissed his sticky cheek, and lifted him from her lap. She took the bits of cake and laid them in the napkin, then gave him a tiny push toward the bed.

Mackie took only one step before his crooked legs bent and collapsed and he fell flat on the wooden floor. He lay there a moment, facedown, sobbing silently. "Well?" Dooya demanded. "Get up, ye clumsy oaf!"

Eilish jumped up, and lifted the child from the floor. "Dooya!" she hissed. " 'Tisn't Mackie's fault his legs are poor."

Mackie buried his face in her skirts, his thin shoulders shaking. Eilish cast Peter a despairing glance. Peter shook his head, his own black eyes shining with sympathy. What was there to do? A dirty, half-crippled Irish boy would hardly be welcome in Craven Street.

By the time Peter and Eilish reached the street once again, and Eilish was stowed inside the carriage, she was weeping, too, great painful sobs that tore at her throat and clawed at her chest. Mackie's absence left a raw wound in the pit of her stomach. Peter turned the carriage in the street and drove away from Seven Dials, while Eilish wept, haunted by Mackie's silent, tear-streaked face, his dull acceptance of her betrayal.

When they reached the Strand, Eilish's crying had grown shrill, almost hysterical. As if outside herself, as if looking in through the windows of the carriage, she told herself to stop. She knew she should stop, knew she had to stop. But it was all coming up at once, like a waterspout on the Thames—her disappointment over the concert, her heartbreak over Mackie, adding to all the sorrow her young heart already held—the mother she had never known, the death of her father, the breaking of her glasses, her ill treatment at Dooya's hands. She sobbed until she had no breath, and then she hiccupped helplessly. She had tapped the very wellspring of grief, and she couldn't find the way to stanch its flow.

When she stopped crying at last, it was from sheer exhaustion. She lay limp and spent against the plush seat, drawing huge shuddering breaths, punctuated by hiccups, like a child after a tantrum. Some time passed before she realized the carriage was not moving. She put a hand to her face, knowing her eyes and lips must be swollen, her cheeks blotched and ugly. She turned her head to look out.

Peter stood beside the carriage, his head averted, his collar turned up against the cold.

With a last convulsive sniffle, she put her hand to the door, opened it, and stepped out.

She found herself, not in Craven Street, but standing on Westminster Bridge, facing south over the river. The pierced towers of St. John's and the Gothic spires of Westminster Abbey thrust up above the fog. Peter leaned on the stone railing, staring down into the bleak, smoky flow of the Thames. Eilish pulled her cloak tightly around her shoulders, and joined him.

"Ta, Peter," she said. Her voice was hoarse with tears. "I'm sorry about all that."

He turned to her, and she saw that despite his round, cheerful features, his black eyes were lined with care, full of sadness. He said heavily, " 'Tis a terrible thing to be without choices."

"Aye," Eilish said. "So I know. And you? How have you learned this grievous lesson?"

"Have you forgotten, miss?" he said. "I'm a slave."

"Aye," she said sadly. "So you are. You and I are much the same. Slave, housemaid, prostitute, street musician—they were all one."

"I suppose we are," Peter answered. His full lips shone darkly, his tongue surprisingly pink when he spoke. "There were two of us, you know, who came over from America with Mr. Franklin. But King ran off—never knew where. Not a word to me, either. Just—gone."

"But you didn't run off."

"No. I doubt King is better off, wherever he is."

"Are you awfully lonely, Peter?"

He nodded. "Like you, miss."

"You should call me Eilish, Peter. We're slaves together."

"Perhaps." He bowed slightly, and gave her a poignant smile. "And now, if you're feeling better, miss, we'd best be on our way."

"Aye. I suppose we must." Eilish turned to step back into the coach.

She had thought they were alone on the bridge, but to her left, just approaching the span, she saw a small person just crossing Bridge Road. It was difficult to see through the mist, but the lad, or lass as it might be, appeared to have oddly short-cropped hair and wore a strange sort of short, wide garment with a turned-up collar. The face was very white beneath a halo of silvery hair.

Elish's head spun with the dizziness of a fey spell. Why did she think the person was a girl, a young woman? With that hair, those odd clothes . . .

She peered through the fog, trying to see more clearly.

Beside her, Peter opened the door to the carriage and said, "Miss?"

Startled, she turned her head to him, and when she looked back, the thick fog had swallowed the odd figure.

"Peter," she whispered. "Did you see her?"

"Who?" Peter said, looking about. "See who?"

Eilish didn't know how she knew, but she understood, sure as sure, that the slave Peter could never have seen the fair-haired lass. She had come just for Eilish.

15

Boston, May 2018

SARAH Rushton wore her ice-blond hair in a perfect chignon, small diamond earrings glittering quietly beneath the smooth wings of hair. She used a pale, shining lipstick, but no other cosmetics. At fifty-five, her jaw was firm, her features chiseled. Her cheeks were marked with lines that were vertical and attractive, as if she had deliberately selected them, and her eyes, under faintly sagging lids, were a vivid china-blue. Charlie's blue. Erin's blue. The doctors and nurses under her supervision knew how those eyes could snap, and so did Erin.

Sarah leaned back in her chair at the head of her elegant dining table, linking her fingers before her. "Tell me about your brother, Erin," she said in her light, slightly dry voice. "And his new enthusiasm."

Erin hesitated. Even thinking about Berrick's clinic made her stomach quiver, but that had nothing to do with Charlie. Her mother and Mal were watching her, and she shrugged. She would never tell them about that. Instead she said, "Charlie's doing a lot of physical therapy. He took the joystick off his chair, and he rolls it everywhere himself. I can't get him to use the power."

"And what about this clinic, this neurophysiologist?"

Erin hesitated again. "Charlie likes him," she managed.

"Evidently. I wonder why Dr. Berrick hasn't published anything about his work."

"Well, he did publish on the net . . ." Erin began, then stopped. Why should she defend Eugene Berrick?

Sarah Rushton gave a delicate snort. "The net." She made a small, deprecating gesture. "It's hardly the *New England Journal,* is it? Though I understand in his residency he had good results with aphasia."

"Aphasia? That's speech, isn't it?" Erin said.

"Indeed it is. I don't know how that could help Charlie. I'd feel better if Dr. Berrick's credentials were more impressive."

"He's young, Sarah." Erin didn't know if she spoke for Charlie's sake or out of the habit of contradicting her mother. She remembered, with disturbing clarity, Eugene Berrick's startling eyes and wonderful hands.

"It's not just that, Erin. He didn't go to good colleges. And he did his internship someplace odd—Spokane, wasn't it? Some hospital no one's ever heard of. That's probably why he hasn't published—he may have tried and been rejected."

"Charlie doesn't care about that, I guess."

"No." Sarah's smooth lips curved in a slight smile. "That seems to be my job."

Erin said, "Dr. Berrick seems to know what he's doing. He's very—" Very what? What had she meant to say? Sarah was watching her with that familiar, cool expression. "He's very focused," Erin finished lamely. "Intense."

"I wish I knew more about him. I'm not sure this is a good idea, but your brother insisted." Sarah sipped water again. "Do you think I should interfere?"

Erin opened her mouth, not knowing at all what she would say. She wanted to resent Eugene Berrick, she wanted Charlie to be with her, the way they had been before. But she also wanted to disagree with her mother, on almost everything. And there was something vulnerable about a young physician struggling to overcome the wrong credentials, a lack of connections. As Erin searched for an answer, the telephone chimed, and the housekeeper came into the dining room immediately afterward.

"Dr. Rushton, the hospital needs to talk to you." Sarah rose, folding her napkin and laying it on the table.

When she left the room, Mal said, "Do you think Charlie's okay?"

"Oh, I guess. I just wish he wouldn't stay there," Erin said. "Doing all that crazy stuff in the clinic—while I have go to London alone!"

"You won't be alone," Mal said in a wounded tone. "I'm coming to London, too."

Compunction further muddled Erin's already confused feelings. "Oh, Mal. I'm sorry I said that. I just meant—without Charlie." She tried to summon an apologetic smile.

His freckled jowls trembled slightly as he nodded. "I know, I know. Not to worry."

Sarah returned by the time coffee was served, and they spoke of the next day's concert, and the night flight to London. Charlie called, and they each took a turn with the phone in Sarah's study. Mal had a new commission to discuss, and Sarah pressed Charlie for details about his work with Dr. Berrick. He smiled cheerfully at her, assured her all was well, he was improving, he would tell her all about it when the time was right. Erin marveled at how well he could manage Sarah.

When it was Erin's turn, they talked about *Moving Mars.* "I've just about got the fingerings," she said. "I'll work on it in London. They've given me practice time at St. John's."

Charlie nodded. "That's great, E. I love St. John's—I'm sorry not to be going with you."

"You could join me there," she said eagerly. "Catch the supersonic commuter! It flies out of Seattle."

He shook his head. "Can't," he said. "Really, I can't.

I'm making progress, I'm sure of it, and so's Gene. Can't leave now."

"It's Gene now? What happened to Dr. Berrick?"

Charlie grinned. "Abducted by aliens," he said.

Erin didn't return the smile. "I don't know what you see in him," she said.

"Yes, you do," he said softly.

"How can you know that, Charlie?"

"I just know," he said. "How about you? You getting over the other day?"

"Sure I am. Forgotten," she said with complete dishonesty.

"Oh, right," he said, shaking his head at her. "Just like that."

She gave a mirthless laugh. "Well, I'm not foaming at the mouth or anything. Yet."

"Listen, E," Charlie said soberly. "You take care of yourself."

"Me? I'm not the one spending every day with a mad scientist."

Charlie put out his hand to touch the screen. "You know what I mean."

She matched her fingertips to his. "Yeah. I'm okay," she said. "I really miss you, though."

"Call me from London."

"I will."

"Work on *Mars*."

"I am, beast."

"I am, too," he said, smiling again.

"But I thought it was finished."

He wiggled his eyebrows. "Wait till you see, little girl, just wait till you see!" He blew her a kiss and broke the connection.

She sat for a moment, her arms wrapped around herself, staring at the wall of medical reference works beside the phone console, and then around at the room. Her mother utterly disdained the trend for period. Her house was furnished with expensive contemp furniture, all titanium and recycled fabric, angular lines, gray and black and silver with dashes of scarlet. The phone console was state-of-the-art, with dual screens and position-sensitive cameras. Even the Bösendorfer in the living room was new, with the brightest tone of any piano Erin had ever played. It was a beautiful house. Sarah had owned it for twenty-five years, but Erin still felt, when she was there, that she was just visiting. She doubted that in all her life she had spent more than an entire year under its roof.

London, May 2018
The Victoria Inn, in Belgrave Road, was a converted nineteenth-century townhouse, with small suites papered in Victorian stripes and floppy cabbage roses, furnished with bentwood chairs and velvet sofas. Mal preferred places with more mod cons. "At least a phone console!" he begged. But Erin rebelled at the mention of a Marriott or a Sheraton. She would have liked something even older, but the little hotel was within a reasonable distance of St. John's, and made a good compromise.

They landed at Heathrow just after dawn. Erin, tired after the evening's performance, had slept a couple of hours and then wakened. Everything was quiet in the first-class cabin. She lifted the little window shade and caught her breath at the wealth of stars sparkling against the velvety backdrop of the night sky. She left the shade up to feel their cool light on her face as she dozed again. What must it have been like, she thought dreamily, to have been able to see the stars above the cities, before the proliferation of electric lights faded them to invisibility. A star-filled sky was a marvel the period neighborhoods could never re-create.

When the limousine delivered them to the Victoria, the concierge recognized them at once, and pleased Erin by calling her madam. They left their luggage with him, ate a quick breakfast, and went on to Smith Square with the glass harmonica cases.

An ad screen glimmered in the outside wall of St. John's, scrolling Erin's picture, the program, and the date of the concert. The house manager met them in the atrium between tall white Corinthian columns, shook Mal's hand, gushed over Erin. "Delighted, Miss Rushton, simply delighted to have you back. Such a lovely old instrument, so charming to hear it in our hall! The BBC were here just yesterday, getting ready for the netcast. Such a pleasure!"

Mal saw to the instrument cases while Erin strolled into the hall. St. John's was the real thing, a masterpiece of the English Baroque, the perfect ambience for the slender sound of old instruments. The players of the Atheneum of Ancient Music all used period instruments. Some were repros, of course, like her own. But some—Baroque violins, double basses, a harpsichord—had been made even before this church, with its openwork turrets and marble floors, had been built.

Erin wandered to the low stage that had been an altar centuries before. She tipped her head back to look up into the arch of the ceiling, tasting the life of the old building, the essence created by the thoughts and desires and regrets of the people who had trodden its floors, breathed its air, laughed and cried between its walls. The atmosphere of St. John's was charged with memory.

When Mal and the driver came in with the harmonica cases on a dolly, Erin said, "I love coming here, Mal."

Mal said gloomily, "I just hope they give you a contract for next year."

Erin laughed. "Oh, come on! Old music isn't a trend here—it's what they do, for godsakes! Do you have to be so gloomy?"

"It's looking thin, Erin, that's all. Looking thin."

She turned away in exasperation. "Well, we're here now, anyway. Come on, let's get it set up. I want to play for a bit."

At stage right, they unpacked the three trunks that carried the glass harmonica. The spindle came out of a long rectangular box, the disassembled cabinet out of a flat, heavy one. The speed control and cleaning supplies fitted neatly into a third. Mal and Erin lifted the spindle out by its brackets and nested it carefully into its case. Erin set about removing the foam pads and cleaning the cups with alcohol while Mal connected the foot pedal and plugged in the universal current adapter. Erin went to the nearest washroom to scrub her hands. When she returned, the power was on, the harmonica ready. Mal had gone off somewhere with the house manager, and Erin had the stage, and the hall, to herself.

Worklights shone on a litter of folding chairs and empty music stands. The scarlet curtains over the immense east window were open, but a gray morning fog muted the daylight. No sound penetrated the thick walls, not the street noise, nor the cheery sounds from the café tucked into the crypt beneath the church. The newly cleaned glasses glowed in the soft light. Erin felt pleasantly disconnected, floating in some space between reality and dream.

She dropped her sweater on a chair. When she put her foot on the pedal the cups spun smoothly and silently. She touched one of the smallest glasses, and the ethereal, ineffably glassy tone rang freely in the unobstructed space. Erin felt the tone in her hand, in her arm, in her solar plexus. It occurred to her that Gene Berrick could be right, that sound could transcend the merely auditory. Surely music was felt in the body as much as in the ears? And perhaps, most particularly, the music of the glass harmonica. It pierced, it soothed, it moved. She saw it in her audiences. She felt it in herself.

With her eyes half-closed, she picked out the old, old melody of "Barb'ry Allen." She couldn't remember where she had learned it. She didn't know much folk music, but she supposed she might have heard it at school.

She played it once through, then again, adding a simple

harmony. Tonic, dominant, subdominant, tonic. She whispered a few of the words, half on, half off the tune:

> *"In Scarlet Town, where I was born,*
> *There was a fair maid dwellin'*
> *Made every lad cry well-a-day,*
> *And her name was Barb'ry Allen . . ."*

The domed ceiling rang gently, a long decay stretching the life of every note. The music rose and swirled into the arching ceiling, and the silver-blond hairs on Erin's arms rose in response. She shuddered with a sudden chill, and looked down at her instrument. The light reflecting in the nested crystals was mesmerizing, dazzling her eyes. Her forehead throbbed. She felt momentarily dizzy, as if an unseen hand, a protoplasmic finger, had touched her just between her eyebrows.

She pressed the power control with her foot, and the spinning glasses slowed and stopped. The last note drifted away from the stage, up into the dome, and died. Erin stood very still, staring at the glasses. She was afraid to lift her eyes.

"Erin?" It was Mal, calling from the foyer. She drew a harsh breath.

"Yes!" she cried. Gritting her teeth, she looked out into the hall. There was nothing there. No one there. She took a wobbling step back, away from her instrument, and sat down abruptly on one of the folding chairs. Mal came in, and made his way across the broad floor toward her. He was slightly stooped, walking slowly, looking about him with his usual doleful air. His appearance was so ordinary, so expected, so indisputably real. Erin was very, very glad to see him.

16

F OR weeks, Franklin had often been away from Craven
Street, leaving early in the morning and not returning
until well into the evening. Eilish spent most of the days
of his absence simply lying on her bed, feeling dull and ill.
She shed no more tears, but she mourned for Mackie, and
accepted her illness as punishment for abandoning him. If
she felt at all well, she rose and went to the laboratory to
play the armonica. It had been moved there after the concert, to stand in the light from the tall windows. The early
spring sun showed dust covering everything in the room,
the grinding tools and glass tubes and wires of Mr. Franklin's various experiments, the desks and worktables and
chairs. Franklin flatly refused to let Bessie in with her dusting cloth.

Eilish pulled the silk covering off the armonica to play
for half an hour, perhaps forty minutes, before nausea
would overtake her. One day she vomited upon leaving the
laboratory, and Cook, coming upon her, insisted upon calling Mrs. Stevenson.

Mrs. Stevenson sent a note to her own physician, who,
though he declined to come himself, sent Peter back with

a bottle full of a potion meant to "fortify the blood," according to the bill that came with it.

No one had ever given Eilish medicine. Cook persuaded her to drink the first dose, sitting up on her bed, her nose pinched shut against the acrid smell of it. It was watery and brown. The taste reminded Eilish of the way Dooya smelled. She gagged, and a good half of what she had swallowed came back. Cook patiently wiped Eilish's face with her apron. "There, there, dear, now, now, lass, 'twill be all right."

Eilish's eyes reddened with tears of weakness. "So kind you are to me," she murmured.

"Nonsense," Cook said. " 'Tis only my Christian duty."

She covered Eilish with the quilt and fluffed her pillow. "Now, Mrs. Stevenson says you're to rest until teatime. Mr. Franklin will be back for tea, and there's to be some sort of news."

"To do with me?" Eilish whispered.

"Something to do with you, I think," said Cook with a wink. "Because you are to take tea with Mr. Franklin and Mrs. Stevenson!"

Eilish's mouth watered, and she swallowed hard, afraid she would vomit again. Something to do with her. A concert? Perhaps a chance to redeem herself! She prayed it would be a concert. She would not deceive herself this time, she would know 'twas not only her instrument, but Mr. Franklin's. She would give her best early on, she would be ready to clean the glasses if someone made them dirty, she would be ever so polite and careful . . .

She glanced at the open wardrobe, where the fine dress still hung. The white linen scarf lay pressed and folded on the dresser. She must contrive to feel better, to grow stronger. To practice more. When Cook left, she got up to open her window a crack and steal a breath of cold fresh air. Cook and Mrs. Stevenson were convinced that London air was unhealthful, and they kept every window of the house closed and locked. But somehow the air from outdoors, sooty and damp though it was, made Eilish's head feel clearer. She made certain her door was closed before she lay down again.

As teatime drew near she rose. She washed her face and brushed her hair, tying it back with a wide white ribbon. Several curling black strands escaped to dangle about her face. She tried plastering them back with water, but they sprang free as soon as they dried, and she gave it up. She drank some of the water, which Cook didn't approve of, either, but which tasted good in her mouth, diluting the effects of the doctor's nasty medicine. She straightened her dress and brushed her shoes, then sat on the bed to await her summons.

She heard the clock strike five, when tea was usually served, and then the half-hour. Still there was no tea bell. Eilish almost decided to take off her shoes and lie down again, but at a quarter till six the bell sounded at last. Eilish stood and smoothed her skirt. Her hands still trembled, but her head felt more or less clear. Walking carefully, she descended the stairs to Mrs. Stevenson's parlor.

Mrs. Stevenson sat opposite Mr. Franklin with the tea tray between them. Franklin nodded to Eilish, rather less cheerfully than was his wont. "Hello there, Eilish Eam," he said. "I hear you've been ill. I'm sorry I haven't been here—the King's Council have taken much pleasure in discomfiting me. I hope you're feeling better?"

"Yes, thank you, Mr. Franklin." Mrs. Stevenson indicated the chair to Mr. Franklin's left, and Eilish sat down. She accepted a cup of tea, holding it gingerly on her lap. She would sooner have rejected it than risk a spill with her shaking hands, but she determined to hide her weakness. Surely this trembling would soon subside, and she would be her old self again.

"Good, good," Franklin said. He looked away to stare into the coal fire, and then, abruptly, he burst out, "There's no help for it, Margaret. I'm going to have to go back to America."

"Oh, must you, Benjamin?" Mrs. Stevenson cried. "Can you not persuade them—"

"I have tried, over and over," he said heavily. He sighed, and took off his spectacles to polish them. "The money is gone, and cannot be replaced."

" 'Twas not your fault, Benjamin."

"No, no, 'tis true, Margaret. Not my fault. But, you remember, I have been here five years. Family duty, as well as patriotic duty, calls me."

Mrs. Stevenson sighed. "What a shame dear Deborah will not sail."

Franklin gave a morose chuckle. "She barely sets foot from our house, Mary. You have never met such a homebody."

"Well, in any case, you cannot go until after your visit to Oxford."

Franklin smiled at that. "No," he said. "Certainly not."

Eilish took a careful sip of tea and waited, eyes cast down, wondering. Why had they called her here? She knew nothing of such matters. Less than nothing!

Abruptly, merrily, as if all his woes had suddenly vanished, Franklin cried, "And what is this to do with you, eh, my girl? I expect you want to hear about your next concert, do you not?"

"Oh, aye, Mr. Franklin."

"Oh, aye, indeed." He put on his glasses and then peered over them. "Our friends were greatly impressed with your performance, Miss Eam, and are clamoring for another. How does St. John's Church strike you?"

"Why, Benjamin!" Mrs. Stevenson exclaimed. She turned to Eilish. "Oh, my dear, how exciting! St. John's is one of the Fifty New Churches, you know! Commissioned by His Majesty! In Smith Square, so very elegant. What an honor for you! Benjamin, who will be there?"

"Members of the Royal Society, of Bray's Associates, and Lord Bute, King George's advisor. Lord Bute has made St. John's available to us. I hope to introduce my armonica to the whole of society! Several musicians have expressed interest, too—William Croft, music master for the Chapel Royal, and Edmund Delaval, of Cambridge."

"How lovely! Don't you think so, Eilish?"

"Oh, aye, Mrs. Stevenson. Ta, Mr. Franklin. 'Twill be very exciting."

Franklin smiled and nodded. "Indeed, indeed." And then, quick as the lightning he was so fond of, he was off on another subject. "Now, Margaret, Dr. Pringle is laying plans to bring his patient here—the one I told you about."

"Oh, the nerve case, is it not, Benjamin?"

"It is. I'll get Peter to set up my apparatus. Collinson will be providing the Leyden jar, and if it arrives when I'm not here, don't let Bessie touch it! Wait for me, or Peter, to carry it up to the laboratory. If you could just see to refreshments, after the patient has gone home—Dr. Pringle and I will be tired, I fear, and in need of sustenance! And I expect members of the Royal Society will want to observe." He rose, bowed to both women, and made to leave the room. At the door, he turned back. "Miss Eam—I understand Mrs. Stevenson procured a decoction for you from her own doctor?"

Eilish nodded.

"Be sure you take it all, then," he said. "We want you strong for our concert, do we not?" His smile was avuncular, and he nodded several times. "Yes, strong and healthy."

"And when is the concert to be?" Eilish ventured.

"This Friday evening," he said, "five o'clock at St. John's. 'Tis to be an evening of new instruments! You, Miss Eam, will play for perhaps twenty minutes, and I will speak about the armonica. Then there will be a performance on the pianoforte—Jacob Kirckman, the Saxon, has completed one. See to Miss Eam's dress and things, will you, Margaret?" And he was off.

•   •   •

THE moving of the armonica to the church of St. John
was harrowing for all concerned. Peter, perspiring, eyes
flashing white from nervousness, was responsible for carrying the spindle with its fragile cups, while Eilish trotted
beside him, watching for stones or roughness in the path
that might cause him to trip. Mrs. Stevenson and Polly, with
Mr. Franklin, rode to St. John's in a hired curricle, since
the various bits of the armonica took up most of the space
in the carriage. Eilish sat inside the carriage, cradling the
spindle on her lap. Upon their arrival she relinquished it to
Peter with the greatest care.

They moved cautiously up onto the porch of the church,
Eilish too busy worrying about the safety of the fragile
glasses to look about her. Not till they were safely inside
the church did she lift her eyes from Peter's burden. She
caught her breath. Above her arched a gilded, majestic ceiling. The floor beneath her feet was cool marble, the hang-
ings and draperies elegantly embroidered. Eilish turned her
eyes to the front of the church, to the raised floor of the
altar. A sudden dizziness came over her, but not the old
illness. It was the fey feeling, the eerie sense of being in
two places at once, and it seemed, for one crystal moment,
that she saw herself already there, already playing. She
shivered.

"This way, miss," Peter said. Eilish startled, and turned
to him, and the moment was gone.

He led the way to the front of the church. Another instrument, looking rather like an overlarge harpsichord, was
already in place on the raised floor of the altar. It was
square, made of some dark wood, with white and black
keys like the harpsichord's. Nearby, to the right of this
strange creation, Franklin was already arranging the case
and the foot treadle for the armonica. Peter gently settled
the spindle into its case and Eilish set about cleaning the
glasses. Franklin reached past her, touching one inadver-
tently, and she bit back a reproach. She took her cloth out
and cleaned the glass again, giving all the others another

swipe while she was at it. Her butterfly was back, trembling beneath her bosom.

Franklin looked her over. "You look lovely, my dear," he said. She smiled, feeling shy. "Now, no need to be nervous," he said. "Just relax and play as beautifully as you did before."

"I will," Eilish said with bravado.

Franklin chuckled, and his eyes twinkled mightily through his odd spectacles. "Of course you will, Eilish," he said softly, with something like affection. "You're a brave girl."

Moments later Polly Stevenson came in with the old lady Eilish remembered from St. Paul's Church in Covent Garden—Aunt Tickell, that was. Polly seated her aunt and then approached the altar with small, swift steps. "Now, Eilish," she said, almost before she was in earshot. "We must straighten that scarf, and try to smooth your hair a bit." She fussed over Eilish for a moment, nattering at her the while. Eilish suffered these attentions as patiently as she might. She had sworn a solemn vow to herself that all would go smoothly on this occasion.

There was the usual delay, and it was extended by a pompous speech by the curate of St. John's, who rambled on and on about the role of the church as musical patron, quoting Papa Haydn and Johann Bach. At last, when she thought even her vow of patience would be worn through, the moment arrived for her to play. She had brought a dampened small towel with her, and she carefully wiped her fingers one last time before she rose to stand beside the armonica.

Mr. Franklin was mercifully brief in his introduction. Soon Eilish was seated on her little stool, her feet on the treadle, her fingers poised above the spinning crystal cups.

She repeated her program of the first concert, feeling confident because she had performed it before. She played "Barb'ry Allen" and "Highland Laddie" and the other familiar songs. There was a fair amount of conversation throughout her performance, but Eilish Eam, street musician, was used to that. When she played "Eileen Aroon," there was a little flurry of activity in one of the middle rows. Eilish glanced up, and saw that one of the ladies had apparently fainted, and was being revived with smelling salts. This was not unusual, either.

Eilish renewed her concentration. Nothing must distract her. In moments of relative quiet, she was struck by the dynamic quality of the sound in the spacious church. Each tone flew upward into the high, curving ceiling, and returned enhanced, haloed, to her ears. It was as if the very angels listened and approved her music. Her slender bosom swelled with elation. This was music—real music. And surely, from the vault of heaven, her da was watching and listening.

She paused briefly to wipe her fingers once more, and to surreptitiously clean the glasses. She saw Franklin watching this procedure with a small frown. She gave him an impish smile. His brows flew up, but his eyes crinkled and his lips twitched as if he would laugh.

For her last piece, Eilish played one of the melodies of Mr. Handel, which her da had learned from Mr. Pockeridge. Sweetly, spinning out the notes, the armonica sang the melody of "O Sleep, Why Dost Thou Leave Me?" It was a slow tune, simple and pure, and the glasses sang it as if the great composer had meant it just for them. The audience recognized the melody, and favored it with a collective sigh. When it was finished, and the applause begun, Eilish allowed herself a quick glance from beneath her eyelids at Mr. Franklin. She saw him smiling, pleased, and she felt a rush of satisfaction. Whatever happened now, whatever the rest of the evening might bring, this moment was worth all of it, all the illness and embarrassment and hard work of the past months.

This time Eilish understood her role. She curtsied once, twice, and then moved quickly away, leaving the armonica to Franklin. She went to sit at the back of the church, in the darkest and emptiest of the pews. Only Peter sat there, and she took a seat next to him. As Franklin gave his little lecture on the properties and construction of the armonica, she listened, her heart pounding with excitement and, at last, joy at the success of her performance. Peter nodded to her, his eyes flashing white, his dark cheeks creasing. She leaned back against the hard pew and wrapped her arms about herself, wishing she could hold in this feeling of exhilaration, this thrill of accomplishment, to savor it over and over again. She felt as if this—exactly this sensation—was what she had been born for.

There was an intermission, during which the assembly got up and moved about the church, admiring the architectural details, talking together. Not a few people went to the armonica, and Eilish knew their hands were on it, their greasy fingers smudging her glasses. She told herself it didn't matter, she could clean the cups in the morning. If only they wouldn't break one!

After perhaps half an hour had passed, the assembly seated itself once again. Eilish relaxed next to Peter. Her work for the evening was completed, and she looked forward to hearing this new, strange instrument, the pianoforte. Mr. Franklin had told her that though the first ones had been built on the Continent, some fifty years before, a few emigrant Saxons were building them now in London, and this was to be a rare treat. The pianoforte was rumored to be the next rage. Miss Marianne Davies, well-known as a harpsichordist, would be the performer.

Marianne Davies was young, though not so young as Eilish. She was dark, and small, dressed in an elegant silver satin gown with a tiny waist and fitted bodice, her small breasts thrust up by her stays to make delectable mounds above the décolletage. Her skin was a smooth pale brown, her fingers slight, her arms quite bare. Eilish stared at her. Suddenly her own fine dress became drab and ordinary, the kind of dress worn only by persons of the working classes.

She understood, her heart chilling, that next to Marianne Davies she must seem like just what she was—an Irish orphan from Seven Dials.

And then Marianne Davies began to play the pianoforte.

As the instrument was new, Miss Davies played the repertoire of the harpsichord, Bach, Scarlatti, and of course Handel. The sonority of the big instrument, the clarity of its upper tones, the full-throated depth of its lower tones, filled the church to bursting. All conversation ceased the moment the music began, but Eilish didn't notice that. She was overcome by the beauty of Marianne Davies's music.

Eilish didn't know how it could be, that she could hear so many different melodies in one piece of music, and yet hear them all as part of a whole. She only knew that the limpid lines of Bach, the crisp and agile passages of Scarlatti, the simple emotions of Handel, were lovely beyond bearing. Miss Davies played as if without effort, her well-schooled fingers moving almost invisibly over the ivory keys. There was applause between her offerings, but not from Eilish. Eilish froze, holding her breath, waiting, yearning for the next piece. And the next. And, at the end of the final selection, she was shocked to find her cheeks wet with tears.

Candles were being lighted in sconces around the church as the assembly rose to take their leave. Eilish sat on, wiping her face, trembling with emotion. Peter bent down to her.

"Miss? What is it, miss? Are you unwell?"

Eilish looked up into his dark, kindly face. It seemed the most beautiful she had ever beheld. "Oh, no, Peter, no!" she cried. "It was just—'twas so utterly, so perfectly—perfect! Have you ever—have you ever in your life? So wonderful! Oh, if only I could learn to play like that!"

And at the thought, more tears welled and her throat closed tight. She turned away from Peter, from the ladies and gentlemen passing by her on their way out of St. John's as if she was—no, because she was—only a servant.

No, she thought. *I could never learn to play like that. No one would teach me. Not Raffer Eam's daughter. Not a penniless Irish orphan from Seven Dials.*

17

London, May 2018

THE Atheneum of Ancient Music never played Zeitler or Rushton, or any music later than early nineteenth century. Erin had been engaged for an all eighteenth-century program. They would play the Mozart quartet, of course, and the little solo Adagio in C minor, the Naumann Quartet for Strings and Glass Harmonica, and the Reichardt. The rest of the program was Handel and Haydn, only strings and winds and brass.

The first day of rehearsal they ran through all the glass harmonica pieces in the morning. The orchestra's Baroque style was faultless. Tempi were easy, ornaments were in agreement. There was almost nothing to change. Erin found herself released for the day before one o'clock.

"I'd like to walk," she said, as she and Mal emerged from St. John's. The early morning mist had burned away in the mild sunshine, and the atrium columns glowed an opalescent white.

"Well, a short one," Mal said. "I need to get back, make some calls."

"I meant, alone," Erin said. At Mal's frown she added quickly, "Really, Mal. You go back to the hotel. Look, it's the middle of the day. All kinds of people around."

It was true. The Footstool, the little café below St. John's, had a steady stream of customers, and the square was full of people enjoying the sun. Many wore the same reff T-shirts Erin and Charlie wore, and the thick rubber sandals that were popular at home. They carried the ubiquitous denim jackets and they cut their hair to look as ragged as possible, short or long or very long. Some wore remnants of native costumes over jeans. A babel of languages drifted past, Asian, African, Middle Eastern.

Mal said, "I'll worry about you, out on your own. I promised your mother . . ."

Erin touched his arm. "I know, Mal, but I was a kid then. I'm a grownup now. I'll be okay. Just a bit of time alone. Some exercise."

"Where are you going?"

She gestured vaguely east. "The Gardens, the river. Just a walk."

The tall black taxicab Mal had ordered pulled into the Square and the cabbie jumped out to open the door. "Go on," Erin repeated. "I'll be back for tea, okay? Don't worry."

Looking glum, Mal climbed in the cab. He gave a small, tired wave as it pulled away.

Erin waved back, trying not to look relieved. She slung her sweater over one shoulder and strode out into the Square. She crossed Millbank Road in an enclosed pedestrian overpass, and turned left, walking quickly until she reached the path into the Victoria Tower Gardens. There she slowed her pace, ambling northward. Old-fashioned dogroses and cow lilies flanked the path, and above them stretched banks of daisies and marigolds and rich yellow forsythia. Erin turned in a circle, her face lifted to the English sunshine. She inhaled the complex perfumes, exhilarated by the very Englishness of the flowers. Off to her right, through the light shrubbery, the Thames sparkled darkly green, cleaner than it had been in centuries.

The breeze from the water carried a rivery tang. Shallow river barges, molded hulls painted scarlet and azure and emerald, paraded up and down the river, ferrying passengers from one end of London to the other. Union Jack pennants snapped an idiosyncratic rhythm to the melody of the water.

The breeze freshened, and Erin shrugged into her sweater and pushed her hair back with her fingers. She walked past the Millennium Obelisk, its pediment lapped by shallow waves, approaching the Victoria Tower pier just as a red barge docked and a dozen or so people disembarked. On an impulse, she pulled out her multicard and thrust it into the scanner. She followed several other passengers aboard.

She sat in the bow, her sandaled feet propped on the bulwarks, the collar of her sweater turned up against the wind. She didn't know which way the barge was traveling, but she didn't much care. It was lovely to sit and watch London slide by. It was rather like looking into a viewwindow, though there were lapses—cars of different periods, architecture ranging from Gothic to classical to contemp. And, too, the people in this scene weren't actors, clean and well-fed and healthy. London had not succeeded in corralling its homeless and indigent, moving them out of the city. The socialism entrenched in Britain in the twentieth century had not given way in the twenty-first. American democracy had been less constraining.

But such thoughts were too serious for the sweetness of the day. Two gulls weaved back and forth above the barge, calling to each other in a tritone pattern—*awk,awk,awk,awk*. Erin laughed up at them, stretching out her arms, exulting in her youth, her strength, her independence.

The barge carried her all the way to the Tower and back again. It was a slow trip, with many stops, many exchanges of passengers. Erin lost track of time, and she lost count of the piers. There were so many, dotting the embankments on both sides, all flying the colorful barge flags. It didn't seem to matter which was which, or where she was. She thought of the hour only when she began to get hungry. Her eyes were sun-dazzled, her cheeks wind-stung. She saw the shrubbery of what she thought was Victoria Tower Gardens, and she left the barge.

As she stepped up onto the pier, she glanced about in confusion. Nothing was familiar. She must have mistaken the stop. She looked about for assistance.

A uniformed woman nodded at her approach. "May I help you, madam?"

Erin said with a little laugh, "Oh, yes, please. I guess I'm on the wrong pier."

"Yes, madam," the woman said, with an air of having said the words a hundred times. "This is Westminster Pier. Which did you want?"

"Uh—Victoria Tower Gardens, I think. Closest to Smith Square?"

The woman looked more closely at Erin. "Yes, miss. You've left your boat too soon." She pointed to the south. "Do you see the four spires there, off in the distance? That's St. John's, in Smith Square. It's just up Bridge Road, here, and down Millbank Road. Bit of a walk, of course, two kilometers or more. You could wait for another boat."

Erin followed the pointing finger. In the near distance was an ornate Victorian monument, the usual horses and carriage and writhing figures. Beyond that rose the roofs of Parliament and the tall column of Big Ben. If she stood on tiptoe, she could just see the towers of St. John's in the distance, slim rectangles of blue sky visible through its slotted spires. "Thanks," she said. "I'll just walk down Millbank and catch a cab."

"Very good, miss."

Erin skirted the ugly monument and mounted a short ramp to the street. She looked right, toward Millbank Road. To her left an old bridge, renovated and widened, spanned the Thames.

A walkway had been added to the bridge, and a steady

stream of pedestrians crossed back and forth over the river. Erin glanced toward the hurrying people, and then looked again. One of them—a woman, or a girl—stood unmoving, bent over the railing as if looking for something in the swirling water below. Erin froze, staggered by a shock of recognition.

The girl was small, dressed in an oddly long, full skirt and a flowing overcoat. Curling tendrils of dark hair lifted in the wind to flutter about her face. She turned her head in Erin's direction, and sunlight glimmered on one white cheek.

Erin's intake of breath dried her throat. She knew that figure. She knew the face, and the hair. It wasn't possible— was it? What was she—Erin's wraith—doing here?

A traffic light changed, and several cars rushed past while Erin stared. Her eyes stung with sunshine and wind, but it didn't seem to matter. Her forehead throbbed, and her heart pounded. The face was so pale, the eyes huge. The girl put a hand up to push back her hair, and Erin saw how thin, how fragile, her hand was. She realized her own hand was up, holding her blond fringe out of her eyes. For a long, time-stopping instant, their eyes locked. Erin almost called out, *Who are you? Why do I see you? What does it mean?*

There was a moment of stillness, the cars stopped at the light, the wind drowning all other sounds. Hardly knowing where she put her feet, Erin plunged across Bridge Street.

People were in her way, blocking her path, slowing her down. She shouldered through them, murmuring excuses, driven by a need to hurry, to see, to discover. The girl had been perhaps a quarter of the way along the span, standing quite still, just—just there! Erin worked her way to the spot, and stood panting, frantically looking about. She looked left and right, she stood on tiptoe to see to the ends of the bridge. She even bent to look over the railing, down into the moving green water. Nothing. The girl had gone. But where? How could she have disappeared so quickly? That coat, the long skirt—she could hardly blend in with the jeans and reff clothes of the crowd.

Erin's head whirled. She turned her back on the river, leaned against the railing. The girl hadn't disappeared. She hadn't been there at all.

The crowd of people, walking in twos and threes, pressed on. Erin gripped the railing behind her with both hands, and closed her eyes against the reeling dizziness. When it subsided somewhat, she opened her eyes again, and turned to look out over the water. She looked down at her hands on the railing, her own small, white, slender fingers. Something about them filled her with a nameless, helpless grief. Her chest and throat ached as if she had been weeping, and real tears sprang to her eyes. Tears for whom? For what?

She stood still, letting the tears flow. It was the strangest feeling, weeping that way, yet not knowing why. It was as if someone else's tears were falling from her own eyes. After a time, the tears ceased, but still she stared down into the river, wondering. When she lifted her head at last, she caught a whiff of something on the breeze, some sharp, spicy scent, gone before she could name it. She shook her head sharply, and dried her cheeks with her hands. Several people were watching her with concern, and Erin forced herself to move, to walk off the bridge, go down into Bridge Street. A taxi came along, and she hailed it.

She slid her multicard into the scanner. "Victoria Inn, please," she said. The taxi drove around Parliament Square and up Victoria Street, turning west toward Belgrave, while Erin stared blindly out the window, her arms wrapped tightly around herself.

She couldn't go on this way. She would have to go back to Seattle. She would have to enlist the help of Gene Berrick, whether she liked him or not. She knew of no one else who could help her put a name to these bizarre experiences. And if she went on having visions, without understanding them, she would go mad.

That is, she told herself, if she hadn't already gone right out of her mind.

THEIR rooms at the Victoria Inn were adjacent. Mal had ordered tea, a meal he never missed when they were in England. Erin washed her face and hands, and took time combing her hair, collecting herself, before she knocked on their connecting door and went through.

Mal was seated at the desk, using an audio-only phone. He waved his hand at the rolling cart that held a teapot in an old-fashioned cozy, a plate of cookies—no, biscuits, Erin reminded herself—and sandwiches. It was an ordinary and comforting little scene, and Erin's anxiety receded as she moved into it. Little pots of this and that filled the tray, and she went to lift the lids and peek in at the contents. She was really hungry now.

Mal said into the phone, rather testily, "Well, I think you're making a mistake. At least think it over. Let me call you next week. It's a great new piece—I'll get Charlie and Erin to send you a recording when they're ready." He listened to a few more words, and said goodbye. He put the phone down, and turned a dour face to Erin.

Her heart sank. "What's the matter, Mal?" she asked. "Who doesn't want me now?"

"That was Toronto, actually. And it's not that they don't want you, you mustn't think that. It's just audiences. One day they want old instruments, period music, and the next they want something else."

"And now they don't want *Mars*?"

"We'll send them a recording. If they don't want it this season, maybe next year."

"Charlie won't like that."

Mal nodded, already chewing. "Yeah, I know. But I'm more worried about your season, Erin. We need contracts for next year."

Erin sat down across from Mal. None of it seemed important right now. She kept seeing, in her mind, that slender dark-haired figure, leaning over the bridge railing. She kept feeling that remembered, faraway sorrow. "I don't know," she said, half to herself. "Maybe I should take some time off."

He stared at her in puzzlement. "Erin—you want to play, to concertize! Don't you?"

"Well, sure," Erin said. "Of course I do, but . . ." Mal's bloodshot eyes searched her face, uncomprehending. She took a deep breath, energized by her idea. "I could spend some time with Charlie. Not worry about things for a while." She reached for a cookie—biscuit—and grinned suddenly. "Unless we're broke?" she asked.

Mal shook his head. "Oh, no, you're not broke. Far from it. It's just—it's my job, to get you concerts, to keep you working. It's business. It's what I do for you."

Erin reached across the cart and touched Mal's freckled hand with hers. "It's not all you do for me," she said. "You've taken care of me since I was eleven, Mal. On the road, off the road, in the concert halls, everything. That hasn't been just business, has it?"

He stared down at her hand on his, and she realized how rarely she touched him voluntarily. Poor Mal.

"I'm going back to Seattle, Mal," she said quickly. "After the Academy concert. I'll take the commuter and be there Sunday morning."

"But they've asked you to give a matinee performance at Franklin House, Sunday afternoon. They arranged it—you know, the Friends of."

The anxiety, the confusion and dread, rose abruptly in Erin's breast. She shook her head vehemently. The last place she wanted to be just now was Benjamin Franklin House. "I can't. Truly, I can't. You have to believe me, Mal. I want to go to Seattle."

He frowned. "Why can't you play at Franklin House? Seattle can't wait one day?"

Erin didn't dare tell him. Mal always talked to Sarah,

and if Sarah knew her other child was having psychic—or psychotic—episodes, she'd have her in a psychiatrist's office in a heartbeat. There would be no arguing with her over something like that. "There's something—something I have to work out with Charlie," Erin said carefully. "Uh— *Moving Mars.*"

Mal looked doubtful. "Well," he said noncommittally. He sighed under the weight of his responsibility. "Well, okay. Sarah won't like it! But I'll go back to Boston and try to explain. And I'll order your ticket for Seattle."

"Thanks," Erin said. She patted his hand and then picked up three biscuits at once. "Mal, take some time off too, why don't you? Take a vacation."

"I don't know, Erin," he said sadly. "Two gigs next year, that's all you've got."

"Never mind," she said. "One slow year won't hurt us."

"Oh, I don't know," he repeated. "I don't know what your mother will think."

"Who cares?" she said. His eyes went wide at that, and she laughed. "Look, Mal. I'll work with Charlie on *Mars,* and when it's ready we'll make a big splash. He says he's cooking up something special, so it should sell itself. You go someplace, relax. Charlie and I will call you from Seattle, wherever you are!"

Mal sighed again, but he nodded as he took another sandwich. "At least use a decent phone, okay? So I can see you!"

She laughed. "We will. I promise!"

18

London, June 1762

A LITTLE tangle of dogroses grew beneath Eilish's bedroom window. They had small pink blossoms and curving thorns and were known to be hardy, for which she was grateful. Every morning, when Cook wasn't looking, she leaned out her window and poured her daily dose of medicine into the dogroses. As far as she could tell, the medicine hadn't hurt the flowers, but it did hurt her. It burned her throat and boiled in her stomach. She loathed the taste and the smell of it. By the end of May, the bottle was empty. No one suggested obtaining more medicine. Eilish was feeling stronger, and if her head ached, she kept it to herself. When her hands trembled, she hid them beneath her apron or in the folds of her dress.

From time to time, since the concert at St. John's, people had come to hear the armonica, and Mr. Franklin—well, Dr. Franklin, now, since he'd gone off to Oxford and received an honorary degree—Dr. Franklin sent for Eilish to give a demonstration. She played for them, the same Scottish and Irish and English tunes. She did her best to make them interesting, adding more complex harmonies, even little, hesitant ornaments such as she had heard Miss Davies

play on the pianoforte. They seemed to enjoy her perform-
ances. They always wanted to try the armonica for themselves, obliging her to clean it afterward, but she swallowed
her temper and did this with as good a grace as she could
muster. Often they offered her a little money, and this she
accepted, curtsying and thanking them politely.

Whenever she had a few coins put together, she sent
them to Seven Dials with Peter. Peter invariably declared
that all was well in the O'Larick household. They had decided, she and Peter together, that it was harder on Mackie,
more upsetting, if she herself went to see him. Eilish suspected that Peter felt it was hardest on her, and hoped not
to make it worse. She doubted he would reveal anything
that might worry her, but she couldn't think what else to
do.

Mrs. Stevenson was in a tizzy today. A number of scientific gentlemen were expected at Number Seven in the
evening. Dr. Pringle was bringing his patient, the "nerve
case," and Franklin was busily making preparations. Eilish
knew little about it, except that members of the Royal Society who were interested in electricity, and there were apparently many, wanted to watch an experiment.

Polly had come in from Essex for the occasion. She
drove Cook and Bessie and Peter wild with orders that con-
tradicted Mrs. Stevenson's, Franklin's, even her own. She
wanted her dress pressed, she wanted the refreshments prepared early and then decided they should be made at the
last minute to keep them fresh. She wanted the hall swept,
and then brought in fresh flowers, dropping leaves and dirt
on the polished wood. She even told Bessie to dust the
laboratory. Eilish took unseemly relish in hearing Franklin
himself put a stop to that.

She stood before her looking glass, tying her hair back,
buttoning the old blue dress. It had always been too large
for her, even with the weight she had gained when she first
came. Now it seemed looser than ever, as if the waist had
stretched. She frowned into the mirror, wishing her cheeks

were full and round like Polly's, with a nice blush to them. Her own were flat and white, her chin as sharp as a bureau corner. She smoothed the dress over her thin body. She must try to eat more today, she thought, she really must. At least to drink Cook's nice cocoa. She hurried down to the kitchen, determined.

Cook was turning out cakes and biscuits at a great rate, and roasting a huge fish for a savory pie. She gave Eilish her chocolate and a piece of buttered bread, and then turned back to the oven. Eilish ate as much as she dared, wary of being ill again, then tied an apron over her dress and began scrubbing pans and washing cups. Peter came in to eat a quick meal standing up beside the table, and hurried out again. Polly sent Bessie to fetch her a tray, and Cook, with an exasperated sigh, dropped what she was doing to make fresh tea and toast two slices of bread.

"Mrs. Tickell is spoiling that young woman," she grumbled as Bessie went out with the tray. "Plain Polly Stevenson will be thinking she's Queen Charlotte."

"Aye," Eilish said, stacking the clean cups on a shelf. "But 'tisn't it all about Mrs. Tickell's fortune?"

"Indeed." Cook tut-tutted as she went back to her work. "And Miss Polly doesn't half hate having to live in Essex to get it!" Eilish giggled, and Cook laughed.

Toward evening, Dr. Pringle's private carriage, bearing the royal arms, turned into Craven Street. Liveried footmen stood by as the doctor climbed down, then gave his hand to a small person heavily shrouded in a hooded cape. From her window Eilish watched them come up the walk and into the house. She hid behind her door, listening as Franklin ushered the doctor and his cloaked companion up the two flights to his laboratory. The two men's voices carried well, making inconsequential conversation. The third person did not speak.

Soon other men began arriving, on foot, in hired curricles, one or two in their own carriages. They were to observe the "experiment," and then to have a late supper in

Franklin's parlor. By the time they were assembled, perhaps eight or ten of them, darkness had fallen. Oil lamps were lit in the parlors. Eilish had a candle in her room, but she didn't light it. Instead, she knelt on the landing, as near the stairwell as she dared, and listened to the goings-on two floors below.

A pool of yellow light spilled from the laboratory until someone closed the door. There was still light from Franklin's parlor, next door, but the second-floor landing was dim, the stairs murky. On the ground floor, Polly and Margaret Stevenson sat in Mrs. Stevenson's parlor. Polly came out several times to peer up the stairs; Eilish drew back so as not to be seen doing the same thing. She could not regret Polly's frustration at not being allowed to observe the experiment.

The conversation in the laboratory died away, and all of Number Seven was quiet. A mechanical sound came through the laboratory door, an abrasive noise, as of scrubbing, or a steady brushing. There was silence for a short interval, and then, all at once, a small crackling explosion. Eilish had never heard such a sound. In the laboratory there was a gasp, and then a long, agonized scream.

Eilish jumped, and pressed her hand to her lips to keep from crying out herself. Her eyes felt stretched and dry, her throat tight with horror.

The men in the laboratory spoke together in low-pitched, excited voices for two or three minutes. When they fell silent, the rubbing sound came again. And again the little explosion, and again a horrifying shriek. This time the patient—it must be a girl, the voice high-pitched and strident—went on screaming and screaming, a sound that scraped Eilish's nerves raw. A deep voice spoke soothing words Eilish couldn't catch, and the screaming subsided into hopeless sobs that seeped out from beneath the laboratory door like water spilled out on the floor. The men's voices rose again in vigorous discourse, evidently undisturbed by the misery of their subject.

Eilish almost sobbed herself when she heard the rubbing sound resume. The patient began to scream immediately, louder and louder, till it seemed her throat must burst. Eilish leaned forward to peer down the stairwell. When the little explosion crackled into the night, it seemed that a blue light flashed in the dark house as if the door to the laboratory were the very door to hell. The scream gave way to a gagging, and then a dreadful high keening like that of a dying animal. The men spoke loudly, to be heard over the sound, and one or two of them even laughed—laughed, by the angels!—as their victim wailed. Eilish was about to go back into her room, unable to bear the sound of the poor thing's suffering, when the laboratory door opened, the men's voices suddenly filling the stairwell. Several men trooped to the other door, going into the parlor with much clapping of backs and hearty exclamations. The keening died away to a monotonous, wordless moaning.

Minutes later, Polly and Mrs. Stevenson came quickly up the stairs, followed by Bessie and Cook with the trays of food and drink. Eilish peeked round the banister as they filed into Franklin's parlor. A moment later, Dr. Pringle and Franklin emerged from the laboratory, closing the door behind them. They, too, went into the parlor. There was no sign of their patient.

Soon the hum of social conversation filled the stairwell. Cook came out of the parlor and went downstairs, while Bessie remained to serve. Eilish stood up, and crept, slowly and silently, down the stairs. When she reached the first-floor landing she crossed it hastily, hoping not to be seen by the members of the Royal Society or by Polly or Mrs. Stevenson. She put her hand on the laboratory door and turned the knob without making a sound.

The lamp had been extinguished. Only a bit of moonlight shining through the tall windows illuminated the room. Eilish slipped in, closing the door behind her.

The moaning went on without interruption. Eilish waited

for her eyes to adjust to the darkness, and then moved down the room, closer to the source.

Franklin's apparatus, consisting of glass tubes, a large piece of soft material, and a glass jar with a wire protruding from its stopper, was arranged around a long table. On the table, the patient lay strapped down with wide leather belts. Above her was another long wire, strung through small loops that hung in their turn from a wooden pole. Now she was crying, saying over and over, "No, no. No more, no. No. No, Mama. No."

Eilish moved to her side and bent over her. The girl's eyes flew open and she drew breath to scream again.

"Hush, now, hush!" Eilish whispered, her finger to her lips. "I'm not going to hurt you. Are you all right? I came to see if you're all right."

"No more," the girl groaned, turning her head from side to side. One leather belt constrained her chest, another her middle, and a third her legs. Her hands, Eilish saw, were tied to the table, and the ends of the wire were poised over her body. "No more," she wept piteously. "It hurts, it hurts. No more." She was thick-featured, with wispy, ill-washed hair and dirty fingernails.

"Hush, now," Eilish murmured again. "I think it's all over."

Eilish saw now, as she observed the girl, that she suffered from tremors of the hands and head. Perhaps every half minute she would quiver, her body jerking like a puppet on its strings. It was disturbing to watch. Her lips were slack and wet, her eyes rolling. "No more," she moaned again. "It hurts."

The door opened, and Franklin came into the laboratory. Eilish stepped away from the table, holding her hands behind her back as if to prove she hadn't touched anything. Franklin pushed his glasses down his nose and squinted at her above them.

"Eilish? Is that you? Good girl! You'll sit with our patient, won't you? Excellent!" He turned without waiting for an answer and left the laboratory. Eilish heard the men in lively conversation until Franklin closed the door on his way out.

The girl on the table moaned and rolled her head back and forth, back and forth. "Poor lass," Eilish said. "Poor little lass. Was it so awful, what they did?"

The girl only went on crooning, "No, it hurts, no. No, Mama."

Eilish was certain she was a half-wit. There would be no conversing with her. But it was sad to see her suffering, the poor dumb creature. "Be still, now, lass," she said. "Listen, shall I play you a tune? You listen to this, and don't worry now. I'm sure 'tis all over."

At the far end of the dust-covered room, the armonica waited in its place. Eilish slipped off the cover and pulled her little stool up to it. She adjusted the treadle and began to play, no particular tune, just hoping the sounds of the crystals would relax the poor creature on the table. After a few moments, the moaning slowed and quieted. Heartened, Eilish played "Barb'ry Allen," and then, as the girl only whimpered from time to time, she played an even slower melody, the old lullaby "Baidhin Elhemhi," for which she didn't know any English words. When she stopped, all was silent in the laboratory.

She went to the girl and bent over her. The thick lips were loose, the dull eyes closed. The girl was sleeping, and it was a curious thing to see. She lay quite still now. Even her tremors slept, the unbalanced nerves dormant. On tiptoe, careful not to wake her, Eilish retreated. She covered the armonica, and then stood by the great windows to look out into the London night. The dark city was dotted with the gentle lights of oil lamps and tallow candles, and above it the sky was ablaze with stars. Eilish wondered what Mackie might be doing at such an hour. Would he be sleeping? Was he frightened? Silently, she breathed against the cool glass of the window, "I pray ye be not alone, sweetheart."

Eilish waited half an hour for Franklin and the others to return. They burst into the laboratory, talking and laughing, voices gone loud with port. The girl in the leather bindings startled and woke and began to cry again, all at once, as if she had never stopped.

"Quiet, now, Rosemary, quiet," Dr. Pringle said roughly. At the sound of his voice she cried harder. Between them, Franklin and Pringle unstrapped the leather belts and lifted the unfortunate Rosemary, her face now distorted with ugly weeping, to a sitting position. Pringle managed to get her to her feet, and she stood before all of them, blubbering open-mouthed.

"Observe!" Franklin cried. Their faces turned to him. "Her tremors have gone!" he proclaimed. Every face turned back to Rosemary.

Eilish stared at her, too. She knew perfectly well that when she had come in, even while the suffering Rosemary had been strapped to the table, the girl's head and hands and body had been subject to violent spasms. But now, even though she stood with her head hanging, mewling like some half-drowned kitten, the half-witted girl's body was steady.

They watched her for several minutes, the gentlemen exclaiming in wonder. Franklin stood beside the sniveling girl, pointing. "You see, my friends, 'tis as I suspected! The application of electricity to the appendages has forced a balance among the subject's nerves. Whereas she suffered from a congestion of energy in one part of her nervous system, and a lack of it in another, the charge of electricity going through the body has relieved this imbalance, and she stands before you, as I predicted, free of her tremors!" He thrust his glasses up on his forehead and beamed.

"And will this state of balance persist?" asked one of the gentlemen.

"That we cannot tell as yet," Franklin answered. " 'Twill be part of our inquiry."

"Perhaps regular treatment will prove effective," Dr. Pringle said ponderously. "As this girl is in my household, she will be under my observation. I will keep you informed."

Rosemary's weeping had subsided, and now she sniffled wetly, wiping her unattractive blob of a nose with her hand. Dr. Pringle picked up the hooded cape and threw it unceremoniously over her. He guided her with a firm hand toward the door.

"Here, Richard," Franklin said, gesturing to Eilish. When Eilish stepped forward from her place by the window, several heads turned in surprise. "Miss Eam can see your patient down to the carriage. There are several details of my apparatus I would like your thoughts on."

Dr. Pringle dropped his hand from Rosemary's back, and she stopped immediately, as if she had no will of her own. Eilish went to her. The girl's body was thick and soft beneath the cape, and Eilish had to exert some force to get her to move. As she maneuvered her out of the laboratory, the men were already deep in conversation again, crowded around the apparatus.

As Eilish drew Rosemary down the stairs, Polly came out of Mrs. Stevenson's parlor. Her cheeks were rosy, her eyes narrowed. "What were you doing up there?" she demanded of Eilish. "Why were you in the laboratory?"

Eilish smiled as sweetly as she could, though her head was beginning to ache. "Why, Miss Polly," she said. "Dr. Franklin needed my help, didn't he? And 'twas my pleasure to provide it."

She guided Rosemary's heavy steps down the last flight, leaving Polly glaring after her. The carriage was waiting in the street, the footmen standing beside it. Rosemary, with Eilish's hand under her elbow, obediently climbed in. As Eilish put her hand on the carriage door to close it, she saw the first tremor return, Rosemary's head and hands quivering with a convulsive shudder. Poor hapless girl. Her trials were not finished.

Eilish, her head aching sharply now, long past ready for her bed, ascended slowly to her room. Mrs. Stevenson's parlor door, on the ground floor, was closed. On the first floor, the men still clustered in the laboratory, where Franklin was holding forth, answering questions, receiving congratulations. 'Twas a good thing, Eilish thought as she climbed the last flight of stairs, that she had removed Rosemary when she did. The sight of her returning tremors would quite have spoiled Dr. Benjamin Franklin's success.

19

Seattle, May 2018

WHEN Erin deplaned in Seattle and trudged wearily up the jetway, she was startled to see Gene Berrick's tall form, the usual jeans and white shirt, leaning against a supporting pillar in the waiting area. Alarm flooded her, driving away her fatigue. "Where's Charlie? What's wrong?"

Berrick straightened and reached for her bag. "Charlie's fine," he said. "He was tired yesterday, and I told him he should sleep in this morning. I had to come out of the city anyway."

"He's been pushing too hard, hasn't he? I knew he would. You have to watch that with Charlie."

"He's okay, I think. We're keeping an eye on him. How was your flight?"

"Fast," Erin said. "Hardly long enough to get any sleep."

"And the concert last night?"

Erin glanced up at him. He looked different here. In the natural light he seemed more human somehow, his features a little softer, his eyes warmer. His hair had less gray in it than she remembered, and was straight and thick.

"The concert was okay," she said. She pushed her hair

back and rubbed her eyes. They felt gritty from lack of sleep and airplane air.

They walked a few steps in silence. Erin couldn't think of anything to say to him. Except the truth, of course. And a moment later she blurted, "I saw it again in London. It's getting worse. If I don't figure this out, I'll go nuts."

"You saw it during the concert?"

She shook her head. "No, I saw it on a bridge, for god-sakes. Figure that one out! And I felt something in St. John's—maybe I would have seen something. I was alone. I didn't look."

"Frightened?"

She felt ashamed of her fears, and that made her angry. "Of course I'm frightened," she snapped. "Have you ever been haunted?"

With exaggerated mildness, he said, "No, can't say that I have." His finely cut lips curved in a restrained smile, and she felt even more angry.

"Listen, you'd be scared, too, feeling like you never know what's going to happen, what you're going to see. I don't know if I need a shrink or a bloody medium with a crystal ball!"

He nodded as if she had said something intelligent. "How about a neurophysiologist?"

Absurdly, even with her temper flaring, Erin thought how beautiful his face was, his profile like carved dark stone. She gave a gusty sigh. "I guess I have to try it."

He gave a short, dry chuckle. "Such enthusiasm. Maybe you'd prefer the crystal ball."

She had to laugh at that, briefly, wearily. "No, I don't think so. Somehow I think binaural beats are more pre-dictable." She rubbed her eyes again, overwhelmed by sleeplessness and anxiety and confusion. "I'm sorry I was rude, Dr. Berrick. I'm awfully tired."

"It's all right. And call me Gene, okay?"

"Okay. Gene." She liked saying it. It was short, clean, masculine. It suited his saturnine face, his long legs, his wonderful eyes. He looked down at her, and she glanced away, embarrassed to be caught staring.

"Tell me about the concert," he said.

She shrugged. "The audience was happy, the orchestra was happy. It's just so predictable. Early music style, early music sounds, they've gotten it down to a science. It's not flexible anymore, it's not—expressive, I suppose. At least, not expressing anything new."

"Not like Charlie's pieces."

"Oh, no! Nothing like that at all. Do you know Charlie's music?"

"Actually, I do. I had one of his discs already, and when he came to me as a patient, I bought the other one."

"I didn't know you liked classical music," she said.

"Well, I didn't hear any when I was young," he answered, his tone suddenly flat. "But I'm making up for it now."

She glanced at him again, wondering what had happened. His narrow face was closed—or was that simply his usual composure? She said, "I missed playing the *Requiem* and I can't wait for the premiere of *Moving Mars* in San Francisco. Something fresh. I must have played the Mozart Adagio and Rondo about a thousand times."

He answered, "I think the best artists are the restless ones." It felt like a compliment, but she wasn't sure. She didn't know how to answer.

Since Mal had taken the glass harmonica to Boston, and the suitcase with her concert clothes, Erin had no extra luggage. Berrick led her down into the underground parking area, a part of the airport Erin had never seen. He put his multicard into a scanner, and moments later a valet drove up in a small, ugly utility van. Berrick held the passenger door for Erin.

She stared at the brown, battered vehicle. "This is yours?" she blurted.

He was already on his way around to the driver's side. He answered as he folded his long legs neatly into the confined space. "Hardly a limo, is it? I transport things fairly often," he said. "I have a delivery to make on the way into the city. Hope you don't mind."

"No, of course not." She looked around at the interior of the van. It was shabby and well-worn, but clean. " It's just that I thought everything had to be period in your neighborhood. Twenties, or teens, or something."

"True. I have to park this under my building."

The little van was obviously old, and it rattled. Berrick drove out of the parking garage and briefly onto the freeway, turning off after a mile or two into a narrow, four-lane road. A steady light rain began that slicked the streets and rolled in wayward stripes down the windshield. On this road there were no limos, no period cars, almost no other traffic. They passed dilapidated buildings, some boarded up and covered with graffiti, others collapsed in on themselves in a mess of weathered wood and broken timbers. Erin's eyelids grew heavy, and she dozed, but when Berrick turned into a gravel road, the jolting woke her. Ahead in the distance she saw the masts and cranes of industrial shipping. The gravel road ran between fields empty of buildings, animals, or crops. As they topped a rise, rows of green and gray and brown canvas peaks came into view.

"The tent city," Erin said in surprise.

"Yes." He pulled up before a plain trexboard office building and parked between two trucks. "Well, the government calls it a refuge area. But everybody else calls it the tent city." The rows of tents stretched away to the east and west. A few leggy shrubs leaned dispiritedly against the office building, but otherwise there was not a blade of grass, not a single tree. Huge Dumpsters lined the driveway, and bits of equipment, trailers, tractors, and portable toilets faced them on the other side. Erin had never seen anything so utilitarian as this place, so completely without grace.

Gene said, "It's not very pleasant here. Not what you're used to." The clear gray eyes assessed her. "You'd probably rather stay in the truck."

She felt as if he had challenged her, and she said quickly, "No. No, I'll come with you." She hid her trepidation. All the bad news seemed to come out of the tent cities, the violence, the tragedies, but she didn't want him to think she was afraid. She opened her door.

He nodded. "Fine." He reached behind the seat to bring out a neat black leather satchel.

"What's that?"

"My medical bag."

"Oh, of course," she said, feeling foolish. She was used to thinking of him in his clean, polished clinic, or seeing patients in a waxed and spotless hospital ward. This place—this place was dirty. Disorderly. The stained and rusting Dumpsters, when she walked past them, smelled of refuse and rot, and insects buzzed around their lids.

The building turned out to be as plain on the inside as on the outside, mostly one large room dotted with biocomposite desks, a couple of fullscreens, and one single-screen phone console parked in a corner like an afterthought. Several people were working at the desks, and a middle-aged woman, in neat reff slacks and blouse, rose as soon as she saw them.

"Gene!" she said warmly. "Thanks for coming!" She stepped forward and took Berrick's hand in both of hers. Erin was shocked to feel a stab of—what was that, jealousy? It couldn't be.

The woman went on, "You have the medicines in your van? Shall I send Roberto out?"

"Hi, Anne. Yes. The truck's open."

Anne went to her desk and spoke into an intercom. When she had a response, she came back. "Have time for a couple of patients?"

He held up his bag in answer. She nodded, smiling, keeping her hand on his arm, and turned to walk briskly toward the back of the little building. Erin trotted after them, feeling out of place and forgotten. Outside, they turned left down a long glassphalt path running between the rows of tents. "Anne, this is Erin," Berrick said as they walked. "Erin Rushton."

The woman nodded and said hello. It was clear Erin's name meant nothing to her. Erin said, "Nice to meet you."

The rain had stopped, but everything glistened wetly, the path, the gravel edging, the canvas roofs. The sky was the same gray as the glassphalt they were walking on. Erin shivered with cold and fatigue. It was hard to believe it was spring in this sunless city.

They stopped at a small, olive-green tent, and Anne called someone's name. A dark woman appeared, lifting the flap that served as a door. "The doctor's here to see Joey," Anne told her. They all went inside, including Erin, though she stayed close to the entrance. She hoped all this would be accomplished quickly, so she could go home, see Charlie, sleep. Get away from this confident woman who was so familiar with Gene Berrick.

A bare bulb hung from the center of the tent roof, and a small electric stove, shielded from the canvas by some sort of panel, stood beneath a vent. There was little furniture, a couple of folding chairs, a small square table, two beds at the sides. The tent smelled of cooked food, body odor, and something like disinfectant. The floor was canvas, too, and had been swept so often there were broom marks brushed into the material.

Gene crouched down before a thin child slumped in a battered wheelchair. The child smiled up at him, showing beige, crooked teeth. He tried to lift his head, and it wavered on his thin neck.

Erin hardly knew Gene Berrick's voice when he spoke to the child. "Hello, Joey. How's it going with you? Your mother?" As he spoke he put his hands on the child's arms, legs, touched his throat and felt the back of his neck. "That old chair giving you trouble, my friend?"

The child responded with noises that only approximated speech, and were accompanied by strings of saliva that dripped down his narrow chest. Gene helped him to hold up his head, gently wiped the drool from his chin, and worked his wasted limbs, murmuring quietly to him throughout. He knelt and put his long arm under the ancient wheelchair, trying to adjust something. When he stood, he shook his head. "The lever's broken off," he said to the mother. He bent and touched Joey's cheek, looking into his eyes. "Sorry, my friend," he said, very clearly. "I can't fix it today. But I'll try to think of something."

Erin was appalled. She wanted to run from the tent, hide in the van. Never had she seen such poverty, such misery, such illness. Charlie's hospital rooms, his doctors' offices, his therapy clinics, had all been ordered, fully stocked, antiseptically clean. Only stubbornness, and an unwillingness to have Gene and the authoritarian Anne think her naive, kept Erin in the odoriferous tent. When the visit was over, advice given, prescriptions recorded, Erin stepped out to hold up the tent flap for Gene and Anne. She drew deep breaths of the fresh air, forcing her face into impassivity. Neither of them seemed to notice her at all.

Walking away, Gene and Anne talked about the availability of donated physical therapy services, the cost of wheelchairs. Erin followed, her arms wrapped around herself, her head lowered. She looked out from beneath her ragged fringe of hair to observe the people who came to the tent doors as they passed. A few looked like people she could have seen anywhere, on the streets of Seattle or Boston, in the squares of London. Others were clearly ill, or impaired. Some were obviously and openly under the influence of opiates or intoxicants. She was stunned by their sheer numbers. It hardly seemed possible there should be so many people without homes of their own. What must it be like to live in such a place, where nothing was yours, and you could expect nothing but what others chose to give you? Whatever euphemism was used to describe these places—refuge areas, canvas communities—couldn't erase the reality. Tent cities were the price the cities paid for their clean and orderly streets. And these were the people paying it.

They turned in at a long gray tent where Gene examined an adult patient while other adults and a quiet flock of big-eyed children watched. The patient was a man with one pant leg, empty, pinned up at the knee. No one mentioned how he had lost the leg. It appeared Gene had treated him before. The subject of discussion this time was availability of prostheses. Gene asked Anne to call Social Services one more time, and to use his name. Erin saw Gene touch the man's shoulder, offer him a hand to shake. All eyes watched them leave the tent, but no one spoke, not even to offer thanks.

The three of them circled around the end of the row. Clotheslines, discarded appliances, bits of broken furniture littered the muddy gravel beside the path. As they neared the office, they passed a playground with a swing, a play structure of red and yellow plastic, a rubber play surface like the one at the Llewellyn School. Charlie had fallen on a play surface like that, when he was six. Erin hoped none of the children here had Friedreich's; the engineered virus, Charlie's "smart bug," had been staggeringly expensive. Even maintaining it was costly. What would have happened if Charlie had been born into such a place?

They had been at the tent city no more than half an hour, but when Erin got back into the van, she was exhausted, worn out by lack of sleep, the cold and wet, and the dismal scenes she had witnessed. Berrick eyed her, and said, "You need to rest."

She nodded. "I do. But, Dr.—I mean, Gene—what's the matter with the little boy? Joey?"

"He has cerebral palsy. We're trying some neural boosters, but they haven't helped much. A better diet, better support, would make a big difference. He's a sweetie."

Erin hated herself for not being able to think of the poor, twisted child, the drooling little boy, as a sweetie. And she could have wept with relief as they drove into the clean, spacious Seattle streets. Berrick turned off the freeway and drove up the hill beneath the monorail track. The sky was still heavy, but here, where the houses were circled by tidy lawns, where lilacs and rhododendrons bloomed in orderly beds, the unseasonal weather seemed charming, Seattle-like. Berrick parked in front of St. Mark's and lifted Erin's bag out of the truck.

"Are you coming in?" she asked, barely stifling a yawn.

"No, I'll see you tomorrow," he said. "We'll talk in the clinic. Say hello to Charlie for me, and get some rest. Both of you."

"Okay," Erin said. He backed the truck and pulled away. Erin toiled up the steps, almost asleep on her feet.

They hadn't gotten around to programming the scanner, so she had to buzz the apartment. There was a long pause while she waited for Charlie to answer. She pictured him maneuvering himself into his wheelchair, rolling to the door to press the button on the intercom. The answering buzz came at last, and the elevator opened. When she stepped out on the third floor, Charlie was waiting in the hallway, still in his bathrobe. "Hey," he said.

"Charlie!" She dropped her bag and went to hug him. "Did you just get up?"

"I overslept," he said. "Then it didn't seem worth getting dressed. Come on, give me your bag. Let's go inside."

She retrieved the bag, but she wouldn't let him take it. He looked awful. His face was pale as milk, except for the dark circles beneath his eyes, and he was thinner than she could ever remember seeing him. She followed him into the apartment, where everything looked the same. Only Charlie was changed.

"Charlie, what's going on? You look wiped out."

He said wearily, "Look who's talking. You look like you walked here from London. Want some coffee?"

She followed him into the little kitchen, and she saw how his hands shook as he reached for the coffeepot. She tried to help him, but he refused her. "Let me do it, Erin, okay? Talk to me. Tell me about the concert."

BEFORE they went to the clinic the next morning, the twins sat down at the dual-screen phone in the condo and called their mother's house. She was already at the hospital, but the housekeeper told them she was sure Charlie's old Jazzy wheelchair was still in the basement storage room. Erin explained the situation, and the housekeeper promised to ship it the next day. Charlie added, "No need to tell Sarah about this." The housekeeper raised her eyebrows, but she didn't argue. It was always easier not telling Sarah.

A cool sun was drying the wet sidewalks as they left the building. Erin walked close to Charlie, not helping, but watching him. His hands were steadier today, and his color was a bit better. "Are you working with Gene every day?" she asked.

He led the way into the monorail stop and angled his wheels onto the platform. "Except Sundays," he said. "Day of rest, right?"

"I guess so," she said. She felt slightly ridiculous, now that she was here, reluctant to put on Gene's headphones and electrodes, let him watch her brain on the damned projection. It made her feel exposed, naked, and she didn't like it. How could she expect to summon her wraith at will? The whole thing seemed preposterous. Maybe she should just come to her senses, take control, make it all go away. She hadn't told Charlie what had happened in London, and she didn't understand that either.

Charlie was out of breath and perspiring when they reached the clinic, Erin walking helplessly behind him. She hadn't realized before how often she assisted him. It was automatic for her to reach out and push the chair, to have him lean on her shoulder as he transferred from wheelchair to fixed chair, to pick things up for him so he wouldn't have to bend and stretch and strain. She could see how the muscles of his arms had grown in the past weeks. Even his neck was thicker. If only his hands wouldn't shake. She tried to remember when he had last gone to Philadelphia, had his smart bug checked. She was sure it hadn't been more than a year. Would Gene know if the Friedreich's was returning? She shivered and hugged herself against the cool morning breeze.

In the clinic, Gene seemed as remote as he had at their first meeting, as if the events of yesterday had never occurred. His power to concentrate was incredible, she thought. Charlie always told her that when she was performing, the theater could burn down around her and she wouldn't know it. Perhaps at those times she seemed just like this, distant, apart, dwelling in her own world of music. Did other people feel closed out then, cut off from her?

Charlie went through his routine first, just as before. He did seem to be moving a bit better, his swinging gait slightly more coordinated. But it could have been, Erin thought, just that his arms had gotten stronger, and he manipulated the walker better. Still, the trek across the floor and back took a little less time, and when he fell into the wooden chair at the end he threw her a triumphant look. Gene, who hadn't watched Charlie at all, but only the projection of his brain scan, was delighted.

"Look at this, Charlie. Let me play this back for you. See here? And here? This shows that the impulse is searching for a new path—look, it tries this one, and then this one. Now this one, see?"

Erin watched the image, and the slender spears of light representing the firing of the neurons, but it told her nothing. Gene mapped it with a grid that would print the patterns on paper for him to study later. Charlie was grinning, tired, but happy. "Great, that's great," he said. Gene handed him the paper, and Charlie reached for it.

Erin was dismayed to see his hand waver, his fingers clutch air once, twice, before he could grasp the sheet. She opened her mouth to speak, but Charlie was so happy, so excited. She closed it again. Gene's eyes were already back on the projection, his profile unreadable.

Charlie was drinking juice. Gene turned to Erin, eyebrows lifted, glasses shoved up on his forehead.

She took a deep breath and stepped forward. "Okay," she said. "I guess it's my turn."

20

SELF-CONSCIOUSNESS made Erin awkward as she seated herself in the wooden chair. Her arms and shoulders thrilled with nerves, as before a concert. Berrick's precise fingers pressed the little electrodes to her temples and fitted the headphones over her hair. When he saw her watching his hands, he smiled slightly. Her cheeks warmed, and she averted her eyes. When he was finished he patted her shoulder, and she jumped.

Charlie had rolled close to the desk, keeping out of Berrick's way, but sitting where he could see the scan projection clearly. He had been pleased, but not surprised, when he learned that Erin was going to try to deliberately call up her wraith. She glanced across at him, biting her lip, wishing she could be as matter-of-fact about all of this as he was.

Berrick dimmed the lights and initiated his program. The oddly atonal sounds pulsed irregularly in Erin's ears, almost below the range of her hearing. She stared at the wall of equipment in front of her, avoiding the sight of the projection of her brain, the little spears of light that would now be flashing through it. The binaural beats met in the middle of her head, making her brain itch. She didn't feel, as she had with Charlie's program, that she wanted to move. She did feel anxious, hyperalert. She found her hands clenched into fists, and she opened them, stretched her fingers, tried to relax her tense thighs.

The tones changed, and the tiny electrical charges began at her temples, perceptible only because she knew they were there. Erin was surprised to feel her eyelids droop. She blinked and stretched them wide. In the cool dimness of the clinic, the machinery glowed white and silver, the gray floor-tiles clean and shining. Charlie and Gene waited, expectant.

Nothing happened.

She had no sensation of time passing. She felt blank, empty. The sounds stopped, as if at some randomly chosen moment, the barely sensed stimuli at her temples faded. Gene came to crouch before the chair and look up into Erin's face. "Nothing?" he said. His eyes searched hers as if they could see right through the irises and into her mind.

Her throat was tight. "Not a thing," she said. She was alarmed to feel her lower lip tremble, like a child's. She berated herself for her cowardice, but the whole thing seemed so bizarre. She felt an absolute fool.

"Okay," Gene said. He came to his feet in one lithe movement. "That was only our first attempt. I wrote two programs yesterday—"

"But maybe we should just—"

He said, "I'm trying to induce the same brain wave state that sparked your experience when you were here before. The trick is that I don't know in which segment of Charlie's program you had your vision, so I have to experiment a bit. Ready?"

Without waiting for her answer, he went back to the Moog. Erin wrapped her arms around herself. She had asked for this. She would have to see it through.

An hour later, Gene removed her headphones and the electrodes and helped her out of the chair. Her legs shook

and she wavered on her feet. Charlie had a glass of juice
ready. Berrick said, "Come on, guys, we'll go out in the
other room. Be comfortable."

In the Edwardian parlor, Erin sat at one end of the loveseat, the juice glass on the piecrust table before her. Charlie
rolled his chair close to her, the wheel touching her foot.
Gene sat on the edge of the armchair, leaning forward,
glasses pushed up on his head.

"I tried both the theta and beta states. Theta is for im-
agery, beta for heightened mental function. We go through
those with Charlie's programs, and that took some adjusting, too. But in this case, with a nonspecific psychic experience, there's no way to plan. We watch the brain scan,
but we don't really know what to look for."

"It's crazy," Erin said flatly.

"No, it's not crazy," he said. He put out his hand and
took hers in long, strong fingers. She stared down at their
two hands, his dark and hers so pale. "Erin, fifty years ago
some very interesting experiments were going on in something called remote viewing. Before the wackos got hold
of it, it was serious scientific research. A subject would stay
in a closed room, with drawing materials, while a team of
two would go to a randomly chosen location. The subject
would draw his impressions of whatever the location looked
like. Sometimes the subject even drew the impressions before the team arrived at the location."

"Was that telepathy?" Charlie asked.

Gene shook his head. "Probably not. McMoneagle felt
it was memory, remembering from his own future, when
he knew, when he had learned, exactly what the target location was, what it looked like."

"Memory?" Erin said weakly. "Backwards?"

"Backwards, forwards, it doesn't matter," Gene said.
"It's Einstein." Erin, lost, looked to Charlie for help.

Charlie was nodding, as if he understood perfectly.
"Space-time," he said.

"Exactly,"Gene answered. Erin stared at them both.

"What are you talking about?" she asked. "I'm having insane visions, and you're talking physics!"

Gene nodded, his face intent. He didn't seem to realize he was holding Erin's hand, even absently stroking her fingers. "You know what the space-time continuum is," he said. "Einstein proposed that time is like a—call it a ribbon, with folds and bends and a surface that can be affected by gravity, say, or speed. If the folds of the ribbon get close enough, it may be a fairly simple process to transfer information from one fold to another. Future or past is not significant."

"All times exist at all times," Charlie put in, nodding.

Erin shook her head, tired and confused. All she could get out of this was that neither Charlie nor Berrick believed she was losing her mind. She hoped that wasn't because they were both nuts themselves. "Are you telling me you think I'm—remembering—from the future?"

"Maybe. Or the past," Berrick said, giving her hand a final pat as if all was settled. "Drink your juice, Erin. We'll try again tomorrow. I'll try a different approach, work through the alpha state. Bit less intense than the beta. And of course, different brains respond differently to the same stimuli. I recorded your scans, I'll study them tonight."

Erin drank the thick, salty juice while Charlie and Berrick talked on about techniques for programming, like two peers. Another patient arrived, a middle-aged man on crutches. Gene said goodbye, and Charlie and Erin left the clinic.

The flamboyant blooms of the rhododendron by the door were already fading, drooping in the late afternoon light. Erin picked a fragment of rusting pink as they passed. By the time they reached the condo her fingers were sticky with nectar.

CHARLIE made a meal of organic semolina pasta with cilantro pesto and toasted pine nuts. Erin cleared the dishes while Charlie rolled the Akai out from beneath the old piano. When she finished in the kitchen, she joined him. He pointed to the synthesizer.

"See this?" he said. A little array of gray metal cylinders had been added to the Akai. To Erin they looked like ballpoint pens cut neatly in half. They also looked vaguely familiar.

"What are those, Charlie?"

"Sensory emitters," he said, with an air of triumph.

"What?"

"Sensory emitters," he repeated. "Like the ones Gene uses. Gene does augmented binaural beats, and I'm doing augmented sensory music!"

That was why they seemed familiar. Erin stared at her brother, perplexed. "Charlie—what the hell is augmented sensory music?"

He wiggled his brows and grinned. "Let's find out, little girl."

He made Erin lie back on the couch and he turned the Akai so the emitters were directed at her. He had made a synthesized recording of the first movement of *Mars*, though he explained that the sensory effect would be considerably less without the strings and flute and glass harmonica. "But try it, E. Tell me what you feel." He touched a few buttons, and sat back to watch her reaction.

The synthesized music was colorless, of course, but Erin was used to that. She knew the piece well, and her mind supplied the resonance, the timbre, the flavor of the actual instruments. It was what the emitters did that startled her.

It was a tickling sensation, beginning in the tips of her fingers, in her eyelids, on the back of her neck. It grew gradually in intensity, a stimulus that ran up her arms, that flooded her face and her throat, that made the backs of her knees throb. And it had—she searched for a word.

"*Affect*," she finally whispered.

"Exactly." Charlie looked smug. "Augmented sensory

music will have enhanced affect. For those who can feel it. Some won't, of course."

"And Charlie—some will hate it."

"Oh, yes," he said complacently. "There will be resistance." He chuckled. "If we're lucky, lots of resistance. And *Moving Mars* will be the first! They'll feel the wrench of the gravity, the ripple of the disrupted atmosphere— they'll feel the bloody planet *move!*"

WHEN Erin finally went to bed, she was exhausted, physically and emotionally. It was early, and the northern sky was not yet truly dark, but clouds lay over everything like a downy blanket. She snuggled beneath the white comforter and watched the pale organdy curtains bell under the draft from the heat register. Charlie was still working at the Akai, the sounds muted and subtle. Erin slept.

When she woke the condo was quiet. The curtains hung still now. The silver sheen of a half-moon glowed on the polished hardwood floor. Erin sat up abruptly, the comforter pulled up to her chin. Her nerves throbbed as if Charlie's sensory emitters were still directed at her.

Her wraith stood in the room, no more than four feet from the bed.

Erin's breath caught in her throat. Her forehead prickled, not painfully, but with a disturbing intensity. Gooseflesh pimpled her arms and her legs. She didn't feel dizzy, or confused. But she wasn't entirely sure she was awake.

The ghostly girl, her face as pale as the moonlight, looked up, directly at Erin. Her eyes were enormous, round, fringed with black lashes. She brought her hands together before her, linking the fingers as if in prayer.

Erin clutched the comforter, and whispered, "Who are you?"

The girl's lips moved. She shimmered, wavered, as if her image might evaporate. Erin cried, "No! Don't go!" She put out her hand, but what could she touch? What could she grasp? It would be like trying to hold a cloud.

There was a sound from Charlie's bedroom. "Erin?" he called.

"Charlie," Erin said, carefully, not taking her eyes from the vision. "She's here."

Charlie's voice was as calm as if supernatural visitors were an everyday thing with them. "Do you want me to come in?"

The image trembled and steadied. Erin stared at it, trying to memorize every detail. The hair, tied back with a ribbon. The great eyes, the long lashes. The full lips, a short, straight nose sprinkled with freckles. She looked very young, perhaps thirteen or fourteen. Her dress was too long and too large for her. Her lips parted as if she were speaking, and she made a gesture with her little hands. There was no sound. It was all weirdly, inexplicably familiar.

"Yes," Erin called softly to Charlie. "Please. Hurry."

The girl in the vision touched her hair, smoothed her dress. She smiled at Erin, and then she turned her back. Erin saw how long and thick her hair was, falling halfway to her narrow waist. The girl moved away, as if to walk out of the bedroom. By the time Charlie had gotten into his chair and rolled into the bedroom, she had faded through the wall as simply as if a door had opened and then closed behind her. Erin sat staring at the blank wall.

"She's gone," she said.

"Where was she?" Charlie asked, breathless from hurrying.

Erin pointed. "There. If she was here at all."

"Fantastic," Charlie said.

Erin fell back against her pillow. "Omigod, Charlie. I wish I understood this."

"Wow," Charlie exclaimed. "I wonder why you saw her tonight, instead of today in the clinic?"

"I don't know. I was pretty nervous today, with Dr. Berrick. He's so intense. I felt like a bug on a slide."

"It's not like you to be nervous," Charlie said.

He rolled close to the bed, and Erin sat up again. "Charlie—do you smell that? That—I don't know what it is! Do you smell it?"

He shook his head. "Sorry, E. Nothing."

"Wow, it's like—it's spicy. No, now it's gone. Oh, god." She put her hands to her hair, knowing it was standing up every which way. "My head feels strange, like my brain swelled and then shrank back to normal. It feels—stretched."

"Cool," Charlie said, grinning at her. "Maybe you'll get smarter."

"Or weirder," she answered. She got up, and found it cold in the bedroom. She found an enormous terry-cloth bathrobe in the closet and put it on. It dragged on the floor and wrapped around her ankles. "Charlie, you want some chocolate?"

"Chocolate? Like candy, you mean?"

"No, like cocoa. Hot chocolate."

He laughed. "I don't know if we have anything like that, but okay. Come on, let's go check the server."

They found some packets of chocolate for the hot-server and sat looking out at the lake while they drank it. The water was glassy and still, with icicles of moonlight laid across it. Erin told Charlie everything she had seen, how it seemed she and the wraith had tried to communicate, how young the girl appeared to be. "Are you afraid to go back to sleep?" Charlie asked at last.

"I don't feel afraid at all, right now," Erin said. "I suppose I'm getting used to it. I just want to understand it."

"It has to be important," Charlie said. "Or else why is it happening to you?"

"Maybe it's not important," Erin said. "People see ghosts, don't they, and it's just scary. It doesn't mean anything. And those remote viewing experiments—they weren't really meaningful, either. Just interesting."

"You think this could be a random experience?" Charlie said.

"I almost hope so," she said slowly. "Because if it means something more—I don't know what to do about it."

"I wish I could see her," Charlie said.

"So do I, believe me."

When they left their cups in the sink and went back to bed, clouds were rolling in again, covering the moon with strands of gray fleece. Charlie squeezed Erin's hand and said, "Sleep well. Call me if you need me." She kissed the top of his head.

Before she drew the comforter over her, she took a last look at the spot where the wraith had stood. The room was much darker now, the organdy curtains and the polished cotton of the comforter making ghostly white patches in the gloom. Erin lay back on her pillow and stared up at the ceiling. Even with Charlie asleep in the next room, she felt isolated and lonely. I suppose, she thought, some things you have to work through alone. No one can help. No one can go through it with you.

But as she turned on her side and closed her eyes, Gene Berrick's lean brown face rose in her mind, his fine hands, his clear gray eyes, and she felt comforted.

21

London, July 1762

PREPARATIONS were under way for Dr. Franklin's return to the Colonies. While London baked under the July sun, Peter had to drive back and forth between White-hall and Craven Street, from Fortnum & Mason's to Bar-clay's to Goodwin's Court, as Dr. Franklin wished to be well-supplied with the tailored suits he could not get in America. The political situation in the Colonies had grown tense, and Franklin's usual ebullience was subdued. Mrs. Stevenson was much grieved to lose her famous and con-genial tenant, and Eilish heard her more than once trying to persuade him to put off his trip.

"And William's marriage?" Mrs. Stevenson kept saying. "Should you not stay to see your son marry?"

At that Franklin growled some uncharacteristic response. Eilish knew none of the details of this, but it was not hard to guess that Franklin was not pleased with William's choice.

Polly came in from Essex often, perhaps once a month, and she and Franklin went all about the town, shopping and visiting his friends of the Royal Society. When Franklin had to go to court, Polly moped about the house, giving everyone pointless orders, until Cook threatened to give notice, which drove Mrs. Stevenson almost into hysterics. Eilish retreated to the laboratory.

She had her own concerns. If Dr. Franklin left Craven Street, where was she to go? She had no purpose here, other than playing the armonica. She supposed she could become the kitchenmaid. Polly would no doubt be pleased by that, but Bessie would be furious.

Into the midst of all this confusion came a message from Seven Dials. Rose Bailey's little brother Thomas came round the back of Number Seven asking for the blackamoor.

Bessie answered the door, and then bustled downstairs to the kitchen, fat cheeks puffed with distaste. "There's a scrap of a lad asking for Peter," she said. "Dirty Irish, I'll be bound. Allus said 'twas a mistake to bring that element into the house! I didn't let 'im in, I can tell you. One look at the mistress's lovely things, and we'd none of us be safe in our beds ever again!"

Cook tut-tutted at her, but Eilish jumped to her feet. "Peter's gone up to the Royal Society meeting with Dr. Franklin," she said. "Who wants him?"

Bessie counted herself at least one social level above Eilish Eam, since Eilish was Irish and an orphan and from Seven Dials to boot. Turning her back on Eilish and speaking pointedly to Cook, Bessie said, " 'E says 'is name's Thomas Bailey. Now, is that dirty Irish, or isn't it? 'Tis like the Old Bailey, where they say there's more Irish spoke than English!"

''Tish tush, Bessie," Cook said. " 'Tisn't Christian to go about making such remarks."

"Well, won't be me what talks to 'im," Bessie announced. She tossed her gray head and flounced out of the kitchen, her footsteps heavy and loud on the stone flags.

Eilish knew Thomas Bailey. "I'll go," she said, but her heart pounded with dread as she climbed the stairs to the first floor.

Thomas Bailey stood on the back stoop, his hat in his hand, his freckled cheeks flushed with the importance of his mission. He cried, "Hi, Eilish," the moment she appeared. "I walked all this way from Seven Dials! Walked right here like I bin doing it all me life!"

"Thomas," Eilish said breathlessly. "Why did you come? What's happened?"

"Rose said to come and tell you, right away. That you would want to know."

"What, Thomas? Is Mackie ill? Hurt? Tell me, hurry!"

"No, no, 'tisn't him, not the lad. 'Tis his ma. Dooya. Dooya O'Larick. She's gone and got herself kilt."

"Thomas! No! How could that be?" Eilish felt as if her knees would collapse. Her head began to ache immediately, and her mouth went dry. She took a wobbling step outside, closing the door behind her. Shaking, she moved down the steps and led Thomas to the stable, where the two of them could sit on a hay bale. "Dooya dead?" she murmured. "For true? I can scarce believe it."

They sat on the scratchy hay, and Thomas jammed his cap back on his head. " 'Tis true," he said, pulling a long face. "Dooya was working, like she does, under the Dials. She found a bad 'un, it seems. He stuck her with his knife so he wouldn't have to pay her, Rose says. Dooya made it back to the Clock and Cup, but she never made it up the stairs."

Eilish sat stunned for a moment, her hands to her cheeks. Dooya dead? It didn't seem possible. Dooya of the heavy hands and the resonant snores and the loud voice. How could all that life be gone? "Oh, by the angels, Thomas, 'tis a terrible thing. Where's Mackie, then? What's become of him?"

"Rose took him in, but the Runners was called, and they told the priest! They'll have Mackie in the orphanage in two shakes. Rose says we can't afford another mouth to feed."

Eilish put her hand to her breast, where her heart

pounded with hopelessness. "Oh, no, Thomas. I don't know what to do! What did Rose want me to do?"

"Well, Rose says if you can send a bit o' money, she'll manage for a while." He grinned, a monkey grin full of confidence. "Here's a grand house, Eilish. Surely someone here can give you some money!"

"You don't understand," Eilish said miserably. "I'm a servant in this house, for all I give concerts and such. If someone gives me a shilling, I always send it to Seven Dials. But I never know when that's to be."

"You give concerts, Eilish? Proper concerts?" Thomas's eyes were wide with admiration.

Eilish took no pride in her concerts at this moment. She had to see Mackie, had to talk to Rose. What would she do? What would become of poor Mackie, another Irish orphan with no one to care for him?

The back door of the house opened, and Cook appeared, still in her long white apron, holding a napkin-wrapped bundle. "Eilish?" she called quietly. "I thought perhaps your caller would be hungry."

Eilish got off the hay bale and went to the door. "Oh, ta, Cook. 'Tis ever so kind of you."

Cook gave her the bundle, watching her face closely. "Bad news, I fear," she said. "You look that pale, dear."

"Aye," Eilish said. "The news is very bad."

She gave Thomas the napkin, and he sniffed it appreciatively and tucked it under his jacket. "What shall I tell Rose?" he asked.

"I don't know," she said. "I just don't know, Thomas. Tell her to wait, and not to let them take Mackie! I'll try to do something. I'll try to get some money. Please, tell her to wait!"

EILISH, weighed down with anxiety, went slowly up to the laboratory. She couldn't mourn Dooya O'Larick, though Dooya had given her a home after her da died.

Dooya had reaped the reward of her sowing, Eilish knew that. But Mackie! Eilish seemed to see his great round eyes everywhere, hear the faltering step of his feet, see the fearful crookedness of his short legs.

She had not so much as a penny. Franklin had been away from home a great deal, and no one had come to hear her play in weeks. She played every day, of course, for herself, or for Mrs. Stevenson, who found it soothed her nerves, but there wasn't any profit in that. She supposed Cook might help with some food, perhaps a cast-off bit of clothing. But money? Oh, what was she to do?

She scrubbed her hands in the washbasin, and cleaned the armonica, then sat down on the stool and pumped the treadle. She began with the oldest, simplest melody she knew, "Eileen Aroon," that her da had told her dated back to the fourteenth century. She played the little Welsh lullaby, "Ar Hyd y Hos," and then she played the Irish one, "Baidhin Elhemhi," as if Mackie were right beside her. The song of the crystals reached right into her breast to squeeze her heart. Tears wet her cheeks, but she didn't notice them until they dropped onto her wrists.

She played until her fingers were wrinkled from the water and her ankles cramped on the treadle. Her tears dried under the caress of the music. She felt lifted out of herself, free of her aching body and anxious heart. It seemed, briefly, that someone stood at her shoulder, someone stronger, wiser than she. She turned her head, but caught only the echo, the shade of it.

Late in the evening, long after tea, Dr. Franklin returned home in the carriage with Peter at the reins. Franklin walked slowly, heavily up the stairs, dragging his gouty foot. He came into the laboratory and found Eilish still sitting at the armonica.

Franklin smiled wearily at her, adjusting his spectacles. "Good evening, my dear," he said. "Have you been practicing?"

"Aye," she answered. "So I have."

He looked at her more closely. "Something is troubling you, Eilish?"

She met his gaze. "Aye. A great grief, Dr. Franklin."

"Ah. Poor lass." He put out his hand and drew her to her feet. "This is a time for woes, I think. I, too, have a great grief, and nothing for it but to return to America. I'm loath to go, but I must." He drew the silk cover over the armonica. "Come, Eilish, let's sit in my parlor. Bessie will bring us something to eat, and you will tell me your grief. Perhaps I will tell you mine, though I think you'll not understand it. 'Tis almost more than I can understand myself."

Bessie, her lips pursed in a sour little knot, brought them a pot of tea and fresh scones and jam. Franklin had a tot of brandy as well. He propped his bad leg on a footstool, and took a deep sip of brandy while Eilish sugared her tea. She loved Cook's buttery scones, but the thought of Mackie, motherless this very night, took away her appetite. Though the armonica's sweet voice had purged her tears, her heart still faltered under its load of worry. She drank, and then put her cup in its saucer and stared into the little fire that crackled in the hearth.

When she looked up, she saw that Franklin had put his spectacles up on his brow and was watching her with gentle eyes. She was surprised by that. Though she often enjoyed his company, she had not thought of him as someone who would concern himself with the troubles of a servant. Peter had to run hither and yon at his master's orders, without regard for the hour or the weather or his own inclinations. But now Franklin nodded to her, saying, "Do tell me, my dear. Let us share our burdens here, in this cozy parlor, and when we fare out into the world again, we shall be the stronger."

Eilish said, " 'Tis kind of you, sir. I fear there is nothing can ease my burden."

Franklin's lips curved upward in a shallow mockery of his old jolly smile. "Let us discover if that is true."

Eilish gave a deep sigh. " 'Tis my old home that troubles

me, Dr. Franklin. There has been a death, and a child, a little child, has been orphaned like myself."

Franklin's eyebrows rose, but he waited, only taking another sip of brandy and rolling about it in his mouth as if the taste were too good to swallow too soon.

"They are so poor in Seven Dials, sir," Eilish said slowly. "I had no home but for that of one of my da's old friends, and she a Gin Lane whore." She blushed a little. "Forgive my talking blunt, sir. 'Tis naught but the truth."

He nodded, his eyes heavy, his mouth drooping. "Truth can be painful, my dear. I have come to terms with a great deal of it lately. As to prostitution—the ways of God's creatures are often twisted, are they not?"

"Aye," she said. "When my da died, Dooya O'Larick allowed me her back cupboard to sleep in. She needed a bit of help with her gossoon—her little boy—I stayed with him nights while she worked. And now she's got herself murdered, and little Mackie, that never had a father, has no mother neither. And he's the crookedest legs you ever saw, that will hardly carry him. He can't go to be a chimney sweep, or a pickpocket, or work for the costermonger, he's that frail."

"Ah," Franklin said heavily. "And so 'tis the orphanage for him, is it not?"

"I fear so."

"Of course, you know I'm bound for the Colonies at the end of summer."

"Aye."

"I wish I could help your little friend, Eilish. I can't ask Margaret to take in a crippled Irish boy."

"No, sir. I know that very well."

"And where is the boy now?"

Eilish watched the small flames dance in the fireplace. "He's with a family I know. They run a pub called the Clock and Cup. The oldest girl takes care of all the wee ones, and 'tis no easy task. She's a good girl, but there's so many mouths."

"Well, now, Eilish Eam," Franklin said. His smile was sharper now, and his eyes began to twinkle. "Many will say I've spent a good bit of money that wasn't mine to spend. But here you've been my helper and my aide all these months, and not asked for a penny! Suppose we were to figure your back wages—would that be a help for young Mackie?"

Eilish looked at him, her mouth a little open, her heart hardly daring to credit his words. "Back wages?" she breathed. "Wages? For playing your lovely little armonica?"

"Exactly!" he cried, truly smiling now. He put his spectacles back on his nose. "Hand me that bit of paper, there, and the inkwell. Let us do a few sums. Good Lord, it's gotten to July, hasn't it? And we began our little project November last!"

Eilish stared, entranced, as he dipped a quill into the ink and made rapid black marks on the paper. "November, December, January—my, my, the time does pass. Let us say, a shilling a week? It's a good wage, don't you think, when room and board are included as well? And I do demand your services at odd hours. So, yes, a shilling . . . I make that thirty shillings, or one pound ten." Franklin put down the pen and smiled at Eilish. "One pound ten, my dear. Would that help your young friend, d'you think?" He reached into his pocket and counted out coins until he reached exactly that amount.

Eilish could hardly believe it. She had never held such a sum. The coins were heavy and cool, gold and silver together, weighing down her palm. They were alive with history, fairly vibrating with stories to be told. Her headache receded almost to nothing, and her heart beat fast now with joy and relief. She put out her hand to touch Franklin's plump one. "Oh, ta, Dr. Franklin. 'Tis so kind of you, ever so kind. 'Twill certainly keep Mackie out of the orphanage, and give the Baileys a bit o' luck to boot! Angels bless you, sir."

Franklin sat back in his easy chair, and, as Eilish had done, stared into the fire. "If only thirty shillings would solve my problems," he said sadly.

"How many shillings would it take, sir?" Eilish asked. "To solve your problems?"

He gave a rather bitter chuckle. "Well, my dear. A mere four thousand pounds should set things straight."

Eilish opened her mouth, closed it, opened it again. "Oh, la, Mr. Franklin!" she said at last. "Who could own so much money other than King George himself? What a terrible trouble it must be!"

"Bad enough, Eilish, bad enough."

Shyly, she said, "And is that why you must return to America? Leave Craven Street?"

"That's not all of it," he said heavily. "There are other things—political things. My home, Pennsylvania, suffers under the ill rule of its governors. I'm needed there."

"Will you ever be back?"

"I hope so, my dear. I hope so."

And then, the big question poised on Eilish's lips, anxious to pop out into the warm air of the parlor. She feared to ask it. She feared more not to ask it. "Mr.—I mean, Dr. Franklin. Are you taking the armonica with you to America?"

He stared at her for a moment in complete amazement. "Taking—taking the armonica? Oh, my dear! I am so sorry! You must be beside yourself with worry!" He grasped her hand and patted it with his other hand, over and over. "No, no, Eilish. I am not taking the armonica! You are to stay here, to live here with Margaret, who is happy to have you, and you are to play my armonica whenever you wish, and for whomever comes to hear it. I never thought—oh, my dear, I am so sorry. No, no, your place in this house is secure, I promise!"

At that very moment, as Franklin held her hand and smiled down at her so charmingly, Polly Stevenson entered the parlor. She stopped and stared down at the two of them, her face ugly with her fury.

"Why, Polly! I thought you had returned to your aunt Tickell!" Franklin cried, all unaware. He jumped up and held a chair for her.

As Polly sat down, she looked at Eilish with cold eyes in a pinched face. In Seven Dials, such a look would have been followed by screeched insults. In Seven Dials, such a look might have occasioned an exchange of blows.

Here in Craven Street, what ensued was an icy conversation, brittle as thin glass. "Why, no, Benjamin," Polly said precisely. "I could not in good conscience leave London while your affairs are not yet in order. I was quite certain you should need my help."

"How true, Polly," Franklin said. His distracted look returned. "Yes, yes, I probably will avail myself of your generosity."

Polly, with an air of settling things, nodded her head at Eilish. "Eilish," she said. "I believe Cook was asking for you."

Eilish looked at Franklin, who was staring into the fire, and then back at Polly. She stood up and smoothed her dress. "Aye," she said. "I'll be off then." And to Franklin, "I thank you again, Dr. Franklin, from the bottom of my heart. You have mightily eased my mind."

He smiled up at her, his glasses sparkling with firelight. Polly frowned, watching the two of them. Eilish spoke in a voice as sweet as one of Cook's cinnamon cakes, as liltingly Irish as she could make it. "Is Dr. Franklin not the most wonderful man to walk the earth? Ah, and I thank the angels for 'im."

She walked out of the parlor with Polly's eyes scalding her back. In the doorway she turned to give Polly Stevenson a wide grin. She could almost hear the crackle of Polly's temper in the air of the parlor as she walked away.

22

Seattle, June 2018

To keep her hands in practice, Erin spent an hour each morning at the vintage Chickering. Its yellowing ivory keys were smooth and cool under her fingertips, and its hammers, except for the broken one, struck cleanly against the old strings. She was in the midst of a Haydn sonatina when the buzzer sounded from the foyer of St. Mark's and Charlie went to answer it. Erin didn't realize someone had entered the apartment until she came to the end of the second movement. At the cadence she looked up, startled by the tall silhouette against the realwindow. "Gene!"

"It's nice to hear you play," he said.

She lifted her fingers from the keyboard. "You surprised me."

"I called him," Charlie said. "I told him what happened."

"Oh. That." Erin rose from the piano bench and walked to the window, feeling oddly self-conscious. The water of the lake was steel-gray in the morning light. She touched her hair, trying to remember if she had brushed it. She was fairly sure she had washed her face.

"I have some time before my first patient," Gene said. "Do you want to talk?"

Erin looked up into his dark face, and then back to the lake. Her pulse beat quickly in her throat. His nearness distracted her, and she wished she had stayed at the piano. "I don't know what to say about it," she told him.

"Charlie thought you might want to pursue it."

"She does," Charlie said, rolling up behind them. "And we do. Come on, let's go give her some breakfast and then we'll pry it out of her."

Erin demurred. "Gene probably doesn't have that much time."

He glanced at his watch. "I'll make time," he said. "Use your phone?" At Charlie's assent, he walked over to the phone and spoke to it briefly. Erin hurried back to her bedroom to check her appearance, brush her hair again, and pull a newer T-shirt over her jeans.

The little brown van had a retractable ramp, and Charlie rolled up it and latched his chair behind the passenger seat. Gene drove up over the hill and on past his building. One of the repro cars went by, the fringe over its isinglass windows fluttering. Uniformed gardeners worked here and there on lawns and shrubs and swept the driveways. The whole neighborhood, Erin reflected, was neater than her bedroom. She remembered the clutter behind the rows of the tent city, and felt vaguely guilty.

Berrick parked his van among a half-dozen other non-period vehicles in back of a one-story, rectangular building. A sign over the roof said Silk City Diner in lurid yellow neon.

The interior of the restaurant was brilliant with chrome and red vinyl and sparkling glass. Berrick led the way to a booth, and he and Erin slid in on the scarlet banquettes, facing each other. Charlie's chair fit neatly under the end of the Bakelite table. A woman in a midcalf flowered dress and a short, frilled apron laid menus in front of them, and brought mugs and coffee and cream in a little pitcher shaped like a cow. Painted metal signs advertised bizarre items like Cornflake Pancakes and Salisbury Steak and

Eggs and Grits. Erin was thankful to see that the menus offered yogurt and fruit and Kashi.

The waitress came back, and they each chose something. Gene leaned forward, elbows propped on the table, eyes glinting. "Now, Erin. Tell me about last night."

Erin took a sip of coffee. It hardly seemed possible, in the clear light of morning, that she had seen a ghost the night before. "I woke up, and she was there," she said, with a little shrug. "I thought maybe I was dreaming, but Charlie spoke to me, and I wasn't. She was gone when he came in, but it was easier to see her than usual. And it was like—" Erin broke off, shaking her head.

"Come on, E," Charlie said mildly.

She spread her hands. "It was like we saw each other. That's impossible, isn't it?"

"And what happened?"

"She—she sort of—smiled. Then she turned, like she was going to leave. And she did. Leave, I mean. Sort of vanish, I guess."

"How did you feel?"

She shrugged. "I don't know. Scared. Weird. Not scared of this girl, this ghost—it's the reason I'm seeing her that scares me. If there is a reason. And I can't control it! I mean, I'm not making her come and go, anything like that. I guess what I felt last night—" She paused. "I felt lonely," she finished, looking away.

Charlie found her hand under the table and squeezed it.

"What did you do last night, before you went to bed?"

Charlie dropped Erin's hand and averted his eyes. She hesitated, confused by his response. She chose her words carefully.

"Well . . ." she said slowly. "I listened to Charlie's new piece—*Moving Mars*. Some of it." She looked at Charlie again, but he was avoiding her glance. Instinctively, she omitted mentioning the augmented sensory emissions. Charlie's face relaxed, and she thought she must have done the right thing. But why? What would Charlie have to hide?

"Ah," was all Gene said.

Her anxiety made Erin's voice sharp. "Listen, Gene. You're a scientist," she said. "Why are you bothering with this? I'm sure you just think I'm crazy. Having mental trips."

"You don't think it can have a scientific explanation?"

"I don't think it has any explanation."

He leaned back, and gave her his restrained smile. "I do, Erin. And I think you should listen to it."

She stared at him. "What does that mean?"

"I mean, heed it. Pay attention. Your mind, some level of your mind, is prompting you to figure something out, to discover something."

"So you do think it's coming from my own mind!"

"In a sense. Space-time, remember? All times exist at all times?"

"Nope," she said. "I don't get it. Personally, I think I'm going bloody insane."

He said quietly, "I'm no psychiatrist, Erin, but I can safely say you're perfectly sane."

"Kind of messy, though," Charlie put in. Erin made a face at him.

Gene went on, "You're having a psychic experience. That's neither inconsistent with science nor necessarily consistent with insanity. Psi has been called quantum interconnectedness—all of space-time is available, all the time. It's not magic."

"Can you say that in English?" Erin sighed.

He chuckled. "You could be picking up something, something your subconscious knows is important, and can't get to you any other way."

Erin mulled that over while the waitress set their food before them.

No one spoke of Erin's wraith again until they had eaten and their coffee mugs were refilled. Then Gene said, "Erin, I'm intrigued by the way you had your vision in London, on the bridge."

"You mean, without music?"

"Without music, or binaural beats, or any other stimulus. One theory in space-time is that, as in the remote-viewing experiments, location is meaningless. But another view holds that the space part of space-time is significant. It may be that in London, you're closer, spatially, to the experience you're trying to access."

"Like seeing ghosts in old houses!" Charlie said gleefully.

"Oh, jeez," Erin groaned.

Gene took off his glasses and polished them with the napkin. "You could go back."

Erin shivered. "Go back?" she whispered through a suddenly dry throat.

"If you want to learn what it is," Gene said. His voice was level, ordinary. "Why not?"

Erin shook her head. She didn't dare speak. If she did, she knew that what would come out of her mouth would be, *Because I'm afraid.* And she could not, she would not, admit that. Gene's eyes sparkled at her through his old-fashioned glasses, and she had the dismaying feeling that he had heard her thought. She stuck her chin out and looked away.

Back at St. Mark's, the twins prevailed upon Gene to wait with his van for a moment in the driveway while Erin hurried up to the apartment. Moments later she maneuvered a wheeled pallet out through the foyer and down the ramp.

Charlie beamed, and waved at the large carton on the pallet. "For your patient, Gene."

Gene looked blank. "My patient?"

"The little boy!" Erin said. "Joey. At the tent city. This was Charlie's wheelchair, his pediatric chair. It's in perfect condition, and it's a lot newer than Joey's."

"Jazzy 2860," Charlie said. "Two-motor midwheel drive, power adjustable seat and angle, cam-strut foldable frame. Directional joystick, voice recognition remote control." He grinned and drawled, "And speed!"

Erin laughed, remembering. "You should have seen Charlie when he was ten! He barreled around the Llewellyn like this was a racing jalopy."

Gene put his hand on the box, and stood that way for so long that Erin began to wonder if they had made a mistake, offended him somehow. When he looked up his eyes were dark, the same steel-gray of the lake in the morning. "Charlie. Erin. Do you know what this chair cost?"

Charlie shrugged. "No, not really. What difference does it make?"

"To you, perhaps, none at all. To Joey, and to his mother, a very great difference. They won't know how to thank you. I don't know how to thank you. It's overwhelming."

"Erin's idea, actually," Charlie said modestly.

When Berrick turned his gaze on Erin, it was like being caught in a spotlight. "Come with me," he said. "Come with me, Erin. To give it to him."

Erin had no desire to revisit the tent city, to smell the crowded tents and see the hopeless faces. But she didn't want Gene to know that. She gave him a breezy smile and a shrug. "Sure." She felt Charlie's amused glance on her, and she tossed her head for his benefit. "Why not?"

THEY went out to the tent city the next day, while Charlie kept a physical therapy appointment. It was a rare morning of glorious blue sky and sweet air, and no pale visions had haunted the night before. Erin dressed carefully, a neat sleeveless blouse and her best jeans, her hair carefully brushed. She rolled her window down to breathe the fragrance of summer as Berrick drove.

"Would you like to drive for a while?" he asked her.

"Can't. I never learned."

"You've never driven a car?"

"No. I've never had the opportunity or the necessity. Everywhere I go, there's taxis, limos, trains—monorails!

Hotels, airplanes, theaters, restaurants—a musician's life."

Cedar shrubs, enormous rhododendrons, and blankets of blue-flowering vinca flanked the highway out of the city, but all of that vanished when they turned off the freeway. On either side of the narrow road leading to the tent city, hedges of blackberry bushes rolled in untidy heaps. The tent grounds had been dug out of the lowlands with heavy equipment, leaving only packed dirt that now sprouted broadleaf weeds and enormous dandelions.

"Did the government do all this?" Erin asked, waving her hand at the rows of tents, the little office building.

"Corporations, mostly," he answered. "Salving their consciences with money. Government coordinates the funds and services."

"You sound angry. But it's better than if they did nothing, isn't it?"

His features were still, in that controlled way she had come to recognize. His voice was expressionless. "Most of these folks would rather be offered work." She had no answer for that.

Anne came out to meet them when they pulled up before the office. Together they unloaded the pallet and rolled it down the glassphalt path.

Everything was the same inside the tent, except that the warmer weather intensified the intimate smells. Gene brought the Jazzy wheelchair out of the box, and lifted the twisted body of the little boy into it. Joey's head bobbed about, and he made excited, unintelligible noises. Gene adjusted the chair, shortened the armrests, attached the head supports that Charlie had never used. His hands were gentle and precise and infinitely beautiful to watch, Erin thought. She wished she didn't feel repelled by the odors, by the tent, by the damaged child.

Gene took a long time explaining the switches and the power to Joey's mother, and setting the voice recognition program for her voice. They experimented, the mother ordering the chair this way and that on the canvas floor, Joey crowing like a happy infant, joyously drooling, his wide smile showing his uneven teeth and pink tongue.

Erin felt as if she couldn't breathe the close air. Perspiration ran down her neck and ribs, and nausea rose in her throat. After what seemed a very long time, Gene shook the mother's hand and bent to say goodbye to Joey, looking directly into his eyes, touching his cheek. At last Anne and Gene came to the tent door, and Erin was poised to make her escape.

Before she could step over the canvas sill, Joey's mother came to her, putting out her leathery hand. "Thanks a lot, ma'am," the mother said. She was missing a tooth in the front of her mouth, but she smiled without embarrassment. "Means a lot to Joey." Erin realized, belatedly, that she was meant to shake the woman's hand.

With Gene's eyes on her, and Anne's, she extended her small white hand. The other woman's palm was rough and dry, but Erin saw, looking down at it, that it was perfectly clean. She shook it, once, twice, and managed to say, "I'm very glad. My brother will be, too."

Outside the stifling tent, she gulped lungfuls of the fresh summer air, smelling blackberry bushes, drying refuse, sunbaked bare dirt. Anne and Gene walked ahead, talking, and Erin followed, feeling ashamed. It was such a small thing she had done, to receive such gratitude. It had cost her so little. And it wasn't enough.

23

London, August 1762

EILISH huddled in her room, her hands over her ears, trying to shut out the sounds of poor Rosemary's witless screaming. It was still light, Franklin and Pringle having begun the poor creature's "treatment" just after tea. A hazy dusk lay over London, and Bessie was lighting the lamps, stamping around the house as if her footsteps could drown out the cries issuing from the laboratory. If the rest of the household were shocked by the noise, no one spoke of it. Cook had pursed her lips when she heard Dr. Pringle was bringing his patient again, and muttered something about infernal practices, but that was all. Polly was away in Essex, and Mrs. Stevenson was in her own parlor with the door closed.

Eilish shuddered and pulled a pillow over her head. Rosemary was screaming herself hoarse two floors below. Eilish heard and felt each plosive shock as if it were being applied to her own body. Franklin knew that the girl's tremors had returned by the time she reached home following the first experiment. He was determined to redouble his efforts to "balance her nerves." The horrific session went on and on, the sound of friction being created, the pause, and then the nauseating pop of the electrical discharge, followed by Rosemary's shrieks. Eilish thought she would be sick with the strain. At a point where she felt she could bear it no longer, a gloomy silence fell. Cautiously, warily, Eilish put down the pillow and sat up. Her room was dark. Night covered the city in a sooty blanket, and only a few of the brightest stars shone through the murk.

A knock at her door preceded Franklin's voice. "Eilish? Eilish, are you in there?"

She jumped off the bed and hurried to the door, straightening her rumpled dress as she went. She found Franklin standing in the hall, his spectacles slipping down his nose, wild fronds of gray hair escaping from its narrow black ribbon. His cheeks and lips were fiery red. "Eilish," he said rather hurriedly. "Our patient is very distressed. Could you come and sit with her? Our treatment cannot take its full effect until she has calmed somewhat."

"Aye, Dr. Franklin," Eilish said. She smoothed her hair back with her fingers as she followed him down the stairs.

Over his shoulder he said, "Perhaps you could play, Eilish. The sounds of the armonica are often soothing to the nerves, don't you think?"

Eilish answered, "Aye." In truth, she thought some people experienced rather the opposite effect. But 'twas not a time for arguing.

Dr. Pringle stood watching from the parlor door as Franklin and Eilish passed into the laboratory. On the table, strapped down as before, the luckless Rosemary moaned, rolling her head back and forth, her hands and feet jerking spasmodically. Franklin said, "I'll leave you now," to Eilish, and made a hasty exit, closing the door behind him.

At the sound of the door, Rosemary whined, the same litany as before. "No, no, Mama, no. It hurts. No, Mama."

Eilish went to her. "Shush, shush, lass," she said softly. " 'Tis all finished for the night. Now I'm going to play for you, as I did before. Do you remember?" The girl's hands and feet convulsed, a hard jerking that made her body strain

at the leather straps. She went on moaning as if she had
not heard Eilish's voice.

"Now, listen, Rosemary," Eilish said as she walked to
the basin to scrub her hands. "Listen. This torture of yours
is sure to be at an end soon. 'Tisn't for the likes of us to
understand all their doings, but at least 'tis coming to an
end for the time. Dr. Franklin is off to America at the end
of the month. I doubt your Dr. Pringle will find another to
do the same work." She dried her hands, and pulled the
cover off the armonica. "Hush, now, Rosemary. Here's a
bit o' music for you, lass."

For answer, Rosemary's body shook in an enormous
spasm. Eilish clucked her tongue and shook her head. "Poor
idiot colleen," she murmured. "What could God be thinking, to give you fits and make you mindless to boot? Poor
lass."

She wet her fingers and put her feet on the treadle. She
began to play "Barb'ry Allen," sweet and slow. After one
turn through the melody she began to sing, her voice no
more than a breath:

> *"They buried her in the old churchyard,*
> *Sweet William's grave was nigh her,*
> *And from his heart grew a red, red rose,*
> *And from her heart a brier."*

Rosemary quieted, her spasms lessening. Eilish wet her
fingers again.

> *"They grew and grew o'er the old church wall,*
> *Till they couldn't grow no higher,*
> *Until they tied a true lover's knot,*
> *The red rose and the brier."*

Rosemary lay quiet, her eyes flickering, her moaning
stopped. Eilish smiled over at her. "That's the way, lassie.
Easy, now. Just you listen to Mr. Franklin's pretty armon-

ica." She played "Highland Laddie" and "Massacre at Glencoe." The lamp guttered and went out, but she didn't need it. She knew the feel of the crystals better than her own face, and she caressed them with a firm and practiced touch. The vibrations crept up her arms and into her breast, comforting, comfortable. The girl on the table lay quietly, head to one side, her thick lips loose and open. Eilish could barely see her in the darkness, but she was certain she slept.

Eilish went on playing just for herself. It was quiet in the house, Pringle and Franklin conversing in the parlor, Mrs. Stevenson and Cook and Bessie and Peter all gathered in the basement kitchen for their supper. Eilish played a nameless sweet melody that had been growing in her head for several days, toying with it, adding harmonies and ornaments and little flourishes, pretending she was Miss Marianne Davies, and that an audience hung on her every note.

Eilish had no idea how much later it was that she became aware of the presence at her elbow, that otherness that was neither human nor demon, memory nor ghost. It was like a reflection, though there was no glass. She turned her head toward the dim outline, the oddly cropped hair, the slender features. She felt no fear at all, only connection, warmth, recognition. She played for the other now, as well as herself.

When she could play no more, her fingers red and chapped, her ankles tired, she drew the silk over the armonica and stood up. Her fey companion had gone. Rosemary slept beneath her leather straps, her thick lips trembling slightly as she snored. Eilish went to the window and looked out into the moonless night, turning her face up to the few hardy stars that twinkled through the clouds. She supposed those same stars had sparkled on her ma and her da, indeed on Saint Brigid herself. She expected they would continue to sparkle when Eilish Eam no longer inhabited the earth.

At length Franklin and Pringle came back into the laboratory, throwing open the door to the lamplit stairwell, talking at full volume, heedless of the quiet within. Rosemary immediately startled and began to whine. Eilish hurried to her side. "No, no, hush now, lass," she murmured. She undid the wide leather belts, one by one. Franklin and Pringle stood watching, commenting as if they were alone.

"You see, John," Franklin exclaimed. "Her nerves have subsided once again, having fallen into balance."

Indeed, Rosemary lay before them without the slightest tremor of head or hands. Her heavy features were slack, her head hanging as if she were still more than half asleep.

"I do, Benjamin," Pringle answered ponderously. " 'Tis remarkable what science has achieved in our lifetime. I must tell His Majesty about this development. One of his lords has a daughter . . ."

"Ancaster, is it not?" Franklin said. "I have heard of the child."

"Yes, that's the one. My lord Ancaster has taken his daughter to every spa in Europe searching for a cure, without result so far as I know. You must return soon from the Colonies, Benjamin. We will try your electrical treatment on the daughter of the duke."

Eilish brought Rosemary to a sitting position and helped her to climb down from the table. Franklin said heavily, "I cannot say when that will be, my friend. Truly I cannot. Matters are at a pretty turn in Philadelphia, I fear."

"I will keep the king's ear for you in your absence."

Franklin grasped the physician's hand and shook it firmly. "I'm grateful to you, John, deeply grateful. But I'll see you once more before I sail."

"Yes, yes, I'll bring this patient next week. One last treatment before you go."

Eilish cast a hasty glance at Rosemary. The girl had not understood, but still, Eilish doubted she would lie down so docilely a third time to be tortured with Dr. Franklin's electricity. Even a dumb animal would eventually grasp what the table and the leather straps promised. The gormless creature stood, without a will of her own, waiting to be driven away like the poor beast of a thoughtless husband-man.

Dr. Pringle gathered up Rosemary's cloak and tossed it over her, leaving it to Eilish to tie the ribbons and adjust the hood. Eilish herded the girl down the stairs and out to the street, where the carriage waited. Pringle and Franklin followed, still conversing. Eilish closed the carriage door on Rosemary. She saw no signs of returning spasms. Perhaps the girl would have a little relief for a time. Eilish went back into the house, in search of the supper she had missed.

The kitchen was dark and cool, but Cook had left the fire banked, and the kettle still steamed on the hob. Eilish found a match and lit two candles. As the wicks flamed up, they cast dancing shadows onto the armchair at the end of the table. Eilish glanced at the shadows once, and then again. "Aye," she whispered, nodding to herself as she set about her preparations. " 'Tis a night for such things."

The large knife was waiting by the wheel of English cheddar. She used it to cut a half-dozen slices, and carried a fresh loaf and two plates to the table. She put tea in the pot, and poured the simmering water over it. While it steeped she set out two cups.

When Franklin came in, he said, "Ho ho, my dear! Expecting me, were you?"

"Aye, Dr. Franklin," Eilish said with an impish smile.

"And how would that be, Eilish, since I almost never come to the kitchen?"

Eilish poured the tea, and fetched the sugar bowl and spoons from the sideboard. " 'Tis because I'm fey," she said. "I have the gift. Like me ma, and me grandma, and so forth. I saw you there, in that chair, in the shadows of the candlelight. So I knew."

"A handy talent, my dear," Franklin said. He sat down in the armchair with a little groan, and lifted his swollen leg to rest on the straight chair opposite. "Would you could see what lies ahead for me in America. Or if I will soon again be in happy England."

"The gift chooses what it will say," Eilish said. "We take what it gives and ask no more."

"Ah, yes," Franklin said tiredly. "I must confess I treat with the Deity the same." Eilish didn't understand this remark, but hunger was upon her, and she let it pass. The two of them sat sipping their tea and munching white bread and yellow cheese in a companionable silence. When the cheese was finished, Eilish brought a pound cake from the sideboard and cut several pieces.

Franklin took a slice, but he didn't eat it. He stared into the shadows beyond the candlelight, absently fingering the cake to crumbs. "Do you know, Eilish," he said softly. "I would give anything to live in a future time."

The strange dizziness seized Eilish's skull. She shook her head to clear it. " 'Tis a strange idea, sir," she said. "Are you thinking the future will hold something the present does not?"

Franklin dropped the remnants of pound cake on his plate. "Ah, my dear, how can I explain? There are such wonders in the natural world as we have only begun to guess at. Electricity is just the beginning. There is also magnetism, and there are those great and ancient bones found by the Ohio River, that we will someday understand. The functions of the body are a miracle of nature still to be divined—and one day, some great and fortunate man will learn how the stars are constructed. The universe has great and wonderful secrets! The more we learn, the more we know we have to learn. I have only begun my studies, yet I am no longer a young man. I will miss the greater part of it, and that grieves me deeply."

Eilish gazed across the table. She saw Benjamin Franklin, but the room around them faded, the sideboard and the fireplace and the great sink drawing back from her as if a tunnel had closed around her vision. She saw only Franklin's tired, good-natured face, his curling gray hair, his dark eyes that usually twinkled with good humor behind his glasses. She heard her voice echo against the stone flags of the floor, though she spoke without volition. "Take heart, sir," were the words. "You will see it all."

"Eh?" he said, pushing up his glasses to stare at her.

Eilish blinked, and shifted in her chair. "What did you say?"

"No, not I, Eilish. You said it. You said I will see it all," he told her. "You said, 'Take heart, sir, you will see it all.' "

Eilish's head ached with the dull throb that had become a familiar companion. She peered at Franklin across the table, assuming it was fatigue that made her vision blur and her eyes tear. " 'Struth, did I?" she said. "Then perhaps you will."

"But how could that be, Eilish?"

"Aye, how should I know? And you the natural philosopher!" She tried to smile, to soften the words. She rubbed her eyes, trying to clear them. "You see how the gift plays us, Dr. Franklin. It gives what it will, and no more. Oh, sir, I must get to my bed, I'm that tired."

He put his bad foot on the floor and rose with some difficulty as she left the table. He stood up, exactly as if she were a lady, and he a swell rising from courtesy, but she didn't remember that until later. What she remembered, as she closed her eyes at last, was the gentleness of his voice as he said, "Good night, Eilish, my dear. Sweet dreams and good rest."

24

London, September 1762

THE entire household of Number Seven stood in a ragged row in Craven Street to bid Benjamin Franklin farewell. A hired driver perched on the driver's seat of the carriage, the reins in his hands, charged with bringing the carriage back after Franklin's trunks and bags had been loaded aboard *The Carolina*. The horse had been sold, and would be collected the next day by its new owner.

Peter had already said goodbye to Eilish in the kitchen. She had been clearing away the remains of an almost untouched breakfast. No one in the house had much appetite this day. Peter stood by the sideboard, his tricorn hat in his hand, his dark eyes mournful. "I hope to see you again one day, miss, but 'twill not be my decision," he said. His full lips drooped.

"Why, Peter," Eilish said. "Are you not glad to be going home?"

" 'Struth, miss," he said. "Glad or sorry makes no difference in my life. But now you will have to go to Seven Dials by yourself, won't you, and 'twill be hard. Who will help you?"

She touched his arm. She would have liked to embrace

him, but feared to offend. "Peter, you've been so kind. 'Twill be a gloomy house without you."

He nodded. His eyes reddened and he looked down at his feet.

Eilish's eyes burned, too. Hurriedly, she said, "Here, Peter," and thrust a small parcel at him, wrapped in a bit of paper left over from a Fortnum's delivery. He unwrapped it awkwardly, and exclaimed when he saw the little embroidered handkerchief. "But, miss! Your mother's bit of linen!"

"Yes, Peter. 'Twill keep you company on your voyage. And you will know I'm thinking of you faraway in America."

"Oh, miss. I shouldn't take it."

"Please, Peter. 'Twill please me to think of you having it."

He nodded then, and tucked the gift into his breast pocket, inside his greatcoat. He swallowed, and whispered, "Thank you, miss."

Now they were outside, in the muggy summer air, under a leaden sky. It was time. "Goodbye, friend Peter," Eilish said, her voice choking. The blackamoor bowed from the waist before he climbed up beside the carriage driver.

Franklin spoke to each member of the household. He gave Bessie a coin, and a little purse to Cook. He embraced Margaret Stevenson. He and Polly embraced as well, long and lovingly, with many assurances of frequent letters and an early reunion. Eilish was last in line.

She stood at the iron gate, her arms wrapped about herself, though she was overwarm in her heavy blue dress. The horse stamped its feet and tossed its head, and Peter spoke soothingly to it. Eilish couldn't look at Peter, she found, and now she didn't want to look at Franklin. He came to stand before her, putting one strong finger beneath her chin to turn her face up to him. "Do not be unhappy, my dear," he said. "Dear Margaret has promised you shall have a home here as long as you like."

"Ta, Dr. Franklin," Eilish said. She caught her trembling lip between her teeth.

"And you have the armonica to play, to practice until I return," he went on, twinkling down at her through his divided spectacles. "I will expect a concert on my very first day back."

"Aye," she said. She wanted to say more, wanted to make a pretty speech of thanks for his kindness and the pleasure of his company, but her eyes burned and her tongue froze. She could only drop her head to stare at her shoes and try with all her might not to cry.

The carriage rocked and creaked as Franklin climbed into it. A moment later they were on their way, amid a flurry of waving handkerchiefs and farewells, *bon voyages* and pleas to return soon.

Eilish stood mute and miserable beside the gate. She was overwhelmed, utterly shaken, by the sure knowledge that somehow, for some reason, she would never meet Benjamin Franklin again in this life.

TWO weeks after Franklin's departure for America Polly Stevenson came to Craven Street with her aunt Tickell in tow. She was to stay for the season, and was suitably burdened with hatboxes, portmanteaus, and trunks. She announced on the very first day that in Dr. Franklin's absence, she would be taking charge of the promotion of his armonica. On the second day, she brought a new person to Number Seven Craven Street.

"Eilish," Polly said. "This is Miss Marianne Davies, the harpsichordist. Miss Davies, this is Eilish Eam. She assisted Dr. Franklin in the manufacture of his new instrument, and has played it quite a lot."

"How do you do, Miss Eam," Marianne Davies said with a gentle smile. She was smaller than Eilish remembered, with soft dark eyes. She wore heavy white powder on her cheeks to conceal the scars of smallpox.

Eilish curtsied to her. "Miss Davies," she said warily, unsure of what this visit meant.

"Eilish," Polly said crisply. "You are to show Miss Davies how the instrument works. When she is satisfied she understands it, please escort her to the parlor for tea." In a quite different tone, she added, "Miss Davies, do send Eilish for me if you need anything until then. Dr. Franklin will be so pleased to know you are investigating his latest invention." Her back straight, shoes crunching on the carpet of glass dust, Polly swept out of the room, leaving Eilish and Marianne Davies alone.

"To begin with," the tiny lady said to Eilish, "please call me Marianne. I'm only a musician, like yourself." Her smile glowed with small, even teeth like little dusky pearls. She was too thin and small to be pretty, Eilish thought, but she was like a nightingale, small and brown and plain, yet enchanting.

"Ta," Eilish said. " 'Tis kind of you, miss. But of course I'm just an Irish orphan. A servant in this house."

"We are musicians, my dear," Miss Davies said. "We are all servants of the Muse."

Eilish didn't understand the reference. To cover her ignorance, she hurried to the armonica and drew off the silk cover.

"Oh, isn't it lovely?" Marianne Davies cried. "Of course, I heard you play it at St. John's, but I confess to quite muzzy eyesight, especially at any distance—and I am far too vain for spectacles! I could only see the gleam of your glasses!"

" 'Tis the loveliest thing I ever saw," Eilish said. And then, on an impulse, she blurted out, "Miss Davies. Your playing—on the pianoforte—'twas a miracle. 'Twould make the very angels weep to hear it."

"How kind of you to say so."

Eilish sighed. "I would give my life to be able to play such music."

Marianne Davies chuckled. "Nay, my dear, you mustn't say that. 'Tisn't worth your life."

Eilish didn't agree, but she held her tongue.

"Come now," Miss Davies said, crossing to stand beside Eilish at the armonica. "Play the glassychord for me."

"Glassychord?"

" 'Tis what the papers call it—Benjamin Franklin's glassychord. What do you name it?"

"Dr. Franklin calls it the armonica, after the Italian."

The tiny lady's smile broke out like sunshine through clouds. "Does he? And you? 'Tis a far more euphonious word, indeed. Then I shall do the same!"

Eilish didn't know what euphonious meant, but she forbore to ask. She had no wish for Miss Marianne Davies, so educated, so charming, to find her stupid. Instead she pulled out the stool for the armonica, sat down and began to pump the treadle. She would demonstrate the one skill in which she had absolute confidence. Soon the crystal tones sang out into the laboratory, and Miss Davies stood listening, sharp little features alight with an expression of profound joy.

On that first day, and many days thereafter, Marianne Davies and Eilish Eam spent long hours over the glass armonica. First Eilish would play, and then Marianne would imitate her. They would discuss the result, and Eilish would suggest this hand position, that finger adjustment. Marianne was so quick, her fingers so deft, that Eilish might have been tempted to envy, but the older woman was as kind and merry as she was talented. Though Eilish had a more or less constant headache now, she could disregard it during their time together. And it seemed as though her own fingers learned from Marianne's, that they were more sure, more flexible for having a model. Marianne's hands danced across the crystal cups, the fingers precise as the fluttering of a honeybee over the white petals of a lily.

Inevitably, the two musicians had to be called away from the ʼrmonica to have their tea. Polly, though the collaboration had been her own doing, became quite irritated with the intensity of their concentration. "Surely, Eilish," she would often say after Marianne's carriage had borne her away, "you could accomplish as much in half the time. Why must you keep her so long in that laboratory amongst all the glass dust and paraphernalia?"

Eilish would toss her head at that, and make some peppery reply. Mrs. Stevenson tut-tutted at her daughter, trying to smooth things over. Cook chortled privately in the kitchen. It was Polly's idea, also, that Bessie should clean the laboratory before Marianne Davies' visits, but Eilish would have none of it. She stood in the doorway, blocking the way as Bessie aproached with bucket and mop and cloth in hand. "Dr. Franklin said not," she said. "You just ask Mrs. Stevenson! You're not to set a foot inside this room!"

"But, Eilish," Polly said several times. "Both you and Miss Davies come out with your eyes streaming and your noses red from sneezing. 'Tis all that dust, surely!"

"Till Dr. Franklin returns, nothing will be touched," Eilish said stoutly. Privately, she thought there might be some truth to what Polly said, but she could not pass up the chance to twit her. The flames of Polly's jealousy were all too easy to fan. Sometimes, when she was alone in the laboratory, Eilish opened the windows and carefully dusted the shelves amongst the bits of glass and tube and wire Dr. Franklin had left. She would have swept the floor as well, but there was no broom to be had without Bessie's knowing. She had to leave the bits of glass that crackled under the feet of anyone who came in. As the weeks passed after Franklin's departure, no one but Eilish and Marianne Davies and, once or twice, Dr. Pringle entered the laboratory. Dr. Pringle cared nothing for the untidy floor.

In late September, when Pringle had come in search of the Leyden jar used to "treat" Rosemary, he asked Eilish to play the armonica for him, saying he had missed hearing it. While she obliged, he sat nodding, tapping his fingers on his knee. At the end of her short recital, he pulled a shilling from his waistcoat pocket and pressed it on her. " 'Twas a pleasure to hear it, Miss Eam. It puts me in mind of my friend Benjamin," he said. "I thank you."

Eilish curtsied and said, "Thank you ever so, Dr. Pringle." He patted her shoulder as he left. She ran to the kitchen the moment the door closed behind him.

"Cook!" she cried. "Oh, Cook, look what Dr. Pringle has given me!" She held out the coin on her palm.

"Now, isn't that nice, Eilish? Such a nice man, he is," Cook said. "No wonder he and Dr. Franklin are so fond of one another."

"Aye, and missing each other," Eilish said. 'Twas not a good day for her, her head aching and her stomach uneasy, but she was delighted with her windfall. "Cook—I must go down to Seven Dials, somehow. To take this to Rose Bailey, for Mackie's sake. 'Tis a long time since I sent Dr. Franklin's money to her."

" 'Twas a tidy sum, that," Cook said.

"Aye," Eilish agreed. "But there are a great lot of Baileys, and now Mackie added to their number! 'Twould be lovely to see him." All at once, she felt overcome with longing to see the boy's round cheeks, his red thatch of hair, his sweet wide smile.

" 'Tis a bit of a walk to Seven Dials," Cook said.

"Aye, but I think I must do it, Cook. Miss Davies isn't to come tomorrow. I'll set out just after breakfast."

"Then," Cook said, with a touch of her floury finger to Eilish's pale cheek, "I'll get busy and make a cake with these raisins Mrs. Stevenson just bought. Wouldn't your lad like that?"

ARMED with a substantial amount of cake, a packet of tea, and some stubs of candles Mrs. Stevenson had deemed too short to use in the parlor, Eilish walked out through a mild September morning. Carriages passed often while she was still in the Strand. When she turned northeast into St. Martin's Lane, the road was noisy with the rumble of carts and curricles, but by the time she reached Monmouth Street, she found mostly walkers like herself. Her persistent headache seemed to lessen as she walked, and she vowed she would get out more, take more exercise.

As she drew closer to Seven Dials, she noticed the meaner clothes, the dirty faces, the worn boots on the passersby. She found herself pulling her skirts aside to avoid brushing those not so clean as herself. "Oh, la," she laughed when she realized it. "See now, Da, what a fine lady your lass has become? Too choosy by half, you'd be saying, were you walking beside me!" This she muttered under her breath, but no one paid her much notice in any case. The costermongers were out in force, and the cries of "Cherries! Buy my cherries!" and "Old clo', old clo'," rang out around her. London was at work.

Eilish approached Seven Dials with some care. It had been many months since she last was here, and she knew she looked much different than in her days of playing in the streets of Covent Garden for pennies. One or two leering men spoke to her, and one raffish boy approached as if to lighten her pockets, but she spoke to them sharply in Irish, and they laughed and backed away. Still, it was with relief that she pushed open the door to the Clock and Cup.

Rose's da was behind the bar. He had no more than half a dozen customers, the hour being early, but he was deep in conversation with one of them. Eilish went on into the back of the house, where the family lived in three crowded rooms. Here she found Rose, with the seven-year-old twins that had cost their mother her life, and Mackie, now four. They were all sitting on a bench round a plank table, peeling potatoes and turnips for the night's kidney pie. Rose looked up at Eilish's entrance. "By the angels," she cried. "Look who's come for a visit!"

The children's faces turned to the door, and Mackie,

who had been peacefully scraping at a misshapen turnip
with a broad knife, began to instantly wail. "Eilish, Eilish!
Hi, Eilish!"

"Oh, Mackie, me darlin'," Eilish said, laying her parcel
to one side and holding out her arms. "Oh, gods, how I've
missed you!"

Mackie dropped the knife, and the turnip went rolling
across the rough boards of the floor. He struggled to lift
his little legs over the bench, to run to her. She saw that
though his legs had grown longer, and thicker, they were
if anything more bent than ever. The twins beat him to it,
bringing desperate tears to his eyes as he struggled. Eilish
hugged the twins, and then hurried to Mackie. He was halfway across the floor to her, swaying, wavering on his poor
bent limbs. She seized him up in her arms and held him
tight, as if she would never release him again. He buried
his face in her neck and wept hot tears into her collar.

EILISH stayed through the day, chatting with Rose, holding Mackie on her lap. His tears dried and he began to tell
her as much as he could in his childish way about the manner in which he spent his days. He went to fetch a toy to
show her, and Eilish gave Rose the shilling. Rose said,
"Must be a grand house, where they hand out shillings so
easy."

"Well, not so easy, perhaps, Rose," Eilish said. "And I
never know when one is coming. But every one comes my
way is yours, I promise!"

" 'Tis a great boon to us, to be sure," Rose said, tucking
the coin into a battered tea caddy above the hearth. "But
'struth, Eilish, there's still a bit left from all that what you
sent us before."

"I'm glad," Eilish said. Mackie returned, his progress
pitifully slow, carrying a little wooden soldier in his hand.
His round cheeks were pale, his thatch of red hair patchy.
Eilish caught him to her in a sudden rush of anxiety. Above

his head, she met Rose's eyes. "His legs get no better, do they?" Eilish murmured.

Rose shook her head. "No. No better. Neither me da nor me can see what work he'll do. The twins run back and forth for Joseph the costermonger, and Thomas has a lovely job for one of the Jews down at the Rag Fair, selling old hats and wigs. But Mackie—"

"He needs the country," Eilish said. "Fresh air and green grass and clean water."

"Aye, and who doesn't?" Rose said tartly. "But for the Irish in London—'tis Seven Dials or Newgate, and naught else!"

"Unless 'tis Craven Street," Eilish said without thinking.

"Aye," Rose said. " 'Twould seem things are a sight nicer in Craven Street!"

Mackie turned his face up to Eilish with his wide, sweet smile. "I go with Eilish now?" he said innocently. And to Rose he said, "Craven Street. I go."

Eilish hugged him close. "Nay, Mackie," she whispered. " 'Tisn't possible. But I'll come to see you every chance I have, though 'tis more than two hours walk! I promise!" She laid her cheek on his tangled hair. "I don't know what else I can do, Rose," she murmured. "I couldn't do better for Mackie if I came back to Seven Dials."

"True enough," Rose said. "No street player could make so much money. And 'tis a much better life you have there."

"I miss Mackie so," Eilish said, her throat growing tight.

The two girls gazed at each other until Rose, shaking her head, said, "You'd best be on your way back, if 'tis a two hour walk. You don't want to be on the streets too late."

"Nay."

Mackie didn't cry as Eilish left, but his eyes were dark, his smile gone. As she trudged back down Monmouth Street, her head began to ache again with a leaden pain that made her eyesight blur. By the time she reached Craven

Street, the pain had spread to her chest and her stomach, so the tea that was laid ready had no appeal to her. She climbed the stairs to her room and lay on the bed. The memory of Mackie's little, resigned face gave her a greater pain even than her poor head, but she was too tired to weep. Eventually, she slept, lying there still dressed, and didn't wake till morning.

25

Seattle, August 2018

THE bike path along Seattle's Green Lake was crowded. Skaters, cyclists, and joggers zigzagged around Charlie's chair, and Erin trotted beside him as he barreled down the glassphalt.

"Charlie, you're a speed demon. I can barely keep up."

He grinned up at her. His blond hair had grown long over the past months, and its ragged fronds waved in the light breeze. "You're not pushing this chair anymore. You're getting out of shape, old lady," he said.

She stuck her tongue out at him, and he laughed. She sidestepped to dodge a small boy on a tricycle. "Where did all these people come from? Have they been hibernating?"

Charlie slowed his spinning wheels to turn toward a narrow grassy area studded with picnic umbrellas over cast-iron tables. "When the sun shines, they all come out at once. They have to—summer comes late and leaves early here."

"It's beautiful, though," Erin said. The air was intoxicating, fragrant with the scents of newly cut grass and blackberries ripening in the sun. Emerald- and olive-green shrubbery hung over the banks of the lake, and the water was a burnished blue, its surface rippling with the wakes of small boats.

Charlie had finished the final score and program for *Moving Mars,* and this was their celebration. Erin dashed ahead to claim a picnic table. "Come on, Charlie, let's grab this one, close to the water."

She dropped her sweater on the chosen table to claim it. Charlie had found a picnic basket in a closet, an ancient heavy wicker affair with bottle holders and an array of tarnished utensils in the lid. He lifted it easily onto the table and brought out a straw-wrapped bottle of Chianti.

Erin wore shorts and a string T-shirt, rubber sandals and a flat cap. Charlie squinted up at her through the sunlight. "You cut your hair again," he said. "You look like a teenage boy."

She pulled one of his long, wispy locks. "And you're an Italian cherub."

Charlie pushed his fingers through his mop. "I like it. I'm aiming for a queue, like Mozart. A black ribbon and powder on my head."

They set out the picnic, cheese and whole wheat French bread, early peaches and fresh tomatoes, smoked salmon. Erin picked up one of the tomatoes and munched it as if it were an apple. Charlie laughed at her. "You're unbelievable," he said. "You eat like a Percheron, and you're still so skinny."

"I'm not skinny," she said, wiping tomato juice from her chin. "I'm slender—big difference."

"Room at this party for one more?"

It was Gene Berrick, in jeans and dark glasses. "Hey," Charlie said. "You got away from the clinic!"

"For an hour or two, anyway," he said.

Erin hastily put the half-eaten tomato on a napkin and tried to wipe her fingers dry on her shorts. She saw with chagrin she had left red streaks on the white fabric. "Hi," she said, feeling the blush in her cheeks. "Glad you could make it."

"So am I." He pushed up the dark glasses and gave her his quiet smile. The silver in his dark hair gleamed in the sunshine.

Charlie worked the cork out of the Chianti bottle and poured wine into plastic glasses. When they each had one, Gene lifted his. "To *Moving Mars*," he said.

"*Mars*," Erin and Charlie said together, and they all drank.

"Have you sent it off, Charlie?" Gene asked.

"Yup," he said. "They've had a rough outline to look at. But now it's finished!"

Erin said, "They're going to love it."

"Let's hope so," Charlie said.

"When's the performance, then?"

"September," Erin told him. "We'll go down the week before for rehearsals." She added wryly, "It's the only gig I have before Christmas."

"Hey," Charlie said. "The work comes and goes. Waves on the ocean."

She sighed. "I guess so. There's kind of a lot of beach right now."

Gene's clear eyes rested on her. "Do you really mind so much, Erin? If things are slow for a while?"

She had to smile at him. "No, I guess not. But Mal worries . . . and then, you never know if it will pick up again."

They sat for a pleasant hour, eating, talking of music and food and good weather. Around them other people talked and laughed, enjoying the sun and the breeze and the water. At length Gene began to extricate his long legs from beneath the little table. "Thanks for lunch," he said. "I'll have to get back. I've got—"

An ugly noise interrupted him. Someone shouted, and other voices rose, too, a swell of harsh noise that broke the peace of the afternoon like a stone shattering glass. Around them people abandoned their picnics, craning their necks in the direction of the commotion. Mothers called their children to them, and held them in protecting arms. Gene came swiftly to his feet, and Charlie turned his chair to try to see.

The racket was coming from a little crowd clustered at the north end of the park. Erin could see waving arms, heads bobbing up and down. The yelling went on, and the knot of people swelled as the curious ran to see what was happening. A police siren wailed almost immediately, growing louder and more strident by the second. Gene put on his glasses to see better. He made an angry noise in his throat.

"What is it?" Erin asked, but he was already striding away.

He was at the scene when two blue-uniformed police arrived, hurrying down from the parking lot toward the disturbance. Erin could just see Gene's lean figure bent over something on the ground. He straightened when the police reached him, and there was apparently some discussion. Gene, taller than either officer, stood with his arms folded. His dark glasses glinted, and he lifted one hand in a small gesture toward the watching crowd.

Erin could see better, standing, than Charlie could from his wheelchair. "It's a person, I think," she said. "On the ground. Maybe someone's hurt? Oh, no, maybe not. He's getting up now."

The police had the man between them, holding him up or keeping him from running off, Erin couldn't tell which. They moved up the path toward Erin and Charlie, Gene following. He had a phone in his hand and was speaking into it.

As the little procession went past, Erin saw the dirty clothes, the unkempt hair, the unshaven face of the man between the officers. He walked uncertainly, stumbling, depending on the hands of the policemen. She stared after him as Gene returned, still talking on the phone. When he dropped it into his pocket, she asked, "Who was that? What was he doing here?"

"I don't know who he was," Gene said. "I don't think he does, either. He was sleeping under one of the tables."

"But what happened?"

Gene enunciated with care, clipping his words. "The clean citizens who use this park tried to roust him, and he treated them to some street language." He replaced his glasses carefully, slowly. "And something else, I couldn't tell what—something rude. Probably smelly."

Erin squirmed inwardly, remembering her reactions to Joey and his mother and their tent.

"What happens to him now?" Charlie asked.

"The police will take him to the refuge area. I called Anne."

Erin said, "You're angry."

He turned his face toward her, his eyes invisible behind the glasses. "They threw garbage at him," he said in a featureless voice. "Nice-looking people with good clothes and new shoes and picnic lunches. He's drunk, or drugged, or mentally impaired, maybe all of those things. He swore at them. So they threw things. And then they pushed him."

"Hey, Gene," Charlie said uncomfortably. "You did what you could."

Gene nodded. "Right. And he'll get filed with a lot of other people just like him."

Erin wanted to touch his arm, to comfort him somehow. "Why are you upset, Gene?" she asked. "You can't save everyone."

Gene turned to watch a scarlet spinnaker swell with wind on the lake. "I've known a few people like that," he said. Charlie and Erin glanced at each other, distressed, unsure. After a moment, Gene leaned back against the iron table, one long leg crossed over the other. He stared up at a trio of white gulls circling against the sapphire sky. The twins watched him, waiting.

"I was born in '90," he said finally. "My mother was a fifteen-year-old girl whose parents kicked her out of the house when she got pregnant. I never knew her. I never knew who my father was—I don't know my genetic background at all. I grew up in what was called 'foster care.' We don't have that anymore, but at the time it meant a succession of houses filled with other kids like me, parentless, homeless, hopeless. Some of the houses were fine, some weren't. Some of the people did it for love, some for money. But like a lot of other kids, by the time I was twelve, I was on the streets. I've slept under a few picnic tables myself."

He glanced up the slope behind them, where the police car, contemp and official, was slowly cruising out of the parking lot. "When I was fourteen, the citizenry voted to clean up the streets," he said. "They cleaned me off the streets, and others like me."

"What happened to you?" Erin murmured.

The dark glasses glittered. "What else? No one's allowed to be homeless anymore."

"The tent city," she breathed. He nodded. She tried to imagine him, his elegant figure, his fine hands, in one of those dark and reeking tents. Her heart sank.

"Was it awful?" Charlie asked softly.

Berrick shook his head. "No. Not awful. No worse than the streets anyway. The bad part is trying to get out of it. No one wants to give someone a job if that's all the address they have. No one wants to give a scholarship to someone from a refuge area."

"But you must have gotten one," Erin said.

"Yes," he said. He took the glasses off. His eyes were dark, his mouth hard. "I had to take the SAT twice. Someone on the board decided I must have cheated the first time. They made me take it again."

"Jeez," Charlie said.

"How awful," said Erin.

Gene looked out at the sailboat again. "Yeah. I sweated that second one," he said.

•   •   •

WHEN Erin and Charlie, sunburned and windblown, entered the condo, the phone console chimed. "Miss Rushton, you have a message."

It spoke again when she didn't answer immediately. "Miss Rushton, you—"

"Okay, got it," she said. "Playback."

The screen clicked on, showing Mal's freckled, droopy face. "Hi, Erin, Charlie," he said. "Good news! Call me when you get in. Erin, San Antonio wants you back, they want both of you! Underwood's out after just one season— now they want *Mars*. They've heard it's going to be different. Is it, Charlie? You need to tell me so I know what to say to the p.r. folks. Anyway, it's short notice, and we should talk. Sarah sends her love." He gave a small wave, and the screen blanked.

"Would you like to respond, Miss Rushton?"

"Later," Erin said. The console clicked itself off.

Erin bent to hug Charlie, and did a pirouette in the center of the living room. "Charlie, this is terrific! Whew, what a relief. Ol' Underwood got what was coming to him! And *Mars*—it's going to be a big success, I know it is."

"Sounds like the word's out," Charlie said.

"Have you told Mal? About the augmented sensory program?"

He shook his head. "He wouldn't get it, anyway."

"I suppose the New Music Group has been talking, and the word spread, then?"

"No doubt." Charlie was smiling, pleased.

"This is great! And I'd better get to work! Get my instrument out here so I can practice."

"But E—what about London?"

She stopped dancing. "London?"

"Gene suggested you go back."

A chill crept across her sunburned shoulders. She felt a sudden, childish resentment at Gene Berrick for casting a pall on her enthusiasm, however unwittingly. She stuck out her chin. "Well, I might. Some time, maybe. But not now. Now I work on *Mars!*"

IN the shower, Erin stood under warm water, letting it sting and then soothe her sunburned skin. As she lathered her hair, she leaned against the stainless steel grab bar. It was slick with water, and her backside slipped on it. She caught herself, laughing, then suddenly stopped, and stared down at it. The bar—and the bath chair, which she had moved out of the shower before she turned on the water—and all the other paraphernalia that went with Charlie's disability, all the familiar aids and equipment, nagged at her, jarred her good mood.

She turned off the water and wrapped herself in a thick white bath sheet. The mirror in the bathroom was full-length, so that a person in a wheelchair could see as easily as a person standing. Erin stood before it, toweling her hair. A premonitory tingle in her forehead made her look around, startled. She didn't see anything. But she felt—she sensed something. She had the distinct sensation that someone was standing at her shoulder. She sniffed. There was that scent again, that spicy, foreign perfume.

She swallowed her fear, and murmured, "Tell me. Please. Tell me what it's about." But though she listened in stillness for several moments, there was nothing to hear.

26

London, 1762, 1763

THE dreary, wet autumn wore on through All Souls, into Advent, and on to Christmas with no glimpse of the sun, but Eilish gave no thought to the weather. Marianne Davies came to Craven Street almost every day, and she and Eilish spent countless hours working over the harpsichord and the glass armonica. They were the best times Eilish had known in her life. She often thought, gazing out her bedroom window into the London night, that she would have been truly and perfectly happy, were it not for her worry over Mackie.

Marianne Davies enchanted Eilish with her quickness of thought, her flashing musicianship, her mercurial temperament. Her tiny hands wove magic on the harpsichord and, in a dazzlingly short time, on the armonica. She made a transcription for the armonica of Mr. J. S. Bach's "Where Sheep May Safely Graze" that made Eilish sigh with delight. When Eilish played the old Irish tunes, Marianne Davies would sit with her eyes closed, her hands clasped beneath her chin, her face rapt. Tears often rolled unchecked down her cheeks, and sometimes she would be unable to speak for long moments afterward. Often she exclaimed, " 'Tis the music of heaven!" More than once, she embraced Eilish and then wept upon her shoulder.

Mrs. Stevenson would nod as she left, and say, "A very nervous type, Miss Davies."

"She is a true *artiste*," was Polly's answer. "Very highly strung. She is an exceedingly refined musician—not at all what we are accustomed to, of course, in this house."

Eilish understood perfectly the intent of such remarks. When Polly turned away, Eilish cast a cross-eyed, tongue-out grimace at her back. Mrs. Stevenson covered her mouth with her hand and cleared her throat. Cook suddenly found reason to cough loudly. When Polly was obliged to return to Essex for Christmas, no one in Number Seven regretted her departure, not her mother, not Cook nor Bessie, and certainly not Eilish Eam.

On Boxing Day, Eilish went to Seven Dials with a carton of food and small gifts, all collected by Cook and Mrs. Stevenson, to give to Mackie and the Bailey children. She found Mackie feverish and out of sorts, and she stayed late into the afternoon, hoping to soothe him. An icy rain fell throughout the day. By the time Eilish walked back to Craven Street, in the early winter dusk, she was wet through.

Cook was watching out for her. When Eilish stepped up in from the back stoop, Cook folded her immediately into a heavy woolen blanket she had kept warming by the fire. "Eilish, my dear, you're shaking like a leaf! You've taken a chill! Whatever were we thinking, letting you go out on such a day? Bessie, Bessie, call Mrs. Stevenson! Eilish will need the doctor!"

Eilish was indeed shivering, the fever already begun, and she couldn't stop the chattering of her teeth long enough to protest the calling of the doctor. She stood in trembling misery in the warm kitchen while Cook stripped off her sodden cloak and her wet dress, everything but her undershift. Cook scrubbed her with a dry towel and then wrapped her again in the warm, scratchy blanket. She plied her with hot chocolate and put a warm compress on her chest.

It seemed Cook's efforts were in vain. By morning Eilish was truly ill, her chest racked with coughing, her throat afire. Mrs. Stevenson brooked no refusal from her physician this time, but insisted that he come in person to see Eilish.

On the third day of her illness, the doctor arrived, a portly middle-aged gentleman with a curling wig and grimy hands. He peered at Eilish through thick smudgy spectacles, and listened to her chest with a little contraption made of a tube with a bell on each end. She thought, even in her fever and choking misery, that she would faint when he brought out a silver stylet and a metal cup. She tried to shake her head, to tell him no, to plead with Cook to stop him, but she coughed so hard she couldn't speak at all.

The doctor took her wrist in an iron grip, and pierced the vein on the inside of her elbow with a sharp stab of the stylet. She watched in horror as her own red blood spurted into the stained bowl, turning dark, joining with the other stains that represented the other poor souls the worthy physician had attended. Her head spun as if she had been doing somersaults, and her stomach lurched.

As the doctor stanched the flow of blood with a bit of rag from his pocket, Eilish wondered distantly at the absence of pain in the wound. Her chest and throat hurt far worse than the prick of the doctor's little knife. A great rushing filled her ears, as if a storm had swirled up in her head. A heartbeat later the storm closed over her, and she was lost in a thick darkness as the agony of her body gave way to the nightmares of fever.

She dreamed of Mackie, sooty and bleeding. She dreamed that Mr. Franklin's boat was tossed in a seaquake, its masts dipping and swaying below towering waves. Again she dreamed of Mackie, of Mackie screaming. She dreamed that Polly Stevenson stood between her and the armonica, refusing to let her touch it. She dreamed of Marianne Davies's small, neat body laid out in a shining black coffin. And yet again, Mackie, wailing with pain and fear. She tried to reach him. Her legs strained, the muscles trembling, but she could not move.

From these dreadful imaginings Eilish woke into physical misery. Every inch of her body ached. Her lungs were afire. Cook or Mrs. Stevenson was often with her, coaxing her to drink a salty broth or pouring the doctor's muddy potion down her burning throat. Sometimes, if she woke alone in the night, she felt that other, that strange presence for which she had no name. She reached out her hand to it, her fingers searching and searching. As her fever rose and fell, the presence took on the attributes of nightmare, elongating until its head brushed the ceiling, or flattening until it was like another blanket over her hot body. Surely, she thought in her more lucid moments, she was glimpsing the tortures of hell.

The worst of it all was the medicine. Eilish had not the strength to push open her window and pour it into the dog-roses. Cook held her head for each dose, seeing that she swallowed every bit, no matter how she gagged. "There, there, dear," Cook would say. " 'Tis for your good, Eilish. Drink it down, now, good girl. I'll bring you a nice jelly that will take away the taste."

It was almost the end of January before Eilish woke on a cold, sunny morning to find her chest beginning to clear. Her head ached, but it seemed to her that it had always ached. Her stomach was still uneasy, but there was such joy in drawing a deep, full breath, in feeling her tortured lungs fill with sweet air, that she felt giddy with hope. Cook sponged her face, and brushed her hair, and gently propped her up on pillows.

She also brought a large box of fancy pralines to the bedside. "Now, here you are, my dear," she said. "You must try one of these today. Miss Davies sent them for you, and I've not let anyone else touch them! She's been calling so often to see if you're better."

"Ta," Eilish whispered hoarsely. "Kind of her."

"Indeed. Very. Now rest, Eilish. I'll bring up some broth as soon as I've given Mrs. Stevenson her breakfast." She bustled out, her long apron flapping slightly. Eilish heard her murmur as she shut the door, "Thank the good Lord Miss Polly wasn't here for all this. 'Twould have been a misery, to be sure." Eilish almost found the strength to smile.

Before tea on that same day, Marianne's dark little head presented itself in the partly open doorway. "Eilish?" she whispered.

"Oh, Marianne!" Eilish breathed, and then suddenly, inexplicably, began to cry. They were weak sobs, and very few tears, as if her body had no moisture to spare, but she couldn't stop them. After the slow, painful, and lonely nightmare of her illness, the blessed sight of a friend's face—a true, angel-sent friend—was too much for her.

Marianne ran to her bedside and gathered her up in her thin arms to hold her like an infant, though Eilish was a head taller than she. Eilish wept her thin tears onto Marianne's neck, and then coughed viciously into a handkerchief, finally falling back, completely spent.

"There, there," Marianne said, pushing Eilish's hair back from her brow. "Now you'll feel better, dear." And somehow, Eilish did.

Cook brought tea to the bedroom, and Eilish and Marianne sat together over it. Neither ate much, Eilish being still too ill, Marianne being a poor eater at the best of times. They said little, but being together was enough. Marianne spoke of her concert tours, and her piano students, and her sister Cecilia, a singer who gave concerts all over Europe. Not until she was ready to take her leave did she tell Eilish the greatest news of all.

"Now, Eilish, are you feeling strong enough for something quite exciting?" she asked, her brown eyes twinkling, a slight flush staining her cheeks.

"Aye," Eilish said, attempting a smile.

"We have had an invitation," Marianne said with a little

flourish of her hands. "An invitation to play the armonica for His Majesty and Queen Charlotte!"

"Oh," Eilish said faintly. She blinked, hardly able to comprehend what it meant.

"Yes, sweetheart," Marianne said. She patted Eilish's cheek. "So you must get well as soon as possible. We— you and I, together—will play a little afternoon recital at court! But not until you're strong again. I have told them so."

Eilish could not imagine saying any such thing to anyone from the court. She blinked again, and felt the welling of her tears of weakness. Marianne bent and kissed her cheek. "No, no, Eilish, don't be upset. I'll come again tomorrow, and bring some of my mama's beef tea for you, and we'll talk about it." She straightened, and her eyes clouded suddenly. She clasped her hands together, and Eilish could see how they suddenly trembled. "You will be well, won't you, Eilish, dear? Promise me!" Her voice shook, and the pitch rose. Eilish summoned all her strength to put out her hand to her.

"Aye, Marianne," she whispered. "Soon."

THE weeks of convalescence were long and empty. It was February before Eilish was allowed out of her room, though she sometimes crept in secret down to the laboratory simply to look at the armonica. She dared not play it lest Cook or Mrs. Stevenson scold her. The late winter weather was gray and changeable, and the air in the house so close and stale, she thought she would smother. She yearned to walk freely through the stableyard, out in the street. She dared not mention returning to Seven Dials, for fear of Cook's becoming upset, but she felt in her bones that the constant headache that tortured her would be eased by fresh, cold air. At night, she pushed up the sash, but in the morning, Cook or Mrs. Stevenson always closed it again. She still spent the better part of each day in her bed.

And there was the medicine. It smelled of rotten eggs, and tasted like something scraped off the cobblestones of Covent Garden. Each dose was followed by an instant bout of nausea. The worst part was that when the first big bottle was finally empty, another appeared in its place. The doctor came three times to bleed her, and each time the bruised wound took longer to heal. She wore a cotton compress on the inside of her arm for a week or more after his visits, and it throbbed at night when she tried to sleep. The last time, red streaks formed up and down her arm, and Cook tutted over it, shaking her head, muttering to herself. She stamped out of the room in search of Mrs. Stevenson while Eilish lay trembling and sick on her bed. Mrs. Stevenson came to look at the arm, and ventured that perhaps Eilish had been bled enough.

"Indeed," Cook said. "Dr. Franklin would not have liked the look of this."

"No, no, I am sure you are right," Mrs. Stevenson said, wringing her hands. " 'Tis such a worry. One hardly knows what to do."

"Dr. Franklin said most ailments get better on their own, did he not?" Cook said boldly.

"Oh, dear, Cook, did he?"

"Aye. He put no great store in physicians, as I recall."

"Oh, dear. Oh, dear."

Eilish lay listening, her arm aching, hardly caring what they said. She had dreamed of Mackie again, Mackie with blackened scabs on his knees and elbows, crying, always crying. She couldn't go to him, she couldn't send for news of him. Had it not been for Marianne Davies and the prospect of playing the armonica with her once again, she could have found no reason to go on breathing.

Marianne came each week, bringing little gifts. Once she brought a tin of the face powder she herself used so liberally, and another time a tiny bottle of scent. She sat beside Eilish's bed, patting her hand or her arm, and told of her concerts, her audiences, what she had played, who had attended. She didn't play the armonica, vowing she would not, until Eilish was beside her.

It was to Marianne that Eilish told her nightmares. Marianne clasped her hands beneath her chin, the easy tears making runnels in her heavy powder. "Oh, how terrible!" she cried. "What do you suppose they mean?"

Eilish knew Marianne was easily upset. She wondered, vaguely, if she should protect Marianne from her frightening dreams, but it was such a relief, in her weakness, to talk of them. When she dreamed of Mackie, she woke with an ache in her breast that was indistinguishable from the pain of her illness. And so they talked together, and Marianne often wept, and then repaired her powder with liberal dustings from Eilish's tin. After she had gone, the room was fragrant with the smell of the powder and her expensive scent.

The weeks stretched on and on, until one day Eilish saw through her window little splashes of soft green enlivening the London landscape. She asked Cook what day it was.

"Why, Eilish, 'tis the end of March already!" Cook said. "And Dr. Franklin gone these six months. You, poor lass, have been abed for three."

Eilish stood up, shaky on her legs, and went to the glass over the dresser. She could hardly believe what she saw. Her cheeks were as white as if she had powdered them. Her body was as thin as Mackie's, her hands trembling as if with a palsy. Her hair, always so abundant, hung limp and straight about her face, every hint of curl vanished.

The brown bottle of the doctor's medicine still stood on the dresser, and the very sight of it made Eilish's stomach turn. Cook was smoothing up her bedclothes, tidying the room, picking up the chamber pot to be emptied. When she had left, Eilish went to the window with the bottle in her hand. She thrust up the sash and leaned out to look down into the dogroses.

The little tangle of vines showed green beneath the brown of last year's growth, the curving thorns gleaming white. Eilish pulled the cork from the bottle and poured every last, reeking drop of medicine straight into the thicket. She closed the window, and placed the empty bottle back on the dresser, then collapsed onto the bed to rest from her exertions.

After a time, she tried to dress. Raising her arms with difficulty, she brushed her hair and tied it back with a ribbon. It hung in a dispirited tumble down her back. She washed her face, and then, in a last effort to make herself more presentable, she splashed an abundance of Marianne's powder on her face, sneezing painfully when it clogged her nose, but persevering. She was as sick of being abed as she had been sick of pneumonia. Today, she promised herself, today at last, she would play the armonica.

27

Seattle, August 2018

I T was obvious, the moment Erin opened the clinic door, that Charlie and Gene had been arguing. A painful silence greeted her. Charlie was pulling on his gloves. He turned his face away, but she had already seen the angry scarlet blotches flaring on his cheeks and throat. Gene was bent over the Moog. When he stood and faced Erin, his features were rigid, his eyes opaque as storm clouds.

"What is it?" she asked. Neither of them answered. Charlie maneuvered himself neatly and swiftly into his wheelchair and spun out of the clinic without even glancing at Erin. She gaped after him, then whirled, fists on her hips, to glare at Gene. "What happened?" she demanded. "And don't give me any patient confidentiality nonsense. I'm not leaving till you tell me."

For a moment she thought even Gene might not speak to her. He leaned against the edge of his desk, arms folded, chin dropped. Beyond the closed rear door, the exercise machinery whirred and clicked. Ted's quiet voice was audible as he encouraged his patient.

The blue and red shape of Charlie's brain scan still shone above the projector, empty now of the white spears of light. Its blankness disturbed Erin, and she averted her eyes.

Gene switched off the projection and the Moog. He looked around at the equipment-lined walls and made a guttural, angry sound in his throat. "Erin," he said. "I'll explain, but can we get out of here? I need space. Air."

They walked out into the shadowed reception parlor, where the curtains were drawn against the August sun. There was no sign of Charlie. Gene opened the outer door and held it for Erin. "Don't worry, he's okay."

"But something's wrong," she said.

"Yes. Mind a walk?"

Gene's legs were long, and he paced quickly up the sloped sidewalk, past the monorail kiosk, and on. The air was breathlessly hot, the late afternoon sky a blaze of clear blue. Erin had to struggle to keep up as he strode beneath a canopy of heavy-branched maples, of cottonwoods with pale leaves that fluttered at their passing, an occasional shaggy hemlock. Erin would have enjoyed the walk if she hadn't been angry. No, not angry, afraid. The two emotions felt almost the same. She had noticed a pronounced tremor of Charlie's hands that morning. He had struggled to simply pour coffee. All day, she had tried to convince herself it was fatigue, or her own imagination. Now she had to hear what Gene would say, but she feared it, too.

He walked in silence, squinting into the glare. His lips were set, his hands stuck deep in his jeans pockets. Erin glanced up at him from time to time, anxiety squeezing her heart.

They walked for fifteen minutes. Erin was panting and perspiring when he finally made an abrupt left turn and passed through an open stone gate. She wanted to resent his arrogance, object to being dragged across Seattle like a dog on a leash, but when she saw where they were, she forgot to be angry.

Before her lay a Japanese garden, softly green and blue and brown, tucked between rolling hills. A path ran between tiny sculptured hedges and past shallow pools dotted with lilies. A small scarlet bridge spanned a reed-filled stream. Gene slowed his steps as they crossed it, giving Erin a moment to look down into the water beneath, where gold and blue koi fish swam among drifting water plants. Beyond the stream a flowering cherry tree shaded an arbor around a tiny stone temple. Gene Berrick threw himself onto a wooden bench beneath the tree, leaning forward with his chin on one fist, staring at the path under his feet.

Erin collapsed beside him, taking deep breaths of the leaf-scented air, turning her face up to let the breeze dry the damp strands of hair clinging to her forehead. She had never seen such a restful place. The little temple sheltered a fat smiling Buddha covered with gray-green lichen. Erin gazed at it, striving for patience, waiting for Gene to be ready to speak.

At last he said, "Ambition is a dangerous thing." His voice was dry and deep. He was so close that she felt the radiant warmth of his long body next to hers, and her skin tingled with awareness. She kept her eyes on the Buddha.

"I thought—if Charlie learned to walk in my clinic, as a result of my research—" He broke off, and leaned back against the bench, crossing his long legs, folding his arms. "I care about Charlie," he said. "I want him to walk because he should walk. And because he wants it. I also want—wanted—"

Erin looked up into his face, saw the old pain and the new mingle in his eyes.

"I wanted," he said, "to succeed for myself. To validate my work. I wanted to prove that a guy from the tent city could do it. City college, state university, residency in a backwater hospital. That none of that mattered. That I could be the one to make the breakthrough."

"Gene. What happened?"

He met her eyes with the air of one making a confession. "Charlie asked me to raise the power on the augmentation, and I did. Twice."

She waited, her mouth slightly open, for the rest of it.

"And he developed intentional tremors in his hands, which he hasn't had since he was ten."

The blood drained from Erin's cheeks. "It's true, then," she whispered.

Gene Berrick's eyes were tortured, but he held her gaze. "It's true. I'm sorry."

"Will they get better? His hands?"

He drew a deep breath. "Well, of course I cut the power back. That's what Charlie's angry about. But you understand, the nature of ataxia is imbalance. As we tried to force the new neural path to form for Charlie's legs, we've evidently stressed other, established neural paths. The brain operates on electrical impulses, which is why the emissions work—and why we had to stop immediately. I can't risk further imbalance. Other things can go wrong, too."

Erin closed her eyes. She didn't want to hear about other things. She saw Charlie in her mind, reaching for the coffeepot, his hand wavering, trembling, missing. Three times he had tried, before his fingers succeeded in closing around the handle. When she opened her eyes, she said, "Maybe he should stop your program entirely." She knew how harsh a statement it was, how awful that would be for both Gene and Charlie, but she couldn't help it.

"I suggested that," Gene said. He turned his head, allowing his eyes to rest on the gentle curves of the stone Buddha. "We argued. I agreed to go on with the augmented binaural beat program, but at the lower power level. It will just take longer . . . or it won't work at all. I don't know which."

"But he was improving," Erin said. "I saw it."

"Right. But maybe not enough to actually walk, not to walk like you or I do. Maybe with canes—if his hands get better." His voice faltered. He shook his head as if to cast off weakness, and looked away into the soft green vista of the gardens. "He won't accept that. He's ready to sacrifice his hands for his legs."

"No. He can't do that. His hands are too important! His music—"

Gene cleared his throat, staring at the Buddha. His profile was as stiff as if he were himself carved of stone. He was as much in pain as Charlie, and she wanted to comfort him. She wanted to be comforted. "Gene," she said huskily. "It's not your fault."

His eyes flicked to her, and away again. "Then whose?"

"I've lived with Charlie twenty-three years," Erin said. "And I know when he sets his mind on something . . . you can't imagine how many different methods he's tried to walk again."

"I have an idea."

Erin put her hand on his arm, felt the tight sinews, the throb of his pulse under her fingers. "There's nothing wrong with wanting to succeed," she murmured. "To be recognized. It's natural."

"Yeah. I know." Strain pulled at his mouth. Erin felt the effort with which he controlled his emotions, the intensity of the discipline that shut him away from her. It was a wall she couldn't breach. She wanted to put her arms around him, to melt his rigid posture, join her own sorrow with his. Instead she took her hand from his arm, sighing, and looked back at the smiling Buddha in his cozy coat of lichen.

WHEN Erin reached the condo, she found Charlie with his headphones on, working with the Akai. She motioned for him to take the headphones off, and when he did, she said, "I thought *Mars* was all finished."

He shrugged. "Just tweaking it," he said. He reached to touch one of the emitters, to twist it to a new angle. "It's never finished."

"Are you okay, Charlie?"

"Sure," he answered, without meeting her eyes. "Fine."

"What would you like to do about dinner?"

"I don't know. I'm not very hungry." He replaced the headphones.

Erin bit her lip, watching his hands on the slide panel. His fingers trembled slightly, and she saw that he supported his wrist with his free hand as his fingers moved. "Charlie!" she said, but he didn't respond. She watched a moment more, wondering what it was he was actually doing. She had packaged up the score for *Moving Mars* herself, including the augmentation program, and shipped it to San Francisco. What was Charlie up to? What was left to do? She gave it up, and turned away to the little kitchen.

She found halibut in the fridge, and a basket of blackberries. She wasn't sure what to do with the fish, but she unwrapped it and found instructions inside the package. She put it in a baking dish and turned on the oven. There was a jar of Italian herbs in the cupboard. She sprinkled the fish with the herbs and then, impulsively, poured a cup of white wine over the whole before she set it to bake. She washed the blackberries and arranged them in a crystal bowl, and set the table with plates and flatware. There was a loaf of French bread in the stainless steel breadbox, and she set that out with a cruet of olive oil. It didn't look like much, but she wasn't feeling very hungry either. She went to the realwindow to gaze wistfully down at Lake Union. It was crowded with sailboats, spinnakers in every color, molded hull boats motoring through the long summer evening. The scene was as gay as any viewwindow's. She leaned her forehead against the glass, feeling bereft.

"Hey," Charlie said behind her.

She turned. He had rolled his chair into the kitchen, and he nodded at the oven. "Good work," he said. "The prodigy cooks!" His blue eyes twinkled at her, tired, affectionate.

"Well, I'm trying. Think of it as experimental."

"Looks great," he said. He rolled his chair to her side. "Sorry about today, E."

"It's okay. I talked to Gene."

"I'm not going to try to explain," Charlie said quietly. "You know already, I think."

"Charlie, you have to give it time."

"How much time? Lifetime?"

"Don't make yourself worse trying to get better!"

He poked her in the ribs. "Don't worry about me."

She snorted at that, and he chuckled. "Okay, then, worry, but keep quiet about it, okay? Now, how about a salad in case you've ruined the fish?"

NOT until after dinner, with the dishes washed and put away, did Erin bring up her idea. "Charlie . . ." she said tentatively.

He was at his slimscreen. He wasn't using the voice program, but she noticed he was hunting and pecking with his forefingers. He looked up. "Yes?"

"I have an idea. About San Francisco."

"Let's hear it."

"I think we should invite Gene to the premiere."

Charlie's eyes shifted away, and Erin, in a rush of intuition, knew he was hiding something. Fear washed over her again. But what could she do? What could she say to her brother? It had all been said already.

When his eyes came back to her, they were guileless, the clear, summer-sky blue she was used to, and he gave her his old, sweet smile. "It's a great idea, E. Do you suppose a doctor from the tent city owns a tux?"

28

London, March 1763

IT was late in March before Cook and Mrs. Stevenson decreed between them that Eilish was well enough to resume all of her former activities. Her first thought, when they set her free, was to see Mackie.

A long walk, of course, was out of the question, and Eilish cast about for a way to reach Seven Dials. There was no horse and carriage in the stable, with Dr. Franklin away in America, nor would there have been anyone to drive a carriage. She had a little money, but not enough to hire a curricle. At last, presuming upon friendship, she mentioned her need to Marianne.

"The little boy?" Marianne cried, the quick and easy tears filling her eyes. "Oh, the one from your nightmares! Why, we must go and see him. We'll go together—I'll take you in my own carriage!"

"Marianne—" Eilish hesitated. She couldn't visualize Miss Marianne Davies in the Clock and Cup. " 'Tis a kind offer, truly. But Seven Dials is not a place for a lady like you."

"But, Eilish, dear, if it's all right for you to be there—"

Eilish touched Marianne's slender hand. "I grew up

there," she said gently. "I know the way they are, the way they talk, how to watch out for myself. I was going to ask if you could loan me your carriage, just for one morning."

"And of course I will! But I am coming, too," Marianne declared. Her moods always shifted as quickly as clouds before the sun, and now she beamed with enthusiasm and generosity. "We'll take all sorts of good things—we'll go to Fortnum's first! You'll see, 'twill be a party!"

Eilish was torn between concern for Marianne's sensibilities, which she well knew to be fragile, and her own craving to see Mackie, to have news of him. In the end, her need to see Mackie won out, and she accepted her friend's help. On a windy and cloudy afternoon, they set out for Seven Dials in the carriage, with Marianne's servant sniffing his disapproval at their destination.

Marianne looked stylish in an emerald wool pelisse, her small face almost lost in its huge collar. She kept her hands warm in a matching muff. Eilish was wrapped in a borrowed woolen cloak, much too large and a nasty brown color, but very thick and warm. Cook had insisted she borrow it. She was still thin and white, and as weak, Cook said, as a half-starved kitten.

At Fortnum's they bought wrapped cakes and sacks of dried fruit and a large wheel of cheese. Marianne chattered gaily throughout their shopping expedition, laughing with the clerks, gently chaffing Eilish, ordering her man around with cheerful tyranny. Her high spirits lasted until they rode into Seven Dials, and the carriage stopped directly before the Clock and Cup, but when they climbed out, Marianne's prattle died away as she took in the squalor of the neighborhood, the road strewn with the empty bottles and unsavory leavings of the night before, the windows opaque with grime. Eilish's heart sank as she watched her friend's cheeks go pale, her eyes grow wide. She cursed herself for her selfishness. She should have refused to bring Marianne here!

Marianne's servant cut his eyes from side to side as he held the carriage door. He said in a low voice, "Please, Miss Davies, do hurry. 'Tis not a fit neighborhood for you, nor for me for that matter."

"Now, now, Albert," Marianne said, though Eilish saw how her little pointed chin quivered. "This is Miss Eam's home. These are—" Her throat dried, and she coughed. "I mean to say, these are her friends."

Eilish was greatly relieved to see Thomas peeking from behind the pub door, and she waved him out. He ran to her, grinning, puffing his chest with importance. "Thomas!" she said. "You stay here, with Albert, and sing out if anyone gives him trouble!"

"Aye!" he cried. "None of these dirty buffers'll bother your carriage, Eilish!"

Marianne fished in her reticule and brought out tuppence for Thomas. He accepted it with a solemn nod, and took up a post beside the carriage, arms folded, eyes narrowed fiercely. Eilish and Marianne, their arms full of packages, stepped inside the pub.

The bar was full of people, most of them men. Every face turned as the two well-dressed women came through the door, and all conversation ceased. Eilish and Marianne froze under the weight of so many strange and hungry eyes. Marianne whispered faintly, "Eilish! You grew up here? *Here?*"

Rose Bailey was behind the bar. She cast down her towel and hurried through the press of customers to meet them.

"Hi, Eilish!" she exclaimed. "Why, whatever is the matter with you? You're as pale as a ghost." She caught sight of Marianne Davies, hanging back behind Eilish in a sudden fit of shyness. "And who's this?" Rose said under her breath. "Seems like a lady to me. No place in the Clock and Cup, I'll be bound."

Eilish gave a nervous laugh and said, "Oh, Rose, this is my great friend, and a very kind lady indeed. Miss Mar-

ianne Davies, the harpsichordist! Marianne, this is Rose
Bailey."

The two women nodded warily at each other. Eilish said,
"Rose, where's Mackie? We've all sorts of treats for
Mackie and the boys."

Rose said slowly, "Why, Eilish, the boy's not here just
now."

"But—but where would he be?" Rose hesitated, her
mouth open, her color up. Eilish felt the clench of her belly
beneath her heavy coat. She wavered on her feet, suddenly
light-headed. Rose saw, and put out her hand to take Eilish's arm.

"Ah, Eilish, ye'd better come back and sit down. Come
now, come on. Ye've been ill, haven't ye, poor lass? Aye,
and 'tis all that rich food, I have no doubt." Over her shoulder she said, "Please come this way, miss. Sorry about the
mess—'tis all these great lads I have about, and no time to
tidy up the place."

Eilish leaned on Rose's arm. Her feet seemed suddenly
to belong to some other body than the one she inhabited.
She stumbled past the bar, over the sill and into the back
room. Marianne followed, staying very close to Eilish and
Rose, and casting nervous glances over her shoulder at the
dark barroom.

The back room was empty, a clutter of dirty plates and
dishes left on the sideboard and the plank table, the fire in
the hearth gone out. Their feet crunched on cinders. Bits of
clothing and cast-off shoes lay in the corners in puddles of
gray soot. Through the open door, they saw the boys' un-
made beds. Rose helped Eilish to a chair, and then hurried
to close the bedroom door. "Me brothers aren't much for
housework," she muttered apologetically.

Marianne murmured her understanding, and gingerly
took a seat beside Eilish. Eilish held herself tightly under
the heavy cloak, trembling as if with cold. "Where is he,
Rose?" she said through a tight throat. "Where's Mackie?"

"Why, Eilish," Rose said again. "The lad's gone out to work. For the chimney sweep."

The room turned abruptly around Eilish, and she gripped the table before her with both hands to keep from falling. "No—he can't," she rasped. "His legs . . ."

Rose said sharply, "Everyone here works, Eilish. I'm no catchpenny, I hope, but me boys have to eat. 'Twas either understrapper to the chimney sweep, or the beggars' corner for Mackie. 'Tis no worse for him than for t'others."

"But, Rose—" Eilish could hardly see Rose Bailey for the black stars littering her vision. Marianne put her arm around Eilish, and Eilish leaned her head against the older woman's slender shoulder. "Oh, Marianne," she breathed. "He's just wee. Just a wee lad."

"He's five years old!" Rose snapped. "Me brothers were all working by five."

"But, Rose, they worked for the costermonger, or fer yer da," Eilish said. She sensed Marianne's strange look at her relapsing accent, but she couldn't help it. Just being in Seven Dials was enough to make her feel she had never left. "Not climbing up in dark chimneys, scabbing their knees, tearing their fingers."

"Nay, you've forgot," Rose said stubbornly. "Thomas worked for the chimney sweep, till he got too big. Mackie's all right, Eilish. He's all right."

"Eilish," Marianne murmured. "The boy's not here. We must leave our gifts and go."

"No," Eilish moaned. "No, I must see Mackie."

" 'Twill be hours," Rose said, gently this time. "He doesn't come back till suppertime. The sweep gives him tea, and then he comes home for supper."

Tears slipped down Eilish's cheeks. Feebly, she tried to dash them away. Her head hurt so fiercely she could hardly think. "I dreamed it," she whispered miserably to Marianne. "I saw him in my dream. Crying. Bleeding."

Rose said through tight lips, "They bleed at first, Eilish, then they scab, and they don't bleed anymore. Their knees and elbows get tough. 'Tis no different for Mackie."

Marianne pulled Eilish to her feet. She spilled their gaily wrapped packages across the table in a colorful jumble and left them where they fell. "Come, dear," she said. "There's nothing you can do here. Come, Eilish. You don't belong here anymore."

Eilish was too weak to resist. Leaning on Marianne's arm, she stumbled out through the pub, into the street, and allowed herself to be lifted up into the carriage. She didn't look back at Rose, who stood in the door of the Clock and Cup, twisting her apron in her hands.

THE spring was long and wet that year, and Eilish felt just as dour. Her strength did not return in full until the middle of June, and her heart felt as if it would never be strong again. She planned another trip to Seven Dials, but until she was strong enough to walk, it seemed she would never make it. Marianne Davies, amid many protestations of affection and devotion, flatly refused to carry her to "that awful pothouse" ever again.

They were to play at Hampton Court at the end of the month, and Marianne came every day to Craven Street for their practice. She had made a breathtaking transcription of Mr. Handel's "Come unto Him, all ye that labour," from *Messiah*, and she played it over and over, changing the fingerings, practicing the trills that required such steady work on the treadle. She listened to Eilish's Irish and Scottish and English folk songs, and made suggestions and corrections in such gentle terms that Eilish finally laughed one day and said, "Marianne! I grew up in Seven Dials—I'm not a genteel lady like yourself! Just tell me what I need to fix and I'll fix it."

Marianne laughed and threw her arms around Eilish. "My darling girl," she said, kissing her soundly on the cheek. "Would that more artists were as courageous!"

Another day, when Eilish made a hesitant suggestion

about sustaining a tone, Marianne burst into helpless tears, her head in her hands, her thin shoulders shaking. When Eilish ran to her, tugging at her hands, begging to know what the trouble was, Marianne suddenly began to laugh, sobs and laughter mixing together in a hysterical soup of emotion. "Oh, Eilish!" she cried. "I fear you have found me out! I am really no musician, no artist—I am a hack, the worst kind of amateur, a *fakir* of music! What will His Majesty think of me? Her Majesty? They will know, they will understand, and I shall be ruined!"

"Marianne!" Eilish cried. " 'Tisn't true, you know it isn't!" But Marianne only cried harder, her thin shoulders shaking. She couldn't calm herself, Eilish could see. She cast about for what to do, how to help her.

Eilish ran to the parlor and tugged one of the stuffed velvet armchairs around the corner and into the laboratory. She set it near the armonica, and ran to get the matching footstool. "Here, Marianne," she said to the weeping, trembling woman. "Here, lass, sit down now. Put your feet up—there. Now you're going to close your eyes, and I'm going to play for you. Just listen to all my silly old songs, and soon you'll feel better." *I hope,* Eilish thought privately. She had never seen an attack of nerves, and thought, in truth, she hadn't an idea what to do about it. There was only one thing she knew how to do well, and that was play the armonica. She would offer that to Marianne, and leave the rest to the angels.

She deliberately avoided the music they had chosen to play at court. Instead, she played the oldest and sweetest tunes she could think of, the ancient ones her da had taught her, that she had grown up hearing hummed and whistled in Seven Dials. "Faerie Queen," and "Joice's Tune," and the old "Planxty McGuire." She let the crystals sing with their own delicate voices. It seemed to her that the vibrations of the glasses could reach out to touch Marianne, to stroke her jangled nerves with their plaintive, soothing fingers. And it was the oddest thing—when she got to

"Barb'ry Allen," a whiff of spicy scent tickled her nostrils. She smiled. 'Twas as if Dr. Franklin himself was at her elbow.

After a time, Marianne's sobs quieted to sniffles, and then to the tiniest little hiccups, like those a bird might have. At last she simply lay listening in the big chair, her head back, her damp handkerchief clutched to her bosom. Her features smoothed and her eyelids ceased to flutter.

Eilish went to sit on the arm of the chair. Marianne opened her eyes and reached for her hand. "I'm much better now," she said softly. "Thank you, my dear. 'Tis amazing, how soothing the glass music is. 'Tis as if it goes directly to the center of one's soul, of one's heart. I felt my nerves simply settle, fall into harmony, in the most miraculous way!"

"I'm glad enough for that," Eilish said. "Without you, 'twill be no concert at court at all!"

"Oh, I know, I know," Marianne said. "But I do suffer from nerves, Eilish. I have since a child. There wasn't anything my family could do." She smiled, and she looked her old self again, her soft brown eyes shining. Her tears had left tracks in the powder on her cheeks, but her lips no longer trembled. "You have healed me, Eilish, my dear little physician! And now, we'd best get on with our practice."

Those days of June were filled with their music, the strains of the glass armonica and occasionally of the harpsichord drifting out into Craven Street like the zephyrs of early summer. But after Marianne went riding off in her carriage, back to her own home, Eilish was left alone with her worry over Mackie and her own failing health.

She hid her illness from Marianne. Her head hurt constantly, blurring her vision, making her hands tremble. Her stomach was often a misery of pain and nausea. She dared not confide in Cook or Mrs. Stevenson. She was terrified of being bled again, and though she had dutifully drunk two entire bottles of the doctor's foul-smelling medicine,

she could face no more of it. When she was able, she
walked out in the Strand, or down to Westminster Bridge,
to breathe the river air. She tried to eat Cook's lovely meals,
but she was so often sick that it seemed easier not to put
anything in her stomach at all. And, of course, at night, she
dreamed of Mackie, and wrestled with her guilt. Only at
the armonica did she find any peace. She spent as many
hours there as she dared, in the dusty comfort of the laboratory, the music rising from her fingers to ease her heart
and soul. It was all the consolation she had.

ON the great day, Eilish rose early. She packed up the
armonica with care, allowing no one but herself to wrap
and pad each precious cup. Marianne's man carried the bits
of the instrument downstairs and stowed them inside the
carriage. Eilish put on her concert dress once again, tying
the linen scarf as artfully as she could around her shoulders
to hide the thinness of her bosom and her arms. Marianne
wore a creamy satin dress with a square neckline and a
neckband of pleated silk ribbon. The underskirt of her dress
was ruched silk, all the same cool ivory color. It set off her
dark skin and deep eyes to perfection. Eilish exclaimed over
her.

"Oh, Marianne! You're as beautiful as—as—oh, la,
ye're a sight for the angels!"

Marianne laughed lightly. "And you, Eilish, dear."

Eilish said, "Ta," but privately she thought Marianne
was being untruthful. Her hair was no longer an abundant
cloud of curls, and her skin had a grayish tinge, as if
touched by the London fog. She glanced once into the
glass, and swore she would never look again.

They entered the palace through the Outer Green Court,
the carriage bumping over the bridge above the moat and
through the Great Gate House. The armonica was unloaded,
and Marianne's servant carried it in for them, leaving a
stableboy to deal with the horse and carriage. Eilish stared

open-mouthed at the rich linefold paneling, the carved
hammer-beam roofs and ornate furnishings of the palace.
It seemed there were elaborately dressed ladies and gentlemen in every corner, all along the route to the Queen's
Presence Chamber. She tried to see everything, to watch
over the armonica, and to keep from stumbling, all at the
same time.

They set up the instrument, and Eilish carefully cleaned
the glasses. They arranged and rearranged the stool, the
treadle, the bowl of water. And then they waited.

Marianne had warned Eilish that His Majesty was often
very late, and Her Majesty the same. To get them both in
the same room at the same time could be a challenge, and
therefore, though they had been asked to present themselves
and the "glassychord" at three in the afternoon, they were
prepared to wait for quite some time. In the end, however,
it could not have been more than an hour, Eilish shifting
her feet with nervousness, Marianne variously forcing back
tears or giggles, pacing with anxious steps. A chamberlain
came to announce that Their Majesties were approaching
the Presence Chamber. Marianne and Eilish immediately
took up their posts beside the instrument, and when the
royal party made its entrance, the King and Queen surrounded by a gaggle of ladies and gentlemen, they both
dropped into the deepest curtsies they could manage.

George III had just passed his twenty-fifth birthday. He
was smooth-cheeked and round-eyed as a boy, lean and
smiling. His three years on the throne had so far not marked
him at all. His Queen was a bony woman with a long, thin
face. She wore her blond hair heavily powdered, arranged
over a high cage, and hanging in tight ringlets. Her narrow
body was made to look even more severe by the deeply
pointed, stiff bodice of her gown of gold-embroidered
linen. The King looked at the armonica with only idle curiosity, but Her Majesty was quite taken with it, coming
close to have a better look. Eilish took a step back, terribly
afraid of saying or doing the wrong thing. Marianne, how-

ever, who had met the Queen before, rose to the occasion.

Queen Charlotte's voice was high and nasal, with a heavy German accent. "So this is Mr. Franklin's glassy-chord? These are the glasses?"

"Yes, ma'am," Marianne said. "You see, the treadle is just here, and it is pumped with the feet, like this." She sat down and demonstrated. As the glasses began to revolve, the Queen gave a little exclamation. "Yes, ma'am," Marianne said. "And we play it this way." She put her little fingers on the spinning crystals and played a sweet triad in D major, then a chord in G, one in A, and back to D, with a nice passing tone.

"How lovely," Charlotte said. "We look forward to your little concert."

Marianne stood and curtsied, saying again, "Ma'am." Eilish, not knowing what else to do, curtsied with her.

There was still some time to wait, as the courtiers arranged Their Majesties and themselves in some specific order, the logic of which eluded Eilish. Eilish and Marianne stood shoulder to shoulder, and Eilish could feel Marianne trembling. "You're shaking," she whispered. "But you didn't seem at all nervous!"

Marianne didn't look at her. " 'Struth, I feel I could be sick."

Eilish had been feeling quite sick with nerves herself. She must, though, she thought, be strong for Marianne. Perhaps if she pretended calmness, she would feel it. "Never mind," she said with a lift of her chin, patting Marianne on the arm. "We shall do the armonica a proud turn today." And at that she did feel more calm, at least a bit.

When at last the moment arrived, it was a great relief for Eilish to sit at the armonica, dip her fingers into the water, and begin. She played "Eileen Aroon" and "The Fair-haired Child," and "Baidhin Elhemhi," and though the courtiers, and even Their Royal Majesties, talked and visited throughout, a polite patter of applause sprang up at the end of each tune. When Marianne sat down at the armonica, however, a silence fell in the Queen's Presence Chamber. Eilish looked up in surprise, having forgotten, since they had become so familiar, that her friend was a well-known and respected harpsichordist. The Queen now rested her chin on her fist, leaning forward in her enormous, elaborately carved chair. Though King George spoke to her, Charlotte was intent upon Marianne and did not answer.

Marianne played "Where Sheep May Safely Graze" and a simple sonatina of Papa Haydn's that had been written for the harpsichord. Her technique was a marvel, each bit of melody emerging from the greater texture to shine like the golden threads adorning the white linen of Her Majesty's gown. And then, very clearly and slowly, Marianne played "Come Unto Him."

The applause for this was enthusiastic, filling the high-ceilinged chamber. Even Her Majesty rose and came forward to congratulate Marianne. Afterward, of course every courtier wanted to touch the armonica, but Eilish was so relieved at their having comported themselves well that she didn't mind in the least. Marianne smiled and curtsied, and looked perfectly serene.

It wasn't until they were on their way home in the carriage, after what seemed an interminable time waiting until Their Majesties and their attendants were quite finished with looking at the armonica and trying out its sound, and then the long effort of packing the cups and disassembling the spindle, that Eilish saw how strained Marianne truly was. She laid her head against the plush seat of the carriage and closed her eyes. The powder on her face was a desiccated and cracked mask, and her closed eyelids looked bruised. She choked on a tiny sob, and tears ran down her cheeks.

"Why, Marianne," Eilish said, tired herself, and fighting her headache. "What is it? Whatever is the matter? I thought everything went so well!"

"Oh, no, no, Eilish, did you not hear? My trill, in the Haydn, it was deplorable! And the Handel—how Her Maj-

esty must despise me, to so poorly represent her country-
man! Oh, I will never play again, I swear it! Never!"

And though Eilish protested, and praised her performance at length and in detail, Marianne would not be con-
soled, but cried and lamented until at last, in a state of utter
exhaustion, she fell asleep with her head on Eilish's lap.
Eilish held her, stroking her hair, and watched out of her
window as the carriage made its slow journey back to Craven Street.

29

San Francisco, September 2018

"CHARLIE, can't you leave it? You can't still be tweaking the damned program!"

Erin stood in the center of their suite at the Marriott, her hands on her hips. She knew how sharp her voice sounded. It was fear making her strident. Charlie, wearing headphones, was bent over the Akai. He had been, it seemed to her, working at the Akai for weeks on end, with breaks only for sessions with Gene and physical therapy. It was late, past midnight, and a heavy fog had rolled in off the Bay.

The face he turned to her now was white, with eyes stretched too wide. Strands of hair escaped his ponytail and hung in sweat-darkened fronds over his forehead. He pulled off the headphones and tossed them onto a couch. "Leave it, Erin," he said hoarsely. "Go back to bed."

"Charlie—you're the one that should go to bed! You'll be a mess tomorrow."

The first *Mars* rehearsal would begin at ten the next morning. They had met with the New Music Group's artistic director already, and Charlie had supervised the arrangement of the sensory emitters around the stage. The augmented sensory program was complete, loaded, coordinated with the score. There was nothing more, there could be nothing more, for Charlie to work on.

"I'll go soon," he said, looking away from Erin, out into the night. Yellow city lights winked faintly through a silvery fog.

Erin tried to speak more gently. "Charlie—what's wrong? Why are you still at it?"

He didn't answer. He rolled away from the synthesizer and went to the window. She took a step toward him, but the angle of his head, the set of his narrow shoulders, constrained her.

"*Mars* will be fabulous," she said weakly, searching for something to make him respond.

"I think so, too."

"So—why are you still—"

He spun his wheelchair around, fast. He had grown very strong in the last months. "Erin," he said. His voice was tight. "I'm your brother. I love you, and I know you love me. But you can't do everything for me."

"But I don't even know what you're doing!" she said, her voice rising with tension.

"You don't need to know," he said. He pulled up one corner of his mouth in a semblance of a smile. "Gotta do some things myself." He turned the chair again to face out into the night. The city's glow made a halo for his blond head.

Slowly, unhappily, Erin went back to bed. But she lay awake, staring up at the blank ceiling, for an hour before she slept.

IN the fifth row of the Titus Theater, Erin sat with the artistic director of the New Music Group to listen to the first reading of *Moving Mars*. She would go up to her instrument after the read-through, to add her part, but she wanted to see what the augmented sensory program would feel like from the house. The director, a taciturn man of about fifty, sat with the full score on his knees. The houselights were up. A few other people were scattered around the theater, musicians of the group who didn't have a part in *Mars,* some relatives, one or two of the press who had asked to observe the rehearsals. Charlie sat alone, in a darkened back aisle, his wheelchair glinting in the shadows.

The conductor turned to the house, shading her eyes against the lights. "Everyone ready out there?"

The director called, "Whenever you are," and turned on the score light he had clamped to the seat in front of him. The houselights dimmed, and conversation quieted.

Erin had spent months on *Mars*, and she knew the music thoroughly, not just the glass harmonica part, but the strings and the winds as well. What she didn't know was how they would supplement the augmented sensory program. She leaned deeply into the plush of her seat and closed her eyes. She only just stopped herself from crossing her fingers.

Erin was accustomed to having a physical reaction to music, but when the music of *Mars* began, her response was profound, even alarming. The emissions began with the first notes of the violin, and intensified when the flute entered. Erin's eyes flew open, and she gripped the arms of her seat. She had to restrain herself from jumping to her feet.

She had an almost irrepressible urge to dance, to whirl as the planet whirled, to act out the complexity of human emotions that spilled from the stage. She stared, openmouthed, at the orchestra, her mind supplying her own missing part, her fingers and toes and eyelids and knees throbbing under the stimuli of the sensory emitters. When the planet moved, Erin felt as if her blood rocked on real waves of disrupted gravity as the planet settled, like a great ship docking, into its new home in the continuum. She felt the gigantic globe's instantaneous transmission through the vastness of space, and she gasped for air at the shock of it, the intensity, the ecstasy.

And all of this, her mind recognized, without even the glass harmonica. How much stronger, how deeply affecting, would *Mars* be when glass music was added?

When the reading was over, Erin found herself perspiring, her mouth dry, her eyes burning. She glanced at the director, sitting next to her. He gave her an uneasy smile. She looked around at the others in the hall. Some leaned forward, listening, interested. One sat back against his seat, his hands gripping the armrests as Erin had done. Another paced at the back of the hall, shaking his hands as if they were wet, or as if they hurt.

Charlie was right. Reactions would vary widely.

There was going to be an uproar at the premiere of *Moving Mars*.

Erin got up and went to where her brother sat motionless, staring at the stage. She touched his shoulder, and he jumped. "Sorry," she said quickly. "But did you like it? Are you pleased?"

He looked up at her. His eyes had darkened to indigo. His hands were clenched together in his lap. "It's perfect," he said hoarsely.

"Charlie—we'll rehearse with the glass harmonica now. But I think you should go to the hotel. Sleep."

"I don't need to sleep."

"You look like hell," Erin said sharply.

He managed a wan smile at that. "Hey, that's my sister speaking. Go on, get up there. Let's see if you've still got your stuff."

"I know the piece, Charlie," she muttered as she walked away. It was easier to feign irritation than to admit her anxiety. Not about *Mars*—she was certain Charlie was right. It was perfect. But she was afraid for Charlie.

Being in the center of the music was quite a different experience. Erin was able to hear the piece as pure music, with the emitters pointed away from the stage, out into the audience. But she saw that the person who had been pacing at the back of the hall after the first reading lasted only a few moments into the second before escaping out the front doors. Several others were up and moving after just a few bars. And before the piece was half done, the director stood up and clapped his hands together, twice. The conductor whirled, outraged at the interruption. She clicked her baton on her stand to stop the music, and then stood, arms folded, glaring at the director.

Charlie rolled swiftly down the aisle, and the director hurried along the row of seats to confer with him. Erin turned off the power of the glass harmonica and waited, straining to hear their voices. Around her the players murmured and shifted, retuned their instruments, made marks in their scores. The director was shaking his head, Charlie was speaking swiftly, gesturing. It was too far away to see the tremors of his hands, but Erin knew they were there. She had seen the difficulty Charlie had at breakfast, how he held his coffee cup with both hands.

She was just about to leave the stage when the director turned and went back to his seat. Charlie rolled close to the stage and gave instructions to the man operating the sensory emitters. He glanced up at Erin and the other players. "Turning 'em off," Charlie rasped. "For now."

WHEN the rehearsal broke for lunch, the director signaled to Erin and to Charlie to join him and the conductor in his office. It was a small room, especially with Charlie's wheelchair crowded in among the other chairs. Erin stood, tension knotting the back of her neck. Charlie's gloved hands clutched the wheels of his chair as he waited with his jaw set, his eyes hard. The conductor looked bewildered.

"What is it? What's the problem? It's a great piece!"

The director nodded. "Musically, it's great. It's the augmented sensory program."

"What about it?"

"He thinks it's too strong," Charlie said. Erin was surprised at the level tone of his voice. He looked as if he wanted tc shout.

"It makes you want to come right out of your seat," the director said gloomily. "It was okay the first time, but when the glass harmonica is added—it's too much! I'm worried about liability. I'm afraid there'll be a riot!"

"Ah. *Rite of Spring*," Charlie said. His lips twisted.

Erin gave a little gasp of incredulous laughter. "Stravinsky?" she said. "You think *Mars* is going to shock them that much?"

The director protested, hands spread in a gesture of helplessness. "We can't afford any kind of disturbance! We're a small organization, a new hall—new music is always struggling to be heard, and we get plenty of criticism as it is for the stuff we try."

Charlie murmured, with a flash of his old humor, "That's why they call it new music."

The conductor put her hand flat on the desk. "I think we should go for it. If we're gonna go down, let's go down in flames. I mean, you're talking about *Rite of Spring*—now, a hundred years later, that's standard repertoire!"

There was a long silence after that. Erin bit her lip and stared at the floor, wishing there were a window to open, or a fan. Charlie put his head back against his chair and closed his eyes, his face white with fatigue. The conductor glared at the director. The director finally, under the pressure of silence, gave in. "Okay," he growled. "But we warn people."

Charlie sighed and opened his eyes. "Okay," he said. He turned his chair, maneuvered through the cramped space, and left the office. Erin followed.

She was startled, as she crossed the stage, to see Ashley Adams's thick figure waiting backstage. Charlie rolled away toward his dressing room, and Erin stopped to greet Ashley. "I didn't know you were coming," she said. "What are you doing in San Francisco?"

The broadcaster waved her unlit cigarette in Charlie's

direction. "Doing a piece on your brother and this augmented music," she said with a grin. "The station actually
paid for me to be here. Think Charlie will talk with me?"

"I'll have to see if he's up to it. We've had kind of a
bad morning."

"Look, ask him, will you? I'll take the two of you to
lunch. Get you out of this place for a while."

Erin left Ashley in the corridor and went to knock on
Charlie's dressing room door. He didn't answer. She listened for a moment, and then put her hand on the knob.

The door bumped against something, and Erin saw the
tire of Charlie's wheelchair in the opening. Alarmed, she
pushed the door farther, and put her head around it.

Her brother was standing, about two feet away from his
wheelchair. Standing on his feet, without assistance. His
face was scarlet with effort, and he swayed. But he was
standing, more or less erect, completely without support.

"Omigod, Charlie . . ." Erin breathed.

He didn't answer. He took another step, a wavering,
crooked step, but he didn't fall. Erin slipped in through the
door, around the wheelchair. Charlie put up a hand and
said, "Don't help me."

"I won't," she whispered. "But for godsakes, be careful."

He gave a little, breathless laugh at that, and took another step. Two steps more brought him to the chair before
the dressing table and he collapsed into it with a grunt of
relief. He took a deep, noisy breath, and met Erin's eyes in
the mirror. "I walked," he wheezed. His hand faltered, once,
twice, as he tried to push back damp strands of hair from
his eyes. "Did you see? I walked."

"I saw."

He gave a shaky laugh. "If only Gene were here," he
said, and the end of his sentence was almost a sob.

"Charlie—how?"

"I've been working. On my own."

"But—"

He threw up his hand to stop her words. The hand made a semicircle, back and forth, back and forth, out of his control. Erin pressed her fingers to her lips to keep from crying out. Charlie didn't seem to notice. "I have to do it for myself," he said. "I have to. Please don't argue with me, Erin. Not now, for godsakes. Erin—I *walked*."

THE twins sat with Ashley Adams on a rooftop, an open-air restaurant designed to look out over the cityscape. Cool sunshine shone on their table, but many floors below them the city lay drowned in fog. The curving top of the Golden Gate Bridge arched above the mist, glowing brilliant orange in the sunlight.

Ashley smoked. The waiter had asked, with the greatest courtesy, to see her card, and then wheeled a personal ventilator up behind her chair. It whirred quietly, processing the thin gray stream from her cigarette.

Charlie ordered carefully, searching out menu items uncontaminated by processing or pesticides or additives. Erin simply ordered what he did, local clams and oysters, pasta made on the premises, marinated California artichokes. Ashley ordered an enormous corned beef on rye and a martini. She sucked on an olive and fixed Charlie with her cheery gaze.

"So," she said. "You're setting the musical world on its ear, they tell me. So to speak."

Charlie smiled at her. He was much recovered, his hair smoothly brushed back into its ponytail, his face composed again. Only his hands betrayed him, and Erin saw that he kept them linked in his lap when he could. "This morning," he said dryly, "they compared me to Stravinsky."

"Sacre du Printemps?"

"Don't say that on your program, Ashley, okay?" Erin said hastily. "That won't be good for Charlie or the New Music Group."

"No, I won't. But the buzz is this augmented sensory

stuff might be dangerous. That they might make the audience sign forms, like the one I signed so I could smoke."

Charlie chuckled. "I don't know what they think's going to happen."

"Well, you know what happened in Paris, when *Rite of Spring* premiered."

Charlie said, "Don't worry, Ashley. No one's going to dance themselves to death during *Moving Mars*."

Erin's heart lurched. The unwelcome words, *Except maybe Charlie,* sprang into her mind and she shivered, suddenly cold in the September sunshine.

30

San Francisco, September 2018

DESPITE Ashley Adams's promise, the rumors about *Moving Mars* flashed through the musical community. The Titus Theater held six hundred people, and before the second rehearsal began, every seat was sold. On the night of the performance Erin and Charlie, arriving at the theater by limo, stared from the car windows in disbelief at the throng waiting at the front doors. People were shouting, waving tickets in the air, pushing at those in line. Scalpers slipped in among the crowd, hiding their brisk business from the watchful eyes of half a dozen police officers.

"Well, you wanted to make a splash, Charlie," Erin said lightly.

"A lot of those people are going to be disappointed," he replied. "They'll barely notice the difference."

"Yes, but there will be a few . . ."

"Oh, yes. There should be a few."

The limo worked through a press of traffic, contemp taxis, retro limos, a few private vehicles. The stage door was in an alley in the back, for which Erin was grateful. Charlie was highly recognizable in his wheelchair, and his picture, blond ponytail and slight form leaning in a relaxed way against the arm of his chair, had been in the *Chronicle* and the *Examiner* and an underground paper. They made their way up the ramp, Erin carrying her dress bag over one arm, her score under the other. Charlie was striking in his blue and silver tux. Mal had arrived the day before, and had spent the day at the theater conferring with the artistic director and the public relations manager. They found him pacing the corridor to the dressing rooms, his tux rumpled, his gray hair not as smoothly combed as usual.

"Mal?" Erin said as they came near. "Everything okay?"

He came to take her dress from her, and he nodded to Charlie. "Yeah, sure," he said nervously. "Everything's fine." He glanced over his shoulder. "Sarah's here."

"She is?" Erin followed his glance. "Where?"

"More to the point," Charlie said. "Why?"

"Oh, you know," Mal said vaguely, waving a freckled hand. "All this fuss."

They all went into the dressing room. Erin pulled off her T-shirt and jeans and put on a long slip. Charlie had decreed no black for *Mars*. He had picked out Erin's dress himself, a swirl of azure and vermilion and silver silk with long fitted sleeves and a deep V-neck. It clung to her slender hips and waist and pooled around her ankles. She pulled it on and turned for Charlie's inspection.

"I love it," he said. "You look like one of those movie goddesses from the thirties."

Mal sighed, and Erin shot him a glance. "You don't like it," she said.

He shook his head. "Oh, Erin, it's not that at all. It's just—you look so grown-up," he said dolefully. "And you're beautiful. Truly beautiful. I can't think of you as a child anymore."

Erin stared at him. "Why, Mal," she said, surprised to feel a lump in her throat. "What a nice thing to say." Impulsively, she went to kiss his cheek. He cleared his throat, and patted her shoulder.

She was brushing her hair when Sarah came into the dressing room.

Sarah looked perfect, as she always did. Her dress was long, a deep midnight-blue, and she wore silver earrings and a silver clasp in her pale chignon. She pressed her cool cheek to Erin's, and then, bending, to Charlie's. "You're both looking well," she said.

Erin turned to the mirror and began applying a glossy lipstick. "Why didn't you tell us you were coming, Sarah?"

Sarah smiled at her in the mirror. "A surprise," she said. "I haven't seen Charlie in months, and of course I wanted to hear the new piece."

"Oh, of course," Erin said. She saw Charlie's warning glance, and she turned away from the mirror to wash her hands, being very careful not to splash the dress.

"Glad you're here," Charlie said politely.

"Charlie," Sarah said. "I haven't had a report from Dr. Berrick. Are you making any progress? It's been some time now."

"We're making some progress," he said noncommittally.

"Well then," Sarah said. "That's good. I'd like to hear about it." She stood a little uncertainly in the center of the room. "Well, good luck with the piece, darlings."

"Thanks for coming, Mother," Charlie said.

Mal said, "We should get to our box, Sarah." He held the door for her. "It will be wonderful, kids, I know it will."

"Hope so," Charlie said.

"Of course it will," Sarah said. "And so much press!"

Charlie chuckled. "Very true." When the dressing room door closed behind Sarah and Mal, Charlie said wryly to Erin, "Damage control."

"What?"

"That's why Sarah's here. Damage control. There was a teeny clip in the *New York Times* about augmented sensory music, and how if it caught on, it would destroy classical music as we know it. Sarah and Mal are already on the p.r. thing. Make sure the press is positive. 'Crippled boy and child prodigy create cutting edge of music.' "

Erin made a face as she dried her hands. "Jeez. You have a future in the tabloids, I think, Charles Rushton."

"Hope I won't need it," he muttered.

The stage manager knocked on the door. "Five minutes, Miss Rushton."

She called her response, and then looked down at her brother. "Charlie, why didn't you tell Sarah? That you took some steps on your own?"

His grin was lopsided, wicked. "I'm going to surprise her," he said. "I'm going to walk into the Boston house at Christmas."

Erin laughed. "But there won't be any press."

"That's the idea."

Charlie opened the dressing room door for Erin. As she passed him, he said, "Listen, E. Play the hell out of it, okay?"

She bent and pressed her cheek to his hair. "Oh, I will, Charlie. I will."

ERIN had never heard such a hush at the beginning of a concert. The applause as the conductor made her entrance, and then Erin hers, was polite, but the air in the theater was thick with suspense. The clapping died away quickly, leaving an uneasy, breathing silence in the hall.

The holographic projections began with the planet spinning slowly above the heads of the audience, a muddy red, ponderous globe. The color of the planet changed gradually, beginning the transition to blue and green, dark at first and then gradually brightening. When the flute entered, and after it the glass harmonica, the planet began to glisten with lights scattered across its face in clusters of white and yellow and silver.

Charlie had written the first melodic phrases as starry fragments—not the warlike Mars of Holst, but the colorful Mars of Bear. The alien world came alive as the music spoke of life, love, conflict, progress. Underlying rhythms grew more complex. The strings and the winds and then the glass harmonica each had exposed moments, individual passages. And through it all, Erin knew, the sensory emissions were intensifying the experience of those in the hall. Despite the emitters being directed away from the stage, she could feel some of the stimuli, at her elbows, on the back of her neck, in her temples.

The conflict grew, and the harmonies clashed and piled one upon another. The danger became a physical sensation.

Moving Mars was undivided, a seamless sweep of music in which each new idea welled and grew and spilled into the next without break. At the moment of decision, the moment the planet moved, the audience in the hall gasped as one being. Someone cried out, and someone else laughed like an unruly child. Erin felt like laughing herself.

The music swelled in a crescendo built upon all the previous melodic and rhythmic and harmonic material. Every player in the ensemble was involved, *embouchures* abuzz, fingers flashing, arms and elbows and hands engaged. Erin pressed all her fingers against her spinning glasses. The cadence was a huge crash of sound that rose to a nearly unbearable volume and then was cut off, abruptly, dramatically, with a great slash of the conductor's baton. In the sudden, echoing silence, the maestra grinned triumphantly at the orchestra, and then laid down her baton and turned to take her first bow.

But beyond the footlights the uproar had begun.

People jumped to their feet. Some were shouting, some were hurrying to the exits, others were clapping and calling for the composer. The surge of emotion from the hall was palpable, a wave, a tide as powerful as any sensory emission. Erin, alarmed, took a step back. She felt exposed, vulnerable. She had never thought of a concert crowd as dangerous, but at this moment, she was afraid of the audience. She looked around for Charlie. He was behind the proscenium, leaning forward in his chair, looking out into the audience. He was smiling—no, he was grinning, enormously, delighted with the disturbance he had created.

Just as Erin glanced back into the house, someone, a man, jumped up on stage. He put his hand directly on the footlights, which Erin knew were burning hot, but he seemed not to feel it. He was young, with wild hair and eyes, and he came right at her—or at her instrument. She couldn't tell which.

She cast about for help, but every single orchestra player was staring, mesmerized, into the tumult in the hall. Charlie saw, and began to roll toward her, but his way was blocked by chairs and stands and the conductor's podium.

Erin stepped in front of the glass harmonica as the boy pushed past the cellos and stumbled toward her. She had no weapon, nothing but her hands, but she held those out as if to block his way. He came closer, mumbling something in a choked voice, and she saw that tears rolled freely down his cheeks. She took another step, hoping to keep him from her precious instrument. He was six inches taller than she, and far heavier, and he lunged forward, almost falling. She put her small body in his path, and thrust her shoulder against his chest. She planted her feet, grunting as she tried to stop his lunge, his reach toward the crystal cups gleaming under the stage lights.

And then a tall figure in a charcoal tux, old-fashioned glasses shining in the brilliant stage lights, put a long, strong arm between Erin and the intruder. She gasped with surprise, and relief.

Gene Berrick held the hysterical boy, gripping his shoulders, pulling him back from Erin, from the glass harmonica. His low, pragmatic voice cut through the clamor. "Calm down, son. Take a breath. You're all right. Calm down." Seconds later, Charlie reached them, having worked his way around the back of the orchestra.

Erin gripped her brother's arm, her knuckles white. "Charlie, did you know it would be like this? This—hysteria?"

He grinned up at her. "Well, I didn't know some music-crazed kid was going to jump up on the stage and come after you, but otherwise—yeah, I had an idea."

Gene turned around now, a hand under the youth's arm, allowing the boy to take one step toward the glass harmonica. He was saying quietly, "There, you see? It's just an instrument. These glass cups revolve, and Erin puts her fingers to them to make the sound, like rubbing your wet finger around the rim of a wineglass. You see? Now, Erin and Charlie have things they need to do. I'll walk you back. And I think we'd better do something about that burn."

He turned the boy around and led him away. An older man was waiting anxiously at the footlights, and Gene conferred with him a moment, then handed the young man off to him. Soon he worked his way back to Erin and Charlie. Around them the musicians, having given up on applause and bows or any other orderly end to the performance, were hastily packing up their instruments and leaving the stage. Chairs and stands were overturned, and programs lay tossed on the floor.

"So what was with the kid?" Charlie asked Gene.

Gene Berrick stood with his hands in his pockets, looking down at Charlie with a bemused expression. "I expect you have a pretty good idea, Charlie Rushton," he said laconically.

"Yeah." Charlie laughed and backed his wheelchair. "Come on, E, let's get this thing off the stage before somebody crashes into it."

"I'll help," Gene said. A stagehand brought the padded box from backstage, and Gene and Erin lifted the spindle and cups and fitted them inside. Charlie reached to unplug the speed control. Erin looked away from his wavering hand, glancing up at Gene. Gene was staring at Charlie, at the hand that reached once, twice, failing to grasp the heavy cord. Gene bent and seized the plug to pull it from the outlet. Charlie quickly turned his chair away, and Gene watched him with a bleak expression in his eyes.

Erin bit her lip, gazing out into the hall. The stage manager had turned the lights up full, and that seemed to settle the crowd. Many people stood beside their seats, looking bewildered. Others thronged the aisles, some staring up at the stage, some talking excitedly together. Near the stage, leaning against the wall with her unlit cigarette dangling from her mouth, Ashley Adams watched the scene. She caught Erin's eye, grinned and waved the cigarette. In the wings, Sarah Rushton stood with her hands on her hips, her face a mask. A reporter stood with her, asking questions, writing down her terse answers.

Erin and Gene finished packing up the harmonica and made their way out to the loading dock, the stagehand following with the cases. Charlie came after, the scores in a fat pile on his lap. Sarah and Mal had both disappeared, but Ashley was waiting for them.

"Hey, kids," she said jovially. "How's about a postmortem? Bar at the Marriott?"

ERIN went to her room to change into jeans, and then came down to meet Gene, Charlie, and Ashley in the cocktail lounge of the hotel. It was a converted cable car, fitted right into the main floor. Everything in the Marriott was thirties, the lobby lined with waxworks of prisoners at Alcatraz, one viewwindow showing workers high in the cables of the Golden Gate Bridge and another opposite that featured oyster sellers on the Wharf. Erin stepped up into the cable car, where the others were waiting at a table built out of the original turnstile.

Charlie started to move his wheelchair, to make room, but Gene stood up. "Here, Erin," he said. "Sit by me." He was still in his tux, and she had a moment now to appreciate his appearance. His lean form was dramatic in the narrow-lapeled suit. He wore a pale gray collarless shirt underneath the jacket, and it set off his brown skin and clear eyes to perfection.

She slid in on the banquette next to him. "I forgot you were coming," she said ingenuously.

"More important things on your mind, perhaps," he said.

"Oh, sorry," she apologized. "It's been a strange night. But I'm so glad you're here!"

"What would that boy have done?" Ashley Adams asked, with a boisterous laugh. "Carried Erin off the stage? Or smashed the glasses?"

"I think he was just trying to understand what happened to him," Gene said. "He was particularly sensitive." He glanced at Charlie. "It was certainly effective," he said. "And affecting. Maybe more than you expected."

Charlie laughed and waved a hand, then caught it back in his lap. Erin noticed he hadn't picked up the glass of Campari that had been set before him. "I expected it," he said. His eyes were defiant. He looked like a child caught with his hand in the cookie jar.

"Really," Gene said. The tension between them made Erin squirm.

Ashley, unaware, leaned forward, her martini half-consumed already, her cigarette feeding its stream of smoke into the personal ventilator behind her. "I didn't feel that much," she said. "What am I missing? The music was wonderful, though, Charlie. Beautiful score, really incredible. But the sensory stuff—I suppose my sense of the drama of the piece was enhanced, but I don't know that I had an augmented experience."

Charlie cast a sidelong glance at Gene as he said, "It affects different people differently."

Ashley looked at Gene. "What do you think, Dr. Berrick?" she demanded.

"I would guess that Charlie's emissions play directly on the limbic system," Gene said. "Seat of emotions."

Charlie nodded. "Since everyone's brain and nervous system has its own characteristics, everyone reacts differently to stimuli—music, for example, or poetry, or a painting—or sensory emissions. Especially when it's combined with the glass harmonica—"

"Why?" Erin interrupted. "What does it have to do with the glass harmonica?"

Charlie chuckled. "Come on, you can relax, E. But you know glass music has a particularly intense effect. You feel it, I know you do. I feel it."

"What's it like, then, if you're sensitive?" Ashley was intent, her cigarette dangling from her fingers, her bright red lips pursed.

Charlie said, "Some feel their hair stand on end. Some feel nervous, or emotional, or like they want to dance. Some, apparently—" He shrugged. "Some—like Erin's visitor—have a sort of *gestalt* experience. All over. And they can't distinguish their physical reactions from their emotional ones."

"So the Stravinsky thing wasn't far off," Ashley said, crushing out the cigarette in the ventilator receptacle.

"Maybe not," Charlie said with a laugh. "Ask me in a hundred years."

Later, Gene walked Charlie and Erin up to their suite. Charlie said good night and disappeared into his bedroom, and Erin and Gene stood beside the enormous realwindow, looking down on the soft lights of San Francisco. The Bay Bridge was a glowing bracelet in the distance.

"Did he steal it from you?" Erin asked bluntly.

Gene Berrick glanced down at her. He looked relaxed, his glasses pushed up on his head, his brow clear.

"You're not upset," she said, surprised.

"No," he said. "Not really. Charlie already knew about augmented sensory emissions when he came to me. I suppose he—let's say borrowed—my techniques, but it doesn't matter."

"But did you think he pushed it too far?"

"No. No, I think it was exciting—and beautiful. I've never felt anything quite like it."

"So you're sensitive to it."

"Very." He turned and leaned against the window frame, looking out at the city. "Your playing was magnificent, Erin. I haven't heard you play before. And there *is* something about glass music . . ."

Her lips parted as she watched his fine profile. Her whole body still sang with the adrenaline of the performance, her arms, her thighs, the small of her back. She didn't think she had ever felt so utterly alive. What would he do, this restrained, disciplined man, if she stepped close to him, touched his cheek with her palm, pressed herself against his long body? And how could he not feel the energy between them? It was like the pull of gravity between two worlds, a force drawing them together. She had to fight it, pull back, grasp at something to restrain herself.

Breathlessly, she said, "I guess you were my hero tonight."

He turned back to her, smiling. "You weren't in much danger." He hesitated, uncharacteristically. Finally he said, his voice low, "Erin. You were so lovely, in that dress—I could have—I could hardly—" He shook his head.

She almost took the step. She could feel, in anticipation, his hands, his lips.

But he tore his eyes from her face, and looked out to follow the winking lights of a plane approaching over the bay. "Listen, Erin. Watch Charlie, would you? I'm worried about him."

"You noticed his hands," she said.

"Not just that," he said. His face was very still, remote again.

"What, then?" she asked, despairing.

"The sensory emissions—you felt them." She nodded. "Very tactile," he said. "I think Charlie's been experimenting on himself."

"You mean, because you wouldn't do it . . ."

He turned back to her, and there was that pain in his eyes. What must it be like to live with that old pain, always with you? Still his voice was utterly controlled. "No, I wouldn't do it. But I—without meaning to—I taught him how to do it himself."

"You couldn't have stopped him. Charlie's set his mind to walking again."

"But I don't think I made the risks clear to him."

"It wouldn't have made any difference! He's brilliant— he must have known. It's been his passion for fifteen years. You should have seen some of the things he's tried, some of the quacks he's been involved with."

"And now I'll be one of those. The quacks."

She winced at the bitterness in his voice. She dared to seize one of his hands in both of hers. "No," she said tensely. "Not one of the quacks. A fine doctor, a brilliant one, who was willing to put it all on the line for Charlie."

He turned his hand to hold hers with strong fingers, and hope flamed in her. "We'll see," he said bleakly. They stood like that for a moment, and again she almost did it, almost bridged the distance. But as she was trying to make up her mind, he squeezed her hand and released it, and she felt suddenly shy again. She gave him an awkward smile, and turned back to the night view of San Francisco.

CHARLIE called out to Erin, early in the morning. She woke from a heavy, sweet sleep, from a dream she didn't want to leave. She sat up, blinking, searching for the clock. "Charlie? Charlie, what is it?"

"Erin," he called again. His voice was high and full of fear. "Erin, I need you. Please. God, Erin. I can't see."

31

ERIN ran from her bedroom to Charlie's, her heart in her mouth, her nightgown tangling around her legs. He was sitting up in bed, wearing a pair of silk pajama bottoms. His hair hung in loose fine strands past his bare shoulders. His face was utterly white.

"Charlie?" Erin gasped.

He turned to her, and she saw that his eyes were glazed, unfocused. They shifted slightly from side to side, as if trying to make something out in darkness. "Erin," he repeated. "I can't see."

Cold terror gripped Erin's heart. She moved slowly, as if wading through frigid water, to her brother's side, and sat down on the bed next to him. When he felt her weight sink into the mattress, he reached out to her, and she caught his blundering hand in hers. She could scarcely speak for the tension that closed her throat. She croaked, "You can't see anything? Nothing at all?" He shook his head in misery, and closed his eyes. Erin put her arms around him and held him to her like a child, her cheek on his tousled hair. "Oh, god, Charlie," she said, over and over. "Oh, god."

They sat like that for some minutes. Erin didn't know

who was trembling more, she or Charlie. She dared not try to stand until they were both a little calmer. When she felt a semblance of control return to her muscles, she helped Charlie into his chair and wheeled him out into the sitting room. "We have to call Gene," Erin said, her mouth dry with fear.

Charlie nodded. "He'll be furious with me," he said in a low tone.

"What? Why?"

"Because I've been using augmented sensory emissions to boost his program."

"Moving Mars?" Erin breathed.

He nodded.

"He won't be angry! He'll be terrified! I'm terrified!"

"He should be angry," Charlie said. "This will totally screw up his results."

"Results? Dammit, Charlie! Who cares about results? You can't see, and you're worried about Gene's results?"

"But you don't know—" Charlie said miserably. He stared over her head, his eyes blank, his mouth twisted.

"What?"

"Mother threatened to stop our work. Said the results didn't justify the program, the research didn't support his thesis. She said—" He broke off.

"What, Charlie? What did she say?"

"I was supposed to be in the exercise room with Ted, but I eavesdropped on their phone conversation. In Seattle. She said something nasty about his training. Said she'd report him for unethical experimentation. You should have seen her—cold as ice, threatening him."

Erin could imagine the way Sarah had looked, and she knew too well how Gene must have looked. She remembered the day in the park, his closed expression, his immobile features. Her heart ached, for Charlie, for Gene. She rolled the chair to the window. "Can you see the light, Charlie?" she asked. He shook his head. She turned the chair toward the center of the room, then spoke to the phone console.

It flicked on, but before she could ask for Gene's room, someone knocked on the door. Erin hesitated. How were they going to hide this? She had no idea at all. With a sinking heart, she opened the door.

Sarah Rushton stood in the doorway, wearing a black tunic over narrow trousers, carrying a gray leather overnight case. "Good," she said by way of greeting. "You're both up. I hoped I could see you before I go back to Boston."

Weakly, Erin said, "Hi, Sarah." She hurried to stand beside Charlie's chair. He reached for her hand, finding it on the first try, and squeezed her fingers, hard.

Sarah didn't seem to notice. She stepped in, dropping the overnight case on a chair and casting a cursory glance around the suite. "Such a madhouse last night—but I think we can keep the press calm about it. Mal and I worked till very late—I called some people I know here, at the *Chronicle*."

Erin stared at her, frozen.

"It's a good piece, Charlie," Sarah went on, smoothing her hair with both hands. "I don't know about the sensory augmentation—where did you come up with such an idea?" She stopped, and fixed the two of them with a steel-blue gaze. "Are you two all right? What's happening?"

Charlie smiled in his mother's direction, and rolled his chair a little forward as if he might go to her. Erin couldn't think of a thing to say or do. "We're fine," Charlie said. "Little short on sleep. Lot of excitement last night."

"Yes." Sarah eyed them, and fiddled with her diamond earring. "Well, I feel certain there's no real risk to audiences, Charlie, but still, it might be a good idea to moderate it a bit. It's groundbreaking, though, and that can't hurt your reputation—Mal agrees with me, by the way."

"Oh, good. Mal," Charlie said blithely. "And the sensory

augmentation is just something I've been—been working on. Got the idea from Dr. Berrick."

Erin cast about for something, anything, to say. Charlie gazed up at his mother as if she were as clear as ever, standing there. What if she moved? What if she came close?

And suddenly, as if she had snapped out of a daydream, Erin knew what she needed to do. She had to get Sarah out of the hotel suite before Charlie's act collapsed. "Mother," she said quickly. "Have you got time for breakfast before you go? I'm famished."

"Well—I have a little time, I guess. Not long. I could have some coffee, at least."

Erin said, "Great. Let me just throw on some jeans."

She hurried, not bothering with underwear. She heard Sarah speaking to Charlie, and his answer, but she couldn't understand the words. She dragged a brush through her hair, and reached for her toothbrush, then decided it would take too long. She dashed back out into the suite, her sandals in her hand.

Sarah turned a startled face to her. "You're going like that?"

Erin looked down at herself. The reff T-shirt had been on the floor under the bed, and her jeans had been crumpled up on a chair. Her clothes were as wrinkled as if she had pulled them out of a wastebasket. "Oh, well," she said with a laugh. "Call it casual."

"Call it messy," Charlie said.

Erin looked at him, thinking, hoping, that perhaps his sight had cleared, but she knew by the way he held his head that it had not. Her heart quivered with anxiety. She grinned fiercely at her mother. "Come on, Sarah," she said.

Sarah looked at Charlie. "Charlie, darling? Don't you want breakfast?"

He shook his head. "I've got some exercises to do. Have a good flight."

Sarah went to her son and kissed his cheek, drawing

back to look into his face. He smiled as comfortably as if
it were any of a hundred farewells they had made, and Erin
opened the door to hurry Sarah away. As she closed it, she
looked back. Charlie was leaning forward slightly in his
chair, staring blindly at the door. His face was rigid with
fear.

SOMEHOW Erin made it through breakfast with her
mother. Sarah told Erin all about her call to her friend at
the *Chronicle*, and the assurances she had received that the
bedlam of the night before would be downplayed, that
Charlie's music, and Erin's performance, would receive un-
biased reviews, at least in that newspaper. Erin told her
about Ashley Adams, and that she thought NPR would go
easy on it as well.

"That's good work, darling. That will please Mal—he's
worried about the San Antonio engagement," Sarah said.
"But I think it's going to be all right." She looked at her
slender gold watch. Despite her lack of sleep, Sarah's hair
and face were as always, perfectly groomed. "I'd better get
a cab, Erin," she said. "I'm booked on the commuter at
nine."

Erin walked with her to the entrance of the Marriott to
wait for the taxi. As they said goodbye, Sarah looked carefully at Erin. "Is Charlie all right?" she asked. "He seems
distracted."

Untruthfully, Erin said, "I think he's okay." Truthfully,
she added, "He's been working night and day on *Moving
Mars*."

"I wish this young doctor of his would keep in touch
with me."

"I'll ask Charlie about that."

Erin stood and waved and smiled as the taxi carried
Sarah away. The moment it turned the corner, she charged
back into the hotel and punched the elevator button, once,
twice, three times, burning with anxiety and impatience.

In the suite she found Charlie sitting in his chair, Gene crouched before him with a pencil flash, searching his eyes. "Oh, Gene, thank god."

He glanced at her briefly, then back at Charlie. "There's no physical evidence of damage to your eyes," he said in a level tone. "Whatever's going on here is neurological. We'll have to assess it back at the clinic."

"I know," Charlie said.

Erin said, "He's been using the augmented program on himself."

Gene flicked off the flashlight. "He's thrown his system out of balance. The neural paths are dislodged, shocked out of their pattern. It was his hands, now it's his eyes. It could have been something else—his hearing, sense of smell— almost anything."

Erin was almost afraid to ask. "Will he be able to see again?"

"Wish I knew," Gene said.

"I stood up yesterday," Charlie said, as if defending himself. "It worked, Gene. I stood up, without support, and I took a few steps. On my own."

"You took a terrible chance, Charlie," Gene told him.

"I know." Charlie hung his head, and Erin's heart ached with pity. He whispered, "I'm sorry, Gene. Sorry I jeopardized the work."

Gene's dark hand on Charlie's shoulder, touching his head, reminded Erin of the way he was with little Joey. His voice was gentle, too. "Don't worry about that now, Charlie. Let's get you home."

Erin pushed Charlie's chair into his bedroom, and helped him to find his toothbrush, brushed his hair back and tied his ponytail for him. She packed his clothes, and then went to do her own. As she left the bedroom, he said, "Erin? I'm sorry—I'm really sorry. I just wanted to walk. Just walk, like everyone else does."

She went back and kissed his cheek, glad he couldn't

see the tears that welled in her eyes. "I know, darling. I know."

In her bedroom she looked at herself in the mirror, and thought it was amazing Sarah had been willing to be seen with her in public. Her hair stood out in a ragged aureole, and her clothes were a disaster. She pulled them off and dressed all over again, more carefully this time. She found a silk blouse that was only slightly creased, and she put it on over a long, soft skirt. When her suitcase was packed, she went into the bathroom and brushed her teeth and combed her hair once again. She turned off the light, still looking into the mirror.

In the dimness, her wraith stood behind her, just at her shoulder. Erin's heart pounded as they stared at each other in the glass. The other girl's eyes were shadowed in her white, familiar face. Somehow Erin believed that the pain and fear of the last hours had called her, had brought her to Erin's attention. "I wish I could understand what you're trying to tell me," she whispered. "It's right there, isn't it? Right under my hand . . . but what is it? How can I help him?"

The girl's eyes were old in her young face. Her image seemed substantial, as if all Erin had to do was turn the light back on, and she would be as clear as day. Her hair was drawn severely back, and her blue dress hung like a sack from her thin shoulders. One small hand came up in a gesture that might have been farewell, or might have been sympathy. She didn't turn away, but faded gently, bit by bit, into nothingness, leaving only Erin's face in the mirror. Erin pressed her cold hands to her cheeks. She felt as lost as if she herself were the ghost.

And there was nothing she could do now but turn away, to go and help her sightless brother find his way home.

32

London, autumn and winter, 1763, 1764

MARIANNE'S performance in the Queen's Presence Chamber, despite her misgivings, prompted a number of invitations to play again, in and about London. Polly Stevenson, dashing in from Essex every two or three weeks, was most gratified by these invitations, but Marianne lamented them.

"I'm so sorry, Eilish," she said over and over again. "I've told them it's not my instrument, that I can't come without you."

Polly said, "And why can't you, Miss Davies? 'Tis exactly what Dr. Franklin should have liked!"

They were sipping tea in Mrs. Stevenson's parlor. Eilish was feeling almost well on this day, her head fairly clear, her hands quite steady. Throughout the summer every window in the house was left wide open, and Eilish went walking in the Strand almost every day, breathing hot clean air, feeling almost as young as she truly was.

Marianne said, "I cannot accept these engagements. The armonica is not mine."

"That doesn't signify," Polly said irritably. " 'Tis Dr.

Franklin's instrument. And I have his complete confidence.
I am to promote it in his absence."

"Still," Marianne said calmly. "Were it not for Eilish, I
would not know how to play it."

"That doesn't matter, does it? Surely even Eilish wants
people to hear his invention! And I feel certain 'tis exactly
what he would most desire."

Marianne shook her head, setting her dark ringlets swaying. "We do not know that, Miss Stevenson," she said.
"And until we hear from him on the matter, I prefer to wait.
In the playing of the glass armonica, I shall not plan any
program for myself alone. The concerts will be for Eilish
and me together, or for neither of us."

Polly sighed gustily. At her mother's warning glance,
she subsided, but her plump face was pinched with frustration.

Eilish didn't mind in the least seeing Polly disconcerted,
but she had no wish to hold back her friend. "Marianne . . ."
she began. Polly frowned and shook her head at the familiar
address. Eilish smiled, and repeated, for Polly's special benefit, "Dearest Marianne. I think you should accept one or
two of these invitations. I will go along, to help you with
the spindle and the cleaning of the cups. But of course, the
nobs—I mean, the people of society want to hear Marianne
Davies, not Eilish Eam. 'Tis the nature of things."

Marianne put out her hand to take Eilish's. "No, Eilish,
no. It is simply not fair."

Eilish shrugged. "Me da would've said, 'Fair's nice, but
winning's better.' "

Marianne and Mrs. Stevenson laughed. Polly folded her
arms and scowled her distaste at such a lack of gentility.
Marianne said, "I should have loved to meet your father,
Eilish."

"Aye. He was a treat, he was."

•   •   •

IT was on a chill night late in October when Eilish had a ghastly dream. It was very like the nightmares of her fever, but with a terrible difference. She woke from it sweating and trembling, only just stopping herself from crying out in horror. She threw back the coverlet and got up to stumble to the window. She knelt there, looking up into the moonless, star-filled midnight. "Please, holy angels," she prayed. "Please let it be only a dream. Please." The countless bright stars shone their cold light on her upturned face, and she felt small and alone and utterly powerless. "Please," she prayed hopelessly. "Please."

After a time she went back to bed, but she could not sleep. When the stars faded in the first light of dawn, she rose and washed and dressed. She slipped down to the kitchen as quietly as she could. Not even Cook was about so early.

Eilish had no appetite, but she wrapped a few pieces of fruit and cheese in a napkin and set out for Seven Dials.

The first signs of early morning commerce busied the Strand. Costermongers were loading their carts, and bakers' boys were filling wide baskets with their masters' wares. The day promised to be a gray one, the clouds heavy in the sky. Yet the air was fresh, the dew still sparkling on the dying beds of phlox and asters before the coffeehouses. The pumpkins and aubergines piled in the shop windows wore their autumn colors like flags.

Eilish walked quickly, taking no pleasure in the bustle around her. Her heart kept missing beats, making her press her hand to her bosom, her steps faltering. It had been a terrible dream, a fey dream. She went on praying as she walked, begging any spirit who heard her to take away this tingling of premonition, to erase her gift, anything, if only this nightmare would be false.

The sun was well up by the time she reached Seven Dials, its warmth filtered through the overcast. The smell of horse manure and emptied chamber pots lent their acrid edge to the scents of frying sausages and baking bread, the

whole mingling in a perfume that was purely the essence
of London. Eilish pressed on, hurrying to have it be over,
to *know*.

The Clock and Cup would not open its doors to business
for an hour yet, though the hired maid was sweeping the
front step. Eilish pushed through the door of the pub, step-
ping into a tired fog of spilled beer and old gin. It was dark,
and empty except for the scattered benches and as yet un-
cleaned tables. She went on to the door that led to the
family rooms and walked straight in without knocking.

Rose and her da and the Bailey children sat about the
scarred plank table, dispiritedly picking at bowls of stirabout. The twins' faces were grimy, their hair dark with dirt.
Rose's eyes were puffy, and she looked up at Eilish without
surprise. "Aye," she said in a hoarse tone. "I thought you
would know." Fresh tears started down her cheeks. Rose's
da and Thomas stared into their bowls in miserable silence.

Eilish froze in the doorway. It was true, then. Grief rose
as a scalding fountain in her bosom. Her knees weakened,
and she gripped the doorjamb for support. She whispered,
"How, Rose?"

Rose covered her face with her hands and sobbed, and
the twins, watching her, immediately burst into loud wails.

Thomas spoke up. " 'Twas the sweep's fault," he said,
his mouth twisted with the effort of holding back his tears.
"Rose told 'im Mackie wasn't to go up inside the chimney,
only to do the hearth and the bottom of the flue. But 'e
'adn't any other help, and a great lot of business, with the
winter comin' on. So 'e sent the boy up anyway." Thomas's
voice caught, and he covered his mouth and cleared his
throat, his eyes red. " 'E fell, did Mackie. Fell right down
the chimney, 'ead first. Died right there." Thomas looked
away, shamed, as a choking sob escaped him.

The lights of the kitchen, the darkness from the pub, the
misery of her nightmare, all whirled together over Eilish's
head. She stumbled, and thought she fell. She tried to speak,
but her voice was thick mud in her throat. There were no

tears. It was the fever returned, the burning in her chest, the aching in her head. She thought—she hoped, she wished fervently—that she was to die now, too. She longed to follow Mackie, to go with him to heaven where, surely, the angels were waiting for a sweet little boy who never had a hope in the world of surviving his childhood. Eilish closed her eyes, and waited for the darkness, for the light, for her own journey to begin.

But it wasn't to be.

Moments passed, and she rose again into consciousness, and the awful pain of knowing the truth. They spoke, she and Rose. Eilish, dry-eyed, very carefully placed her napkinful of fruit and cheese on the table before she went blindly, automatically, out into the street again, there being nothing for it but to walk back to Craven Street on legs that still moved, breathing air with lungs that still functioned, hearing the sounds of London with ears that still listened, feeling the pain of loss with every pulse of her heart which, though infinitely damaged, still beat. She knew she would sleep, and wake, many times yet in this life. And each time she would mourn the loss, the untimely and cruel and unbearable reality, of a little motherless boy who would never wake again.

BOTH Cook and Marianne did all they could to console Eilish. They tried to persuade her to eat, to rest, to talk, but she found comfort in none of those things. She shed no tears. She felt as dry as week-old bread, as desert sand. Her chest and her head ached unbearably, and she slept poorly, when she slept at all.

The only surcease Eilish found was at the armonica. From the first day of her mourning she closed herself in the laboratory and played the glasses by the hour, till her fingers were red and wrinkled, until her back ached as badly as her skull, until her ankles stiffened and could no longer pump the treadle. She played until Polly Stevenson pounded on the laboratory door, saying she would drive the whole house mad with her constant music. Marianne came every day, and when Eilish was too exhausted to play the armonica anymore, Marianne played for her. Sometimes they moved to the parlor, where Marianne would play the harpsichord while Eilish listened, staring blankly out the window. And so the weeks of Eilish's bereavement passed, through November, on into December.

Marianne offered, over and over, to teach Eilish the harpsichord. Before Christmas Eilish agreed, more to please Marianne than because she felt any energy for a new undertaking. She sat at the keyboard listlessly, following Marianne's instructions, hardly caring whether her fingers obeyed her or not.

Almost despite herself, she began to learn the different technique, the curving of the fingers, the slight percussive action of the fingertips on the keys that caused the strings to be plucked. There were scales, and finger exercises, and little tunes to learn by rote. At Christmas Marianne brought her a score as a present.

"I can't read any writing at all, Marianne," Eilish said. "How will I ever read these lines and circles and all these little specks?"

"You can, Eilish. I know you can," Marianne insisted. "Come now, for me, dear? Try."

And for love of Marianne, Eilish tried, though her brain felt thick and slow. She sometimes thought she must be unimaginably stupid, and wondered how Marianne could put up with her. But bit by bit, the beautiful logic of written music began to take shape in her mind. In January Marianne went to Bath for a week, to play a harpsichord concert. One cold, wet morning while she was away, Eilish sat down alone at the harpsichord, thinking to please Marianne by practicing her scales. Almost absently, she opened the score that waited there, expecting the usual confusion of lines and notes and inscrutable marks.

It was a very strange thing, Eilish thought later. The

swirl of notes and accidentals and clef marks resolved itself
quite suddenly into a meaningful pattern, as if it were a
faraway sight coming all at once into focus. It was, surprisingly, music. Eilish's hands stole to the keyboard, finding the fingerings, searching out the notes.

She found herself playing a little chorale of Mr. Bach's.
The chords fell under her fingers with ease, the passing
tones and chromatics were logical, and wonderfully musical. The pain in her breast, her constant companion for two
black months, receded. She played on, slowly, stumbling
here and there, to the end of the chorale. At the resolution,
the perfect subdominant, dominant, tonic cadence, she became aware that for the half hour she had been playing,
she hadn't thought of Mackie once. How could that be?
How could she so quickly forget?

In guilt and shame, in a hot and watery surging of grief,
she put her head down on her folded hands and sobbed.
Mackie had been dead for more than two months, and it
was the first time she had wept for him.

She ran upstairs to her room, still crying, and threw
herself upon her bed. Perhaps she would cry forever, perhaps she would die crying. Her throat hurt, her chest burned
with her weeping, but she relished it. It was like putting
out a fire—her tears were the water, her pain the flames.
She poured her tears over the burning wound of her loss,
and finally, after hours of solitary weeping, she fell into a
heavy slumber. Even as she slept, the tears rolled down her
face, so that when she woke, her pillow was sodden.

THE next day Marianne returned from Bath. She came
straight to Craven Street before even going to her own
home. Eilish was in the kitchen, lending Cook a hand with
the washing up after breakfast. Polly Stevenson, in London
for the season, sent Bessie down to fetch her.

Eilish hurried to take off her apron and go upstairs,
where she found Marianne sitting with Polly and Mrs. Ste-

venson. Marianne rose and embraced her, then held her at arm's length to look at her. "Why, Eilish," she said, her small features creased with concern. "Your face is quite puffy—your eyes are swollen. Why, dear," she exclaimed, and embraced her again, "you've been crying at last, haven't you? Poor darling, poor, poor thing."

Eilish hugged Marianne tightly. "Aye," she said. "All yestermorning and most of the afternoon. Like a lost babe, I cried. 'Twas a disgrace."

"Dearest heart, it was exactly what you needed," Marianne said warmly. They sat, Marianne still holding Eilish's hand and patting it. "Tears are so healing, don't you think so, Mrs. Stevenson? Miss Stevenson?"

Polly sniffed. "You're very fortunate, Eilish, that a person of Miss Davies's rank takes such an interest in you. 'Tis most kind of her. I hope you're properly grateful."

"Oh, Polly," said Mrs. Stevenson. "Do hold your tongue."

Polly's cheeks turned pink, and she simmered like a pot on the boil.

Marianne ignored all of this, and only smiled into Eilish's face. "Come now, tell me what you've been doing since I've been away."

"She does nothing but play the armonica till we're driven to distraction," Polly complained. "Or the harpsichord. I do think music is a wonderful and refined accomplishment, but a household needs some peace!"

Marianne fixed her sparkling dark eyes on Polly. "Perhaps, Miss Stevenson," she said, " 'Twould be better if Miss Eam came to me. To facilitate our work together. My household is quite accustomed to hearing music at all hours. My sweet little sister sings her scales, and I play mine, at any time we take a notion."

Mrs. Stevenson protested. "Oh, Miss Davies, no! I promised dear Benjamin—Dr. Franklin—I promised him Eilish would always be welcome here!"

Eilish smiled gratefully at Mrs. Stevenson. "Ta," she

said softly. "I don't know that I deserve such kindness. But I thank you."

Polly opened her mouth, and at a look from her mother, closed it again. Marianne said, "How kind of you, Mrs. Stevenson. You are a worthy friend to such a distinguished man. And perhaps now you will excuse us? Eilish and I have ever so much work to do." She stood up, and held out her little hands with the air of one making a great announcement. "We have an invitation to play the armonica for a *salon*. In Bath, if we can carry it so far! Everyone there is fascinated by the reports of the effects of the glasses' vibrations. They can hardly wait to hear Dr. Franklin's latest invention!"

THEY spent the rest of that day laying plans, Mrs. Stevenson alight with pleasure, Polly sullen with envy and resentment that it was Marianne, after all, who was truly the promoter of the armonica.

Eilish spoke quietly, and smiled when Marianne did. Still, when Marianne went home, Eilish was quite spent, and worn by the renewed pain in her head. She trudged up to her bed and lay down, staring out the window into the roiling gray clouds.

"Oh, Mackie, darling," she whispered. " 'Tisn't that I've forgotten. I'll never forget, I promise. The angels have left me here alone, and I have to carry on, don't I? But I'll never, never forget. I promise you."

33

Seattle, September 2018

To Erin the holographic scan looked very much like it always did, mystifying blue and red lobes pierced by slender shafts of light. Gene froze the projection and pointed to one area of the blue. "Primary visual cortex. Looks like you're getting the impulses, but your conscious mind isn't recognizing them. The augmentation you were using with *Mars*, and then applying to yourself, created a sort of chaos in the firing of the neurons." He pointed to tiny flashes that appeared to go off in random directions. Erin frowned, trying to understand.

Charlie was seated in the wooden chair, the electrodes on his temples and behind his ears, his eyes covered with one hand. "You can't imagine," he said, "what it felt like to me. To stand on my own, to take those steps—oh, god."

Erin stood behind Gene's chair. Gene glanced up at her, but in his concentration, she was sure he barely saw her. "Okay, Charlie," he said. "Put on the headphones now." Charlie obeyed. "This will be long, Erin," Gene added. "You should go home. I'll call you when he's done."

"What are you going to do? What is he listening to?"

Gene touched some buttons on the Moog and then

leaned back in his chair, rubbing his face with his long fingers. Erin knew he'd been up all night writing the program. "It's a straight binaural beat program with minimal augmentation," he said. "It's almost a reverse of the one he was using—to coax his brain patterns back into balance."

"Gene," Charlie said, lifting his head. Erin suppressed a shudder. His eyes flicked left to right, searching, searching, finding nothing but darkness. He said in a voice of utter misery, "Will I lose my legs again, then?"

"I can't say, Charlie," Gene answered slowly. "One thing at a time, okay? Now, just listen, and follow the program. I'll be right here, monitoring the scan. I've done my hospital rounds, and canceled all my other patients for the day. Ted's going to make sure we're undisturbed." He stood, and gestured to Erin to precede him out of the clinic. They walked quietly around Charlie and into the little parlor.

Gene closed the door behind them and stood gazing at the glossy leaves of the camellia that brushed against the glass. "It's important to try to correct this now, Erin, right away," he said wearily. "I know you have a concert in San Antonio—but Charlie may not be able to go. I'm concerned about permanent damage." Worry and fatigue pulled at his mouth, and his eyes were dark.

Her throat closed. "Permanent?"

He nodded. "I have to reestablish a normal pattern from the nerves of the eyes to the visual cortex. I worry about atrophy, that if it goes on long enough, the pathway will deteriorate and Charlie won't ever see normally again. But if we catch it early . . ."

"Like with his hands?" Erin asked.

"Yes. His hands are steady again, you saw that. But it concerns me that he can manipulate his own brain functions this much. We don't know enough, even now, about how the brain works, how it compensates."

"He's willing to risk everything," Erin said in a small voice. "It scares me."

"Yes. It's frightening. But, since you both studied music from such an early age, you have an advantage."

"Charlie was telling me about that. Something like—I don't know, more to work with?"

Gene nodded. "Yes. About five percent more cortex to work with, actually. Brain structure adapts to demand, but it has to start at an early age. And it's cerebellar volume, the seat of intentional movement—it's probably why his experimentation has achieved such dramatic results. Lucky, hmm?" His tone was bitter.

"He's good," she said sadly.

Gene didn't seem to hear her. "I'm missing something here," he said, half to himself. "If Charlie can create this dramatic an effect with augmented music, what the hell's the matter with me, that I can't do it with a controlled program?"

"I told you," Erin said. "He's good. He's always excelled at everything."

He answered with a short, bitter laugh. "More so than I, apparently."

"Gene—you know that's not true."

"I wish I did," he said shortly. "Wouldn't it be terrible if your mother was right? If my training just isn't up to it?"

Erin exclaimed, "You can't think that!"

"But maybe I should. Maybe Charlie should."

"No!"

He turned to look down at her, his eyes bleak. "Brain mapping is the key," he said.

"What?"

"Brain mapping. They're doing great work with it at Brown. I couldn't get into Brown—substandard college degree, they said, and there was that taint on my SATs. They were making real breakthroughs at Harvard, but there wasn't enough scholarship money. I've studied all the material, of course. I did my dissertation on it, after my residency. But maybe that's not the same as really being there, seeing the work firsthand. Maybe your mother's right about me."

Erin seized his arm, hard. Her short nails dug into the cloth of his coat, and she stood on tiptoe to look into his face. "Now, you listen to me, Gene Berrick," she said. "She may be our mother, but it's always, always her agenda, and never anyone else's, not even Charlie's. All that damned refinement—Sarah Rushton of the Boston Rushtons! You know what that meant? It meant poor little Charlie Rushton had to be a guinea pig for engineered viruses—it meant I had to be the best, the youngest, the first of the new glass harmonica virtuosi—it meant we had a private school housemother for a parent instead of our own oh-so-bloody perfect head-of-surgery mother!"

"Erin—"

"No!" she said, knowing she'd shocked him, too furious and scared and desperate with worry to stop herself. Tears of anger scalded her eyes. She beat one fist against her thigh in helpless frustration. "Everybody thinks it's so amazing, this talented Rushton family, brilliant mother, prodigy daughter, poor beautiful Charlie in a wheelchair, such fascinating, newsworthy, Who's Who sort of nonsense, and I don't care! I'd give it all up in a minute if only Charlie could be healthy!"

"Erin," Gene said, shaking his head. He took her hand, and his lips twitched, and she saw he was going to laugh.

She stamped her foot. Her voice rose, scraping from her throat. "Dammit! You just don't know, Gene—I know it's worse for you because of the tent city and all that—but we were at the Llewellyn all the time, Thanksgiving, Easter, stupid Halloween—then to have your work denigrated because of your bloody school—what a bitch she is! I could just scream!"

He seized her other hand, made her open her fist, then took her shoulders and shook them gently. "Erin, relax. It's okay, it's okay."

And she found herself sobbing against his chest, wetting

his white coat with her tears, shaking with fear and fury. He held her just right, long arms firm but not too tight, neither squeezing nor pushing her away. She had wanted him to hold her for so long, but dammit, not like this, not this idiotic way, her blubbering like a spoiled brat, and him smoothing her hair, patting her back, making soothing stupid noises that had nothing to do with anything. And laughing at her. It was utterly ridiculous. How idiotic she must seem, and what the hell did any of it mean anyway?

Poor Gene, his patient blind, her having tantrums, his work falling apart. He might as well laugh. She started to giggle herself. It was all such a disaster, such a bloody great comedy. She tried to stifle her giggles, but that made them worse, and soon she was laughing helplessly, choking on her laughter as much as she had on her tears. Under her cheek, she felt the chuckles that welled from him, too, and that made her laugh even harder, until her face hurt with it. Finally she just stood in the strong circle of his arms, taking comfort in the solidity of his body against hers, the warmth of his hand on her back.

At length, mopping her face with her fingers, she freed herself and stood back. "Omigod," she said. "What was all that about?"

"I don't know," he said. "But I wish I had it on disc." He grinned, really grinned, showing white teeth in his brown face. It was a devastatingly attractive face at that moment, and she had to resist throwing herself back into his arms.

She pressed her fingers to her lips, feeling the laughter bubble up again in her throat. "Wow. I was really on for a minute there."

"Indeed you were." His grin faded, but he looked better, his eyes clearer, his mouth relaxed, still curving. "Listen, we're not going to panic yet. Charlie and I'll have a go at it today, and we'll see what happens. Try not to worry too much, okay?"

"Right." Erin took a ragged breath. "Tell you what—I'll bring around some lunch."

"Thanks."

"Sure."

He hesitated, then added, "But Erin, I mean—thanks for all that you said, too. For believing in me."

Impulsively, she stood on tiptoe and kissed his cheek, daring his reaction. His skin was firm and smooth, just a hint of afternoon beard touching her lips. It smelled faintly of aftershave. And he didn't pull away. "I do believe in you, Gene," she whispered. "And so does Charlie."

"I'm doing my best for him," he said, his eyes darkening.

"You always do your best," she said quietly. "For Charlie, for Joey—all of them. Always."

He looked into her eyes for a long moment, and she thought he might, he just might, bend and kiss her in return. But he turned away, and went back into the clinic, closing the door behind him.

It wasn't until she was on her way out that she realized that she knew the scent on his skin. It was spicy and sharp and familiar. It was the same scent that sometimes came with her wraith.

CHARLIE began to see sporadic bursts of light, then light and shadow, but by the end of the week, he was still virtually blind. He could feel his way around the condo, and around the bathroom, but Erin had to put his chair on voice remote and direct it for him when he needed to go outside. He couldn't use his slimscreen, couldn't work with the Akai. He could play the Chickering, and he could listen to recordings. Erin cooked for him, and cleaned, and made his bed, and dealt with the laundry and the grocery service. Charlie was chastened, penitent, anxious.

Gene worked doggedly, reprogramming the Moog, rescheduling his other patients, trying every approach he could think of to reestablish the neural pathways Charlie had lost.

At the end of one session, Charlie agonized. "God, Gene! What good am I now? What in hell will I do? What's the point of any of this?"

"Charlie, we're not giving up. You can't give up. We'll find the way—"

Charlie shook his head. "Might as well forget it." He was slumped in his wheelchair, the glass of juice half-finished in his hand. Erin stood watching, her arms wrapped tightly around herself.

Gene repeated, "It's not true. The scan shows improved continuity of the pathways, and you're much stronger physically. Come on, Charlie. I think we're going to be able to do this."

"We?" Charlie cried, with a shrill laugh that was almost a wail. He waved the glass in Gene's direction, into his personal darkness. "What's this *we*, white man?"

"Charlie!" Erin cried. "Don't talk like that to Gene!"

And Charlie wept, hiding his face behind his hands, sobbing. "I didn't mean it, god, Gene, you know I didn't mean it. I'm so sorry."

Gene was up, bending over Charlie, his hands firm on his shoulders. "I know you didn't mean it," he said. "Forget it, Charlie. Forget it. It's going to be okay." His voice was firm, but Erin saw the dismay on his face.

She couldn't take it anymore. It was too much, Charlie weeping, Gene hurt, the whole thing reeling out of control. She fled.

She ran at first, and then, out of breath, she walked, for perhaps fifteen minutes, cursing under her breath, damning the disease, the music, the whole awful week. Without planning to, she found herself in the Japanese gardens where she had come with Gene. They were almost deserted now in the autumn afternoon, and she had the paths to herself, the little plashing stream, the leafy alcove where the mossy Buddha kept watch. Hot and sweaty, she collapsed onto the bench in the shade of the cherry tree. For a long time she sat there, until her perspiration dried and her breathing slowed. She sat until the shadows began to grow, to stretch across the little stream and darken the smiling Buddha's face. She didn't see her wraith, but she felt her, a shade at her elbow, a half-heard echo, waiting for her to notice, nudging her to listen, listen. And now, in the gardens, with the little stone god before her, she knew it was time.

If she had to cancel San Antonio, she would. If she had to face her fears, she must. She would take Gene's advice. She would go back to London. It was time, and past time, to try to figure it all out.

34

Bath, April 1764

THE coach trip from London to Bath exhausted Eilish.
The rocking of the coach, on roads deeply rutted by
the wet winter, made her stomach so queasy that twice,
despite her best efforts, the coachman had to stop for her
to be sick in the ditch. Her head ached afresh with every
jolt and bump, and the situation was not helped by her
concern over the safety of the armonica.

Marianne, too, was torn between her worry for Eilish's
health and the effect of the rough ride on the crystal cups.
It was a long, awful day. They arrived late in the evening,
Marianne in tears, Eilish pale and drained and silent. Only
the news, from Marianne's servant, that the armonica was
intact, revived them enough to try to eat a little supper.
They were put in the same room, the two of them tucked
into an enormous bed with canopies all round. They curled
up together, like lost kittens, for comfort, though Eilish
feared she could not sleep for the pain lancing her temples.

Eilish never mentioned her headaches to Marianne, or
the fact that sometimes she could barely lift her head from
the pillow in the mornings, and that when she did, the room
spun around her like a leaf in the wind. The slightest hint

of her being unwell tended to send her friend into parox-
ysms of nerves, often with tears. Marianne was the most
sensitive, the most fragile, person Eilish had ever met. Her
nervous attacks were hard to soothe. Preventing them was
far easier.

Bath was a quiet place, a spa that was beginning to be
fashionable among the London set. The air was clean and
sweet, their feather bed soft as a cloud. Eilish, despite her
fears, slept heavily that first night, and when she woke, her
headache was somewhat improved. She had felt ill for so
long that even a mild reprieve felt almost like returning
health. Marianne was already up, darting about their bedroom like a hungry sparrow. She threw back the heavy
curtains to let in the mild spring sun.

"Eilish, dear! Look what a lovely day it is! Come, get
up, get up! We must set up the armonica, clean the glasses,
speak to Mrs. Selledge about the arrangement of the chairs!
And of course we must practice—oh, this will be a notable
event!"

Eilish put back the coverlet and stood up. Her legs shook
beneath her, but she held onto the carved bedpost to steady
herself. She said, smiling, "Could we at least have a bit of
breakfast first, Marianne?"

Marianne turned to her, glowing like a tiny dark porcelain doll. "Oh, dear Eilish, 'tis good that you're hungry!
Now, come and sit at the dressing table! I'll brush your hair
for you. You must eat, yes, and perhaps drink the waters—
they are said to be very restorative. Perhaps the curl will
return to your lovely hair! That's it, we'll walk to the spa
this morning, and you will drink the waters—"

"Then you must, too," Eilish said, laughing.

"Very well! If you will, I will!"

The concert was set for the weekend, when Mrs. Selledge's houseguests would come down *en masse* from London. Cecilia Davies, Marianne's sister, would be there to
sing some songs of Mr. Handel's and Mr. Purcell's. They

had three days to wait and prepare until they should all arrive.

According to Marianne's plan, she and Eilish went each morning to the spa among the old Roman ruins, where they dipped up brackish, salty water from the mineral spring and drank. The walk to and from the spa tired Eilish, but she did not mention it. She leaned more heavily on Marianne's arm than she had before, but Marianne seemed not to mind. Each afternoon they ate luncheon with Mrs. Selledge and her husband, and then they practiced in the parlor. It was a pleasant interlude, and Eilish felt a bit stronger each day of it. The country air helped to clear her head, and the waters of Bath, if they did not promote her health, at least did it no harm.

The guests from London arrived on the Friday, bringing Cecilia with them, setting the house abustle with servants and trunks and cloaks and boots. Eilish was overwhelmed by such a throng, and having nothing to do and not knowing what to say or where she should be, retreated to the bedroom. She sat curled in the deep bow window, watching the comings and goings in the road at the front of the house. Without intending to, she fell asleep, and dreamed a sad little dream of Mackie. He smiled up at her, the old sweet smile, and his great round eyes were clear and peaceful. She reached out her arms to him and he ran to her on legs as straight and strong as sapling oaks. In her dream, she caught him to her, and pressed her cheek to his tangled hair.

"Why, Eilish, here you are! I have been wanting to introduce you to my dearest little sister, but here you are hiding away!"

It was Marianne, come in search of her. Eilish woke with a start, and found tears on her cheeks. Marianne saw, and exclaimed, "Oh, Eilish, sweetheart, are you all right? What is it, whatever is the matter?" And she herself burst into nervous tears that she dashed away with her small hands as quickly as they fell.

With difficulty, Eilish climbed out of the window seat and took Marianne's hand. "No, no," she said as calmly as she could. " 'Twas only a dream. I am well, Marianne, I am perfectly well." She spoke soothingly to the older woman until her tears stopped and then, with Marianne apologizing profusely for her outburst, they went downstairs to meet Cecilia and the other guests.

AT teatime on the Saturday, the guests gathered in Mrs. Selledge's large parlor. Eilish and Marianne had set up the armonica and the harpsichord in as fetching an arrangement as they could. Enormous bowls of lilies and hellebore flanked the instruments, and a variety of chairs and armchairs were scattered about the room. Cecilia, taller and paler than Marianne, but otherwise very like her, stood with Eilish and Marianne in the hall, waiting until the proper time. They listened to the chatter of the guests, the clink of the wine bottles against the tall, sparkling champagne flutes, and watched the servants dash in and out with trays.

Marianne, twisting her hands nervously, said, "I think it must be time, do you not? What do you think, Cecilia?"

Cecilia opened her mouth to reply, but was interrupted by the precipitous passage of the butler making his way past them into the parlor. A moment later he and Mrs. Selledge, pink with excitement and champagne, emerged, closing the door on the noisy conversation within. The three musicians stood looking at each other, wondering, as Mrs. Selledge and her butler rushed past them to the front door of the house.

A few moments later, they reappeared with a curious little entourage consisting of a small man, his plump wife, two young children, and a tall thin servant. There was a bit of fuss and chatter in a language Eilish couldn't understand. The tall servant spoke a few words and Mrs. Selledge answered. Cecilia, who was good at languages, hissed to her sister, "They are Germans! But they are speaking French with Mrs. Selledge." The servant was carrying the youngest child in his arms, and the older one, a girl, tottered along leaning on her father's arm. It was very clear to Eilish, without understanding a word of their speech, that the children were ill, and that the parents were frantic about them.

There was nothing they could do, with their hostess so occupied, but wait to begin their program until she should be free. They stood awkwardly by, trying not to stare at the dark, small people as they shed their heavy traveling cloaks. Cecilia and Marianne whispered a translation of the conversation to Eilish.

"Oh, the poor babes," Marianne murmured. "They've just come from Calais, by way of Dover, and the crossing has made the children sick. They met Mrs. Selledge and her husband in Paris last year, and are begging for a bed for the night, as there is no hotel available. They have been traveling—oh, what was that? It's so difficult, the French, and their accents—because they are not really German, but from Salzburg—oh, they have been from home a year already. Poor children!"

Mrs. Selledge summoned a maid, and the butler and the maid gathered up the traveling cases of the family and began lugging them up the broad stairs. The family trudged after them, the children's eyes heavy and dull, their little faces pale as milk. Marianne hissed to Cecilia, "Do you know who they are? Did you hear their name?"

"Oh, yes!" Cecilia said, her eyes shining with excitement. "It's those children—those *Wunderkinder*—the Austrian prodigies! They've been invited to perform at Buckingham House by Her Majesty. They perform upon the harpsichord, though they are only tiny! 'Twas all the buzz in London, Marianne—you remember, do you not? They are the Mozarts!"

THE concert went well, though the delay meant that more than a few of Mrs. Selledge's guests had already drunk a good bit of champagne. Still, Eilish and Cecilia, and even Marianne, felt satisfied. Eilish played only Irish folk tunes on the armonica, "Abigail Judge," and "Castle O'Neil," and "Faerie Queen." Marianne played her transcriptions to perfection, and then sat down at the harpsichord to accompany her sister in "Rejoice" from *Messiah,* and "O Had I Jubal's Lyre," and Mr. Purcell's "Sound the Trumpet." All the music was very well received. Eilish felt quite included in the general success, and though the greater attention was paid to the Davies sisters, that was quite natural.

An awkward moment came when dinner was announced. Mrs. Selledge whispered in Marianne's ear, and Marianne, looking stricken, came to Eilish.

"Oh, my dear," she said. "I am so embarrassed. I hardly know how to say—how to tell you—" She paled, and colored, and paled again, and her eyes filled with ready tears.

Eilish took her hand and held it tightly. "Marianne, just say what is troubling you. You cannot upset me, I promise you."

"Oh, Eilish." The tears spilled over, marking the powder on Marianne's cheeks. "It is the dinner—the guests—the table—"

Eilish took a sharp breath. Despite her promise, a little flame of resentment leapt up in her bosom. She quenched it resolutely, smiling brilliantly and exclaiming, "Oh, but Marianne! I am to dine with the servants, of course! I should have been utterly at a loss trying to make conversation in such company." She patted Marianne's shoulder, and took out her own handkerchief to smooth the ruined powder. "There now, you must have a lovely dinner, you and Cecilia. I shall be quite comfortable in the kitchen, and then early to bed. You'll see, I'll be fast asleep while you have to go on making yourself pleasant to society!"

She did her best to suit action to word. While the staff were still running up and downstairs from the kitchen to the dining room with trays and pots and tureens, Eilish walked up to their bedroom. She sat down at the dressing table and brushed her hair before the mirror. She lifted the strands to inspect them, but found no sign of the curl returning. She rose and took off her dress, and put on the lovely dressing gown Marianne had given her for the trip. She was washing her face when the knock sounded on her door.

She went to open it. "Yes?"

It was her hostess, Mrs. Selledge, looking slightly harassed. "Oh, Miss Eam," she said breathlessly. "I am so glad I found you. Will you come?"

Eilish tightened the sash of the dressing gown around her. "Of course. Where?"

But Mrs. Selledge had already turned away, taking her compliance for granted. Eilish followed her down the corridor, around a corner, and up yet another flight of stairs. Mrs. Selledge knocked briefly on a door, and went in.

The room was so large as to be almost an apartment. Two great beds and a cot crowded the space, and a table, littered now with dishes and cups and flatware, had been set up in the center of the room. The two foreign parents, dark faces lined with weariness, sat at the table, and the servant hovered over one of the big beds. Both the children lay on the bed, but at the opening of the door, the smaller one sat up, calling out something Eilish couldn't understand.

The servant spoke to him rather sharply, but the boy paid him no heed. He leapt from the bed and ran to Eilish, seizing her hand. He looked up into her face and demanded, with a tug on her hand, "*Je veux l'entendre!*"

"What?" Eilish looked to Mrs. Selledge in confusion, and then back at the child. The boy looked to be no more than five, tiny and small, with a sharp, prominent nose and enormous dark eyes. He tugged on her hand, and repeated his demand. "*Mademoiselle! S'il vous plait!*"

Mrs. Selledge sighed, and said, "*Wolferl, elle ne parle pas français.*" Then to Eilish she said, "Wolferl refuses to go to sleep until he hears the glassychord. Your instrument.

He heard the concert from the top of the stairs, when he was supposed to be in bed, and now he insists on hearing the 'new glassy instrument,' as he calls it. He and his sister—Nannerl, that is, upon the bed—have been terribly sick since the crossing. Their parents feared to travel further until they were stronger."

The father spoke to the boy, but the child, red-faced, stamped his foot and shook his head imperiously. "*Nein!*" he cried. And then, "*Non!*"

Mrs. Selledge rolled her eyes at Eilish. "Wolferl at least seems much recovered. Their native language is German, you understand, but they have been traveling in France and Holland, speaking French. Will you play for him, please, Miss Eam? I must return to my guests."

Eilish opened her mouth, meaning to assent, but Mrs. Selledge had already withdrawn, hurrying out of the apartment, leaving the door open behind her. Eilish looked helplessly after her, and then at the little boy, and at his parents. They watched her with hopeful, exhausted eyes. She spread her hands, saying, "I'm very sorry. I don't speak a word of your language."

The little boy, standing before her, spread his hands, too, and gave her a sharp monkey grin.

She laughed, and bent down to speak to him. " 'Tis quite the gossoon you are, isn't it, then?" she said. " 'Tis the armonica you will have, and naught else!"

His large brown eyes shone with intelligence and humor. He said something she didn't understand, and she straightened, chuckling. " 'Twon't be much talk between us, will there? All right, lad. Off we go. But none of your nonsense! Though I look like a nob, I'm naught but an Irish orphan from Seven Dials, and ye'll mind yer manners with me!"

Her words were sharp, but she spoke them gently, and his answering smile was sweet. Eilish's heart ached with a spasm of remembered sorrow. 'Twas altogether too much like Mackie's smile. Thank the angels this lad's legs were straight as arrows in their thick white stockings.

As they left, little Wolferl spoke over his shoulder to the servant, in French. Eilish looked back as she led the way downstairs, and saw that the servant was following them, carrying the girl Nannerl. The girl kept her eyes closed, her face turned into the servant's vest. She looked older than Wolferl, perhaps ten years of age. It was hard to tell because they were both so small of stature, like their parents.

Eilish turned up the oil lamps in the parlor and went to pull the cover off the armonica. The moment the cups were revealed, gleaming in the lamplight, Wolferl made a sound of joy, and gave a little jump of pleasure. He did not threaten to touch the glasses, but he stood very close, examining them with avid eyes. Nannerl, still with her eyes closed, lay limply in the servant's arms, though her brother tugged at her sleeve and spoke to her.

"Never mind," Eilish said. "The poor lass can listen with her eyes closed, now, can't she?"

He watched her closely as she sat down and pumped the treadle. When she dipped her fingers in the water and touched them to the spinning glasses, he stood stock-still, his concentration so fierce, it seemed his gaze must burn her. She played "Baidhin Elhemhi," hoping to soothe the little girl's illness, and she played "Eileen Aroon," because she was sure the boy couldn't have heard the tune before. Then she glanced slyly up at young Master Mozart, and played the transcription of "O Sleep, Why Dost Thou Leave Me?" She was rewarded by seeing him catch his breath, his little hands coming to his mouth in surprise.

When she finished the air, she saw that Nannerl had turned her head and was watching her with hollow eyes. Eilish smiled at the child, and began an old Scottish tune Franklin had loved. " 'O Little Sister,' " she murmured to the children, though she knew they couldn't understand. " 'Tis an old ballad of a girl crying for help as the fairies carry her away to Heaval—'tis very sad, but remember, 'tis only an old song, and you mustn't believe a word of it."

She played it through once, and then, lightly, sang the words:

> "Little sister, sister, hu ru
> My love, my sister, hu ru
> Can you not pity, ho ho ill eo
> My grief tonight? hu ru."

Nannerl lifted her head, and a wan smile brightened her face. Like her brother, she had a long, curving nose and small plain features, but beautiful dark eyes. She said something in German, and Eilish spread her hands and shook her head, to show she couldn't understand. Nannerl smiled again, and said something to the servant, who put her down. She walked, shakily, but eagerly, to the armonica. Seated, Eilish was as tall as the girl was standing.

"Hu ru," the girl said, with a little laugh. "Hu ru, hu ru."

"That's right," Eilish said. "That much at least we understand! There now, lass, you're looking ever so much better."

The little dark girl put out her hand, but like her brother, she didn't offer to touch the armonica. She only stroked the very end of the spindle with one small fingertip.

"It's an armonica," Eilish said, with a gesture to include the whole instrument. "A glass armonica."

"Harmonica," Nannerl said. "Harmonica."

Eilish grinned at her. "Close enough, lassie."

The lad looked up at the servant and said something in French. The servant turned to Eilish and said, in heavily accented English, "Wolfgang says the music—" he struggled for the right word—"the tone of the music—" The servant sighed, despairing of the language. He pointed at his chest. "To the heart. No ears. The heart."

"Ah," Eilish said, nodding. "Straight to the heart, and never mind the ears. It could be. 'Tis like that with my little instrument, nor is the young lass the first to be healed by it."

The man nodded and smiled, though she wasn't sure he understood much of what she said. She said to the children, "Now sit right there, both of you—you, too, Wolferl, there with your sister. I'll play one more tune, and then it's off to bed for the both of you. By morning, you'll be right as rain."

Eilish played "Barb'ry Allen," very slowly, the song of the crystals plaintive and sweet in the high-ceilinged *salon*. She sang the old words the way she had learned them, in Irish, since the children wouldn't understand them in any case.

> *"In Scarlet Town, where I was born,*
> *There was a fair maid dwellin' . . ."*

The two children, leaning together, began to yawn, and the servant smiled down at them. And Eilish, at the armonica, felt the presence by her elbow. Her arm tingled as if a cool breeze had touched it. She didn't look up. It wasn't necessary. She knew that the other, that faint shade, was with her, listening, watching, learning.

> *"Oh, yes, I ken, I ken it well,*
> *In the place where I was a-dwellin',*
> *I give a toast to the ladies all,*
> *But my love to Barb'ry Allen."*

By the time the song was finished, Nannerl's eyes were closed again, but this time in a comfortable doze that was hardly disturbed when the manservant picked her up once again to carry her upstairs. Her cheeks had gone rosy, as a child's cheeks were meant to be. Eilish went to carry Wolferl, fearful that she couldn't lift him, but she found him light as a feather. He wasn't truly asleep. As she tucked his head onto her shoulder he lifted it to give her a resounding kiss on the cheek, and he snuggled close in her arms as if he had known her all his life.

"Now, where have you been, my lad, that you make so free with strange ladies?" she murmured. But in truth, she didn't mind. A strange family, this one, traveling all over with two young children, and not strong children at that. But such unusual children! Imagine, so tiny, and invited to play at court! 'Twas a wonder. Eilish couldn't imagine such a life. She wondered if they knew their good fortune, these children. Ah, to live surrounded by family, and wealth, and nobility . . . and music . . .

Once Eilish had deposited the children back with their parents, and found her own room again, she was dragging with cold and fatigue and her own illness. She took off the dressing gown and pulled on her bedgown with shaking hands. She fell into the great bed, drawing the coverlet around her, nestling down into the soft feather mattress. And all night long she dreamed of the young Mozarts, bowing to queens.

35

London, September 2018

ERIN couldn't sleep on the plane. She felt wary, as if she were walking too fast in a thick fog, not knowing what might loom up out of the mist. Throughout the five hours of supersonic flight she turned and wriggled in the wide leather seat, trying to get comfortable, trying to relax. The cabin attendant asked if there was anything he could do for her, but what she needed was not in his power.

She had left Charlie with Gene, to stay with him in his rooms above the clinic while she was gone. Ted had offered to help with Charlie's care, and the two of them worked out a rotation. As Erin said her goodbyes, Charlie's blank expression, his unseeing eyes trying to follow her movements, tore at her heart. The logic of a lifetime told her not to leave her brother blind and alone. But it was instinct driving her, not intellect. It was, she thought, like learning a complicated piece of music. First there is the dry ritual of learning the notes and the rhythms and the phrasing. The internalizion of the music, the integration of technique and form and meaning, is an intuitive process. Whether her visions came from her subconscious or from some source that was real in another sense—physically real, temporally, or even spiritually—she would have to immerse herself in them. Integrate them.

Gene Berrick's belief that her experiences had a basis in reality, that she wasn't out of her mind, gave her strength. She trusted him. She missed him. She wished he were with her at the same time that she was deeply grateful he was watching over Charlie.

She checked into the Victoria Inn and tried again to sleep, but now the hour was wrong for sleeping, and she woke too soon, still tired. She gave up trying to rest. She drank some coffee, pulled a warm, bulky sweater over her jeans, and stepped out of the hotel into the cool light of midmorning.

The doorman offered to call her a cab, and she was about to accept, but when she glanced out past the elegant portico of the hotel, she was struck by how gracefully the old and the new dwelt together in this city. She was drawn away, invited by the ageless autumn sun, the sparkling air. She forgot to answer the doorman. She wandered away from the hotel as if in a dream, leaving him standing and staring after her.

She meandered down Belgrave, and turned in the general direction of the Thames. Without conscious decision, she followed every short, haphazard street that opened up before her. Contemp cabs and autos rolled past on the smooth pavement of the twenty-first century, but the shops and houses and hotels she passed were Victorian, or Georgian, or Restoration. She knew as she walked north that there would be even older buildings, sixteenth-, fifteenth-, fourteenth-century structures, renovated, preserved, venerated. People had lived in those buildings, had worked and learned and suffered and cherished.

Erin wondered if their wisdom was lost—or if they could still teach those who came after, those who were listening.

Objective time slipped away from her. She arrived at Westminster Bridge warm with exertion, the pale mop of her hair blown ragged by the wind from the river. She pulled off her sweater and knotted it around her waist as she moved into the pedestrian lane of the bridge and stood in the exact spot where she had seen the slender girl with the dark curls whipping about her head. Had she seen her with physical eyes or metaphysical ones?

There were very few people about. Erin stood looking down into the shining water, letting it dazzle her eyes. She kept her hands on the stone railing, and lifted her face into the wind. She remembered the tears, those tears that had seemed to be someone else's. Through her fingers she felt the vibrations of memory, echoes, as if they had been recorded in the stone. But the presence that had left them was gone, dispersed like a fog burned away by the morning sun.

As she left the bridge, Erin felt a tug to her right, almost as if someone had pulled on her sleeve. Turning to the right meant going in the opposite direction from St. John's, her next destination. She glanced up the Victoria Embankment, past the spires of Whitehall, and wondered. St. John's was to her left, down Millbank. What was it that called her? She couldn't think of anything. After hesitating a moment, she turned left, to make the walk to Smith Square.

A luncheon concert was in progress at St. John's, the strains of Mozart flute quartets floating out over the square. Erin sat on a stone ledge just outside and listened, gazing up at the turrets of the old church and thinking about the people, each with his or her own thoughts and fears and desires, who had gone in and out of its atrium entrance for almost three centuries. When people began to stream out, Erin, moving against the crowd, made her way inside.

The musicians were still on the low stage, putting away their instruments, chatting. Erin waited for them to finish, not wanting to talk to anyone. Then, as the janitorial staff started coming through the aisles, she went up on the stage and looked out into the hall.

The arched nave was misty with sunlight, the gilded columns glinting. Here, too, Erin felt the echoes of the past, but nothing more. She remembered how alarmed she had been, how the chill had crept up her arms and her mind had pulled back. She couldn't summon it now, couldn't call it back. It seemed to be fading, dimming, slipping away. Was she too late?

"Miss Rushton?"

Erin, startled out of her reverie, turned too quickly toward the voice and almost stumbled.

"Why, Miss Rushton! What a pleasure!" The house manager of St. John's hurried up the aisle toward Erin. "Why, Miss Rushton, had we known—I know the members of the ensemble would have loved to meet you. Why didn't you let us know you'd be in London?"

He put out his hand, and Erin shook it, awkwardly. "I—I'm sorry," she said. "I didn't actually know I was coming—I'm just—just on a visit," she finished lamely.

"And Mr. Oskar? He didn't come with you?"

Erin's composure returned at that. "No," she said firmly. "I'm traveling alone."

"Really, really," he said, blinking. "Well, it's a pleasure. Do you have plans while you're here? Do you have your instrument? We would love to have you at one of our noon concerts, if you care to . . ."

"No," Erin answered. "I don't have the glass harmonica here. It's in Boston."

"Ah, ah, I see. Well . . ." He spread his hands. "I'm sorry to hear that. Are you at the Victoria again?"

She nodded, and pulled on her sweater. It was cool in the old church.

The man put his head to one side and regarded her. "Do you know, Miss Rushton, the people at Franklin House were ever so keen to have you play there. And they have a glass armonica—"

"They do?" Erin stopped with her sweater half on. "I didn't know that."

"I believe you—er—had to cancel your last engagement there?" That was true, of course. Mal had arranged it, and

Erin had refused. "And they have acquired a very faithful reproduction of the original armonica, modeled after Franklin's own. The one he gave to Marianne Davies."

Erin finished putting on the sweater, looking out into the empty church. An armonica, at Franklin House. Was this what drew her, when she was on the bridge? She knew the address was Craven Street, of course, but where was that from St. John's? A flutter of nerves tickled under her breastbone, but she steadfastly ignored it. She had not come so far to be frightened off again. She pushed her hair back with her fingers and looked up at the house manager. "Would you call them for me? See if they're interested?"

"Oh, with pleasure, Miss Rushton! I'm certain they'll be delighted! Won't you come this way?" And he led her off toward his office behind the atrium.

THE docents at Franklin House were more than delighted. They wanted to wait three days, to give them an opportunity to set up a netcast, to invite guests, to do advertising. Erin agreed, but asked that she have private time each evening, after the tours of Franklin House were concluded and the exhibits closed, to practice with the armonica.

She called Mal on the Victoria's audio-only phone to tell him, and he offered to catch a plane to London. "No, Mal, I can handle this," Erin said.

"But how about money? What are they offering?"

"Not a thing, Mal. I don't want anything. I'm doing it as a benefit."

There was a little silence. Erin stared at the ceiling, at her toes, at her tousled reflection in the mirror of her suite. She could imagine Mal's look of calculation. Finally, he said, "Okay, okay, Erin, that's probably good. Very good for your rep. Good for your image. Returning to the source, giving back, all of that."

"Right," she said dryly. "So, Mal, I just didn't want you caught off guard. Since they're netcasting it."

"Well, good, Erin. What about a dress?"

"I'm going shopping tomorrow."

"I wish you'd told me you were going to London. I could have helped . . ."

"Thanks, Mal, but I didn't need help. I came for something else." And when he pressed her for what the something else might be, Erin avoided telling him.

"Do you want to speak to Sarah? I think she just came home from the hospital."

Erin thought of Gene's face, the pain in his eyes. "Nope," she said flatly. "She's probably tired. Tell her I said Hi. You two can watch the netcast."

She hung up, and lay back on the narrow bed to stare at the coved ceiling. She would call Charlie, too. But the voice she really wanted to hear, the one she needed to hear, was Gene Berrick's. She sighed, and rolled over, hugging the pillow to her to stifle her loneliness.

FRANKLIN House sent a cab for her just after teatime, when the last tour of the museum would be finishing. It was a short ride, up Millbank, past Westminster Bridge toward Charing Cross. The building that had been Franklin's home in London, now numbered Thirty-six, had been painstakingly restored over a ten-year period and had opened to the public twelve years before. The kitchen in the basement, the family rooms on the ground and second floors, Franklin's rooms on the first floor, had all been brought alive with period or repro furnishings, paintings, lamps, china, and glass.

A security guard met Erin at the iron gate and led her up to the first floor, where Franklin's laboratory had been reconstructed, complete with a variety of mysterious equipment, jars and tubing and wires set up as if to re-create his experiments. Heavy curtains were drawn over the tall windows to protect the artifacts from damaging sunlight.

The armonica rested behind a little burgundy curtain

hung from a gold rope. The guard unhooked it for Erin, and then left her alone in the laboratory. Most of the lights in Franklin House were off, but there was an electric lamp, made to resemble an oil lamp, near the armonica. Erin drew it close, and sat down on the little stool beside the instrument.

It had been beautifully made. The cups were painted with diamonds, as Franklin's had been, to indicate the pitches. Erin trusted the manufacturer had not used a lead paint. She doubted such a thing even existed anymore. The maker had somehow contrived to make the glasses very like those Erin remembered from the instrument in Boston. This spindle was new black iron turning on brass gudgeons with a shining mahogany flywheel, and the wooden case was inlaid and artfully hand-painted in eighteenth-century fashion. It had a foot treadle, of course. No electric power. Erin hesitated, looking at it.

"Well," she muttered. "Marianne Davies did it her whole life. I suppose I can too." She put her feet to the treadle and pumped.

36

London, June 1764

O N a bright morning, Marianne's carriage delivered her
to Craven Street. Bessie ushered her into Mrs. Stevenson's parlor, where Polly and Margaret Stevenson were
having coffee. Eilish, called up from the kitchen, found all
three seated around the table. Marianne was beaming, and
leaped up the moment she saw Eilish to draw her to a chair.

"Eilish, dear, I am so full of news I fear I must burst!"

Eilish sank gratefully into the chair, and leaned on the
arm of it. Mrs. Stevenson offered her coffee, but she said,
"Ta, Mrs. Stevenson. I do not think I will, just yet."

Marianne took her own chair, sitting on the edge of it
as if she might jump up again at any moment. "First! Eilish,
Miss Stevenson—have you heard about the little Mozarts
and their concert on the fifth of June? It was the most miraculous thing—that little girl, only eleven, and her brother
only eight! What magic they make with a harpsichord! Had
I not been there, I should never credit it!"

"Lovely," Eilish breathed.

"Yes," said Polly crisply. "I have heard all about this,
even in Essex. They are calling this little boy a genius, this
Mozart. But they do that so often, do they not?"

Marianne smiled at Polly, too buoyant in her mood to be affected by her skepticism. "Of course, Miss Stevenson, they do. But this I heard with my own ears—'twas a wonder indeed! He plays as if he were already an adult, with years of training behind him. He plays, I swear, better than I do, for all my years of practice!"

"Oh, Marianne, that cannot be true," Eilish said. She laid her head against the back of the chair and smiled at her friend. "You are the greatest musician in England."

"Oh, well, I cannot accept that," Marianne laughed. "And I certainly cannot improvise in the way this little boy does. But wait till you hear the rest of my news!" She put out her tiny hand and covered Eilish's. "Eilish, sweetheart, we were such a great success in Bath that now we have been invited back!"

Eilish's smile faltered, but she squeezed Marianne's delicate fingers in hers. "Lovely," she said again.

"Yes, isn't it?" Marianne beamed at them all. "I think we shall have to expand our repertoire! And Cecilia would like to sing with the armonica, one of the transcriptions! Now, will that not be a triumph?"

"I would love to be present," Polly said stiffly.

Marianne said with delicate tact, "I am certain the invitation will include you, Miss Stevenson. As you are Dr. Franklin's protégée."

Polly flushed with pleasure, touching her hair, smoothing her dress. Mrs. Stevenson murmured, "How kind, Miss Davies."

"Not at all," Marianne said. She smiled at Eilish. "Now, dear, tell me what you think!"

Eilish sat up a little straighter. She looked into Marianne's gentle face, her dark eyes so full of joy on this lovely spring day. She wanted to make her happy, wished she could say the words to please her. But she could no longer dissemble. It was time.

"Marianne," she said, a little hoarsely. "My dear friend. You must play this concert alone, I fear. You will be wonderful, and it will mean so much to Dr. Franklin that you do it. But I cannot. I think, in all truth, I will play no more concerts."

Marianne immediately left her chair to kneel beside Eilish, gripping her hands. "What do you mean, dear? What can you mean by that?"

Eilish saw, above her friend's dark head, that Mrs. Stevenson was watching with a grave air of understanding. Polly sniffed and wriggled impatiently. Pity for Marianne made Eilish's voice soft.

"I am so sorry, Marianne," she said. "I know you will be unhappy. But my health is so poor—I am so weak—it has been days since I had the strength to sit at the armonica, to work the treadle. There is nothing to be done for it."

"Oh, no!" Marianne cried, the quick tears rushing to her eyes. "Oh, no, Eilish, it cannot be true! We shall call a physician, you must come to my own home, you shall rest . . ."

"No, dear," Eilish breathed. " 'Tisn't possible. I am so sorry."

"But, dearest Eilish, you can't mean—" Marianne's eyes searched Eilish's face, and saw the terrible truth there. She burst into heartbroken sobs and buried her head in Eilish's lap.

Polly's eyes had gone wide. "Eilish—are you so very ill? Did no one know?"

Mrs. Stevenson rose and put out her hand to her daughter. "Polly, dear," she said. "I believe we shall leave Miss Davies and Eilish alone for the moment. Come with me down to the kitchen. We will talk to Cook about the supper."

For once Polly did not argue. She stood, murmuring, "Eilish—I'm very sorry, Eilish. I—truly, I had no idea." Eilish nodded to her as she left, and sat stroking Marianne's hair, patting her hand. After a time, Marianne lifted her tear-swollen face.

"If you cannot play—at least you can be there, can you

not, dear? Be there to advise me, to listen, to tell me what needs work, what is all right——"

Eilish tried to smile, but her lips trembled. "If I can, Marianne, I will. 'Tis not that I do not wish it. But I cannot help it, dear. 'Tis not my own will. It has been decided for me."

Marianne, comprehending the enormity of what Eilish was trying to tell her, was shocked beyond tears. She stared, her face white, her eyes stark. "Oh, God," she said. " 'Tis too cruel, that you should fly from me so soon."

"Oh, but Marianne," Eilish said, "I do not mind, after all. I long to see Mackie, and my father. If I cannot have my music, and they are gone . . . what is left for me?"

"Eilish!" Marianne moaned. "I am left for you, sweetheart! I, who love you more than anyone in the world!"

"My sweet friend. If I could stay for you, I would."

"Then I shall not go on without you! I shall never touch the instrument again!"

"Oh, no, you must not say that," Eilish protested. She felt as if she could sustain the conversation no longer. Weakness, fatigue, illness dragged at every limb, and her aching head felt too heavy to lift. Sometimes, at night, she felt that death would be welcome if only to relieve the pain of her head. "Marianne, your sister needs you . . . and your public cries out for you . . . and, only think, there is only you now to give life to the armonica."

"Oh, my dear," Marianne whispered. "I shall pray this is not true, any of it. I shall pray to God to give you back to me."

Eilish closed her eyes. "Ta, Marianne. Or to make it easy for me."

Marianne gave a little cry of grief, and caught Eilish into her arms.

LATE that night, when the household was asleep, Eilish woke with a start to find her bedgown wet with perspiration, her heart thudding in her ears. She lay looking out into the brilliant stars of summer. *'Twould be fair*, she thought, *that I should die alone, right now. Alone, as Mackie died.* She even waited, listening to her heartbeat, feeling her breathing, wondering if this could be the moment. But her heart continued to beat, and her breath, though it was shallow and quick, did not stop.

She threw back the covers and got slowly to her feet, steadying herself on the bedpost. She pulled a dressing gown over her bedgown and moved carefully to the door to listen for any sounds of people about. There were none. The household slumbered peacefully beneath her. Cautious of making noise, of stumbling, Eilish crept down the stairs to the laboratory.

She did not trouble with lighting the oil lamps. She dared not play the armonica for fear of waking anyone, and in any case, she had told Marianne the truth. Her feet were too weak and unsteady to work the treadle. She only wanted to look at it, to touch it one more time. She pulled off the silk cover, and put out her hand to the crystal cups.

They were cool to the touch, shining softly in the starlight, the painted diamonds glowing white. She sat on the stool and dipped one shaky finger into the bowl of water beneath the spindle. Slowly, gently, she rubbed the finger across one small cup. A thin, clear sound, hardly more than a breath, rang out in the empty laboratory. Eilish sighed. So lovely, it was. So enchanting. She had given all of her being, all of her short life, to be able to play it. And now, so soon, too soon, it was to be over.

She would not weep for herself. She deserved no tears. She was being punished for her selfishness, her abandonment of Mackie, her failure to save him. And if she could not save Mackie, what point was there in saving herself?

She dipped the finger again, and poised it over the glasses. But before she could bring it down, she became aware of that other presence at her shoulder. It was rather like peering at her own reflection in the dim and shadowed glass over her bureau. She smiled at it.

"Aye," she whispered. " 'Tis you, is it not? And what do you think of my farewell performance?"

She stroked the glasses one more time, one last sweet, longing note, and then covered the instrument, left the laboratory, and dragged herself up the stairs to her bedroom. She would not see the armonica again.

37

London, September 2018

THE glasses, thicker and duller-looking than the ones on Erin's own instrument, revolved smoothly on the reproduction spindle as she pumped the treadle. She dipped her fingers into the water and pressed them to the spinning cups. It was a richer tone than she was accustomed to, the timbre slightly muted, less focused. She played a triad, and a scale, and then, working to keep the speed steady, she tried a trill. It was quite different, the spacing between the cups, the balance between the work of her feet and her hands. Her trill was muddy and awkward and she gave it up for the moment.

"Good thing I left time to practice," she muttered to the empty room.

Franklin House was quiet around her. The security staff were on the ground floor, and the lights, except in the laboratory where she was working, were off. The imitation oil lamp cast only a dim glow over the armonica. Erin felt she had been set apart from the everyday world. It would be easy to believe she had stepped back in time. Perhaps the lady of the house, powdered and wigged, would look in and offer her tea, or the great Benjamin Franklin, bursting with energy and curiosity, would throw open the door and peer through his bifocal glasses to see who it was playing his latest invention. Or perhaps . . .

Erin experimented with the unfamiliar instrument for half an hour, until her ankles grew tired from the unaccustomed movement. She took a break, standing and walking around the laboratory. Like the armonica, the exhibits were convincing reproductions. A thick glass jar, with coppery wires poking out of its lid, rested on a shelf. A bizarre contraption of straps and ominous-looking metal wires hung above a wooden worktable. Erin went to the door and peeked around the corner, into Franklin's parlor.

The parlor, also, was filled with repro furniture and lamps and paintings, but she thought it must look very like it had in Franklin's day. A snatch of music and laughter rose from the security office downstairs, a television program, or a netcast. It was comforting to hear, a reminder that the world she knew was still there. She went back to the laboratory and the armonica. The car was returning for her at eight, leaving her about an hour more to work.

This time when she pumped the treadle, the action felt much more natural. It was, in fact, remarkably easy. Only once, that time in Boston, had she touched a manual treadle, but suddenly it seemed as if she had always known how to work it. She had often noticed that when she struggled for a new technique, it came to her after a recess, as if her mind went on working on it while her muscles rested. Smiling down at the little instrument, she began one of the old Scottish tunes Benjamin Franklin had been so fond of. "Bonnie Laddie, Highland Laddie," a melody so popular in its day that even Beethoven had composed a setting, rollicked from her fingers, flowed as if the crystals had only been awaiting an opportunity to sing it. Deborah Franklin had said once, upon being wakened by the strains of her husband's armonica, that she thought she had died in her sleep, and was "listening to the musick of the angels." The sound was pure and sweet, fragile and powerful at the same time.

Erin closed her eyes, feeling the placement of the cups, their thickness, their texture. She dipped her fingers again, and began "Barb'ry Allen."

She felt the presence as a warmth by her side, as if someone had turned on another lamp. Her right shoulder, her arm, and her cheek vibrated with it, and she knew. She opened her eyes.

The revenant at her side was as clear as her own hands upon the glasses. Erin dared not turn her head, lest the wraith shimmer into nothingness once again. She dared not lift her fingers from the spinning cups, lest that was the magic, or the medium, which made it possible for her to see. Her mind and her body and the music and the revenant were one. For the moment she shared the space of her existence with that other, ghostly, but very real, presence.

The girl sat beside her at the armonica, her hands outstretched, shadowy reflections of Erin's own. Hers were white, and terribly thin. Her hair, which Erin remembered as a cloud of black curls, now hung in long, straight tresses over her shoulders. Erin carefully slid her eyes to the right, without moving her head.

She was lovely, her eyes a dark blue, black-lashed, under heavy black brows. Her small nose was dusted with gold freckles, and her lips were full and sweet and sad. Her smile was wistful, full of longing. Of farewell.

The demarcation between present and past, reality and dream, blurred and disappeared. Erin felt the vibrations of the glass in her ears and her fingers and her heart, and she saw her wraith as clearly as any hologram of Charlie's.

'Tis like that, my little instrument.

Erin heard the words in her head as if they had been spoken aloud. Goose bumps rose on her arms and her neck. "What?" she whispered. Her melody slowed, stretching, spinning out into long legato notes that dissolved all rhythm into one continuous thread of sound. Her feet worked automatically, forward, back, pumping, pumping. The girl leaned forward, closer to Erin, and then past. Her gaze shifted, and Erin followed her eyes.

The dimness beyond the circle of the lamp seemed to fill with people. Erin couldn't make them out really, except for one child who lay in the arms of a tall man, and one other person, male or female she couldn't tell, lying supine on the worktable under the odd apparatus. The others were truly shades, shifting, drifting with the air. Erin felt absolutely certain that if she turned on the electric light overhead, they would disappear. Only the girl at her side was distinct.

'Tis like that, my little instrument.

Erin became aware that her ankles were cramping, her hands tiring, but she dared not stop playing. She looked at the girl beside her. She whispered, "Like what? What do you mean?"

The great eyes shifted back to her, the lids falling once, twice, as if she were going to sleep. She reached out with one finger and inaudibly stroked one of the spinning glasses.

My little instrument.

In the end, ankles and wrists exhausted, Erin had to cease her music. The revenant beside her appeared to sigh. She stood, turned, and drifted away, leaving Erin alone in an utterly empty room.

ERIN slept badly that night, tossing from side to side, disturbed by dreams in which oddly dressed people did strange and frightening things in the old laboratory. Early in the morning, again with only coffee to sustain her, she took a cab to Thirty-six Craven Street. She was tired, her eyes burning, her ankles aching from the unaccustomed motion of the treadle. She climbed out of the cab and stood outside the iron fence, looking up at the stone façade of Franklin House. Now that she was here, she had to fight a reluctance to go in, to open herself again to these exhausting experiences. But she must. She had to pursue this to the end. For Charlie, and maybe, even, for herself.

The museum was just opening. A bus filled with schoolchildren in green and blue uniforms emptied in front of Franklin House, and a crowd of chattering youngsters trooped in through the iron gate under the supervision of their teachers. A docent met them at the door. Erin stood to one side and listened as the docent gave the children an introduction to Franklin House.

"This used to be Number Seven," she said in high, cultured accents. "When Mrs. Margaret Stevenson owned it, and Dr. Benjamin Franklin lived here. I know you've learned all about Dr. Franklin from your teachers, haven't you?"

There were murmurs of assent from the children. "Oh, isn't that lovely," the docent said automatically. "Well. Dr. Benjamin Franklin stayed with Mrs. Stevenson twice, from 1756 to 1762, and again from 1764 to 1775. We're going to show you all four floors, but children, please respect the ropes that are strung in some of the doorways. Those are to protect the rooms and some of the old furniture that Dr. Franklin and his friends may actually have used. You may go into some rooms, though, and we'll show you which ones. Come now, down these stairs, and you'll discover what an eighteenth-century kitchen looked like!"

Erin followed at a little distance as the children trooped down the stairs and were allowed to wander through the kitchen, to touch the old wooden sideboard, to run their hands over the nocked and worn kitchen table, to exclaim over the ancient stove and the stone sink. She stood in the doorway listening to the docent talk about Margaret Stevenson and her daughter, Polly, and their small staff. She went along as they moved up the stairs to the ground-floor parlor, the Stevensons' living quarters, then on to the first floor, and Franklin's laboratory and parlor.

The students were ushered into the laboratory, though

the armonica was protected from their curious hands by its little velvet curtain. The docent went to the worktable and the odd apparatus hanging above it. "Now, children, you all know from your studies that Benjamin Franklin was very interested in electricity, don't you? Yes, of course you do. Well, this odd contraption here was called a Leyden jar, what today we would call a capacitor. It was used to store and pass along static electricity. Benjamin Franklin and Richard Pringle, the royal physician, gave some patients electric shock!"

The children murmured to each other, delighted with this horrific idea. The docent smiled coolly. "Yes, indeed," she said. "They experimented on some lesser members of society, and then they tried to heal the daughter of the Duke of Ancaster, who was only thirteen, and suffered from seizures. Alas—" the docent gave her audience a cool smile, "the poor girl died subsequently—not here, I'm glad to say, under Benjamin Franklin's treatment! But at Bristol on Palm Sunday. In 1767, that was."

Satisfied with the effect of her pronouncement, the docent led the children around the corner to the parlor. She busily quoted dates and names and events, but Erin didn't hear them. She stopped where she was, staring into the now-empty laboratory. The house felt as alive to her as if the residents of the eighteenth century still dwelt there. She glanced over her shoulder, half-expecting to see someone in a long skirt and an apron, or a brocade waistcoat. Her head felt strange, as if her mind had grown too wide for her skull to hold. She rubbed her eyes.

The docent was explaining the armonica, saying that there would be a little concert the next evening by a contemporary player of the instrument. Several children asked if they could attend, and the docent explained about fundraisers and the need of the Society for money to sustain the exhibits. They made a circuitous tour of the parlor, taking turns sitting in the chair that, their guide said, could have been Benjamin Franklin's. Their teachers stood on the landing, yawning, talking to each other.

The tour wound on up the last flight of stairs. The children crowded onto the little landing trying to peer into the small bedroom that was blocked by one of the burgundy velvet ropes. Erin had to stand halfway up, looking at the backs of the restless children, listening as the guide spoke of William Franklin. "Dr. Franklin's son occasionally came to England with his father, and when he was in London, he stayed in this room. He was away a good deal, of course, and married a beautiful Englishwoman in 1763. I might mention that his bride was not his father's choice, and it was some time before they were reconciled over the matter! Back there, in that tiny room, Dr. Franklin's slave, Peter, slept. But in this room, when William was away, other people would live, other staff or people assisting Dr. Franklin in his scientific work."

The docent turned and faced the children, her eyebrows raised, her voice dropping dramatically. "In fact, it is thought that someone who lived in this room may also have died here. Do you know, children, what the Society found buried beneath Franklin House when they renovated it? Can you guess?" She paused theatrically. The children squirmed with anticipation. Erin froze, her hand on the banister, her feet heavy on the narrow stair.

"They found *human bones*!"

38

T HERE was something magical about having given in
to her illness, Eilish thought. Her body lay on her bed,
wasting, dying, but her mind roamed as free as a summer
dove, touching wherever it would. She felt she could follow
Marianne even as her carriage carried her away from Craven Street. She could sense Cook, working, sorrowing
down in her basement kitchen. She could even, from afar,
touch the distant busy mind of her benefactor, the faraway
Dr. Franklin. And when she slept, Mackie was there, waiting, and she was eager to be with him. "Patience, sweeting," she found herself murmuring when she woke once
again to find herself still in the world. "Soon."

She no longer had the strength to go down the stairs to
the armonica. In fact, for a week she had been unable
to leave her bed, and poor Cook and Bessie had to tend to
her, for which she felt remorse. But there was nothing she
could do about it. They were waiting, all of them, for the
final day, and she more than any.

But in her mind she visited the laboratory, stroked the
glass cups once again, felt the treadle smoothly pumping
beneath her feet, and the strains of music, of glass music,

rise from her fingers. And at night, when the busyness of the active world settled into sleep, she thought herself down to the laboratory and reached out to touch that other, that mysterious shade that sometimes joined her at her little instrument.

This was a great comfort to Eilish, that someone else would sit at the armonica. It had to be in the future, since the armonica had only come into being with her coming to Dr. Franklin. It meant to her that the glass music would not die, but would live on, perhaps with Marianne, perhaps with others, most certainly with that other yet to come.

Marianne came to see her on her last afternoon, and sat weeping beside her bed. "Marianne," Eilish breathed. "Do not cry, my dear friend. I am not sad, why should you be?"

"But, Eilish," Marianne sobbed. "I must go on without you, and I do not see how I shall."

Eilish had no answer, and she had to rest before she could speak again. "Marianne," she whispered. "I need a favor. Will you do something for me?"

"Anything, sweetheart," Marianne said, taking Eilish's white hand in her little brown one. For once, she had left her face unpowdered. The pockmarks showed clearly in her thin cheeks, tears shining in them like little puddles in a rough street. Her eyes were dark with misery.

Eilish rested again. When she had strength, she murmured, "I cannot write, you know. Will you write for me? A note for Dr. Franklin?"

"Of course, dear," Marianne said. She swallowed a sob. "Tell me, and I shall write it at my desk when I am at home."

"Write it all," Eilish said weakly.

"Yes, dear, all. I promise."

Eilish was obliged to rest again before she had breath to dictate. After a few moments she said hoarsely, "Write: 'Dear Dr. Franklin. Please give my friend . . .'" a pause as she drew a shallow, inadequate breath, "'my friend Marianne Davies . . .'" another pause. Eilish felt her eyelids droop, and a great drowsiness overtake her. She forced her eyes open, to see Marianne, tears streaming down her face, bending over her. " ' . . . the glass armonica,' " she finished. She couldn't stop her eyes from closing, though she heard Marianne sob.

The passage of time no longer seemed meaningful. When Eilish opened her eyes once again, she found Mrs. Stevenson, Cook, and Bessie in the room and Marianne seated beside her on the bed holding both her hands. Eilish didn't know if it was the same day or another. Marianne's face was dry now, but her hair was tumbled, as if she hadn't had time to arrange it properly. "Is there anything you need, dear?" Marianne asked in a low tone.

Eilish tried to remember what she had already said, but it seemed very far off and hardly important now. "The armonica," she said, her voice hardly a breath.

"Yes, dear. I know, I will write to Dr. Franklin for you."

"And write . . . 'your friend, Eilish Eam.' "

"I will. Oh—" Marianne brought Eilish's nerveless hands to her breast. "Oh, Eilish, I do love you!"

But Eilish didn't hear Marianne. She heard Mackie's voice. She saw Mackie, Mackie on straight, strong legs, running through brilliant green grass, a bright sun shining on his tousled red head. Eilish ran, too, joyously, feeling strong and rested. She ran to Mackie, and caught him up in her arms to bury her cheek in his sunburned neck, to breathe the sweet little boy smell of him. And it was over.

39

London, September 2018

THE concert in Benjamin Franklin House, Number Thirty-six Craven Street, was a cozy affair, with perhaps thirty people in attendance. On short notice, the Society had turned it into a black-tie event, with champagne and hors d'oeuvres and hostesses soliciting donations. An ad screen beside the front door of the house scrolled Erin's publicity photo with her name in mock eighteenth-century script, and the time for the netcast. Inside, the first-floor laboratory was transformed, velvet chairs scattered here and there in eighteenth-century fashion, beeswax candles alight in branching candelabra. The armonica lay in a golden pool of candlelight. The guests wore tuxedos and long evening dresses.

In the afternoon Erin had taken a cab to Harrod's and found a long ruby velvet skirt and a white silk blouse with a deep, lace-trimmed collar that looked very period to her. As she gave the clerk her multicard, the girl said, "This will be lovely with madam's hair." Erin had to stifle a giggle.

As she was leaving the store, she passed the men's toiletries counter, and was caught by a distinctive smell. When she inquired, the clerk opened a bottle of something clear and held it out to her. "This is bay rum, madam," the clerk said.

Erin bent to sniff the bottle's contents. The scent was spicy, clean, and familiar. Her eyes went wide, and she took an involuntary step back.

"A fine old-fashioned gentleman's toilet water," the clerk said. "Sold for more than two centuries. Would madam care to purchase a bottle?"

She hesitated. "Bay rum?" she repeated.

"Yes, madam. Bay rum."

"I—I don't know," she finally stammered. "Perhaps next time." He smiled at her, and turned his attention to the next customer. Wondering, amazed, Erin hurried out of the store.

For the concert she wore no jewelry and applied no makeup other than a pale rose lipstick. When she came into the room, the murmur of appreciation assured her she had made good choices. She made a mental note to tell Charlie that for once she had gotten the clothes right.

The netcameras were small and unobtrusive, single-angle only, set up on the laboratory worktable. The house manager of St. John's was present to introduce Erin as the "reigning virtuosa" of the glass harmonica. He gave a short talk on the differences between her own instrument and the repro that had been made for Franklin House. Erin bowed to polite applause, and took her seat on the little stool.

She played simple pieces, all from memory. She played the Mozart solo Adagio, following with one of the Zeitler Airs. She played a brief and tuneful "Romanza" Charlie had written for her when they were only fourteen, his first composition for the glass harmonica. And from the first notes, her revenant was at her side. Other hands joined hers on the glasses, not obstructing, but sharing. Thin ankles touched hers on the treadle. The music filled the renovated laboratory, resounding against the tall windows, the glass tubes, the polished floor, and they made the music together. Every cell of Erin's body sang with it.

At the end, the applause was enthusiastic, and there were polite cries for more. One woman, in an expensive evening gown and diamond earrings, stood staring at Erin and the armonica, her eyes shining with tears. Usually Erin avoided the people thus affected by glass music. But on this occasion, she met the woman's eyes and held them.

'Tis like that, my little instrument.

Erin hadn't planned an encore, but the old folk song sprang to her mind.

> *"In Scarlet Town, where I was born,*
> *There was a fair maid dwellin' . . .*
> *Made every lad cry well-a-day,*
> *And her name was Barb'ry Allen."*

Erin knew by the nodding heads and shared smiles that her listeners knew the words of the song. She felt her revenant's pleasure at the choice, and she smiled down at their joined hands. If the audience could see what she saw, could feel what she felt, they would run away in terror, as Erin had been running for months. But now, everything was different.

> *"Oh, father, father, dig my grave,*
> *Go dig it deep and narrow.*
> *Sweet William died for me today;*
> *I'll die for him tomorrow."*

When she finished, she watched her wraith rise from the armonica, turn, and drift across the room on feet that did not quite touch the floor. People spoke to Erin, asked questions, called out compliments, but she didn't hear them. She forgot about the netcast, the cameras, the man from St. John's. She rose from the little stool, picked up her long skirt, and followed the ghost.

They moved lightly, quickly upward. One flight of stairs, a narrow landing, another flight of stairs. On they went, to the small bedroom at the front of the house, where the old bed and ancient bureau with its looking glass waited behind the flimsy barricade of burgundy velvet. The wraith went straight through the curtain as if it weren't there—and of course, for her, in her world, it wasn't. Erin understood that perfectly. For herself, she unhooked the little curtain on its rope of gold, and stepped into the room.

Her revenant stood before the bureau, looking into the cracked and smoky glass above it. She untied the bit of ribbon holding her long dark hair, letting it fall loosely about her narrow shoulders. She sighed, gazing into the mirror, and then went to the big bed and lay down. Her slender body shadowed the white quilt, but made no depression in it.

Erin stood with her back to the bureau, her heart beating fast, her lips dry. She watched as the girl curled herself around a lace pillow, her hair flung out behind her in a splash of black against the white. The girl closed her eyes, and Erin stared at her, her mouth a little open in wonderment.

It was like looking into the old glass and seeing her own reflection, blurred and shadowed and flawed by time. Her wraith—her revenant—could have been herself. Their features were different, their hair, their bodies—yet they were somehow, in some way, the same person.

Slowly, wary of the fragile channel of contact, Erin moved to kneel beside the bed. "What happened to you?" she whispered. "Was it you, down there in the laboratory with Franklin? Was it your instrument first? Are those your bones found beneath this house? Oh, poor child—we don't even know your name!"

The girl's eyes opened, but not to look on Erin. She looked up, past Erin's shoulder, and something made her face light with a sudden, overwhelming joy. Erin wanted to look, too, but she dared not tear her eyes from the girl's face for fear she would slip away from her.

The girl's lips moved. Her arms reached out to hold something, someone. Her pale face was transformed by a radiant happiness that made Erin cry out softly, and press her hand to her own breast as if to capture, and hold, the moment of ecstasy.

Seconds later, the image shimmered, wavered, and Erin reeled with vertigo, as if caught in a whirlpool, as if the room had been turned upside down. She clutched at the bed for balance and closed her eyes. When she opened them, her wraith was gone.

Erin put her forehead against the soft bed. She couldn't cry, not for a girl dead two hundred and fifty years. But she grieved for a life that had surely been too short. And she knew, with a surety that defied all of Gene Berrick's science, that she would never see her wraith again. But she had heard her voice.

'Tis like that, my little instrument. And that was the answer.

ERIN cradled the antiquated phone to her ear and listened to Gene's deep voice on the other end. "He's still sleeping," he said about Charlie.

"I know it's early there," she said. "Sorry if I woke you."

"You didn't. I have rounds to make."

"Oh, of course . . . but I wanted to tell you . . . Gene, he needs the music."

"What?"

"Oh, sorry . . . it's just been an incredible night. But I know what Charlie needs!"

"Pardon?"

Erin could have kicked herself. What a way to tell him. "Oh, god, I sound like an idiot. He needs what you're doing, of course, I mean, that's the whole thing, isn't it? But to help him find his balance—that is, the balance between your program and the way his brain works—oh, I can't explain this. I know it, but I can't put it into words!"

It was frustrating not to be able to see his face, and she was relieved to hear him chuckle on the other end of the line. "Never underestimate instinct," he said. "The intuitive leap."

"Trust you to have a name for it," she said. He chuckled again, and she smiled into the blind telephone. It was wonderful to have his voice sounding in her ear. "Listen, Gene—you remember that old study from the nineties—they used Mozart, I think."

"Yes?"

"Okay, well, it's like you said your program would always have to be individually tailored for every patient, because brains react differently to different stimuli? Well, we already know that in music, of course, because people like different types of music—but who knows better what Charlie responds to than I do? Or than he does, for that matter!"

Gene was quiet, waiting. She marveled how, even now, with her babbling at him from another continent, he could be so composed.

"What if Mozart actually imparts some of his own—I don't know, being, spirit—through the music? And why not? We know music is more than just sound organized by pitch and rhythm and duration. Every instrument has its own properties of sound, of course, its own capabilities, but we can't explain why the music has the effect it does. There's just—there's magic in it!"

Now she did expect him to laugh, but he didn't. He spoke in a tone that took her breath away. "Come home, Erin. Come as soon as you can."

"I will," she said. "But I have to go to Boston first, to get the glass harmonica. And I'll be on the very next plane to Seattle."

"I'll meet you."

"Tell Charlie for me, okay?"

"I will." She heard the smile return to his voice. "Good work, Erin."

The compliment meant more to her than all the reviews she had ever collected. "Gene—" she began, and then found she didn't know what to say.

"I know. We'll talk when you get here. Safe trip."

40

Seattle, October 2018

ERIN wanted to race down the jetway to Gene, but first she had to wait for a skycap, shepherd the glass harmonica cases from the cabin, then wait again for the jetway to be clear to dolly the cases into the terminal. At last, with the skycap behind her, she emerged.

He was there, a neat reff jacket over his jeans, dark glasses thrust up on his head. She put out her hand to him, suddenly shy. He took it, and kissed her cheek as if that were the most natural thing in the world.

She said, "Hey," and he gave her his quiet smile.

"Hey, yourself. Tell the guy to follow us."

With the cases loaded carefully in the back of the battered van, they drove straight toward Seattle, no stops this time. On the freeway, Erin asked, "How's Charlie?"

Gene glanced at her, his dark glasses flashing. "He's about the same. Other than Ted keeping him up on his physical therapy we haven't done any other work. Just backpedaling, really."

She nodded. "Is he driving you crazy?"

"A little." He smiled. "But it's understandable. We set him up with some equipment so he can listen to music, and installed a voice program on his slimscreen. And I brought over his Akai so he could fiddle with it."

"But he promised not to treat himself?"

Gene's smile faded. "Yes. He's scared, Erin. That's not helping the work, either."

They were quiet for a time while he drove. As they were passing the first of the high-rises, he said quietly, "So you saw her?"

She took a deep breath. "I don't know if I can ever explain it to you. Or to Charlie. I saw her, yes, in Franklin House. With the music, and then without it. It was like—it was like she's me. Like a reflection of me, or me of her. I don't have any philosophy to fit the experience."

"I'm sure you know there are some."

"Well, yes—but this is so *personal*. I don't know that some ritualized system could ever fully explain it to me. But it was real. And I'm not nuts."

"I know." Gene reached for her hand and held it, cradling it on his long thigh until they left the freeway and turned up the hill toward Charlie.

WITH Gene's help, Erin set up her glass harmonica in the clinic, at the opposite end from the Moog. When their hands touched, or their shoulders brushed, she felt warmth. The atmosphere between them was pleasantly charged, full of promise.

They had agreed not to tell Charlie about their plan, to let the factor of surprise be an added stimulus, but he surprised them.

He turned his blind face this way and that as Gene helped him from his wheelchair to sit inside the wooden framework. "What's here?" he asked sharply. "Erin? Something's different."

"How do you know, Charlie?" she asked. Nervous now, she stood behind her instrument, her hands apart in front of her. She had washed, and washed, and washed again, wanting everything to be perfect, her tone, her technique to be smooth, nothing to jar Charlie's concentration.

"I don't know—I feel something. Something's changed. Gene?"

"I'm here, Charlie."

Erin could see how anxious her brother was, how his eyes searched the shadows that were all his brain perceived. "Gene . . ." she began.

He nodded, and moved swiftly back to Charlie's side. He put his hand on Charlie's arm, and spoke calmly. "It's Erin's instrument," he said. "We want to try something new. Just listen, and let it work for you, all right?"

"It's the glass harmonica?" Charlie asked querulously. "It's here?"

"Yes," Erin said. The power was already turning the spindle, and she dipped a forefinger and touched one of the cups. The tone spun out, sweet and clear and high. Erin shivered with memory. Charlie visibly relaxed.

"Oh," he said. His face cleared. He put on the headphones, and Gene attached the electrodes to his temples, tucked them behind his ears. Charlie put his head back against the chair and took a deep breath. "Okay. Good. That's good, E. I'm ready, then."

Gene and Erin had spent hours the night before coordinating the binaural beat program with music for the glass harmonica. It had been past midnight when they were finished, Gene yawning, Erin alert, still on London time and having slept on the commuter. Charlie was already asleep in the guest bedroom. Gene ordered a readout of the program and the music, and while it was printing, he made up the couch for Erin.

He brought her a pillow from his bedroom and she stood holding it as they said good night. She came within a heartbeat of asking to sleep in his room, in his bed, but she stopped herself. She thought she knew what his answer would be. When it was over, when Charlie was better, that would be the time. Then they would be free. When Gene turned back at the door to his bedroom, his eyes flashing their clear light at her, she knew she was right. She hugged the pillow tightly, feeling the imprint of his fingers on it.

GENE and Erin both wore headphones like Charlie's, though not the electrodes. Gene began the binaural beats, and she could see by watching his fingers on the augmented synthesizer that he had begun the sensory emissions as well. He nodded to her, and she began to play.

At first she only matched a simple progression of chords to Gene's program, creating a background, an even rhythm, an orderly structure. She didn't want Charlie to have to work to understand it, but her intention was to anchor the sounds of the binaural beats in a basis of tonality. She played for a few moments before she dared a glance at Charlie's face.

His features were composed, his eyes closed, his lips relaxed. His hands, lying palm up in his lap, were still. She looked at Gene, but he was concentrating on the projected scan. Modulating carefully, Erin raised the pitch of her progression. Charlie didn't move, his eyelids didn't flicker.

Erin began the "Romanza." Almost immediately, Gene lifted a hand to point to the scan. The blue lobes revolved slowly against the lines of the mapping graph. She followed Gene's pointing finger and she saw, she really saw, the delicate arrows of light traversing Charlie's brain. It was no longer frightening. It was encouraging. It was necessary. Gene held his finger over the area he had told her before was the visual cortex, and she saw how the lines of light fragmented around it. It made her think of two people trying to meet in a maze, dashing down each promising corridor only to find themselves blocked, hemmed in, unable to reach each other.

She finished the "Romanza" and began on the *Lux Aeterna* of the *Requiem*. Charlie had labored over that movement, struggling with the progression, working and reworking the themes until they melded into one transcendent flow. Gene watched, nodded, adjusted the emissions with his fingers on the sensor panel. Erin played the movement exactly the way Charlie had asked for it, very slowly, *molto legato*, with classical resolutions of the long phrases. She felt, she hoped that she felt, the intensity of her tone reach out, touch his mind, translate through the limbic system, help his brain to balance sense and sensation, intention and motor control. She closed her eyes. *Feel it, Charlie. Let it help you.*

A choked sound made her open her eyes to look at her brother. He sat without moving, his eyes still closed, but tears had begun to stream down his cheeks.

Alarmed, Erin looked to Gene.

Gene's face was triumphant. He nodded to Erin to continue, and his fingers moved again across the sensor panel. Charlie sat listening, weeping. And the spears of light, the fragmented lines of energy, came closer and closer until at last they met, melding into the perfect shape that meant Charlie could see again.

Gene said softly, "That's it."

Erin had come to the end of the *Lux Aeterna.* She lifted her fingers from the spinning glasses.

Charlie wiped his cheeks, and pulled off his headphones. He opened his eyes, blinking several times as if waking from sleep. He rubbed his eyes with his fingers, stretching his eyebrows up, pulling at the corners of his eyelids.

He grinned at Gene. "Hey."

And he turned to Erin. "God, E," he said. "Do you ever need a haircut."

GENE strictly forbade Charlie to try walking on the same day, but Charlie was gay, ebullient, full of hope just the same. "I still don't know why it worked," he kept saying, as Gene brought his juice. "I've been listening to Erin play the silly old instrument most of my life. What's different now?"

"In part, it's the anticipation," Gene said. "The augmented binaural beats are one stimulus, but music, particularly music you know well, is a different, and complementary stimulus. What we know for certain is that part of the pleasure of music is the anticipation, the expectation of a certain harmony or rhythm or cadence—and Erin played music that you had written, in which your expectations are very high. That, combined with the extra energy of the sensory augmentation, transcends the auditory cortex to stimulate the visual cortex—and I hope, in time, the motor and somatosensory as well."

"But it has to be the glass harmonica," Erin said. "There's something about the timbre, the vibrations—something balancing. It's like—listen, have you ever seen an old-fashioned chalkboard? You know—the green thing you write on with white chalk?"

Gene said, "I went to school in the tent city, remember?"

"Okay, right. So, I think the tones of the glass harmonica are like the opposite of the screech of chalk on the board. I mean, that's not all that loud a sound, chalk scraping on a chalkboard, but it makes anyone who hears it want to jump out of their skin. Why should that be? So I don't know the explanation, but the tones of singing glass are just the opposite—you want them to settle into your skin, you want to let that tone inside your head—it's balancing."

"In other words," Charlie drawled, "neither of you has a clue." Erin gave his ponytail a sharp tug.

Gene smiled at his patient. "It will be fascinating developing a theory to fit the particulars. And you'll have to help, Charlie. For now, we'll just be damned glad it works. Medicine advances often enough on hunch and instinct. Let's use what we've got and analyze it later."

"A lot later, please," Erin said, laughing now. "I'm starved."

Charlie got himself into his wheelchair, and they went out in search of a meal. Charlie's eyesight was not as clear as it had been before, as they felt confident it would be again, but his excitement over having it back, even if the outlines of objects and people were a bit fuzzy, was infectious. Gene's relief was almost as heady as Charlie's, and Erin was buoyant.

Once they were seated in a booth of the Silk City Diner, Erin gripped her brother's hand. "God, Charlie. Promise me. Never again. Never, never again."

"Well, I'm still going to do augmented sensory music," he said.

"But not on yourself!"

Gene said, "One of the reasons we had success today, Charlie, is because you're particularly sensitive to the augmented sensory emissions. You've got to be careful."

"I'm going to walk," Charlie said stubbornly. "I am. No, I won't use the program on myself. But from a strictly musical standpoint, *Mars* was great. When people get used to augmented sensory music . . ."

Erin rolled her eyes. "Could we talk about the weather or something?"

"Yes," Gene said, "let's talk about the weather. And wine. We have a lot to celebrate."

They pored over the wine list together, arguing, laughing. When the wine arrived and they each had a glass, they toasted.

Erin began. "To your beautiful blue eyes, Charlie. Your beautiful, fully functional eyes!" They drank.

And Charlie said, "To Gene. Best doc in or out of the Ivy League!" They drank again.

At last Gene said, "To Erin. It took guts, Erin, going off in search of your ghost."

Charlie echoed, "To Erin." He and Gene drank, but Erin grew thoughtful.

"I wish I knew who she was," she said.

"You think those were her bones under Franklin House, don't you?" Charlie asked.

Erin nodded. "But she wasn't important enough to be remembered. So I don't know her name, or why she died— or much of anything."

Gene raised his glass one more time. "We know she was a musician," he said quietly. "And we'll remember her. She's important to the three of us." His hand was close to Erin's under the table, and their fingers came together and entwined. His were long and cool and strong, and hers throbbed with the pace of her heartbeat.

"To my wraith, then," Erin said, holding up her glass, swirling the wine inside to watch its ruby glow. "May she rest in peace."

GENE drove to St. Mark's, and he and Erin followed Charlie's chair into the elevator and down the corridor to the condo. Erin walked close to Gene, feeling his arm against her shoulder, almost painfully aware of his thigh brushing hers, his hand reaching past her to open the door to the apartment. Moonlight shone through the rose window, refracting in patterns of crimson and gold and turquoise. Charlie turned his chair in the doorway, and grinned. "Well," he said, wiggling his eyebrows at them. "Good night, you two. See you in the morning."

Erin felt her cheeks flame. "Charlie!" She could hardly look at Gene, but every part of her body reacted to his closeness, every nerve cried out to touch him.

Charlie winked. "Oh, don't worry about me! I can—really, really, I can—take care of myself." He saluted them. "Thanks to you guys."

He turned his chair, and with a jaunty wave over his shoulder, he disappeared into his bedroom. Embarrassed, self-conscious, Erin looked up into Gene's dark face. His gray eyes sparkled like clean water in bright sun, and her body warmed beyond bearing.

"Erin?" he said softly.

She smiled tentatively. "Would you—would you like to take me home, Gene?" she whispered.

He put his arms around her and pulled her close. All she could think was *At last, at last.*

41

Boston, Christmas 2018

THE limo carrying them from Logan Airport pulled up in front of Sarah Rushton's house, and Gene and Erin climbed out to wait for their bags. And for Charlie.

Charlie got out of the limo from the other side, moving carefully, but entirely on his own. He had acquired a beautiful cane of mahogany, carved circa 1940 and inlaid with mother-of-pearl. He leaned on it, careful of the icy glassphalt sidewalk, and led the way slowly, but steadily, up to Sarah's low, covered porch.

Erin and Gene stood back, allowing Charlie to be the one to ring the bell. Gay Christmas lights, blue and silver and white, glowed in looping patterns through the hollies flanking the porch. The housekeeper opened the door and gasped at the sight of Charlie Rushton standing in the doorway on his own two feet. He laughed.

"Shh now, don't tell Mother. Where is she?"

The housekeeper, her hand to her mouth, shaking her head in amazement, pointed toward the living room. Charlie, placing the cane carefully, stepped over the sill and made a measured progress down the polished hallway. Erin and Gene followed.

They found Sarah seated by a tall, slender abstract of a Christmas tree, a twist of elongated silver branches around a gray biocomposite trunk. Red glass beads dotted it here and there, sparkling like rubies in the lamplight. Sarah's sleek blond head was bent over a slimscreen in her lap. She heard their footsteps and glanced up.

"Who . . . ? Charlie? Charlie—god, Charlie, omigod!" She stood, almost dropping the slimscreen on the floor. Hastily, she set it on the chair. "Charlie, you're—you're *walking*—"

He grinned and flourished the cane at her.

His mother gaped, and made a visible effort to compose herself—and then Sarah Rushton did something neither Charlie nor Erin nor the housekeeper nor anyone else had seen her do for years and years. She burst into sobs. They tore from her throat, from her body, the hoarse, ugly, helpless sobs of long-suppressed grief. She covered her face in shame, bending at the waist in an agony of release. "Oh, thank God, thank God," she sobbed. "Oh, Charlie, my son, my baby—I am so sorry—I have always been so sorry—"

Erin stared at her mother in horror. Charlie, shocked almost out of his hard-won balance, leaned against the door frame watching her cry, hardly knowing her.

It was Gene who strode forward, who put his long arm around the weeping woman, who helped her to a chair and found her a handkerchief, who spoke soothingly to her until the worst of her tears were spent. Erin stepped close to Charlie, her shoulder touching his, needing an anchor of familiarity in the sea of confusion.

As Sarah began to grow calm, hiding her face in her hands, wiping her face with the sodden handkerchief, Gene looked up at the twins.

"Erin, Charlie, why don't we give your mother a moment? This has been a shock for her."

Sarah said something in a choked voice, and Gene bent to hear her. When he straightened, he kept one brown, doctorly hand on her shoulder. "She says it's a wonderful shock," he told them, with his quiet smile.

"Sarah—" Erin began.

Charlie moved forward, leaning on his cane, but moving, walking on his own. He went to Sarah and settled into a chair close to her. "Mother," he said. She lifted her ravaged face to him, and Erin bit back an exclamation. Sarah Rushton looked every one of her fifty-five years. But her blue eyes, dark now with tears, were vivid with an inner light.

"Charlie," Sarah said through trembling lips. Erin saw now that there were lines in her slender throat, that her hands were blue-veined. When had she begun to age?

"Charlie, darling," Sarah said again. "I am so happy for you. And so very, very sorry."

"Mother, why? What are you sorry about?" he asked. He took her pale, veined hand.

Sarah blew her nose, and began to pull herself together. The signs of age disappeared as she composed herself, as she regained her dignity.

"I'm sorry," she said, "because it was all my fault, and I couldn't change any of it. It was too late."

"How could it be your fault, Sarah?" Erin asked.

Sarah glanced at her, and then up at Gene Berrick, and the guilt in her face was painful to see. "I should have had the test. I should have known."

Gene shook his head. "It might not have made a difference, Dr. Rushton."

"But we didn't know that, and we'll never know. And all these years—oh, Charlie—"

Fresh tears welled in her eyes. Her son laid his carved cane on the floor and leaned forward. For the first time in more years than Erin could count, mother and son embraced. Gene looked up at Erin, and she saw the pride in his eyes, pride and satisfaction and the wonderful kindness that had made her love him.

"Thank you," she mouthed. He winked at her.

• • •

THEY sat around the dinner table and talked, Sarah, the twins, Gene Berrick, Mal Oskar, long after the housekeeper had served, cleared away, and gone off to her own home. Sarah was completely recovered, her eyes cool again, her hair perfectly smooth. Erin kept stealing glances at her. She had never seen her mother smile as much as she had that evening, particularly whenever she looked at Charlie. If Sarah was not exactly effusive, she was certainly amiable, and the conversation stretched on while the candles in the poinsettia centerpiece burned low.

"So, Dr. Berrick," Sarah said, "I'd like to see Charlie's scans—to see the progression. I'm not at all sure I understand how you accomplished this."

Gene leaned forward. In the candlelight his skin was chocolate, his pale eyes startling. Erin looked at his hand resting on the table, the long fine fingers, and she could barely restrain herself from touching it. Gene said, "I didn't accomplish it, not really."

"Yes, you did," Charlie exclaimed. "It couldn't have happened without you."

"Well, no, but I meant that I didn't do it alone. It was when Erin joined us—" They had made a tacit agreement not to tell Sarah about the setback of Charlie's hands, the loss of his vision. "When Erin brought the glass harmonica to the clinic, Charlie's scans began improving immediately."

"Why should that be?" Sarah Rushton asked.

"A very good question." Gene traced a pattern on the white tablecloth as he spoke. "Of course, the brain's responses to stimuli are idiosyncratic. And we're still learning how the brain compensates for damage. But in Charlie's case, I think the use of music helped to order the neurological impulses—rather like the Parkinson's patients who can walk only while listening to music. And for Charlie, of course, the glass harmonica was the perfect music. Because

he knew the compositions, because the patterns were expected—and it may be that there are properties to the sound
of the glasses that affect the electrical impulses of the nervous system. We're going to do some work on that, do
some experimenting with other patients, and also try recordings as opposed to live music. I'd like to develop a
concrete therapeutic model."

Erin put her hand to her mouth to hide her smile. They
could analyze all they liked. But there was an element to
Charlie's healing they would never understand. *'Tis like
that, my little instrument.* For some things, science had no
explanation.

Sarah bestowed a respectful smile on Gene. "I assume
you'll publish now, Dr. Berrick?"

Gene leaned back in his chair and looked at Charlie. "I
don't know," he said. "Charlie's work shouldn't be com-
promised—"

"Gene," Charlie said firmly. "Of course you'll publish!
We'll just be open about all of it. What difference does it
make where the idea for augmented sensory music came
from? Everyone knows I was in a wheelchair. It makes a
great story."

Gene shrugged. "We'll see. But only in the journals. No
popular press."

"No, of course not," Sarah said "But your university will
want to publish your results."

Mal cleared his throat. "Uh, no popular press? What
about Charlie? The netcasters are begging for interviews,
after San Francisco and San Antonio. This could mean a
lot of work, for both Charlie and Erin."

Charlie laughed, and gave Erin a thumbs-up. "Hear that,
little girl? Fame at last."

WHEN everyone else had gone to bed, Erin and Gene
bundled up in wool coats and warm boots, and went out to
walk the snowy streets and look at the Christmas lights

strung in trees and shrubs and windows. Gene held Erin's hand in the deep pocket of his coat as they strolled together.

They passed a lighted window where several people, adults and children, gathered around a Christmas tree. Laughter filtered out into the cold, along with the syrupy strains of Christmas carols.

"Scenes like that used to break my heart," Gene said softly, squeezing Erin's hand. "Home, family, parents, friends. It seemed as unreachable as a house on the moon."

Erin said, "Looks like a Rockwell painting."

"I want it," Gene said.

"What, a Rockwell painting?" Erin teased.

"No." He looked down at her, his features grave, his eyes sparkling with the colors of the Christmas lights. "A home, a family. All that old stuff that I never had."

"You know, I didn't have it either, Gene."

He stopped walking and faced her. Their breath made ephemeral clouds around them. In the cold air, every sound was magnified, the creak of trees under their weight of snow, the convivial sounds of the Christmas gathering.

"Erin, in a way you did have it. I understand it wasn't perfect, and that you think your mother let you down. But she cares for you, and she provides for you."

Erin felt a twinge of shame. "I know that, I guess. I've never seen her as happy as she was tonight, actually. I didn't know she had that much emotion in her."

"Everyone does," he said.

"Even you?" she said, leaning close to him, teasing again.

For answer, he bent and kissed her, a long, sweet, yearning kiss that left her breathless and wanting. "Especially me," he said. "Marry me, Erin."

She pulled back abruptly and stared at him. "What did you say?"

His face went very still. "I think you heard me."

"Well, Gene, I—I guess I did, but I—"

He turned his eyes back to the lighted window, the colorful scene inside. "Sorry," he said in a level voice. "I thought—maybe I've said the wrong thing."

"Gene—darling Gene—it's just so old-fashioned, so—" Erin giggled. "It's so bloody *grown-up*!"

He looked down at her again, and his lips curved. She threw her arms around his waist and stood very close to him, looking up into his dear dark face, his crystal gray eyes. "Say it again," she whispered.

He held her face between his hands and said, "Marry me, Erin Rushton. Grown-up, old-fashioned, institutional marriage. Marry me."

"You know what you're getting into?" she asked breathlessly. "Musician's life, concert tours, hotel suites?"

"That's why we have airplanes," he murmured. "Do you know about emergency calls, hospital rounds, clinic hours? Marry me."

"Oh, yes," she said, through the frosty cloud between them. "Oh, yes, Gene Berrick. I think I will."

THE day after Christmas, Erin took Gene to see the ancient armonica at the Old State House. They stood gazing at the artifacts in their climate-controlled glass cabinet, the faded blue long-skirted coat and brocade waistcoat, the assemblage of china and flatware and old portraits. The cups of the little armonica were dull and lifeless, their luster dulled by the passing of two and a half centuries. Its iron spindle was stained with rust.

On the facing wall, looms and spinning wheels and assorted Colonial sewing implements were arranged. They leaned close to a deep glass frame to examine items from the Franklin home in Philadelphia. There was a 1785 mezzotint of Deborah Franklin, hanging between a faded and faceless rag doll and a child's silver spoon and cup, now black with age. There was also a bit of embroidered cloth that looked like a linen handkerchief, pressed flat under its own bit of glass.

Erin stared at the little yellowed square. Its edges were brown and crumbling, which made her feel sad for some obscure reason. The embroidery was in some language she didn't recognize. She had an idea it might be Gaelic, or Celtic, but she didn't know. She wished she could touch it. "What is that, do you suppose?" she asked. "That bit of cloth?"

Gene shook his head. "Don't know. Do you want me to find a docent and ask?"

Erin bit her lip, then gave a small laugh. "Oh, no, it's nothing. Don't bother." But she gazed at it for several moments before she was ready to leave it and walk on.

They made only a cursory tour of the rest of the museum before they went back out into the cold air. As they waited for the car to come around, Gene squeezed Erin's arm. "When are you going to tell Sarah?"

"You mean, about you and me?"

"Yes. Aren't you going to talk to her before we leave? Or do you want me to do it?"

"No, no, I don't want you to do it. I don't know, I just— I guess I just want to keep it to myself for a while. Well, me and Charlie, that is."

The car pulled up, and the driver opened the door for them to get in. Quietly, Gene said, "You know, Erin, I'd like to get to know your mother."

"After the things she said to you? About you?"

He shrugged. "We've all made our mistakes. And I think your mother wants to know you better—to understand you. You're very alike, you two."

She gave him a sidelong glance. "Jeez," she said wryly. "Me and the ice queen."

He said, "Give her a chance. Let her get close to you."

"You mean, the way you finally let me get close to you?"

He looked down at her, his fine lips curving, his eyes bright. He bent and kissed her. "Were you trying to get close to me?" he said.

"You know I was!"

He chuckled and put one long arm around her, drawing her close. "It was complicated," he said. "Charlie, and the augmented sensory music, and then your—well, your—"

She poked him in the side with her finger. "Go ahead, say it. My ghost."

"Your wraith," he said, smiling. "I like that much better."

"Yeah, I do too."

"Well, your wraith, then. That made you—almost—my patient, as well. It was an ethics thing."

Erin sighed. "She's gone, you know. I knew she would be, I knew it in London."

"Are you sorry?"

"No!" She laughed, and then added, "Well, maybe a little. Because it was sad, knowing she was gone—but then, maybe she was never there at all."

"Oh, right," he said. "It was all in your little glass-vibrated head."

She drew back and looked up at him, eyes wide in mock surprise. "Why, Dr. Berrick!" she cried. "What was that, a joke?"

He gave a modest shrug. "Lost my head for a moment. I won't make it a habit."

She laughed and kissed him soundly on his cheek.

WHEN Gene's paper on augmented binaural beats appeared in JAMA, the little clinic was inundated with calls, and Gene was besieged with offers from research hospitals and experimental clinics all over the world. Charlie had more offers of commissions than he could fulfill, making Mal beam with satisfaction whenever he called. Erin was bursting with pride, so much so that Charlie started calling her Your Highness and Madame, until she threatened to knock his cane out of his hand.

In truth, he hardly needed the cane any longer. She hardly knew him these days. He walked as quickly as she did, straight-backed and proud. His shoulders had grown broad, his arms and legs filling with muscle. He was several inches taller than she, something she hadn't really noticed before. He was almost through with his next augmented composition, *Noir*, but he wouldn't allow her to start on the score until Gene had checked his program levels. It was to be a dark, unusual work, scored for glass harmonica, oboe, bassoon, percussion, and low strings. When Erin asked him about it, he wiggled his eyebrows and said, "Wait, just wait."

She was happy enough to wait. She and Gene were busy developing a program of glass harmonica music and augmented binaural beats at various levels to be used in conjunction with physical therapy. The little boy, Joey, would be their first subject.

Gene and Erin married in the spring of 2019. Sarah insisted they come home to Boston for the wedding, and she shopped with Erin for a very grown-up dress, white silk with narrow pleats dropping from the neckline, and transparent gauze sleeves. Gene was strikingly handsome in a dove-gray tux. Mal, with tears in his eyes throughout the ceremony, stood up for Erin. Sarah, elegant in black chiffon, was utterly composed. And Charlie, grinning and proud, stood beside Gene. He stood by himself, without his cane, and handed over the ring at the proper time with a glow of pride, as if he had engineered the whole thing himself. And in a way, of course, he had.

Sarah gave the newlyweds a beautiful reception, champagne and sushi and edible flowers on a great white cake. A string quartet played, and as Erin danced in her new husband's arms, she felt one, last fey tingle in her forehead. Later, when she and Gene went outside for a breath of cool evening air, she felt that other, that revenant, at her shoulder, for the space of three heartbeats. It breathed against her cheek, and swirled away into the dark garden, leaving behind it the faintest whiff of bay rum.

Erin smiled after it. Of course, it might not really have been there. It could have been only her imagination. It might have been no more than a bit of breeze kissing a happy bride's cheek. And now it was gone.

TO BENJAMIN FRANKLIN, ESQ., LL.D.

Aided by thee, Urania's heav'nly art,
With finer raptures charms the feeling heart;
Th'Harmonica shall join the sacred choir,
Fresh transports kindle, and new joys inspire,
Hark! The soft warblings, sounding smooth and clear,
Strike with celestial ravishment the ear,
Conveying inward, as they sweetly roll,
A tide of melting music to the soul;
And sure, if aught of mortal moving strain
Can touch with joy the high angelic train,
Tis this enchanting instrument of thine,
Which speaks in accents more than half divine!

—John Dunlap, 1772, Philadelphia

Author's Note

A number of historical figures participate in the eighteenth-century portion of this story: Benjamin Franklin; King George III and his Queen, Charlotte; Marianne Davies, an early player of the armonica who died in an asylum of a malady of the nerves said to be brought on by the vibrations of glass music; the slave Peter, who traveled to England with Benjamin Franklin and his son William; Margaret Stevenson, Franklin's landlady, and her daughter, Polly, who was his student and devoted correspondent; Mary Tickell, Polly's aunt, who required that Polly live with her in Essex in order to claim her inheritance; and Wolfgang Amadeus Mozart and his sister Nannerl, who arrived in London late in April, 1764, having been made very ill by the crossing of the Channel.

Eilish Eam, so far as we know, is fictional. It is true, however, that human bones were discovered beneath the Craven Street house during its renovation.

Louise can be reached by E-mail at LMarley@aol.com. Visit her website at www.sff.net/people/lmarley.

PENGUIN PUTNAM INC.
Online

Your Internet gateway to a virtual environment with hundreds of entertaining and enlightening books from Penguin Putnam Inc.

While you're there, get the latest buzz on the best authors and books around—

Tom Clancy, Patricia Cornwell, W.E.B. Griffin, Nora Roberts, William Gibson, Robin Cook, Brian Jacques, Catherine Coulter, Stephen King, Ken Follett, Terry McMillan, and many more!

**Penguin Putnam Online is located at
http://www.penguinputnam.com**

PENGUIN PUTNAM NEWS

Every month you'll get an inside look at our upcoming books and new features on our site. This is an ongoing effort to provide you with the most up-to-date information about our books and authors.

**Subscribe to Penguin Putnam News at
http://www.penguinputnam.com/newsletters**